Under a Winter Sky

A Fantasy Holiday Anthology

WITH NOVELLAS BY

Kelley Armstrong

Jeffe Kennedy

Melissa Marr

L. Penelope

And an exclusive short story by

Grace Draven

Susan,
Never give up!

Five powerhouse authors of fantasy and urban fantasy bring you a feast of romantic midwinter holiday adventures.

Happy reading!

KELLEY ARMSTRONG
www.KelleyArmstrong.com

"A Stitch in Time" cover art by CoverCouture

Thank you for reading!

Credits
Cover: Ravven (ravven.com)

Contents

Ballgowns & Butterflies

by
Kelley Armstrong

Ballgowns & Butterflies *is the second story in my time-travel Victorian gothic series, coming right after the first novel,* **A Stitch in Time**. *If you haven't read* **Stitch**, *no worries—this novella was written to stand on its own, and you'll be up to speed within a page or two.*

WHEN THE CAR-HIRE driver slows in the village of High Thornesbury, I direct her to the hill instead, where a house looms at the top, barely visible through the falling snow.

"Wait," the woman says. "You're going to Thorne Manor?"

"I am."

"You know them then? The couple who live there?"

"You . . . could say that."

She cranes to look back at me, and I resist the urge to nicely ask her to keep her eyes on the road . . . the impossibly narrow roads of North Yorkshire, now covered in slick December snow.

"Is it true what they say?" she asks.

I'm tempted to make some noncommittal noise, quite certain that I don't want to know what "they" say. But curiosity wins out, and I venture a cautious, "What do they say?"

"That she owns the house—the wife. She inherited it from her aunt. She's a professor in Toronto—the wife, not the aunt."

"I *have* heard—"

The driver steamrolls over my response, her accent sharpening as she warms to her subject. "They say she used to come here as a girl. To Thorne Manor. Then a terrible tragedy claimed the life of her uncle. But the best part is . . ." Her voice lowers to a delicious whisper. "The ghosts. The manor house is haunted, and the girl saw the ghosts. Her uncle did too, the night he died."

My throat closes, swallowing any reply I could make.

The driver continues, "Then the woman inherited Thorne Manor and came back, after over twenty years away. She must not have seen any ghosts that time, because she stayed the summer, and she met a man. A *Thorne.*"

"Yes, I have heard—"

"It's like a story out of one of those romantic movies, isn't it? The American—well, Canadian in this case—inherits a house in the English countryside, and then along comes a British lord, claiming it's his rightful family home. They start off fighting about it, only to fall madly in love."

I sigh inwardly. I should just let her have her version of the story and keep my mouth shut. But I am a history professor after all—I cannot allow rumor to stand as historic fact. Of course, nor can I tell the actual truth, which would probably have the poor woman turning around to whisk me to the nearest psychiatric hospital. Still, I should repeat the narrative we've constructed, the part of our story that is completely true.

"I'm familiar with the couple in question," I say. "The woman knew him when she was a girl. They were old friends, and he has never laid any claim to the house."

"Hasn't he?" She frowns through the mirror at me. "Isn't that suspicious?" Her eyes round. "Oh! It's that other sort of story, then. The one where he *pretends* to fall in love with her to get his hands on the house, which he thinks is his by right."

"No," I say.

"How would you know?"

Because the man *was* the rightful owner of Thorne Manor . . . two hundred years ago. Because as a child, that girl stepped through time and met a boy. Returned as a teenager, and fell in love. Returned as an adult, and won him again and was able to bring him back, both of them now moving from his time—where he is Lord William Thorne of Thorne Manor—and her time, where he is Mr. William Thorne, husband of the current owner. How do I know all this? Because I'm the current owner, the girl, the woman, the wife: Bronwyn Dale Thorne.

Of course, I can hardly say any of that, so I only gaze out at the lights of High Thornesbury as we pass through the tiny village. I know every street of it, in this time and in William's, and my pulse quickens, a smile growing as my hands clasp atop my protruding stomach.

Home. I am home.

When I was a little girl, this was my favorite place in the world. Even after I lost it, first when my parents divorced and later after my uncle died, I would dream of North Yorkshire the way others dream of a childhood home. So many happy memories here. Summers spent exploring these moors, picking bramble berries and picnicking with my dad and my Aunt

Judith and Uncle Stan. So many even happier times crossing over to William's world, secret visits to my most cherished friend and, later, my first love.

I grew up and found love again. Married a wonderful man and lost him, widowed at thirty. I'd had a home with Michael, but Toronto never *felt* like home the way this place does. Now I am back. Back for good, I hope. I had to return to Toronto to teach the fall term, but I've started my maternity leave, expecting a baby in March. After that . . . Well, if all goes well after that, this *will* be my home. I have a lead on a teaching position in York and a few other possibilities tucked in my back pocket.

I'll miss Canada, but I am ready to make this move. I think I've been ready since the day I first visited my aunt and uncle at Thorne Manor, certainly since the day I stepped through time and met William. Now, seeing the village lit up for the holidays, I feel as if I've come home. My first Christmas at home.

The lights fade quickly as the hired car begins the long climb to Thorne Manor. I'm struggling not to press my nose against the cold glass, straining to see the manor house through the falling snow. I think I can make out a faint glow and then—

The driver curses and jams on the brakes just as the headlamps illuminate a coal-black horse, racing around a curve and coming straight for the car. Or so it seems, but when the car follows the turn in the winding road, it becomes obvious that the horse is actually off to the side, galloping down the hill.

"Bloody fool," the driver grumbles.

"True," I murmur.

The rider wheels the stallion around and begins running alongside us.

"Is he mad?" the driver says.

"Possibly. Just don't let him beat us to the house, please, or I will never hear the end of it."

Now I do press my nose to the icy window, breath fogging the glass as I squint out. William lifts gloved fingers in greeting, but I don't think he can see me. He's bent over the horse, and with his black jacket, he nearly melds into the beast. Only his red scarf makes him truly visible, flapping behind him, an obvious concession to my warnings that car drivers aren't accustomed to sharing the road with horses.

The horse seems to have adapted well to his new master's riding habits. After much consideration, William bought him late this past summer. The first horse for his new stable on this side of the stitch. A black stallion, the mirror image of his on the other side. Xanthus and Balois, named after Achilles's immortal steeds.

We continue to the end of the drive, where William swings off Xanthus and lifts an imperious hand for the driver to stop.

Then, before the driver can do more than squawk an objection, William is throwing open the rear door and shoving his head and shoulders inside.

"Finally," he says. "I have been waiting *hours*. You really should have let me meet you at the station." He peers at me. "You aren't dressed for the weather at all. It's a wonder you didn't freeze on the way."

"Hello, William. So lovely to see you."

He grumbles and shoves a thick car blanket into the rear seat, bundles me into it and then glances at the driver.

"That will be all." He hands her a bill. A large one, given the way her eyes saucer. "I appreciate you conveying my wife safely from the station. Please deposit her bags at the end of the drive, and I will retrieve them later."

"I can carry—" I begin.

"I've got it, miss," the driver says. "You ought not be carrying anything in your condition anyway."

I'm not even halfway out of the car before I'm scooped up, the blanket wrapped around me.

"I'm pregnant, William," I say. "Not an invalid. I can walk—"

"Yes, you can. No, you will not. It's cold and it's slippery, and you've come halfway around the world in a single day, while six-months pregnant. You must be exhausted."

Exhausted is one way of putting it. Bone-dead and beat-down is another. I've spent the last two weeks cranked up to double speed, frantically finishing my end-of-term work so I could catch the first possible plane to William.

I'd told myself I'd sleep on the flight. I did not, even though *someone* found a way to secretly upgrade me to first-class, and I had no excuse for not stretching out in my little pod and spending the seven-hour flight sound asleep. No excuse beyond the fact that I was on my way to see William for the first time in two months, and I was so excited I could barely stay in my seat.

No sleep on the flight. No sleep on the train. Definitely no sleep in the car, and I can blame my chatty driver, but by that point, as William and Thorne Manor drew ever closer, it'd taken Herculean effort not to leap out of the car and run the rest of the way.

Now I am here, and it's as if my strings have been cut, every bit of energy evaporating. So yes, I am tired. Exhausted. But my journey is at an end, and I will now crawl into bed and not leave for three days straight. Okay, maybe there won't be much rest *tonight*—I'll definitely find the energy for a proper reunion—but afterward, I'm zonking out.

William fusses with my blanket, making sure I'm swaddled like an infant. I don't argue. I'm in the mood for a little coddling. Also it gives me time to look at him, just look at him, a sight even more welcome than the lights of High Thornesbury.

It's always disconcerting to see William in twenty-first century clothes. That's my hang-up. He had no such concerns. He'd been more than happy to shed his suits and ties for jeans and sweaters. This is a man who's never more comfortable than when working in his stable or riding out on his land. Modern clothes suit his lifestyle much better, even if he does look very fine in an old-fashioned suit.

Today, he's wearing a cable-knit sweater under his jacket. I roll my eyes at that, wondering which local knit him the sweater. When he'd first "arrived" as my fiancé, the villagers had been skeptical. Yes, he was obviously a Thorne—his face bears the strong features that grace a dozen portraits in town—but they didn't know him. They'd taken me in—that wee thing who used to trot about town, that poor girl who saw her uncle die, that quiet widow who came to reopen Thorne Manor at last.

William might be a Thorne, but clearly he was up to no good. Wooing me in hopes of regaining Thorne Manor. Their suspicion lasted about five minutes, and the next thing I know, he's bringing home the best scones from the bakery and the finest cuts from the butcher.

High Thornesbury is very proud of its history, with a million tales of the eccentric and good-hearted family who once inhabited the manor house. The Thornes were a rare example of popular landowners, and William carries the mantle of that legacy with ease. He is as popular in modern High Thornesbury as he is in his own version of it, and I have no doubt someone knitted him that sweater . . . and no doubt that he has already found a way to repay their kindness.

The sweater does look very good on him. Even by modern standards, William is a big man, over six feet tall and broad shouldered. Like me, he's thirty-nine, our birthdays being a mere month—well, a month and a hundred-and-fifty-odd years—apart. His tousled black hair is unfashionably long in his own time, but suits him well here. He has a square face, bright blue eyes and a solid jaw without even a hint of five-o'clock shadow, meaning he shaved for me this evening. Not that I care—he looks very nice with beard shadow, too—but he will always be the Victorian gentleman who must show his lady that she's worth the effort of a late-day shave.

I take off one glove and run a finger along his clean-shaven jaw. His gaze slants toward the road, being sure the driver is gone. Then his hand goes behind my head as he pulls me into a deep and hungry kiss.

"Now that's a far better hello," I say as he lifts his head.

"It seemed rather improper to deliver it while you were in the backseat of a cab, shivering to death in the cold."

I roll my eyes. "I wasn't shivering, William. But yes, it wasn't the best place for a welcome-home kiss."

I snuggle into his arms and let him continue carrying me up the walk. As we reach the porch, I twist, wanting to see Thorne Manor lit up in her holiday finest . . .

The only lights are ones illuminating the porch. The yard is snow-covered and otherwise empty.

William pushes open the door, which lacks so much as a wreath. Once we're through, I discreetly try to look about for a tree or maybe a sprig of mistletoe, even cards on the fireplace mantle.

Nothing. There's nothing.

"Yes, yes," he says. "Stop squirming. I'll put you down soon enough."

A clomp-clomp as he kicks snow from his boots. Then he walks into the parlor and deposits me on the sofa, amidst a nest of piled blankets. Across the room, a fire blazes. A tantalizing odor makes my mouth water, and he disappears into the kitchen, only to return with a basket of warm scones.

"Freya's?" I say.

"Of course. You didn't think she'd let you arrive without sending up a bushel basket of scones. That's the appetizer. Mrs. Shaw left a cold supper on the other side. We'll cross over when you're ready."

A cold supper isn't . . . quite what I'd hoped for. Especially not one served in a nineteenth-century house on a midwinter night. I'd rather stay here and pop something into the microwave oven, enjoy my late dinner with central heating and electric lighting.

Really, Bronwyn? Really? Mrs. Shaw made dinner for you. Freya made these scones for you. William got this fire going for you and came out to meet you with blankets. And you're complaining?

No, the truth is just that I'm disappointed by the lack of, well . . . My gaze slides around the room, which looks exactly as I left it after October's Thanksgiving break.

I'm disappointed by the lack of Christmas. Which is equally shameful. I know William hasn't celebrated the holidays in years. Did I expect him to ready the house for me? He's waiting so we can decorate it together. It's hardly Christmas eve. There's plenty of time.

I'm just tired. Tired and overwhelmed with the emotion of being back here and seeing him and our house. I missed them both so much.

Which reminds me . . .

I sit up as he takes a scone from the basket. "Where's Enigma?"

I'd left my kitten here, with William and her mother, Pandora. Taking the little calico to Canada wouldn't have been fair. This is her home. Yet she can pass through the time stitch, so I'd expected her to be waiting for me.

"She's off doing kitten things," he says. "On the other side. Endless mischief, that one. I think I might have spotted her this morning . . ."

Not disappointed. I am *not* disappointed.

"Give me a few moments to fetch your bags and stable

Xanthus. Then we'll cross over."

He kisses my forehead and then holds a warm scone to my lips. I smile and take it. As I nibble a toasted edge, he heads for the door. Then he turns and glances back, his lips twitching in a smile.

"Any gifts for me in your bags?" he asks. "Best to warn me, so I don't accidentally peek."

"You mean so you know whether there's any *point* in peeking."

His brows arch. "That would be wrong."

"No, William, there are no gifts for you in my bags." I take a bite of the scone, drawing out the moment. "I had them shipped to Del and Freya's. Pre-wrapped. And *very* well taped."

"One would think you don't trust me around them."

"One would be correct."

He shakes his head. Then, at the door, he pauses and looks back at me. "You never did tell me what you want for Christmas. You'll need to do so post-haste, or you'll wake up to a very sad holiday morning."

So he hasn't bought me any gifts yet. He's waiting to hear what I want... when I spent days wandering through wretched shopping malls picking out exactly the right things for him, without so much as a hint about what he'd want.

Not disappointed. I am *not* disappointed.

The door closes, and I slump into the blankets and sigh.

It's fine. Really, it's fine. There are many inconsiderate people in the world, but William isn't one of them. This is all just new to him.

The man has spent the last decade living alone in the

moors, avoiding all but locals and close friends, his family gone, his life shadowed by scandal and rumor. Now, in the space of a half-year, he finds himself married and a father-to-be . . . and living part-time in a world he can barely fathom, a world filled with endless challenges.

It's a wonder he crossed over to meet me at all. In his place, most people would hide in their own century, popping over only long enough to leave a note saying "Meet me on the other side." He not only waited here but found a way to surprise me with a flight upgrade and hired car. And I'm disappointed by the lack of a Christmas tree and presents?

By the time he returns, I'm on my feet, face washed, hair brushed, scone basket over my arm.

"All ready to cross over?" he says as he shakes new-fallen snow from his hair.

"I am." I kiss his cheek. "Thank you for coming to meet me. And for the flight and car."

"Flight and car? Whatever are you talking about?"

"The upgrades?"

His eyes dance. "Must have been pixies. I can scarcely operate my mobile phone. I'd hardly know how to get you . . . what did you call it? An upgrade?"

I shake my head. He's right about the phone—so much tech to learn, so little time to learn it when you're taking care of two houses and two stables.

Luckily, William isn't afraid to ask for help, and our neighbors Freya and Del are more than happy to provide it. Well, Freya is, at least. Del just quietly comes over and cleans out the stable or mows the lawn, and then, if thanked, he'll grumble that *someone* needed to do it.

"We'd best bring a blanket or two," William says, as he puts out the fire. "I'll need to light the fireplaces once we cross. Perhaps we should bring a torch as well? I considered leaving a candle burning, but that bloody kitten of yours would have set the house aflame." He frowns. "I hope she didn't get into our supper. I ought not to have left it out."

So I'm leaving this brightly lit, warm house for a cold, dark one with a potentially kitten-nibbled dinner?

I plaster on a smile. "It'll be fine. I'm just glad to be home."

He leads me upstairs, flipping off lights as we go. We head to my old bedroom—the one I'd used when I'd visited my aunt. It's an office now. We'd debated turning it into a nursery, but we'd rather not need to worry about our baby crawling through time during naps. This is where the stitch is located. A link between my old room and William's.

Why is there a time stitch here? *How* is there one? What even *is* it? There are questions we can't answer and don't care to.

For years, I'd been the only human who could cross. Then came Pandora, William's kitty, and later Enigma. After I put the last of the Thorne Manor ghosts to rest, William was able to cross as well.

Could others cross? It isn't a question we're ready to answer. The few people who know our secret have decided that, as much as they would love to pass through time, they don't dare risk being trapped on the wrong side.

We only hope that our child will be able to cross over. If not . . . well, if not, then we'll have decisions to make, but we trust that if we can—and our cats can—then our child will be able to as well.

We head for the stitch spot without preamble. William takes my hand, and we cross into our other office, which—contrary to his warning—is neither cold nor dark. It's blazing with light and warmth, the fireplace burning bright.

I turn and smack his arm.

He rubs his arm. "Is that how they use mistletoe in your world? Terribly uncivilized."

I crane my neck up to see a green and red sphere hanging over the stitch. It's a kissing ball—an apple covered in foliage and herbs, giving off the most delectable smell. There's mistletoe, of course, with its bright red berries, but also rosemary and lavender, symbolizing loyalty and devotion.

I smile as I gaze up at the ball. Then I reach for William, but he's already bending down to pick up a bright red box.

"Your first gift," he says.

Before I can protest that it's too early, something inside the box scratches. Then yowls piteously. I sputter a laugh and pull off the perforated lid to see a half-grown calico cat nestled in a bed of blankets with a toy and treats. Enigma glares at me with baleful green eyes.

"Hey," I say. "I'm not the one who put you in there."

Enigma continues to glare until I pick her up. Then she settles in on my chest and accepts my petting, even deigns to purr a little.

"I spent all afternoon trying to catch her." He rolls up his sweater sleeves, revealing a criss-cross of scratches down both arms. "Ungrateful little beast. I told her you were coming home, but did she listen? No. Just wanted to chase mice through the barn."

I set Enigma on my desk chair. Then I put my arms around William's neck, leaning back for a kiss. Instead, he scoops me up in his arms.

"There will be none of that," he says. "You have missed your chance and will need to wait for next Christmas. Do you know how much time I spent crafting that kissing ball? Holiday decorating is exhausting. I cannot imagine all the bother other people go to, putting up trees and hanging wreaths. I hope you're quite content with that single ornament."

He knees open the office door. Something smacks the top of it, and I crane my neck up to see a sprig of greenery hanging from a red ribbon.

"Wait," I say. "Is that more—?"

"More what?" he says, deftly swinging me around so I can see it. "Stop squirming, Lady Thorne. You're worse than that kitten of yours."

"Also much, much heavier," I say. "I'm going to suggest you put me down before we reach the top of the stairs. I'm carrying a few extra pounds these days."

"So I've noticed. I've always encouraged your obsession with scones, but you may want to curb your intake. You seem to have developed a bit of a . . . belly."

"Pretty sure I've always had one."

"No, you have a lovely, lush figure, which is currently somewhat unbalanced in the center. I blame scones."

"I blame you."

"Me? I've been in Yorkshire all these months, unable to

feed you a single biscuit or other sweet treat."

"You just have Freya help you mail them to me. In large boxes. Which are much appreciated but still . . ." I lay my hands on my bulging stomach. "Even those treats are not responsible for this. Now set me down—"

"Too late."

He takes a step down the stairs. I shake my head and go very still, which isn't necessary. The Victorian country lord's lifestyle is active enough. Add an insistence on doing one's own property work, and the result is a man who has little difficulty carrying his not-small-even-when-not-pregnant wife down the stairs.

When we reach the bottom, he turns me around again, so I can't see where we're going. I don't miss the kissing ball over the next doorway either, though he pretends not to see it.

"May I walk now?" I say.

"Certainly not. It's pitch black and freezing, and I fear the cats have eaten our supper."

"So I'm imagining the candlelight?"

"You must be."

"And the crackle and heat of a blazing fire? The smell of a hot meal?"

He frowns down at me. "You didn't catch a fever in that airplane, did you? You appear to be suffering from the most dreadful hallucination."

"Including the smell of a pine tree?"

"Indoors? Dear lord, who would do such a thing?"

He takes another step and then pauses, his foot moving something that swishes over the carpet. I twist to see a brown-paper wrapped box with a bow on top.

"That's not a gift, right?" I say.

"Certainly not. Someone has dropped a parcel on the floor."

My gaze drifts over a pile of boxes. "Quite a few parcels, apparently."

He sighs. "I cannot keep up with the post. Boxes upon boxes of saddle soap and shoe polish. Thank goodness you've finally arrived to tidy up after me."

He deposits me on the sofa, and finally moves aside for me to see the room.

I gasp. I can't help it. Yes, after seeing the kissing balls, I suspected he'd done a bit of decorating. Yet this is beyond anything I imagined.

There's a magic to Victorian Christmases, even if it's just our twenty-first century fantasy version, one that didn't actually exist outside a few very wealthy Victorian homes. The appeal for us is the simplicity of the decorations and the emphasis on nature. Brown-paper parcels with bright scarlet bows. A real tree, smelling of pine and blazing with candles. Wreathes and holly and ivy and mistletoe, none of them mass produced in plastic. It's a homemade, homespun Christmas.

That is what I see here. The fantasy, as if William pored over modern representations of that Victorian dream and brought it to life.

Brown-paper gifts piled under the tree, each wrapped in bright, curling ribbon. Evergreen boughs woven and draped across the mantel. Victorian holiday cards tucked into the boughs. Sprigs of holly scattered over every surface.

The tree stretches to the high ceiling, and the sharp scent of pine cuts through the perfume of the roaring fire. The tree is bedecked in red bows and ribbons. No candles—such a fire hazard—but hand-blown representations of them instead. The reflection of the roaring fire makes the glass candles dance, as if they're alight themselves.

When I rise and step closer to the tree, I see pine cones sprayed silver and what looks like silver-wrapped balls, each no bigger than a nickel. William pulls one from the tree and unwraps it to reveal a spun-sugar candy.

He holds it front of my mouth, and I inhale the sweet smell of peppermint.

"It's a bit early in the century for candy canes," he says. "I'd hate to accidentally invent them, so I'm hoping these are an adequate substitute."

I open my mouth to speak, and he pops the candy inside before I can. I laugh and let it melt on my tongue.

"It will do then?" he says, waving at the room.

Tears prickle at my eyes. "It's . . . it's . . ."

"Serviceable? Good. Now I presume you'd like some supper."

I catch the front of his sweater. "I can think of something I'd like better."

His brows rise. "Better than sustenance for our unborn child?"

"I ate a scone. The baby's fine."

"Well, then . . ." He lowers himself to me. "I suppose that cold supper can't get any colder."

"And I don't care if it does."

DINNER IS NOT a cold supper. It's only slightly cool by the time we get to it. Mrs. Shaw knows her employer well enough to leave it in the oven, keeping warm until he finally gets around to eating.

Mrs. Shaw lives in the village, spending semi-retirement with her daughter and grandchildren. Yes, having Lord Thorne alone in his manor house, with only a live-out housekeeper and occasional stable boy is dreadfully shocking, but as I said, the people of High Thornesbury are accustomed to eccentric lords. I'm sure there are plenty of whispers about the fact that his new bride spends so much time in London—while she's pregnant, no less—but an excuse about an invalid relative needing care has been deemed acceptable enough.

So we have the house to ourselves, which is good, considering that William is currently walking out of the kitchen naked, ferrying plates of food in to me, as I lie in front of the fire in an equal state of undress.

It's a veritable feast. Holiday food, to go with the ambiance. There's mincemeat pie, which still contains actual meat in this time period. Plum pudding is served with the meal, being considered more of a solid chutney than a dessert. To drink, there is a peach punch. Victorians love their punch, and being able to make it with out-of-season fruit is the mark of a cook—or housekeeper—who has mastered the art of canning.

The last dish is a tiny plate of sugarplums. William holds one to my lips as he stretches out beside me.

"Dessert before I'm finished dinner?" I say.

"Oh, I apologize. You aren't done yet? You do look very full." His gaze drops to my belly.

I groan. "You're going to keep doing that, aren't you?"

"I must. Freya bought me a book on twenty-first century fatherhood, and it included something called 'Dad jokes,' which it defined as repeating a vaguely funny witticism ad nauseam. I'm practicing."

I roll my eyes and stretch onto my back, taking the sugarplum with me. As a child, I always thought sugarplums were, well, sugar-coated plums. There are no plums involved, just lots and lots of sugar, this particular one having an anise seed at the middle, rather like a jawbreaker.

As I enjoy the comfit, William runs a hand over my belly. I look down to see his face glowing in the candle light.

"Bigger than when you saw me in October?" I say.

"Wonderfully bigger." He leans down to kiss my stomach. "You look well and truly pregnant now."

He's moving up beside me when he stops short, his hand on my belly.

"Was that a kick?" he asks.

"Probably food digesting. I was a bit hungry."

I feel a tell-tale twitch inside me and glance down to see something briefly protrude from my stomach.

"Nope," I say. "That's definitely a kick."

William grins and spends the next few minutes watching my stomach as our baby wriggles and kicks.

"A dancer," he says. "Like her mother."

I snort. "About as graceful as her mother, too."

I finish a second sugarplum and then stretch a hand over my head, fingers brushing a brown-paper parcel wrapped with scarlet ribbon.

William lifts it out of my reach. "None of that."

As he moves it, the tag—cut from a Christmas card—dangles low enough for me to read. I blink and then sit up, catching the tag to double check the writing.

"To William, with love from *Bronwyn?*" I say. "Uh, this isn't from me."

He frowns. "Are you sure?"

"Positive. Freya is under strict orders not to release your gifts to anyone but me. I also didn't wrap them in brown paper."

"How strange. I wonder what it could be, then?"

"One way to find out." I reach for the box, but he whisks it away.

"Uh-uh," he says. "You have made the rules very clear. We do not open gifts before Christmas. Possibly Christmas eve, if I have my way, but *no* sooner."

"I'm the giver of that one, not the recipient. I want to see what I got you."

"It's a surprise."

I thump back onto the pillow-strewn carpet. "You are ridiculous."

"Insults will not earn you more gifts."

I look at the towering pile. "I don't think I need more."

"They aren't all for you."

I crawl over and plunk down beside the stack to begin reading tags. "For me, for me, for me, for . . . Will Jr? Hoping for a male heir, I take it?"

"Certainly not. I picked a name suitable for either sex."

"We're going to call our daughter William?"

"Willa. Will for short."

"Which won't be confusing at all."

He crawls over to sit beside me. "I would love to choose a proper name, but I cannot do it until you give me one of my presents."

I look at the box tagged to him from me.

"Not that one," he says. "The one you're hiding in your magic box."

I look down the length of my naked body.

He sputters a laugh. "Your *other* magic box." He rolls over and pulls my cell phone from my discarded coat. "You have something on here for me, don't you?"

I take the phone, flip through photos and pull up my ultrasound picture. When I pass it over, he turns it this way and that, frowning at the screen.

"Now you're just teasing me," he grumbles. "I know the difference between a baby and a topographical map."

I laugh. "Sorry, but that *is* your child. It's a sonographic view."

I point out the facial profile and limbs, and as I do, his blue eyes light up. Holding the phone, he rolls onto his back to stare at the photo while I munch on candied nuts.

After a moment, he says, "You say the doctor can tell the baby's sex from this sonograph?"

"She can."

He sits up. "And . . ."

"Well, if you were secretly hoping for that proper Victorian heir, you'll be disappointed."

"A girl?" He grins. "We're having a girl?" He lifts the phone to gaze at the screen again. "Baby Willa."

"We'll, uh, work on that."

He pulls me over to him. "In the interest of marital har-
mony, I'll settle for Wilhelmina, but that's as far as I'm going.
Wilhelmina Hortensia Melvina Dale Thorne."

"Melvina," I muse. "I like that."

He pauses. "I was joking."

"No, it's a good one. Melvina Thorne. I think we have a
winner. We're definitely—"

"Oh, look, is that mistletoe over our heads?"

"I believe there's scarcely a square foot of this house where
mistletoe isn't over our heads. We'll need to get rid of it after
Christmas. It's poison, and little Melvina—"

He cuts me off with a kiss and lowers me back onto the
pillows as the phone slides to the floor, forgotten.

As a historian, I specialize in the Victorian era. It has been my
period of fascination since childhood, when I first crossed the
stitch into William's time. That knowledge is extremely helpful
now. I know what to expect from this world. While I can still
be uncertain and cautious, I feel comfortable navigating it,
with few genuine moments of culture shock.

Thus I know what I should expect on waking mid-winter
in Thorne Manor. The room will be freezing cold, with no
maid to slide in and light the fire before we wake. I should be
nestled under layers of blankets and wearing a long, flannel
nightgown—for warmth, not modesty. The windows will be
open despite the sub-zero windswept moors, because a closed
window invites miasma, which will lead to endless ailments.

Even after the fire is going, the ambient temperature will likely not exceed sixty degrees, requiring those endless layers of undergarments.

Instead, I wake naked in a comfortable feather bed with just the right amount of blankets, the top ones peeled back so I don't roast. The fire is roaring, and has never been fully extinguished. William rose earlier and stoked it, and while a big stone house like this is impossible to keep toasty without central heating, the rooms will be warm enough to suit my more modern sensibilities—and my preference for modern underwear, which William fully endorses. One window is just cracked open. We've discussed germ theory enough for my husband to banish period-appropriate notions of miasmas, and for us, a little fresh air is simply preference.

The room is deliciously cozy, that chilly breeze like the welcome ripples of wind on a hot day. The sharp and crisp breeze perfectly counterpoints the perfume of the roaring fire and . . . Is that tea?

I lift up and follow my nose to a steaming cup resting on the nightstand, with two biscuits perched on the saucer.

God, I love my husband.

I love this bed, too, which is going to be my dearest friend for the next twenty-four hours. I'll tell William that I need a little more sleep, and that he's more than welcome to join me later, when we can continue our marital reunion.

I grin and reach for a biscuit. The door swings open, William giving it a kick as he walks in, breakfast tray in hand.

Enigma wends her way past his feet and hops onto the bed to curl up with me. Her mother—Pandora—follows at

William's heels like a loyal hound. It is a picture I have been dreaming about for two months, rising in this bed, seeing William, the cats, the fire, the smell of the moors through the window . . .

I am home, and here I will stay.

William sets the tray on the side table.

"You cooked breakfast?" I say.

"Cooked is a strong word. More like 'warmed up.' But I did put eggs in boiling water."

"Impressive."

"I knew you'd want to rest after your journey."

I sigh in deepest contentment. "Thank you."

As I dig into breakfast, he disappears and then returns with clothing heaped over one arm.

"I bought a few winter frocks for you," he says. "I hope they'll fit. Mary estimated for me, and she'll adjust as needed."

"Perfect. Thank you."

He sets the pile on a chair and lifts the pieces, one at a time. The first is a full rich burgundy skirt, floor length, with pleats for light crinolines. Then a blouse that's obviously been tailored for my belly, simple and white with burgundy buttons. There's also a long fitted jacket in hunter green and a matching winter bonnet. Together, they'll form a simple but stunning holiday outfit.

"Gorgeous," I say.

"I thought they'd be suitable for our day's adventure."

"We're . . . going out?"

He's lifting the gown and can't see my expression.

"We are," he says as he lowers it. "The Festival of the Penitent Rapscallions. I thought you were going to miss it. But you are not."

"The Festival of the . . . what?"

He waves off my confusion. "I'll explain later. We've time for you to eat breakfast and dress, but then we really do need to be on our way. There are rapscallions in need of pardons, whether they are penitent or not."

"Uh . . ."

"Eat. Dress. Your festival awaits, my lady."

WITHIN AN HOUR, I'm bundled into a sleigh. A proper Victorian one-horse open sleigh, complete with jingle bells. I'm nestled in a pile of furs, and then my husband is beside me, and soon we're whipping down the hill to High Thornesbury.

I struggle to keep my eyes open. I swear I'm more tired now than when I arrived. Which, I suppose, may have something to do with the fact that I didn't get much sleep last night. Entirely my own fault. William had been endlessly solicitous of my "condition," and I'd waved off all his concern, avowing that I was only six-months pregnant and there'd come a point where sex would become unwieldy, and damned if I wasn't getting my full share before that happened.

If I'd been more energetic than William expected, then he can be forgiven for not realizing exactly how tired I am post-journey. I could say something. I could even just yawn and lean onto his shoulder, and that would be enough to have him turning the sleigh around and bustling me back to bed.

Two things stop me from doing that. Two things that have me sitting upright in the sleigh, bright-eyed and beatific, smiling and tipping my chin to everyone as we enter the village.

One, I am Lady Thorne now, at a time when that really means something. William may employ minimal house staff, but he understands that it is his hereditary duty to oversee the well-being of "his" town. Many of these villagers farm on his land or tend sheep in his flocks or run shops in buildings he owns. There's something uncomfortable about that for a twenty-first century dweller, but I still remember William's shock when, as a child, I told him we did our own cooking and cleaning. He wasn't aghast at the thought of hard work; he was alarmed about the disappearance of a major source of employment for the working class.

While there are certainly cruel and overbearing—or just plain thoughtless—landowners in Victorian England, the Thornes have always been an example of the way the system was supposed to work. It's still imperfect from a modern viewpoint, but despite my discomfort with being "lady of the manor," it's exactly what I am.

If I must be a lady, then I want to be the best one possible. That means joining William in village life. Playing my role. There's a cringeworthy old saying about the wife being a reflection of her husband, but there's truth of that here. I want to rise to William's example. This festival is important to the village, and our role in it is important, and I'm not going to force him to make my excuses, even if he'd happily do so. How would it look if Lady Thorne only returned yesterday evening and she's already too tired to join the "common folk"?

The second thing that keeps me from bowing out? I'm

about to participate in an archaic Victorian holiday tradition, one unique to this village. The historian in me is salivating, and the little girl who loved all things Victorian is bubbling with excitement.

William steers the sleigh down the snow-packed roads. The sides are thronged with villagers, snaking their way toward the village hall. When a preschool-age boy darts from the crowd, shrieking at the sight of the sleigh, William pulls the horse to a stop lightning fast.

The boy's father runs out, calling apologies.

"No trouble," William calls back. "He only wanted to see if he could outrun my sleigh." William leans over the side and waves a shiny copper coin. "Do you want to try, lad?"

The boy nods furiously.

"Then here is the wager. You must stick to the side of the road there. If you come out into the street, you lose the bet. We race to the village hall."

William shades his eyes. "Anyone else up for the challenge? Boys and girls are welcome to try their luck, but no one over the age of ten. We mustn't make it too difficult on my horse."

People laugh, and a few children come out from the crowd. William asks someone to do the countdown, and then we're off. William keeps the gelding going at a trot, leaving the children struggling. A few give up. When he nears the hall, though, he reins the horse in, and any of the children who kept at it win themselves a farthing.

We leave the sleigh outside the hall, and we're met by Mrs. Shaw's sons and son-in-law who help me down and then escort us in. The hall is already packed with people, more streaming in. There's a small stage erected at the front. On it are two rough-hewn wooden thrones, festooned with holly and ivy. We're led in the back and to the thrones, where we're given holly crowns and scepters.

Once everyone's in, the vicar says a few words, welcoming the villagers to the festival. Then he summons a little girl from a seat near the front. She's about six years old and missing her front teeth. She wears a green dress adorned with enough bows and lace for two gowns. As she draws closer, I can see the dress is a hand-me-down, faded and repaired, but in it, she walks like a princess, her face glowing.

The girl stops before us and curtseys.

"Agatha, isn't it?" William says.

"Yes, m'lord," she lisps.

"Have you committed a misdeed this year, Agatha?"

"Yes, m'lord," she says, barely able to contain a grin.

"Are you ready to make a full accounting of that offense?"

"Yes, m'lord."

"Please proceed."

She straightens. "Last fall, I climbed a fence and stole an apple that had fallen on the ground."

"And what did you do with it?"

"I ate it, sir."

William frowns. "You didn't try to put it back in the tree where it belonged?"

She giggles. "No, sir."

"That poor tree, losing an apple, only to have a little girl snatch it up." He eyes her. "Was it a delicious apple?"

"Very delicious, sir."

"Did it have any worms in it?"

She makes a face. "No, sir!"

"Well, then I suppose one could say that if the tree dropped the apple, then it meant for someone to eat it, and if there were no worms inside, then you weren't stealing *their* food, so . . ." He looks at the crowd. "Does anyone wish to claim the cost of this fallen apple?"

A few low chuckles drift from the audience.

"Well, then," William says. "I pardon you, Agatha, for your misdeed." He taps his scepter to her head. "In recognition of your brave confession, Lady Thorne has a reward for you."

"Two rewards," I say, taking a couple of humbugs from my basket. "One from Lord Thorne, and one from myself."

I pass the girl the peppermint sweets. She curtseys and blushes and can't quite make eye contact with me, but she smiles shyly before scampering back to her seat.

The procession continues. One child after another confessing to some "misdeed" from the previous year, to be "pardoned" by William. As childhood crimes go, they're all innocent enough. I'm sure no one who actually did anything seriously wrong would confess it here. In some cases, I also suspect children concoct a "crime" to join the fun and get the candies.

This is certainly not a Victorian tradition I've ever heard of. William says it's very localized and he doesn't know the origins, only that he'd attended his first as a boy when his grandfather had done the pardoning. I cannot wait to discuss it with Freya, who's a folklorist and has surely heard of it.

When the official pardoning is over, the festival spills into the village square to allow the hall to be prepared for the luncheon. William and I go out with the others and socialize in the square while admiring the decorations.

When we think of an old-fashioned Christmas, the Victorian model is what comes to mind, mainly because most of our traditions surfaced—or in some cases—resurfaced with Victoria's reign, many of them borrowed from her husband's German homeland. Here I'm witnessing what is truly the dawn of the modern British and North American Christmas, and the locals have thrown themselves into the season with typically Victorian abandon, decorating everything in sight.

We're soon called back into the hall, where what waits is not a luncheon but a veritable feast. Everyone has cooked and baked their family holiday speciality, and as the local nobility, we must try it all to avoid giving offense. Boar's head. Ham. Roast goose. Sage stuffing. Vegetables cooked in every possible combination. Mincemeat pie. Cranberry pie. So many pies. And, of course, plum pudding. *Three* plum puddings.

After we dine, it's back into the square for more socializing. William is off talking with a group of men who farm on his land. I'm chatting with the local schoolmaster and his wife when I notice a young woman trying to catch my attention. It's Mary, the teenaged seamstress William hires for our wardrobe.

I excuse myself from the young couple and head toward Mary. Even with the square cleared of snow, I need to haul up my long skirts and coat, and by the time I reach her, I'm very aware of exactly how tired I am, but I banish it with a bright smile of genuine warmth.

"Greetings of the season, Mary," I call as I approach. "It's so good to see you. Thank you for altering my outfit. You are an expert estimator."

"I'm glad it fits, ma'am," she says, "and I didn't mean to interrupt your conversation. I only wished to ask if we might have a word. Not now," she adds quickly. "I know you're busy. Perhaps we could talk tomorrow, when I come to the house?"

"Tomorrow would be fine, Mary, but if there's something you need to speak to me about, I'm happy to hear it now."

"It's not worth troubling you with, ma'am. Just . . ." She casts a quick glance at my midriff, as if not wanting to be indelicate. "Lord Thorne says you'll be staying at Thorne Manor now, at least until the fall."

"We will. My invalid aunt is doing much better. If William and I decide to spend any time in London, it won't be until after the summer."

In other words, if I can't get a local teaching position in the twenty-first century, William has insisted we'll temporarily move closer to wherever I'm working.

Mary nods. "That's what his lordship said. For now, though, you'll both be living at the manor, along with the babe when it comes."

"We will."

"And being a lady, especially one with a new babe, you'll need more staff at the manor. At least a maid. Perhaps even a nursemaid."

"We . . . haven't given it much thought."

"But you will. You can't stay up there with just a live-out

housekeeper." She straightens. "I would like to apply for whatever position you require, Lady Thorne. I do not have experience as a maid, but I'm a quick learner."

"I know you are," I murmur.

"And I *do* have experience with babes. I can provide references for that."

"I thought you liked being a seamstress, Mary."

"Yes, but it's only part-time. Piecemeal work. Father says I need a full-time position. He's found one for me in Whitby, working on a farm. It's either that or I marry George Wilcox, who's widowed with five little ones." She lowers her voice. "I don't know which is worse."

I stifle a smile. "No doubt."

The answer here is obvious. Hire her. I know Mary, perhaps better than I know anyone in the village. She's been at the manor many times. She accepts our eccentricities without question. To her I am simply a formerly widowed American, and any oddities of my speech and behavior can be chalked up to that.

I trust Mary. There's no one I'd rather have in the house, even if I'd still want it to be a live-out position. I don't need a maid—or a nursemaid—but this isn't about me. She needs a job, and I could find enough work to justify a wage that we can very easily afford. So why am I not jumping in to offer her a position?

Butterflies.

What holds me back is a little thing called the butterfly effect, which gets its name from the idea that the mere flap of a butterfly's wings could set about a chain of reactions that cause a tornado.

For the average person, the "butterfly effect" is usually heard in terms of time travel. What if we *could* go back in time? What effect would our actions have on the future? Even if we actively strove to do good, couldn't we unknowingly cause future harm? What if we traveled back in time to stop a killer, only to discover that one of his later crimes had launched a revolution in forensic science or victims' rights, so we've save a few lives only to ruin thousands?

This is the dilemma I struggle with as a bona-fide time traveler. I didn't, at first. As a child, one hardly considers such things. As a teen, quite frankly, I didn't care. As an adult, though, I am keenly aware that I am tampering with history. Even my existence in this world could have unforeseen effects, and I cannot add to that by meddling.

I'm not a monster, though. I won't let Mary be married to a middle-aged man who only wants free childcare and housekeeping. Nor will I let her be shipped off to Whitby, away from her family, her seamstress talents wasted doing backbreaking physical labor. I will find another solution to this problem, and so I tell her I'll think on it, and she tries not to let me see her disappointment at that.

BY THE TIME William bundles me into the sleigh, I'm ready to fall asleep against his shoulder. I'm stuffed with plum pudding and pie, and my brain is buzzing with all the things I saw and heard, cataloguing them for Freya. I'm also making mental notes of names and occupations and the spiderweb of relationships that is at the heart of an English village. I want to be like

William, able to put names to faces and ask people how their sheep are faring or whether their newly wed daughter is settling in well.

Of course, thoughts of married daughters remind me of Mary. The obvious answer is to discuss this with William. He at least needs to know she asked about employment. But when it comes to my butterfly-effect concerns, he has decided not to interfere. I must work this out for myself. His opinion would be that I shouldn't worry about it, and he realizes that could sound as if he's belittling my concerns. So he's keeping mum on the subject, and I agree that's best in general. Still, I would like to know whether I'm overreacting here.

"I spoke to Mary," I say, raising my voice to be heard over the swish of snow beneath the runners.

"I thought I saw you two together," he says. "Did she say when she'll be up tomorrow for the fitting?"

I pause. "She asked about speaking to me when she came to the house, presumably for a fitting, but we didn't set a time. Had she already arranged an appointment with you?"

"I discussed it with her yesterday, when I knew you were on your way home early. The Festival of the Penitent Rapscallions isn't the only thing that you arrived just in time for. There's also the Yuletide Ball at Courtenay Hall."

"What?"

He smiles over at me. "August's family holds a holiday party every year. You finally get to see Courtenay Hall *and* attend your first ball."

His smile widens to a grin, setting his blue eyes twinkling. The first time I met Mary, he'd hired her to play ladies maid for me, as I prepared to attend a ball—a private ball for just William and myself. That was our first night together as a couple, and it'd been the most perfect, magical night ever, meant to fulfill my teenage fantasy of having William sneak me into a Victorian gala.

Now he's giving me a proper ball, at the summer home of one of my favorite people on this side of the stitch: William's best friend, August Courtenay. I'll get to see August and his three-year-old son, Edmund, *plus* visit their estate *and* attend my first ball. Even better, I don't need to sneak in. I am Lady Bronwyn Thorne, an invited guest. A thrill darts through me, and I find myself grinning back at him.

"I thought you might like that," he says, his arm going around me in a quick squeeze.

"When is it?" I ask.

"Tomorrow night."

My smile falters as I inwardly collapse into a puddle of exhaustion. I recover in a blink and deliver a quick kick to my mental backside. None of that. This is the opportunity of a lifetime, and I'm damn well going to seize it. It's only mid-afternoon. I can nap as soon as I get home, and if I'm still tired after that, I'll extend my nap into an all-night sleep so I'm fully refreshed and ready for tomorrow.

I have a holiday ball to attend, and I cannot wait.

So, THAT PLAN to crawl into bed when I get home? It starts to fall apart as soon as we get back to Thorne Manor. William wants to escort me inside and then stable the horses, but I insist on accompanying him into the barn. Horses may be his passion, but they are an old love of mine, one I'm rekindling as fast as I can.

First, I must greet all the horses while trying very hard not to lavish undue attention on my personal favorite, Epona, named after the Celtic patron goddess of horses. The two-year-old gray filly is Balois's offspring, and she's promised to a London buyer once she's old enough to be trained. I don't have a horse of my own yet—I usually ride the gelding William uses for pulling the sleigh, who is a fine horse but more trained for carts than riders.

We're still trying to decide whether I should claim a future foal or buy a young horse of proper riding age. While I would love a horse from William's stock, he has buyers for two years' worth of colts and fillies, and I'm not sure I care to wait that long for a horse to call my own.

An hour passes between feeding treats to the horses and discussing whether or not riding is safe in my condition. The doctor says it is, but William would prefer we didn't take the chance, and I'll grant him that.

When William finally shuffles me into the house, I'm ready for bed. Instead, he steers me to the time stitch, because apparently we have a tea date with Freya and Del, and just enough time to go back to the modern world, change and then drive over to their place.

Sleep. Someday I will sleep. Just not today.

"THERE," FREYA SAYS, closing the door behind William as he heads outside with Del. "They're gone. Now get your deadbeat self onto Del's chair for a nap."

She points at the recliner by the window. It's old and ratty, clearly his contribution to the marital home, and yet it looks like the most comfortable chair I have ever seen. My knees wobble just seeing it.

Freya puts a hand against my back and steers me toward it. When I dig in my heels, she walks where I can see her and crosses her arms.

I lift one eyebrow at her stern expression. "Is that the look you gave your students when they misbehaved? If so, may I tell you why it didn't work?"

"Oh, it *always* worked. I might have been the softest touch at the academy, but that only meant my pupils hated to disappoint me." She looks up into my face. "You are disappointing me, Ms. Dale."

I sputter a laugh. But I do lower myself into Del's chair with an audible sigh of contentment.

"So," she says. "Are you going to tell William how exhausted you are—having flown across the world, six months pregnant, right after exams—or am I going to need to have a word with our Lord Thorne?"

I sigh. "It's not his fault."

"Nope, it's yours." She catches my look and arches her white brows. "Well, it is. He's like a child who just devoured an entire bowl of sugar. His new bride is home, at the holidays no less, and he's too excited to pause long enough to see that the only place you want to visit is your bed."

I sigh again. Deeper. Then I straighten. "Oh, I haven't told you where we went this afternoon."

"Don't change the subject. We're—"

"The Festival of the Penitent Rapscallions."

That stops her. She blinks. "The what?"

I smile. "You mean you haven't heard of it? Aren't you the local historian *and* folklorist?" I lean back in my seat. "Well, I suppose it's not that important. Just a forgotten local tradition that I attended personally and could tell you all about . . . if only you wouldn't rather discuss my need for sleep."

She glares. Which is adorable, really. Freya is barely over five feet tall, plump and white haired, and about as menacing as a Persian kitten.

"Would you like to talk about the festival?" I say.

"Would you like to tell William you're too tired for all this holiday running about?"

"After the ball. I really do want to go to that. Until then, if I can just sit here, with nice cuppa and a biscuit or two to sustain me . . ."

She rolls her eyes but walks to the table and pours me a tea as I start telling her about the festival.

"That is remarkable," she says twenty minutes later, sitting in her own chair, madly typing my observations into her laptop.

"You've never heard of it?" I say.

"I have heard of a local tradition involving pardons, but I was never able to track down details. It seems I was looking in the wrong direction. Pardons are primarily Roman Catholic in nature, mostly associated with Easter and Michaelmas. There's very little Catholic influence here, though, which is why I wasn't getting anywhere. What you're talking about more likely holds traces of Saturnalia."

She chuckles at my expression. "Yes, you'd best not tell the vicar that their beloved festival is rooted in paganism."

"Aren't most, though?" I say as I glance around her living room.

While there's a small tree in the corner, her own decorations suggest a celebration of Yule and the solstice more than Christmas, though they also bring to mind the Victorian decorations William put up, strengthening the commonalities between the two.

The emphasis is on nature, with evergreen boughs and holly, dried citrus slices, mistletoe balls and pine cones. And, of course, candles. So many candles, as if to summon the sun indoors as the days grow ever shorter.

"Saturnalia then?" I prompt. "Roman holiday held in December and one of the precursors to the non-Christian aspects of Christmas."

She smiles. "Correct. Saturnalia celebrated freedom, among other things. Masters would serve dinner to their servants and slaves, who were free for that brief period of time. According to some historians, there was also a practice of pardoning criminals during that time. Your local penitent festival could have its roots there. There are also potential origins closer to home. In the middle ages, the York minster hosted a winter mistletoe service that pardoned wrongdoers. It clearly rose from pagan practices." She taps her keys, making more notes. "I'll take a closer look at the York mistletoe service and see whether the practice spread to any other villages in the area."

We chat a bit more about the High Thornesbury festival

and its possible antecedents. Then I pull my feet under me. "I also had . . . Well, I have a situation I need to discuss with you."

I tell her about Mary.

"And you're hesitating to hire her?" Freya says. "For fear of what exactly? That you might interfere with her destiny to die broken down in a field by the age of thirty?"

I give her a look.

"Well?" she says.

"It won't come to that, obviously. If I don't hire her, we'll find another—less intrusive—way to help. But it's a symptom of an issue I need to deal with. What if, in the correct timeline, she went to Whitby, met the farmer's son, fell in love, and lived both happily and comfortably for the rest of her life? What if, by hiring her as a nursemaid, I sentence her to a life in service, never able to give up the steady paycheck to follow her dreams?"

"And what if, by squashing a bug in Victorian England, you bring about World War Three?" Freya snaps her laptop shut. "Where do you draw the limit, Bronwyn? And at what point is that limit going to interfere with your life, and the lives of your family? Yes, your baby doesn't need a Victorian nursemaid. But maybe she should have one. Maybe that's *her* destiny."

When I don't answer, she sighs and says, "You do realize the butterfly effect is pure fiction. An author's creation."

"No, it's not," says a thickly accented voice from the doorway. "It's chaos theory."

I look up. Del is in the doorway, pulling off his boots, with William coming in behind him. Del had been Thorne Manor's caretaker for years, my aunt hiring him when she stopped coming up to North Yorkshire after her husband died.

My early correspondence with Del referenced his legal name, as he was part of Aunt Judith's will. That name is Delores Crossley. It's almost hard to remember that now, arriving and being confused for about five seconds before I figured it out.

Del presents as male and uses male pronouns. As for the specifics, it's none of my business. He is Del Crossley, caretaker of Thorne Manor, devoted husband of Freya and our friend. He's also a retired physicist, which was more of a shock than anything else. The man looks like he's spent his life with grease on his hands and a pipe clenched between his teeth.

Del walks in and pokes around the tea table before selecting a square of cucumber sandwich.

"Chaos theory," I say. "That's science, right?"

He snorts. "Yes, Dr. Humanities Professor, it's one of those *science-y* things."

He eyes his chair—with me in it—and I start to rise, but he waves a gnarled hand and lowers himself beside Freya, who leans against him briefly in greeting.

"Is it a physics science-y thing?" I ask as William comes in and silently takes a seat near me.

Del sighs, as if I'm asking him to roll a boulder uphill, not talk about a subject he enjoys as much as William likes talking about horses . . . or Freya about folklore . . . or me about Victorian history. We are passionate about our passions, which is probably why we've become such good friends.

In normal conversation, Del's North Yorkshire accent is

porridge thick and liberally salted with local dialect. I think that's partly a choice and partly camouflage. The average retired physicist—or historian—might want people to remember they have a PhD after their name, but Del would be quite happy if most of his neighbors forgot. He wants to recede into village life for his retirement. Hence the accent. When he launches into lecture mode, though, all that falls away.

"Chaos theory is the study of random or unpredictable behavior within systems," he says. "When it comes to time travel, many theoretical physicists disagree with the so-called butterfly effect. They believe that it's ridiculous to think one small action could disrupt a future that has—in the traveler's time—already taken place. According to them, the universe would heal itself."

"How?" I say. "Any change I make here *must* ripple through time."

"Must it? That makes the universe seem an awfully fragile thing." He leans back. "The butterfly effect is a Hollywood gimmick, a constraint to place on time-travel stories. Raising the stakes and all that nonsense. But those writers live in a world where time travel *doesn't* exist. If it does—which we know—the results cannot be catastrophic."

William rises and brings the tea pot over to refresh my cup. "That presumes, of course, that time is linear. Or that my world exists in the same timeline as yours."

"Precisely," Freya says. "I don't think it does. It's like I've said before. Time seems to be stitched together at a point where you two can cross. It's probably also stitched at other points. That would mean multiple layers of time rather than one set timeline."

And so it goes, launching into a heated discussion of the nature of time travel. I join in a bit, but my mind keeps circling back to what they've said about the butterfly effect and chaos theory.

There are no answers here. Oh, I could try to *get* answers. I've already affected William's own timeline. I can check the archives and see whether anything has changed.

I did check once, when I feared I'd never get back to William. I learned that he died an old man in his nineties and never married.

If I check again, will that have changed? Even if it has, does that prove this is one uninterrupted timeline? I'm not sure it does. Maybe only my timeline changes, the effects I've wrought appearing in the archives in my own time, but not in the future one of his. Yes, it makes my head hurt just thinking about that.

But even if I could prove, beyond a doubt, that it is a single timeline, does that also prove that me hiring a girl in nineteenth-century England will have unforeseeable—and disastrous—effects on the modern day? Of course not.

These answers do not exist for me to find. I need to make choices on my own. To decide for myself what I believe and what I'm going to do about it.

DESPITE MY BUSY day, William is careful not to keep me out too long. By dinner, we're back in Thorne Manor, and then it's a quiet evening and off to bed early. Which would be lovely if my racing brain would actually let me sleep. It's not just my brain. Little Melvina is restless too, kicking and squirming, as if she senses my disquiet.

This is, of course, all her fault. Yes, I'm already shoving blame onto my poor unborn child's shoulders. The fault, I think, lies with impending motherhood. Or maybe just hormones. All I know is that five months ago, I enjoyed a glorious newlywed summer with William, unhampered by thoughts of what havoc my existence might wreak on history. We spent most of our time holed up in Thorne Manor—on one side of the stitch or the other—and we interacted with the outside world no more than we needed to do to establish our story as a newly wedded couple.

But then I returned to Toronto, and as my belly grew, I began to think more and more of myself as a mother, and with that came an additional sense of responsibility. It didn't help that I was teaching Victorian history, constantly reminded of the impact people and their actions have had on our past.

Lying in bed that night, my brain ping-pongs from one side of this debate to the other.

One minute, I decide I'm overthinking it. Making too much fuss out of nothing. Hubris, even, to think that my actions could impact history.

Then the next minute, I'm a fretting ball of nerves, setting guidelines and rules for myself, treating William's world like a museum I'm visiting. Stay on the paths. Do not touch the exhibits. Do not cross the ropes. Remember that I am a guest in their world, there to observe and . . .

And do nothing that might actually make a difference, even a difference for the better? If I do that, am I not like a wealthy visitor to the V&A, walking right past the donation boxes to take advantage of the free admission?

William has money. No, he'd correct me—*we* have money. His family had been in dire straits when his mother passed on. He'd barely been able to keep Thorne Manor, which had always been the family's holiday house, with their primary residence in London. William had taken what little capital he still owned and invested in . . . well, he invested in me. In my words. In what he remembered me talking about when we'd been teenagers, all the advances of the twentieth century.

William figured out what industries would become most important, what new inventions were likely to succeed, and while he made a few ill-timed choices, his instincts and his intelligence were enough to make him a wealthy man, all his family's debts repaid with a cash flow that would be the envy of his peers.

Ask William what he does with this fortune, and he'll joke that he uses it very wisely—to allow him to hole up in his beloved moors, with his beloved horses, playing the reclusive eccentric and never needing to set foot in London except by choice. That's true, but he also uses it for good. To help where he can in High Thornesbury.

How do I follow his example—which I desperately want to do—without interfering in history? Or, in worrying about interfering, will I do less good than I could?

These are the thoughts that have me tossing and turning. I wake with a few ideas for other ways to help Mary, but it doesn't solve the problem long term. That I still need to figure out for myself.

THE NEXT DAY passes in a whirlwind of activity. Mary comes, and while I make suggestions for her future, I can tell none of them are what she wants. I offer to help set her up in a proper dress shop, but there isn't enough of a market for it in High Thornesbury, and she doesn't want to move away. I offer to hire her to sew our baby clothes and a new post-pregnancy wardrobe for me, which is great, but what comes after that?

She listens to my suggestions and tells me they're very good and she'll pay them proper consideration. But I hear the hesitation in her words. I see her disappointment, too. It's not as if she's asked for something outrageous. Just a modest position that we'll need filled anyway. My reluctance must feel like rejection, no matter how much I assure her it is no reflection on her.

After my dress fitting, Mary takes the gown into another room to make alterations. Once the dress is done, it's time to get ready. Mary helps with that, as she did the night of my private ball with William. I might argue that I don't need a maid, but for an evening out, Victorian style demands at least one extra pair of hands. As Mary helps, she temporarily forgets her disappointment, and begins chattering away, sharing all the local gossip.

It takes nearly two hours to get ready. First come all the layers of dress, made that much more difficult by my belly. I'm thankful I'm only six months along. I can't imagine how difficult it would be to find formal dress if I were in my eighth month. I suppose the answer there is that if I were in my eighth month, I wouldn't be going to a ball. I have a feeling I should enjoy this side of the stitch as much as I can over the holidays, because not long into the new year, I'll want to be in the twenty-first century, where no one will blink at me going out in public with a basketball under my shirt.

Once I'm dressed, it's time for primping—the makeup and the hair and the jewelry. Tonight I wear the Thorne jewels. The necklace is a huge sapphire pendant circled with diamonds, more diamonds hanging from it. Even the chain is encrusted in diamonds. The ring is gold inlaid with a large sapphire flanked by diamonds. And the bracelet, not surprisingly, is more diamonds and more sapphires.

A fortune in jewels, passed from generation to generation, a symbol of continuity and former wealth, a reminder that the Thornes are a very old and very close-knit family. When his parents' debt had been at its worst, William had been on the brink of doing the unthinkable: selling a piece of the set. That's when he concocted the desperate ploy of using what little capital he had left to invest in the future I'd described. Now I hold the jewels in trust for the next generation.

When I'm finally dressed and ready, I look in the mirror and my breath catches, as it did the first time I saw myself in a proper ballgown. There's a fantasy fulfilled here, one featured in a thousand historical-romance novels, our intrepid young heroine dressing for the ball where she will meet the man of her dreams.

At thirty-nine, I don't quite fit that "young heroine" mold. I'm a middle-aged, very pregnant widow on her second marriage. And yet my story is at least as magical as any in those books I loved. I have married the man of my dreams *twice*. When Michael died at thirty, I thought that was it for me, even if "remarrying" was on the list of things he wanted for me . . . right after "have countless torrid affairs." The affairs never happened. The remarriage did, though, to the man who first captured my heart.

Mine might not be a standard romance story, but it is an incredible one that I am incredibly lucky to be living. Married to the man I thought I lost, starting a family after I assumed that opportunity had passed from my life. I have a home, a family, a community, and a career I love.

That's what I see in the mirror. Me, happy. Insanely happy, adorned in jewels and wearing the most amazing dress. Because while family and home and career are all vastly more important, one can never discount the value of a gorgeous ballgown.

This one is sapphire blue, in a shade to match the jewels. It's empire-waisted, which isn't the fashion, but it means that the waist sits above my belly, allowing the skirt to flow from there. Long-sleeves finish in delicate black lace. There's a black front panel on the full skirt and black trim on the hem. A low neckline to show off the jewels. Victorians may have a reputation—unearned mostly—for prudery, but I've never had more of my bosom on display then when I wear a period-appropriate ballgown.

My hair tumbles past shoulder length. It's threaded with silver, and my refusal to dye it is more proof of vanity than a lack of it. I consider my hair my best feature—even if William would point to other assets. Dyeing out the silver would mean changing the color and possibly the texture, and so I will be vain and leave it long and natural. Mary has curled and pinned it into a gorgeous partial updo that I can only pray will survive the three-hour sleigh ride to the ball.

Mary's gone now, and I'm in front of the mirror, tweaking and turning, making sure everything is right because I know enough about Victorian society to realize it must all be right. It's scandalous enough that I'm appearing in public in "my condition."

As I'm adjusting my décolletage, William walks in, murmuring, "I'll do that for you."

"Yes, and that will be a lovely way to launch my society debut, arriving hours late and in disarray because somehow, fixing my neckline resulted in my dress spending the next hour in a heap on the floor."

His smile sharpens to a wolfish grin. "No need for that. I will hitch it around your hips with utmost care. It'll scarcely even wrinkle." He touches my waist as he moves in closer. "Or perhaps I'll hoist you onto the table here, where there's a nice carpet for my knees as I go down—"

"Stop," I say, my voice coming out strangled. "Please."

He arches one brow. "Are you certain?"

"I am not at all certain," I say. "Which is the problem. We need to be on time, William, and I need to be as presentable as possible. Once I've been properly introduced and everyone has had time to form an opinion of me, *then* you may ravish me in a deserted back hall."

He chuckles, the sound half growl. "If you think I won't take you up on that . . ."

"Oh, I will be very disappointed if you do not, Lord Thorne."

He puts his fingers under my chin and lifts my lips to his in a long, delectable kiss. "It is a deal, then, Lady Thorne, on one condition."

"Which is?"

"That I do not ravish you in a back hallway, but that I do exactly what I just offered, in some suitably empty room. If there is to be any ravishing, it will take place on the ride home."

"In the sleigh?"

"Is that a problem, Lady Thorne?"

I brush my lips across his. "Not at all. Now lead on, m'lord. We have a ball to attend."

UNDER NORMAL CIRCUMSTANCES, there would be no problem arriving late. Fashionably late is a thing in Victorian times as much as the twenty-first century. One never wants to appear too eager. Or one doesn't if one cares about such things, which we do not. In fact, we're going to the ball early, though mostly so that I may have a proper tour of Courtenay Hall and spend time with Edmund before he's sent off to bed.

August Courtenay has been William's best friend since childhood. He's also his business partner. August is the one person on this side who knows the truth about me. Not because William confessed, but the opposite—William had refused to explain anything about me at all. When I'd returned to Thorne Manor at fifteen, William suddenly became less available to his friend, secretive and very, very busy. Presuming the issue was a girl, August set out to solve the mystery and discovered that William had been spotted with a mysterious girl no one had ever seen, one who dressed quite oddly. His first guess was that William had found himself a girl of the fae. I suppose that made more sense than the truth, which August worked out last summer when I returned.

August lives in London, but his family has an estate in North Yorkshire. And when I say "estate," I mean the kind of place that gets used today as the backdrop in grand period dramas. In fact, I'm quite certain modern Courtenay Hall has appeared in at least one production. In the twenty-first century, it's periodically open to the public, and when I visited it as a girl, my mind had been blown by the sheer scope of the place.

I've never been to nineteenth-century Courtenay Hall. This past summer, August always came to us, sometimes bringing Edmund. August's wife, Rosalind, died when Edmund wasn't even a year old. I say "died." William says died. Most of the world says died. Rosalind was apparently known for her moonlit rides on horseback, and one morning, she wasn't in bed when August awoke. Her horse was later found drowned, having apparently panicked and charged off a seaside cliff.

Clearly, Rosalind is dead. What other explanation could there be for the disappearance of a young mother who, by all accounts, adored her husband and son? Well, according to August, she left. Abandoned them. Ignore the fact that she never threatened any such thing, that they hadn't been fighting the day before she disappeared, that she'd never given anyone the slightest indication that she wanted out of the marriage. No, forget all that. Rosalind abandoned him, and he will hear no reasonable argument to the contrary.

William has long since stopped beating his head against this particular wall, and I cannot do it either, however frustrated I might be. I never met Rosalind, but I am offended on her behalf. For a good man, August is making a very stupid mistake—obviously preferring anger to grief—and our only consolation is that he does not share this theory with their son. He tells Edmund only that his mother loved him very much and died tragically.

We leave mid-afternoon because it'll take three hours to get to Courtenay Hall. I am not looking forward to repeating the journey late tonight. All right, given what William promised, I'm looking forward to at least *part* of the return trip. The rest will not be quite so comfortable in the middle of a winter's night.

August offered us overnight accommodations at Courtenay Hall, but his brother vetoed it. Apparently, the earl is a bit of an ass. That's my description of Everett Courtenay. William's is much more colorful. According to the Earl of Tynesford, we do not rate an overnight stay, and if my condition makes the long journey difficult, perhaps we shouldn't attend.

"He means perhaps *I* shouldn't attend," William says as we draw close to Courtenay Hall. "Our marriage may have brought me a measure of respectability, but I am still not acceptable in polite society."

William is referring to the scandal that has dogged him for over a decade. Three young women have disappeared in William's life: his sister, his former fiancée and Rosalind. That count sometimes rises to four. I'm the fourth—the mysterious girl seen with him all those years ago.

William was responsible for none of those disappearances. We solved the two murders, and I laid the spirits to rest. That is not, however, the sort of thing he can say in public.

"The problem," I murmur, "is that while you may have married, I am not someone the earl—or any of his compatriots—has ever heard of. A middle-aged widow from the Americas? Very suspicious."

"Devil take them all, I say." He glances my way, his face shadowed by his fur-lined hat. "They won't bother you. They won't dare. That's the one advantage to possessing such a dreadful reputation."

I shake my head. "I don't care either. I understand why we can't spend the night, though. It *is* his brother's house."

"And by the time his lordship decreed we could not stay, the local inns were full. There are others farther along, though when you see the condition of them, you may prefer to carry on."

"We have blankets," I say. "If you do not mind me curling up in the back . . ."

He smiles. "I do not mind at all. In fact, I believe I packed enough blankets that you may strip down to your knickers and curl up quite comfortably."

"And then the sleigh breaks down, and you're left standing at the side of the road with your wife in her underwear."

He waggles his brows. "That would certainly provide a boost to my reputation."

"Not in the proper direction."

I push my hands deeper into my muff and gaze out at the

winter wonderland. Endless fields of snow stretch to the horizon, with the falling sun painting the world a festive red. I cuddle closer to William as he turns the horse onto another road.

We pass a wagon, and the boys in it all turn to stare at the sight of us. Living this close to Courtenay Hall, they'd see their share of well-dressed couples in expensive conveyances. Our sleigh is certainly a wondrous thing—sleek and gleaming black with a leather seat and fur-trimmed blankets. What these boys don't usually see, I'll bet, is a sleigh like this being driven by the owner himself. We should be comfortably ensconced on that leather seat while a driver conveys us to Courtenay Hall. Personally, I like this much better. It's certainly a quicker ride, with William deftly steering the gelding, knowing exactly how fast the sleigh can safely and comfortably travel.

We turn onto another road, and I lean forward with a gasp.

"Pretty little thing, isn't it?" William murmurs.

In the distance, Courtenay Hall sprawls at the foot of wooded hills. Every window is ablaze with light and a skating rink glistens in the front yard.

We continue down the lane, passing gardens put to bed for the season. I spot a maze, two small ponds, a lake to our left, a grand fountain to our right . . .

"There are follies, yes?" I whisper. "That's what I heard, though when we visited in the modern day they were off-limits to the public."

"There are several follies," William says. "To your right, if you squint, you'll see a pyramid. There's a tower in the woods. Oh, and of course, the Grecian temple on the hill ahead."

I make a noise suspiciously close to a squeal. William chuckles. I have a weakness for follies. Perhaps they carry less mystique to those who grew up in England. Or to those who don't study Victorian history.

The nineteenth century saw a huge rise in tourism, at least among the upper and upper-middle class. Egypt, Greece, Italy, India . . . The English were mad for travel, and if you traveled, you wanted the world to know it. Souvenirs were a must.

Of course, many of those so-called souvenirs are what we'd now call stolen artifacts, and I suspect I'll see a few objects d'art inside that will make me squirm with discomfort. But follies are different.

When the wealthy traveled, one thing they brought back was a blazing desire to reproduce the world in their backyard, which worked best if your backyard encompassed hundreds of acres. Victorians rebuilt architecture from places they'd seen, usually scaled down versions. And by "scaled-down" I mean a twenty-foot pyramid instead of a two-hundred foot one.

"Is the temple life-size?" I ask. "At least big enough to walk in?"

"It's big enough to hold a garden party. That's where August proposed to Rosalind, if I recall correctly. It was our favorite spot growing up. We'd spend hours in there, playing all sorts of boyhood games. It's based on the Temple of Athena Nike in Athens, as perfect a scaled replica as could be managed."

He glances over, a smile playing on his lips. "We could always skip the ball and ride straight there. Spend the evening huddled in blankets on the steps of the temple, gazing up at the stars . . ."

He catches my expression. "And that was a cruel tease. I apologize." He kisses my nose. "We'll return when we can enjoy it properly, preferably in spring. The earl despises the countryside, and he's rarely here. We'll visit when August comes to stay."

"We'll bring little Melvina," I say.

He laughs. "We will certainly bring little whatever-we-name-our-daughter-that-is-not-Melvina."

I'm about to tease him when a figure darts from a doorway. It's a young woman in a maid's uniform, waving madly.

William pulls the reins and the horse stops sharply. "Trying to get yourself killed, Lottie?" He calls. "I know having the master at home is never cause for joy, but surely it isn't all that bad."

The girl—no more than a teenager—giggles and curtseys. "Mr. August told me to watch for you. He's getting ready, and he wanted you to come in this door, if you please, so he might bring young Edmund down for a visit."

The maid stops at my side of the sleigh and curtseys again. "I'm Lottie, Lady Thorne. Pleased to make your acquaintance. May I help you down?"

"I'll assist my wife," William says. "Get yourself inside before you catch your death of a chill."

I smile. "Please do go in. Lottie. But thank you for the offer."

Lottie disappears into the house, and William provides the assistance needed to get off my high perch. Then he carries me straight to the steps, ignoring my laughing protests.

"We'll go in and get comfortable," he says as he sets me down. "If August is getting ready, we'll be here a while. Even with a valet, the man cannot ready himself for anything in a hurry."

"If he takes extra care tonight," I say, "perhaps it means he's ready to look for a new wife."

William's snort says what I already know. August is light years away from that. William is about to comment when we step through the doorway, and a reedy voice shouts, "Uncle William! Aunt Bronwyn!"

We turn as a fair-haired preschooler tears along the corridor. William catches Edmund up, making the boy squeal.

August appears around a corner. William might gripe about how long August spends getting dressed, but the result is exquisite as always. When August does decide to re-enter the world of courtship, scores of eligible young women will be summoning their dressmakers for a new wardrobe, in hopes of catching his eye. He might be the youngest son of an earl, with no title of his own, but he's well-off in his own right, with a face that belongs on a Greek sculpture.

"Bronwyn," he says with a half bow. "You look incredible. I see you brought your stable boy. How thoughtful."

William rolls his eyes. I will point out that William's suit is both fashionable and well-fitting, tailored to his large body. It is not, of course, as fashionable or as well-fitting as August's. If the man has a streak of vanity, it's best seen here, in his impeccable attire.

We embrace, and August waves us into a room. A small sitting room of some kind. In a house this big, there are probably a half-dozen of them. I take a seat, and Edmund launches himself onto me, his squeal drowning out his father's gasp of horror.

"Careful, Edmund," August says. "Aunt Bronwyn is with child, remember?"

I laugh and arrange the boy on my knee. "My lap isn't quite as spacious as it once was, but we'll manage. I want to hear everything I've missed since I've seen you. First, though . . ."

William passes me a wrapped cloth from his pocket.

"Cookies!" Edmund shrieks.

August mock winces. "Biscuits, Edmund. They are called biscuits here."

"But these are cookies," I say. "Because they come from America." From my favorite bakery in Toronto, actually, though I can hardly tell Edmund that. "Chocolate-chip cookies."

This is how I won the heart of August's shy toddler. A very special cookie known only in the Americas. Now, let's just hope he never actually travels to the Americas and discovers no one's heard of a "chocolate-chip cookie" yet.

Aren't you worried about that? my little inner voice whispers. *Rosalind was a baker. Maybe Edmund will grow up to "invent" chocolate-chip cookies decades before their time, and the universe will implode.*

That is, of course, ridiculous.

Less ridiculous than thinking terrible things will happen if you hire a sixteen-year-old girl who is in desperate need of a job?

I brush off the voice and turn my attention to helping Edmund unwrap the cookies as William and August get caught up in some shipping matter or another.

"So," I say when we've freed the treats. "How is Surrey?"

Surrey is Enigma's sister, and another of Pandora's kittens. August gifted her to Edmund after William claimed he'd found homes for all four kittens. She'd been a surprise, and so that's what Edmund named her, Surrey for short.

This is all the prompting Edmund needs. Mouth stuffed with cookie, he launches into a story about his beloved kitten, and I settle in to listen.

BY THE TIME the ball begins, I've almost forgotten what we're actually here for. My mind is still buzzing from a private tour of Courtenay Hall, and it's calmed only a little by helping put Edmund to bed and reading him a story.

When William suggests we may want to "freshen up," I spent thirty seconds wondering why, before I hear music and chatter from the rooms below. Then I look out the window to see a queue of horse-drawn carriages inching down the lane.

William and I stand on a balcony to watch the guests arrive. I lean back against him, his warm arms around me, and we chatter like red-carpet reporters. I *ooh* and *ahh* over the fashions, as couples ascend the wide stairs. William does the same for the horses and carriages. He tells me the names and titles of everyone he recognizes, along with whatever gossip he can dredge up from memory. We spend a perfect half-hour hidden in the shadows, watching the procession.

Then, when the lane is log-jammed with carriages and sleighs, William decrees it time to make our appearance. This has been our plan all along. We'll enter the ball at the busiest moment, to attract the least notice. William doesn't care, of course, but I'd rather avoid as much unpleasantness as possible. My Victorian-ball fantasies only involve wearing a pretty gown and dancing the night away with someone special. Making a splash of any kind is not part of the plan. I am here to enjoy and observe.

Having been in the house for two hours already, we could enter through the rear of the ballroom and avoid being announced. That, however, wouldn't mean we could sink into the shadows. William is too notorious for that, and I am too pregnant.

In a book, we would swan into the ballroom, the butler would announce us, and everyone would turn to stare. And only someone who had never actually attended such a gala would imagine such a thing. We walk in, and it's like stepping into a wedding halfway through the night. There's a quartet playing music somewhere, but I can barely hear them over the din of voices.

If one imagines a Victorian ball would be very sedate, one has—again—never met an actual Victorian. Voices rise as people compete to be heard over one another. Raucous laughter rings out. Someone shouts for a passing serving girl. It's a cacophony of riotous, happy noise, and I am more than content to have our introduction drowned out by it.

"Lord William Thorne and his wife, Lady Bronwyn Thorne," the butler announces.

Only a few people close enough to hear him turn. We begin our descent into the ballroom almost unnoticed. Then the ripples begin, our introduction being passed along on a tide washing out ahead of us.

Thorne? William Thorne? Isn't that . . .

I won't say every head swivels our way, but enough do that if I ever entertained even the vaguest fantasy of turning heads at a ball, I can check that off my bucket list.

While there's something to be said for glances of admiration, am I a terrible person for admitting that this is kind of fun, too? Being the scandalous wife of a scandalous man?

I'd worried I might embarrass William by blushing or shrinking into myself under the weight of wicked whispers and gimlet-eyed glances. Instead, my spine straightens and my chin rises and the tiniest of smiles plays across my lips as the crowd parts for us. I am on the arm of a wonderful man, in a world I never thought I'd see, living a life richer than most people in this room could ever imagine. I am blessed, and if I'm a wee bit smug about it, I'm fine with that.

It's only after a moment that I see *where* the crowd has parted. Where it's leading us. A figure walks our way, a man who reminds me of August in a fun-mirror reflection. I'm sure he was handsome once, but there's a dissolution about him that makes my skin crawl.

It doesn't help that I've heard nothing good about Everett Courtenay, Earl of Tynesford. Yet even without that, I'd still feel that chill. His red nose and pouched eyes speak to a fondness for drink. He's in good shape otherwise, if solidly built. The look in his eyes is what creeps up my spine. It's a haughty sneer that says he doesn't see his equal anywhere in this room, and certainly not in the couple approaching him.

"Thorne," he says, his voice ringing in the now hushed room. "Finally decided to buy your way back into polite society with a bride, did you?"

I blink. Whatever I've heard about the man, I expected a veneer of civility. Or maybe that's what comes with being a member of the upper nobility. You can say what you want, hurt who you like.

"Tynesford," William says. "Good to see you. May I introduce my wife, Lady Bronwyn Thorne."

"Bit long in the tooth, isn't she?"

A titter ripples through the crowd.

"I didn't marry her for her teeth," William says smoothly. "Lady Thorne was a childhood friend, whom I had the good fortune to meet again this spring."

The earl's gaze shoots pointedly to my stomach. "Didn't waste any time starting on an heir, I see? Remind me again when you two got married?"

Gasps mingle with the titters now. Everyone knows what the earl is insinuating. He's actually correct. We married when I was nearly two months pregnant, in a small, private ceremony, with a clerk who was willing to backdate the marriage certificate for us.

"June second," William says. "And yes, we were fortunate enough to begin a family while on our honeymoon. As for an heir . . ." He lifts his shoulders in a shrug. "I'd be more than happy with a healthy baby girl. In fact, I'm quite certain that's what I'm going to get. I'd even be willing to wager on it."

For the first time, a pinprick of interest gleams in the earl's eyes.

"Would you?" Tynesford says.

"I would. I'm so certain, I'd lay ten to one odds on it."

A ripple of surprise through the crowd, almost drowned out by the earl's guffaw. "Well, then, far be it from me to discourage a man willing to gamble at such outrageous odds. Shall we say ten pounds?"

The gasps take on an edge of excitement. Surely William won't agree. If he loses at those odds, he'll owe the earl a hundred pounds, the modern equivalent of over ten thousand dollars.

"Accepted," William says.

The earl's laugh grows louder. "You really are mad, aren't you? All right then. Ten pounds at ten to one odds. Now, see that you don't murder *this* bride before she can give you that child."

William stiffens. His mouth opens.

"William!" a voice calls, as August pushes his way through the crowd. "Finally."

He embraces us as if we didn't just spend two hours together. Then he glances at his brother, as if only now noticing him there.

"Everett," he says, his tenor voice ringing out. "Thank you for entertaining my friends. I hope I didn't interrupt anything."

"No, your *friend* just wagered me ten pounds at ten-to-one odds that his wife will have a daughter."

"Did he?" August looks at me, his brows rising in question.

I dip my chin in a nod.

"Well, then," August says, "allow me to join in the fun. I won't give quite as good of odds, but shall we say ten pounds at five to one odds?"

Tynesford chuckles. "How much have you had to drink tonight, August? All right then. I accept your wager."

"Excellent," August says. "Now please allow me to steal my friends away . . ."

As he steers us from his brother, he whispers, "How certain are we about that?"

"Very," I say.

He exhales. "Excellent. I will look forward to my spring windfall. Come along then. I have so many people for you to meet, Bronwyn. Have you ever heard of . . ." He whispers a name into my ear.

My eyes must round, because he laughs. "Very good. Then we'll begin there."

IT IS THE ball of my dreams. *Beyond* my dreams. My youthful fantasy had been all about the gowns and the dancing. I have the first, and I get the second, with both William and August escorting me around the dance floor until my feet hurt. But it's more than that. It's the people for one thing. I meet some I know from history and some I've never heard of, but if August introduces us, it's because he finds them interesting. I expected to be in a corner with William, and instead I have incredible conversations with bright, witty and fascinating people.

There is also the food. One can never discount the food. Raw oysters are all the rage, and they're here in six varieties. There's sweetbread pate, which I'm sure is delicious, but I've never been a fan of organ meats. Tiny quail with delicate truffles. Deliciously fried rice coquettes. And fruit, every variety of fruit available in this era, showing off the estate's wealth. Imported oranges and pineapples. Greenhouse strawberries and grapes. Platters of exquisite little cakes and one entire tray devoted to Nesselrode pudding—chestnuts and fruits and liquor in a cream gelatin base. Knowing I can't judge the alcohol content—and the Victorians poured with a liberal hand—I take only a nibble or two from William's bowl of pudding. I also eschew all punches except the one August assures me is alcohol-free, a sad little pitcher at the end of a table groaning with bowls of jewel-toned beverages.

The pièce de résistance, though, is the ice cream. Which is . . . Am I being a complete twenty-first century snob to say I get a laugh at the ice cream? Row upon row of tiny silver dishes with a tiny half-melted scoop in each.

Had it been summer, it'd have been difficult to produce ice cream for this many guests, and the treat would be reserved for dinner parties. The Courtenays have an ice house—an insulated and sheltered well packed with ice in the winter. While freezing isn't a problem at this time of year, the sheer effort of churning ice cream in these quantities is a feat, and I pity the staff.

William also makes good on his promise: the one about sneaking off to an unused room, hiking up my skirts and getting down on bended knee. Yep, that's an entirely different sort of historical romance scene, but I've certainly read and enjoyed those too, and I enjoy this enactment even more.

Whatever fears I had about being here, whatever trepidation, it evaporates after we leave the earl and his snarky insults. I'm sure others make some, but I don't hear them. I thoroughly enjoy my evening.

At one point, as the ball begins to break up, William is snared by a man I don't recognize, who wants to talk business. I excuse myself, and I'm heading to fetch another glass of punch when a familiar calico tail swishes from under the table cloth.

Surrey.

I glance around. Thankfully, no one else has seen her. The earl is not a Surrey fan, and this will be just the excuse he needs to ban the kitten from Courtenay Hall. I hurry to another table to grab a scrap of fish and then, with my back to the guests, I coax Surry out, scoop her up and scamper out the nearest exit.

Once in the hall, I pause to get my bearings. Voices waft over from my left, a trio of women by the sounds of it. I clutch Surrey to my chest and turn a corner to avoid the small room where they're chatting.

I make it three steps before their voices reach me with a word that catches me up short.

"—Thorne."

I slow.

"I don't know what anyone sees in the man. He's *brutish.*"

"He might seem it," another says, "but I've heard he's an absolute gentleman between the sheets."

As they titter, I smile. When I first fell in love with William at fifteen, I'd have been horrified to hear such a thing. Perhaps that's the advantage of age and maturity. I'm glad William found pleasure elsewhere and that he pleased women doing it. He may have been a recluse, but he was not a monk.

The women giggle amongst themselves, and I'm about

continue on when one says, "That wife of his, though. I'd heard she was of an age with him, but did you see her? The *size* of her?"

"I know," another says. "I didn't appear in public once people could tell I was with child. It's not seemly."

"I don't mean the pregnancy," the first woman says. "Even without a child in her, she's going to need her gowns specially made. Lord Thorne may be a man of some size, but his hands still won't span her waist."

My cheeks heat. I should walk away. I know that. Yet I stand there, rooted to the spot, and I'm fourteen again, ignoring girls sniping as I buy a cookie from the cafeteria. I'm twelve, overhearing the boys snicker about the size of my breasts. I'm nine, when my ballerina mother canceled my beloved lessons, finally acknowledging I was never going to be ballerina sized.

Oh, I hear other voices, too. William ogling my figure as he plies me with scones. My father telling me I inherited his size—tall and broad and never "thin." My stepmother marveling over how strong I am, how toned from my dancing.

I am big. Tall, big-boned and carrying extra weight even without a baby. I've come to terms with that. I'm healthy and fit and active, and if being a size eight would mean giving up my treats, I'm not doing it. Life's too short.

Yet this still stings. Stings all the more because this is a world where concepts of beauty are shifting. In the early Victorian era, women were more likely to be mocked for being too slender. It was considered unhealthy. By the end of the nineteenth century, fat-shaming and diets will be in vogue.

Even now, attitudes are changing, and in a time when the average woman is a size six, I very obviously do not fit that norm.

So their words sting, but I'm hardly going to let them ruin my evening. I continue down a side hall and find the sitting room we'd used earlier. I deposit Surrey there with more fish, and I promise August will return her to Edmund as soon as possible. Then I ease the door shut behind me and wait to be sure she doesn't howl.

When all remains quiet, I make my way toward the ball only to hear the trio of gossiping women have entered the corridor. To return the way I came means passing them. I should, chin high, but I can't be bothered. Not if I don't have to. There's another way around, and I decide to take it rather than risk any scene that might torpedo my perfect evening.

I head down a hall, and then another and then . . .

And then I am lost.

Seriously? It's a house. You can't get lost in a house.

You can if it's an estate like this, with a dozen bedrooms and a half-dozen sitting rooms. When I spot narrow steps leading up to the second level, I realize I've reached the servant wing.

I'm turning around, orienting myself, when I catch a flicker of movement out of the corner of my eye. I spin to see the hem of a dress flipping around a corner.

"Miss?" I call.

I hurry to the corner. There's a young woman ahead. Light hair. A pale blue dress. Moving soundlessly as her feet seem to float an inch above the floor.

A chill runs through me.

I shake it off. I don't see ghosts. Okay, I *have* seen them, but only at Thorne Manor, and those have all been laid to rest. I haven't seen one since. Nor have I seen one anyplace else.

This isn't a ghost. It's just a maid wearing slippers, a maid who has learned to move noiselessly through the house.

"Miss?" I call again.

She disappears around another corner.

I sigh and lift my skirts to follow. "Miss?" I call. "I'm a guest from the ball. I seem to have lost my way. If you could direct me . . ."

I trail off as I catch a low laugh. A laugh I recognize as the earl's. I slow and turn the corner to see the young woman looking back at me, her pale face in shadow. She lifts one hand, as if in a wave, and I take a tentative step forward. She moves through a doorway, vanishing again.

Another chuckle from somewhere ahead and around yet another corner. Definitely Everett Courtenay. I do not want to bump into him, and I presume the maid's thinking the same, waving me into a side room until he's passed. Skirts lifted again, I jog along the hall and veer into the room she'd entered.

It's empty.

No, it simply *seems* empty. It's a music lounge, complete with a gorgeous little piano and seating that rings the walls. It's also dark, and I walk in, squinting to see where the girl is hiding.

"Hello?" I whisper.

No answer. I take another step and my knee thumps

against a stool. I stifle a yelp of surprise and bend to move it aside, my fingers sliding over crushed velvet.

Something moves alongside me, and I jump, straightening fast.

"Hello?" I try again.

Nothing. The room is silent and still, the only light coming from the hall. I squint and struggle to see, until I've surveyed the entire room.

The maid is gone.

I firmly remind myself that I do not see ghosts outside Thorne Manor. Well, the manor and the moors. Still, they'd all been connected to a single killer, and they've been laid to rest. Therefore this is not a ghost.

Then what is it? A teleporting maid?

No, it's a maid playing a game. I couldn't see her well enough to guess her age. She could be a parlor maid or a between maid, young enough to have a bit of fun with the fancy guests. Or young enough to want to see the ball, and now she's hiding before her master catches her. I thought she was waving me into the music parlor, but she could have been waving me on, telling me which way to go to return to the party.

A perfectly reasonable explanation. And I don't buy it for a second.

I saw the ghost of a woman in a blue dress. Not a maid's uniform, but a lady's dress. A fair-haired woman, small of stature.

When I'd been secretly trying to identify the ghosts at Thorne Manor, I'd asked William to describe Rosalind. Could she be tall and dark-haired? No, the opposite. Tiny and blond.

Like the figure I just saw.

I take a step deeper into the room and whisper, "If you want to speak to me—"

A yelp sounds outside the door. A young woman's cry of surprise, dissolving into nervous laughter. I consider, and then I back up to the doorway to listen.

"Please, m'lord," a young voice says. "I really do need to return to my duties."

A rumble of a male voice, words indistinguishable, but the tone sounding like Everett Courtenay. I hesitate in the doorway and listen. When another girlish yelp comes, I hurry toward the voices without thinking.

Again, the yelp becomes nervous laughter, and I know that sound only too well. A young woman trying to make light of a concerning situation. Trying to laugh it off.

"You should get back to the ball, m'lord," the young woman says. "They'll be expecting you."

"Is that an order?"

More anxious tittering. "N-no, sir. Of course not. I just thought your guests might appreciate your attentions—"

"More than you?"

The giggles take on a note of panic. "N-no, sir. I appreciate your kind words."

"They aren't kind. They're honest praise. You've grown into a very pretty lass."

I stride around the corner to see that the earl of Tynesford has a maid against the wall, his hand cupping her bottom as he leans into her. It's Lottie, the maid who came out to greet us.

Lottie lets out a shriek, a little too loud for the surprise of seeing me. I feign a startled gasp and fall back. Then I laugh softly.

"My lord," I say. "My apologies. You gave me a start. I've been wandering these halls for at least a quarter of an hour, trying to find my way back to the party." I look from him to the maid. "I hope I didn't interrupt anything."

"Not at all, m'lady," Lottie says, a little breathlessly as she squirms away from the earl. "His lordship was just asking if I'd refill the punch bowls when I had a moment. Why don't I escort you back to the ball, and I'll see what needs to be filled."

Tynesford doesn't get a chance to even speak before Lottie is past him, hurrying over to me. I thank the earl for the lovely party. He only glowers at me, and then turns on his heel and stalks off.

I let Lottie lead me down another hall. Then I say, as carefully as I can, "I do hope I didn't interrupt anything you did not want interrupted, Lottie. It sounded as if you might . . . welcome the excuse to escape."

Her fair cheeks blaze bright scarlet. "Yes, m'lady. I did. Thank you. He . . ." She swallows. "He has had a lot to drink this evening."

"Ah. That's a rare occasion, is it?"

Another flush, this one paired with a low chuckle. "It is not, m'lady."

"Does he often 'notice' you when he's in his cups?"

Her gaze drops and her feet move faster. "He didn't used to. Not until this summer. He hasn't—hasn't done anything like that. But Cook did warn me I ought to be careful when he's . . . like this. He surprised me."

"Hmm."

"It's all right, ma'am." She flashes me a smile that's a little too bright. "I'll be fine."

I don't answer. I'm already deep in thought. Looking closer at Lottie, I'd guess she's about sixteen. That explains why she might not have had trouble with the earl before this summer. I could be outraged at the thought that she'd have trouble with him now—she's a third his age *and* his employee.

What I just witnessed, though, is hardly a unique situation for a pretty girl in service. I could blame the Victorians, but I remember a summer job at her age, having to deal with my fifty-year-old supervisor's gaze never rising above my well-endowed chest, with his "accidental" touches that always managed to brush my breasts.

The difference is that I'd been in a temporary position, and I would have quit if it'd gone any farther. I didn't need the money, and my mother would have insisted I quit if she'd known. Lottie doesn't have those options. No more than Mary does. Their choices are limited, and at sixteen, a job is the beginning of a career. It is not pocket money but a means to survive.

I can't offer Lottie a job. She wouldn't want it anyway, I suspect. This is her family in service, and there's prestige in working for an earl. She might change her mind if it becomes more than drunken groping in a back hall. Or *when* it does—I have little doubt it will.

What I can do is inform August. He'll care. He might have had quite the reputation before he married, but like William,

August's reputation features only willing lovers moving in the same social circles. Neither William nor August has anything good to say about men who dally with their housemaids.

Here, I will interfere. There is no question of that. Which, I reflect as we near the ball, answers my other question, too.

If I intend to live part-time on this side of history, I cannot do it in a bubble. It's like hearing a cry for help and telling yourself someone else will respond. I despise such people for cowards, and I have always vowed I will not be one of them. If I heard that cry on a modern street, would I pause with a thought for the future I might be disrupting? Wonder whether it is the victim's destiny to be attacked, even killed? Of course not. And so I shall not do it here.

Del is right. If true time travel is possible, and I am in the same timeline as ours, then the universe will accommodate for that. It will heal itself.

I will not act carelessly, but I will act. I must.

I FIND WILLIAM, and I tell him what I saw in that back hall. With every word I speak, his face darkens, and I begin to wonder whether I should have waited until we'd left. The last thing William's reputation needs is for him to call out his host. He does no such thing, of course, because whatever his reputation may be, he is well-versed in temper management. He is angry and outraged, but he's not about to go hunt down Tynesford, not when anything he does could open Lottie to retaliation.

"August wondered whether he'd prey on the child," William says when I finish. "He has a history of that, which is why

79

the houskeeper prefers to hire older woman and girls who are less to his taste. I believe Lottie was a special case, a dire circumstance."

He glances over my shoulder and then steers me farther aside as a couple approaches, laughing. "The point being that August feared trouble, and he has considered offering the girl a position in his own household. He doesn't particularly need another maid, but he could find work for her."

"That would be wonderful," I say.

He kisses my forehead. "I'm glad you were able to stop him tonight. August has been watchful, but Tynesford knows he's being watched. The man is, sadly, not an idiot. I'll speak to August and he'll offer the girl a change of position."

"Thank you."

"No, thank *you*, for getting lost. The fact that you managed to help that girl means I shall be far less inclined to suffer the guilt of having abandoned you."

"Mmm, pretty sure I abandoned you. The punch bowl seemed much more enticing than a discussion on tariffs."

He puts out his arm for me to take. "Still, accept my apologies with a return trip to said punchbowl, before it is well and truly empty. I presume you did not manage to refill your cup."

I tell him about rescuing Surrey, which I'd left out of the initial explanation. I'd also left out the mysterious disappearing maid. No need to worry him about that. But now that I'm reminded, there's something I need to ask.

"This may sound like a foolish question," I ask as we approach the banquet table. "But when we were touring, I don't think I saw a portrait of Rosalind."

"Ah, no, you did not. That . . . would not be on the tour. Not if August is giving it."

His face reflects the same emotions I feel, that mingle of pain on August's behalf and frustration with how he's handling his grief.

William straightens his cuffs. "There is one picture of her, I believe. One he has not managed to . . . make disappear. Would you like to see it?"

"I would. Please."

WE'RE IN A dimly lit alcove, close enough to the kitchen that the heat from it has me sweating. I can smell roast pork, breakfast for those guests lucky enough to win overnight invitations.

"Where are we?" I whisper.

William motions for quiet and then opens a door into what seems like a cramped sitting room, stuffed with castoff furniture.

"It's for the staff," he says.

"And Rosalind's portrait is here?"

"I believe so." He takes an oil lamp, lights it and raises it. "Yes, it's still here. The cook was quite fond of Rosalind, and I believe the old woman snatched this photograph before August could . . . put it into storage."

He points at a small table where several ornately framed photographs are displayed. When I pause, uncertain, he lifts one and passes it to me.

I lift the picture into the light and—

"Oh!" I say.

I expected some dour-faced formal portrait. There's always a misunderstanding that Victorians didn't smile for photographs, when the truth is that the process took so long that attempting a smile would result in a blurred face. A serious pose was less likely to show the distortion of movement. Yet while the subjects in this picture aren't exactly grinning, they exude a joy brighter than any hundred-watt smile.

It's Rosalind and August, when they'd been courting. She'd owned a bakery in London, quite a scandalous thing for a young single woman, especially one of her good breeding. But she'd been the oldest of three girls who'd lost their parents. To support her sisters, she'd either needed to marry quickly or make use of her stellar baking skills. She chose the latter.

This photograph was taken in front of her bakery. Rosalind holds August's arm, and they gaze at the photographer with a joy so incandescent that just looking at them feels like an invasion of privacy. I have seen August happy, but I have never seen him like this.

As for Rosalind, she is positively ethereal, a beautiful young woman of no more than twenty-two, tiny, with light hair and a face that is as beautiful as her soon-to-be-husband's is handsome.

"She's gorgeous," I say.

"She was many, many things," he says. "That was one of them."

I could be envious, hearing my husband speak this way of another woman. I am not. I know how much he cared for Rosalind. She'd been like a sister to him, years after he'd lost his own.

"I . . . I thought I saw a young woman in the halls," I say. "I mean, yes, I did definitely see one. I presumed it was a maid and went after her because I was lost, but she kept moving. She disappeared into a room . . . after beckoning me. That's how I found the earl and Lottie."

William nods slowly. Six months ago, I'd have tensed, interpreting his careful reaction as doubt, but I know now he's assimilating my words.

When we first reunited, a comment about ghosts had elicited a very clear reaction from him. A very dismissive reaction. Superstitious nonsense. So I'd kept my experiences to myself, only to later discover that as soon as I said I saw ghosts, he believed me. The critical part there was me. If I told him I saw unicorns, he'd believe me, and if he said the same, I'd believe him.

"This young woman led you to Tynesford," he says. "So you could interrupt and rescue Lottie."

Now I'm the one pausing. "I hadn't thought of that, but yes, it makes sense."

"And you thought it might be Rosalind's ghost." He glances at the photograph. "Was it?"

"No." I look at the picture. "The figure was fair-haired and small of stature, and I didn't get a good look at her face, but I'm quite certain it wasn't Rosalind."

He exhales, echoing my own relief.

I continue, "I wouldn't want to think of her trapped here, unable to communicate with her family. I also . . ." I take a deep breath. "August isn't the only one who doesn't want to believe she's dead. That's silly—I never even knew her. I certainly don't want to think of her having abandoned her family, though."

"She wouldn't," William says firmly. "August and Rosalind were having... troubles." He looks at the photograph. "I haven't admitted that, have I? It wasn't the sort of trouble where one abandons one's family, though. Certainly not for anyone as attached to family as Rosalind. She loved August, adored her son and was very close to both her sisters. The problem was August. He could be very jealous, and he struggled with that. He could be controlling, and she struggled with *that*. They would have worked it out. But you wonder why he believes she left. That is it, I think, even if he'd never admit such a thing. He fears he drove her off, and somehow, it's easier to blame her for abandoning them. Do I think she ran away? Absolutely not. Do I think she died? Unfortunately, yes. Do I hope to be proven wrong? That she fell and struck her head and lost her memory, like some gothic heroine, and she'll reappear one day? Yes. Mostly, though, like you, I simply would not want to think of her as a ghost."

He pauses and then says, his voice lower, "That is what I'd hoped for, though, when I thought you were lost to me. That I'd stay at Thorne Manor even after I died. That I'd see you again that way, when you returned. That you might even see me..." He rubs his hands over his face and shivers. "Fortunately, it did not come to that."

I hug him fiercely, my head on his shoulder. I'd thought the same thing... while hoping that even if we were separated forever, he'd have moved on and found peace, no matter how much I'd have desperately loved to see him again.

He hugs me back and kisses the top of my head. I reach up and kiss him properly, a deep one that chases away the memories of that terrible, uncertain time.

"It could have been a maid," I say as we part. "A living maid, who alerted me to the issue and then slipped through a door I didn't see in the dark." I roll my shoulders. "Either way, that particular young woman seemed fine. It's Lottie that matters."

"And it's Lottie I'll speak to August about, posthaste. Let us go find him now." He glances at the photograph. "Best not to tell him this is here."

"I won't."

WILLIAM SPEAKS TO August alone. While August is hardly the sort to blush and stammer at the mention of sex—even in front of a woman—he is still a man of his time, and this conversation will go better without me to hear it. Particularly if the answer is not to my liking. I can't imagine August shrugging off Lottie's dilemma, but he might have already decided against offering her a job at his London home and instead just promise to have the housekeeper and other staff look out for her.

I needn't have worried. The matter is settled in the time it takes me to freshen up in the lavatory. August will offer Lottie a position, and if she agrees, she can quit Courtenay Hall right after the holidays and depart with August and Edmund. The earl will be livid, of course, but it's not as if he gets on with August anyway. Also it's not as if Tynesford can threaten to cut off August's allowance—he did that when August married Rosalind—or threaten to keep him from visiting Courtenay

Hall—access is part of August's birthright. So while I feel bad about giving the brothers one more point of friction, William assures me August is only too happy to whisk an innocent girl from his brother's lecherous clutches.

From there, we depart. August offers to smuggle us into his quarters for the night, but I can only imagine what kind of scandal would erupt if we were spotted sneaking out in the morning. No, we gratefully accept a hot flask of tea from the cook, and then we are off for the journey home.

Once again, William makes good on his promise of an intimate diversion. Or he does after I assure him I am quite awake enough and warm enough to enjoy it. We find a sheltered spot, ensure the horse is comfortable and then get comfortable ourselves in a bed of blankets. It is a wonderful interlude, snow just beginning to fall around us, the night clear and bright with stars . . . though admittedly, I don't notice either until I'm lying there afterward, cuddled with William and staring up at the sky.

The next thing I know, I'm waking in bed. Obviously, I fell asleep. Equally obviously, William did not—he drove us home and carried me up to our room. I remember none of that, though, and I wake snuggled deep in blankets.

I lift my head and find myself looking into Enigma's green eyes as she stares at me accusingly. Then I see the sun through the windows. Bright midday sun.

I blink and reach for my modern-day watch on the night stand. It's almost noon. I blink harder, and I'm pushing myself up when William enters with a steaming breakfast tray.

I smile. "Breakfast in bed again? Careful, I could get used to this."

"I am merely providing necessary sustenance for the long and busy day ahead."

"Busy . . ." I say carefully. Even sitting up sets my entire body groaning, as it whimpers that it would like a few more hours of rest, please.

"Yes, busy," he says as he sets down my tray. "We have a terribly full day ahead of us. First, a sleigh ride. Then charitable visits. Then supper at the curate's. Then either caroling or attending the Sir Hugh's evening of charades." He pauses. "No, I believe we can do both. First the caroling, and then the party, with only an hour's ride between them."

I open my mouth.

"Oh, and decorating. I left off decorating twenty-first-century Thorne Manor so we might do it together. We'll need to squeeze it in somewhere. That won't be a problem, will it?"

I open my mouth. What comes out is a soft whine, audible only to the cats.

William looks thoughtful. "Or—and I realize this is a mad thought—but hear me out. Or we could send our regrets on all counts, postpone the decorating, and you could spend the day in bed."

My mouth opens again.

"No," he says quickly. "That's silly. Forget I mentioned it." He sets the tray before me. "You can't possibly be tired. It isn't as if you slept the entire ride home from the ball, so exhausted that you didn't even stir."

"I—"

"Didn't stir despite driving through a blizzard, with me

cursing the entire way."

"I—"

"Didn't stir despite the fact that we nearly plowed into a sheep."

"A sheep? In winter?"

He throws up his hands. "Exactly my point. A white sheep during a whiteout. Fortunately, your husband is an excellent horse trainer, whose steed scented the beast and stopped for it. Then I had to check the ewe's markings and return her to her owner, who lost her in the fall. Yet somehow, my wife, kept sleeping. Soundly enough that I checked her pulse not less than five times, only to begin worrying that while the signs of life remained strong, perhaps she was suffering some sort of pregnancy-induced coma, one that would explain her not waking despite sharing her open-sleigh bed with a *sheep*."

"With a . . . ?" I peer at him. "Okay, now you're making things up."

He walks to a chair, picks up my discarded corset and plucks off a strand of wool. "There was a sheep. And so, worrying about your health, I shook you awake. Do you remember what you said?"

"No . . ."

"You mumbled something about the woolen blanket smelling damp, and then went back to sleep. Which suggests you were very, very tired. Except, if that were the case, you'd have told me, instead of letting me drag you hither and yon."

"I've enjoyed being dragged hither and yon."

He gives me a stern look. "Perhaps. Yet maybe, in my excitement to give you a perfect first Christmas together, I forgot you are a six-months pregnant professor on holidays, who flew across an ocean to see me. I failed to consider that you may be—humor me here—a wee bit exhausted."

I lift my thumb and forefinger. "A wee bit."

He sits on the edge of the bed and stretches his hands as far apart as they'll go. "A wee bit."

I laugh and twist to fall into his arms, nearly upsetting my tea cup. He rescues it and hands it to me, and I take a long sip.

"Yes," I say. "I should have told you. I just didn't want to interfere with your plans, which were lovely and delightful, and I thoroughly enjoyed them."

"But now you'll thoroughly enjoy a well-deserved day in bed?"

"I will. Tomorrow."

He sighs.

I lift a hand. "Today, I will spend a few more hours in bed. Then I would like to speak to Mary. I wish to offer her a position, if that's all right with you."

His expression tells me I've made the right decision even before he says, "It is most certainly all right with me."

"Then, while I won't have Mary start until after the holidays, I would like to let her know as soon as possible. May we do that?"

"We may. We could stop by her family's home this evening."

"You did mention caroling. Is that really a thing?"

He sighs. "In High Thornesbury, it is most definitely a thing. To my eternal dismay. Eleven months of the year, the villagers know to stay at the bottom of my hill. But come mid-

December, they all begin tramping up, expecting Seville oranges and a cup of smoking bishop. A simple glass of mulled wine isn't good enough, not since that bloody Christmas Carol story. They all want smoking bishop."

"Well, I shall help Mrs. Shaw make the punch, but, since caroling is a tradition, I have an idea . . ."

IT'S EARLY EVENING, and we're bundled up against the winter's chill, walking along the front path of a tidy little cottage I know only too well. In my world, it belongs to Freya and Del. I've passed it many times in this world, and never known who lived there, perhaps not wanting to know, lest they be unsuitable people. But as we make our way up the front walk, I'm grinning with delight.

"Mary's family lives here?" I say.

"Haven't I mentioned that?"

I tug my hand from the muff to sock him, and he yelps far louder than it deserves.

"That is *not* ladylike behavior, Lady Thorne. Yes, perhaps I ought to have mentioned it, but . . ." He glances at me. "I know homes are much larger in your world, and I feared it might . . . discomfit you."

He has a point. I've often thought how adorable Freya and Del's cottage is, perfect for two people. Yet it had once housed an entire family.

"I am a history professor," I remind him. "I know this sort of living situation was much more common." In the great cities, entire families live in places a quarter this size.

"Life is different here," I continue. "It is not always what

I'm accustomed to, but many would argue that people in the twenty-first century don't need nearly the size of homes they buy. Although one could argue that here, too. No family requires a house the size of Courtenay Hall. And Thorne Manor is rather large for two people and their cats."

"Don't worry. It shall be full enough soon. I want at least six children. And a score of staff."

"More like six cats and a score of horses."

"Now that's just ridiculous, Lady Thorne. Horses in the house? They'd trample the poor cats."

"The point, Lord Thorne, is that I realize this size of house is the norm for a village family, and if they are healthy and happy, then I will not be discomfited."

"If it bothered you overmuch, I suppose Mary could live in with us?" There's a note of trepidation in his voice that makes me smile.

"No," I say. "Despite your jest about the score of staff, I know you would not want that, and I could not abide live-in staff any more than you."

He exhales in relief.

I continue, "I will ask that we ensure her earnings well compensate her for the lack of room and board, and if she wishes, she may take rooms elsewhere. That seems a suitable compromise."

"Very suitable."

We reach the front door. William knocks. There's a flurry of commotion inside, and someone peeks out a window, sees our lantern and basket and shouts "Carolers!"

There's a pause, a silent one, and I glance at William, my

brows rising as I wonder whether he's not the only one who isn't particularly thrilled with this custom. Just when I think they're going to pretend they aren't at home, the door opens, and a middle-aged version of Mary stands there, beaming. Then she sees who it is.

"M-m'lord," she says. "Is-is there a problem?"

"No problem at all," he says. "We've come caroling. Is Mary home?"

Another pause. Then Mary's mother invites us in, but the invitation is hesitant, and I get the sense she'd rather we stayed at the door. Having gentry unexpectedly come to call is the ultimate hostess nightmare. I assure her we're very warm and comfortable and will not stay long. She backs inside and calls for Mary, and she returns with Mary, an older man, and an adolescent boy. Also a chair. The boy carries the chair outside for me to sit on. I thank him and say I will sit in a moment.

"First, we have come caroling," I say, lifting my lantern. I also point to the basket in William's hand. Normally, this would be empty—a hint for a modest recompense for our singing, perhaps an apple or a sweet. Ours, though, is full. "And a holiday gift, in thanks for the kindness you have shown, allowing Mary to tend to me."

Mary murmurs something, trying very hard to sound appreciative and not at all disappointed that I've made no mention of her offer.

"Now for the carol." I look at William. "Please tell me your singing voice is better than mine."

"Er, perhaps we should have discussed this *before* we decided to go caroling."

"I take it that's a no." I turn back to the perplexed family. "We apologize, in advance, for our inability to carry a proper tune."

I take a deep breath. Then we sing our song to the tune of that Victorian caroling classic "We Wish You a Merry Christmas."

"We wish to hire Mary after Christmas, we wish to hire Mary after Christmas, we wish to hire Mary after Christmas . . . and John too, if he can be spared."

The family gapes at us.

"Oh my," I say. "That's not how it goes at all, is it?"

Mary's father lets out a boom of a laugh. "It is not, but it a lovely song to hear nonetheless. I do hope I didn't misunderstand the lyrics."

"Easy enough to do with our dreadful voices." I look at Mary. "You suggested you would be available to work for us if we decided to hire additional staff with the baby. I would like to offer you a live-out position, to be assumed any time after the holidays. The salary will be negotiated once we have a better understanding of our needs and your availability, but it will be no less than twelve shillings a week for half-time employment."

Mary goggles at me. "Twelve shillings for *half*-time?"

"That is very generous," her mother says. "I do not think she requires quite so much, but as you said, it can be negotiated."

The average house maid in this era can expect to make about fifteen pounds a year, slightly more than doubled if they aren't given room and board. What we're offering is a full-time wage for half-time work. It's woefully low by modern standards but to go higher would smack of charity.

"We certainly can negotiate later," I say, my smile belying the fact that I don't intend to offer a pence less.

"As for the second part of our song," William says. "I know young John has been seeking employment outside the family farm. With the baby coming and my wife's occasional family obligations in London, I have realized I will require additional stable staff. I wish to make a similar offer to young John. Twelve pence a week for a half-time live-out groom position, to be negotiated properly after the holidays."

"Groom?" John says. "You mean stable-boy, do you not?"

"Am I mistaken that you passed your thirteenth birthday recently?"

"N-no, sir. You are not."

"I have a stable boy, who works after his school classes, and he is but eleven years of age. That would mean, I believe, that you are better suited for the position of groom. Unless you would prefer to be a stable boy."

The boy straightens. "No, sir."

"You are fond of horses, I believe."

"Very much, sir."

"Then we will suit nicely." William lifts the basket. "While we realize it is traditional to collect sweets while caroling, we find ourselves quite overburdened with them. We were hoping we might leave these here."

"Were you not continuing your caroling, Lord Thorne?" Mary asks. "I would join you if you were."

William hesitates.

Mary's mother elbows her daughter. "Lady Thorne ought not to be on her feet any longer than necessary."

"I would be quite fine with a few more stops," I say. "Perhaps you would know who in town might not be otherwise occupied on this evening?"

Mary nods, understanding my meaning—are there lonely villagers whose evenings we might brighten?

"There's the Widow Allen," Mary says. "And Mr. Morris's children have not yet come for the holidays."

"If they do at all," her mother grumbles.

"Then we shall make those stops and perhaps a third. Please feel free to join us, Mary."

"We'll all join you, if that's all right, ma'am," her mother says.

I smile. "That would be delightful. Thank you."

T'WAS THE NIGHT before Christmas, and all through the house, not a creature was stirring, not even a mouse. The last rodent, it seems, had been caught this morning and deposited on my pillow as an early Christmas gift. We have peace now, as we cuddle on the loveseat in the library, watching our blissed-out cats lolling on the carpet.

"What did you call it again?" William asks. "The herb in those toys?"

"Catnip."

"For cats? How intriguing. I've heard of catnip tea for humans." He watches Enigma purring loudly, wrapped around her toy. "I do believe I shall invest in catnip as a cure for the overactive kitten."

"Uh-huh."

"I'll sell it on the pharmacy shelf, right beside Godfrey's Cordial, for fussy babies. Which reminds me, I ought to purchase some of that for little Melvina."

When I glance over, his lips are twitching.

I squeeze his thigh. "Not funny."

"No? I do believe opium addiction is a small price to pay for a quiet baby."

"Which reminds me that's something we need to discuss with Mary. Absolutely no giving Melvina medicine for colic or teething or crying, even if it's an old family recipe."

"Probably best to just request that she not give the baby *anything* unless approved by us."

"True."

Godfrey's Cordial was a well-known "cure" for cranky babies in the Victorian era, along with several similar concoctions. In this time period, the manufacturer doesn't need to list ingredients. The active one in most of them? Tincture of opium.

We can be shocked by that now, but this is a time when lower-class women were expected to put in a full day of backbreaking work at home—plus taking in extra chores, like laundry—while tending to an endless stream of pre-reliable-contraceptive babies. If something would keep those babies quiet while their mothers worked, they'd jump at it, especially when it was an approved medicine.

Even if those mothers had known the truth, opium use is widespread at this time. It's legal and easily available in laudanum, a lovely little sedative to help with everything from restless sleep to "attacks of nerves" to menstrual cramps.

"That reminds me," I say. "If in a few years, the doctor tries prescribing you anything containing a new miracle drug called cocaine, best to refuse it."

"Freya has already made an appointment for me to meet the doctor in modern High Thornesbury. No offense to dear Dr. Turner, but one thing I am fully taking advantage of is twenty-first century medicine."

"Good call." I sip my punch.

"Stop looking at the presents."

"I'm not—"

"You can't take your eyes off them. Particularly this one here." He rises and picks up a gift I couldn't even see, tucked behind the tree.

"Fine," he says. "I surrender to your relentless curiosity. You may open it."

He hands me a long narrow box, unduly heavy. I weigh it in my hands. Then I smile. "You bought me a clothing iron. How delightful."

He shakes his head and motions for me to get on with it. I untie the ribbon and take my time unfolding the paper, enjoying his obvious impatience. Finally I lift the lid off the box. Inside is a brass plate engraved with "Epona."

I look up at him.

"You are as easily fooled as young Edmund," he says. "Did you really believe I'd sell your favorite filly?"

"You said she'd been sold since before her birth."

"And now she is unsold. The buyer was more interested in a colt, and so I convinced him to wait for that, with the added incentive of a reasonable discount."

"So she is mine?"

"No, I simply bought a brass name plate for her door until I find another buyer."

I throw myself into his arms for a fierce hug. "Thank you."

"She will not be ready to ride for a year or so, but you said you'd like to participate in training."

"I would very much. Thank you."

He reaches into the pile of gifts and hands me another heavy box. This one is addressed to Will Jr.

I open the gift, faster this time, and discover another brass plate. This one reads Gringolet—the name of Sir Gawain's horse. Beneath it is the bill of sale for a young gelding pony.

I laugh. "You're already buying our daughter a pony?"

"Never too early to start."

I lean in to kiss his cheek. "She'll love him."

"And now a gift for me," he says. He picks up the one in brown-paper wrapping. "Oh, I am most curious about this present."

"The one you bought yourself?"

"Nonsense. It clearly says it's from you."

He settles into the spot beside me again, his hip rubbing mine. I reach for a candied nut and as soon as I snag one, he tugs me onto his lap.

"I do believe we should open this one together," he says. "Since you seem to have forgotten what you got me."

"Baby brain," I say.

"Undoubtedly."

He pulls the string and I unwrap the paper, which has been

carefully folded and secured without the use of tape.

"Books!" he says. "You bought me a trio of tomes. How kind."

"Because you obviously need more," I say, waving at the overstuffed shelves surrounding us. "I'm not even sure where you'll put three more."

"Not in here, given the publication dates."

"Ah, I see. They're modern books." I lift the first one. "*An Introduction to Baking.*"

"So I can learn to bake for you," he says. "Excellent choice. I can only hope it includes instructions on operating modern appliances."

"Well, this one does. Though not for the kitchen." I hold up an 'idiot's' guide to smart phones.

"Thank you," he says. "I do need that."

I sputter a laugh and then flip to the third and final book. "*A Father's Guide on What to Expect in the First Year.*"

"Now that," he says, "is definitely a modern book. I do believe the current version would have exactly one page, telling me to cede all responsibility to the angel of the household."

I make a choking noise.

"Yes," he says. "I have a feeling *my* angel would like me to change a soiled cloth or two. I also have a feeling that I will want to do so, not only for her, but to fully experience fatherhood."

"Changing diapers is the best way to do that," I say. "All the diapers."

He frowns and flips through the book. "I'm quite certain it

doesn't say that."

"I'll write it in."

He laughs softly and turns me to face him. "So yes, these books are to me *from* me. My way of saying that I intend to be a complete and active participant in your world"—he holds up the phone guide—"and in our household"—he lifts the cookbook—"and in our child's life. While I know you'd expect me to do more than a man of my time and background, you might also make *allowances* for my time and background. That is unnecessary. We are in this together." He puts his arms around me. "You, me and our child-who-will-not-be-named-Melvina."

"I actually had some thoughts on alternatives."

He exhales dramatically. "Thank you."

"I was thinking Amelia. Amelia Judith Thorne."

A moment of silence. "After my mother and your aunt."

I nod. "Is that all right?"

"It is *very* all right. However, if Judith is more common in your day, we could reverse the order."

"I like Amelia Judith."

"Might we sneak in Dale? As a second middle name?"

I smile. "We could do that."

"Amelia Judith Dale Thorne."

"It's quite a mouthful."

"A beautiful mouthful." He bends to my stomach. "Happy Christmas Eve, Amelia."

My eyes fill with tears, and I twist to hug him.

"Happy Christmas Eve, Lady Thorne," he says.

"Happy Christmas Eve, Lord Thorne."

Also by Kelley Armstrong

Rockton thriller series
A Stitch in Time gothic series
Cainsville paranormal mystery series
Otherworld urban fantasy series
Nadia Stafford thriller trilogy

Standalone Thrillers
Wherever She Goes
Every Step She Takes

Young Adult
Aftermath
Missing
The Masked Truth
Darkest Powers paranormal trilogy
Darkness Rising paranormal trilogy
Age of Legends fantasy trilogy

Middle-Grade
A Royal Guide to Monster Slaying fantasy series
The Blackwell Pages trilogy (with Melissa Marr)

About Kelley Armstrong

Kelley Armstrong believes experience is the best teacher, though she's been told this shouldn't apply to writing her murder scenes. To craft her books, she has studied aikido, archery and fencing. She sucks at all of them. She has also crawled through very shallow cave systems and climbed half a mountain before chickening out. She is however an expert coffee drinker and a true connoisseur of chocolate-chip cookies.

www.KelleyArmstrong.com
mail@kelleyarmstrong.com
facebook.com/KelleyArmstrongAuthor
twitter.com/KelleyArmstrong
instagram.com/KelleyArmstrongAuthor

THE LONG NIGHT OF THE
CRYSTALLINE MOON

by
Jeffe Kennedy

Shapeshifter Prince Rhyian doesn't especially want to spend the Feast of Moranu at Castle Ordnung. First of all, it's literally freezing there, an uncomfortable change from the tropical paradise of his home. Secondly, it's a mossback castle, which means thick walls and too many rules. Thirdly, his childhood playmate and current nemesis, Lena, will be there. Not exactly a cause for celebration.

Princess Salena Nakoa KauPo nearly wriggled out of traveling to Ordnung with her parents, but her mother put her foot down, declaring that, since everyone who ever mattered to her was going to be there to celebrate the twenty-fifth year of High Queen Ursula's reign, Lena can suffer through a feast and a ball for one night. Of course, "everyone" includes the sons and daughters of her parents' friends, and it also means that Rhyian, the insufferable Prince of the Tala, will attend.

But on this special anniversary year, Moranu's sacred feast falls on the long night of the crystalline moon—and Rhy and Lena discover there's more than a bit of magic in the air.

Acknowledgments

Many thanks to beta reader Emily Mah Tippetts for a fast and insightful read. Tons of gratitude to Darynda Jones for the daily sprinting sessions, listening to ideas on this novella, and a final beta read full of the best kind of squees. Also hearts to Grace (Darling) Draven for the long conversations and excellent advice.

Thanks and love to Carien Ubink for reading, looking up All The Things, and "general assisting." I'm sorry this isn't the Zyr novella you were looking for.

To Kelley Armstrong, Melissa Marr, and L. Penelope—thanks for trusting I'd get this done in time. I'm thrilled to be sharing pages with you amazing authors.

As always, love and immense gratitude to David, who is there every day, and who makes everything possible.

Thank you for reading!

Credits

Proofreading: Pikko's House (www.pikkoshouse.com)

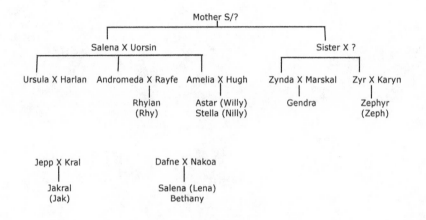

Mother S/?

Salena X Uorsin | Sister X ?

Ursula X Harlan   Andromeda X Rayfe   Amelia X Hugh   Zynda X Marskal   Zyr X Karyn

Rhyian   Astar (Willy)   Gendra   Zephyr
(Rhy)   Stella (Nilly)   (Zeph)

Jepp X Kral   Dafne X Nakoa

Jakral   Salena (Lena)
(Jak)   Bethany

~ 1 ~

C ASTLE ORDNUNG CAME into view as the dragon dropped beneath the thick cloud cover. From Rhyian's perspective on dragonback, the white towers and high walls looked only slightly less white than the snowy landscape. The high queen's crimson banner flapped furiously on the heights, all the pennants of the subsidiary thirteen kingdoms arranged below. Though it was still afternoon, the thick snowfall dimmed the light to a grim gray, so gloomy the thousands of burning torches lining the parapets shone clearly.

Rhy snorted to himself. So much for mossback's much-anticipated viewing of the crystalline full moon. With that overcast, no one would even see it. To think that he could be at home in tropical Annfwn, celebrating the Feast of Moranu in the traditional way—on the beach, shapeshifting, dancing, and drinking in the warm night.

But no. His mother had issued a royal command that Rhy absolutely would attend the ball celebrating the quarter-century anniversary of High Queen Ursula's prosperous reign.

Nothing less could've forced him to attend. Not that Rhy didn't love and respect his Auntie Essla. But it seemed likely Salena would also attend. And he'd rather be anywhere than in the same place as Salena.

Not something he could or would confess to anyone. And even the queen's son must obey royal commands—particularly when his father, the king of Annfwn, did nothing to save him. So there Rhy was, tricked out in the fancy dress outfit his mother had forced him to wear via yet another royal command—the silver-trimmed black velvet making him look like a mossback—plunging into bitter winter, and counting the minutes until the following dawn when he would be free again.

The longest night of the year had a *lot* of minutes.

Hopefully Salena would just ignore him tonight. It would be a big event in a huge castle. They should be able to avoid each other. After all, they'd managed to avoid each other for seven years since the *incident*. And she'd been the one to flee Annfwn, clearly to avoid seeing him ever again. He couldn't imagine she'd want to see him now any more than he wanted to see her.

Zynda landed in the cleared field set aside for the dragons. The cold wind whipped them cruelly as soon as Rhy's sorceress mother released her magic bubble that had kept them warm on the journey. Zynda waited only long enough for them to scramble down the rope-harness ladder before shifting into an elegant ballgown and furred cape. "Brr," she declared, joining them. "I always forget how cold it is here in winter."

"I don't," Rhy replied caustically, but subsided when his mother glared at him. They rushed up the cleared walkway, the torches lining it providing some warmth, though the flames whipped and guttered with the wind.

Guards saluted, shouting hails for Queen Andromeda of Annfwn, some giving Zynda's husband, Marskal, the Hawks' salute, though he was long since retired from the high queen's elite guard. Finally, they made it inside the castle, and for once, Rhy appreciated the thick walls. The stone edifices mossbacks favored might be as confining as a cage, but they did cut the brutal winter winds.

It was like stepping into a different world—and a different Ordnung than he'd ever seen before. To honor the goddess Moranu's rule over shadows and the dark of night, the rugs, table coverings, and other hangings were all in deepest black. They created a somber backdrop for the remaining decorations, which all celebrated the return of light. Silver and gold threads wove through all of the black fabrics, catching the candlelight. Crystal plates and goblets sparkled with fire, everything in silver and gold. White gems of all shapes and sizes studded everything, like thousands of stars, and garlands of evergreen boughs sporting white moonflowers that gleamed like sweetly scented living pearls festooned the walls, windows, mantels, and every other possible surface.

The elaborate crystal candelabras—some suspended by silver wires, others perched in clusters on every surface—held white candles blazing with light. More moonflower garlands dripping with flashing crystals, and possibly diamonds, hung in graceful swoops from the high ceilings.

Scribes sat at black-draped tables scattered throughout the busy reception hall, using flashing crystal implements to take notes for fancily dressed folks speaking earnestly to them. In other places, hammered gold bins held countless rolled scrolls of paper, with empty tables beside them, writing implements at the ready.

Rhy had no idea what that was about, but he had to admit—silently, in the privacy of his own head—that the mossback celebration of Moranu's feast outstripped the one in Annfwn. Certainly more elaborate. But then, mossbacks always did like *things*.

"Rhy!" Astar, wearing a fancy velvet getup very like Rhy's, came striding through the busy hall, his twin sister, Stella, right behind him. His cousin embraced him, thumping him on the back. Stella hung back, giving him her serious smile and a courtly wave. Her sorcery gave her extraordinary healing skills but also made her sensitive to people's emotions and physical pains. She'd learned a lot about shielding herself from the Sorceress Queen Andromeda, but not touching people helped more than anything. Still, a crowd like this couldn't be easy for her.

Rhy gave her a gallant bow, then clasped Astar's forearm. "Happy Feast of Moranu, Willy and Nilly," he said, using their childhood nicknames, originally assigned by exasperated adults exhausted from chasing rambunctious shapeshifting twin toddlers, and now used gleefully by their friends to annoy them. Surreptitiously scanning the throng, Rhy didn't see Salena anywhere. Last he'd heard, she'd been off in the Aerron Desert making it rain. Maybe Moranu would look on him favorably—not that She ever did—and Salena hadn't come tonight.

"I'm so happy you joined us, Rhy!" Stella beamed at him. "We weren't sure you would, knowing how much you hate to leave Annfwn, especially in winter." As dark as Astar was light, Stella looked very much like Andromeda, with storm-gray eyes that shone almost silver like her argent ballgown. Her dark hair—the exact same unusual rusty black as Rhy's mother—was up in a complicated style that shone with red glints where the light hit it.

"I wouldn't have missed this for the world, my gorgeous cousin," he replied with his most charming grin.

"Moranu save us all," Queen Andromeda said in a very dry voice as she joined them. "It's capable of polite speech. Who knew? Happy Feast of Moranu, niece and nephew, it's good to see you."

"It's wonderful to see you, Auntie Andi," Stella replied after Astar finished hugging their aunt for the both of them. "Mother and Auntie Essla are getting dressed now. I'm to ask you to join them in Her Majesty's rooms."

Queen Andromeda dusted off her leather riding pants unnecessarily. "Ah. Time to confront whatever Glorianna-inspired creation my baby sister intends to dress me in."

"Auntie Ami is dressing you tonight?" Rhy asked, beyond surprised.

"Yes." His mother wrinkled her nose at him. "Which is something you'd know if you'd listened to anything I've said for the last three days instead of sulking. Ami insisted on designing gowns for the three of us sisters. Essla, too. We're frankly terrified," she confided.

Even in his rotten mood, Rhy had to smile at that. As the avatar of Glorianna, goddess of beauty and love, his Aunt Ami embraced all things frivolous. "I'm amazed you agreed."

His mother grimaced. "We're all making concessions so this event will be a perfect celebration," she replied meaningfully.

"I'm here, aren't I?"

She straightened his collar, smiling wistfully. "I know you hate this," she said quietly, "but you look very handsome."

He batted her hands away, but relented and gave her a hug. "Good luck. I'll pray to Moranu for you that the dress isn't pink."

"She wouldn't do that to me," his mother replied firmly. "Would she?" She shook her head. "I'll see you all later."

Once Andi left them, Astar clapped Rhy on the back. "It's been too long." He waggled his blond brows. "And we have a bottle of Branlian whiskey waiting to properly kick off this celebration."

Rhy whistled in appreciation. "How did you get that?"

"Being heir to the High Throne might be the bane of my existence, but it does have a few perks." Astar shoved back his golden curls, grinning cheerfully.

"And Jak has promised to bring aged Dasnarian mjed," Stella added. "He sent a message that Jepp and Kral obtained a few casks of the good stuff, and he's bringing one."

"Then we might as well start on the whiskey," Rhy said, "so we'll be ready for the mjed. Who else is here so far of the old gang?" There. He'd asked that nonchalantly enough. *Please say Salena isn't coming.*

"Jak arrived this morning. Otherwise, only we have joined the party so far that I've seen," Astar replied. "But I've had a salon set aside for us to all meet up. Jak is keeping a lookout for the girls to emerge from their primping, and he'll bring them to join us." He smiled, every inch the golden prince. "It will be good to have all seven of us together again."

"Won't it, though?" Rhy said, scanning the crowd again with increasing dread. *All seven of us.* So Salena *was* coming. In fact, it sounded like she was already here. And they were going to be crammed into a tiny room together.

This night would be endless.

~ 2 ~

A ND THERE HE was. Rhyian. Like night made into flesh, Moranu's loving hand all over him, crowning him her Prince of Shadows. Salena couldn't look away.

Amid the glittering crowd, laughing with Astar and Stella, Rhyian stood tall and languid, black hair in glossy disarray as if he'd just crawled out of some girl's bed. Probably had. He wore silver-trimmed black velvet, perfectly tailored. And, even slouching with indolent grace, hands stuck carelessly in his pockets, he dominated the room with dark radiance. Astar, ever the golden prince, dimmed in comparison as he gestured widely, saying something with a wide and happy smile. Rhyian nodded, clearly not paying much attention as he scanned the crowd. Looking for his next conquest, no doubt.

Don't be bitter, she reminded herself. After all this time, she couldn't possibly care what he did.

"You look amazing, Lena," Zeph said in her ear. "Quit fidgeting. You'll soil the white silk, and you can't shapeshift it clean again."

"Don't be smug." Lena yanked once more on the strapless bodice in a futile attempt to cover more of her cleavage. "It's *so* low cut. I don't know what Mom was thinking."

"Your mother may be a librarian, but she's also a woman—and she was thinking you could stand to flaunt your impressive assets." Zeph hooked her arm through Lena's and hugged them together in solidarity. "Rhy won't know what hit him."

Lena gave her a rueful look. "If he even notices I'm here."

If she even wanted him to notice her.

Gendra slipped her arm through Lena's on the other side. "Oh, he *knows*," she said. "He's been in a rotten mood ever since Andi made it a *royal order* that he had to attend tonight."

"She *did?*" Lena studied Rhyian from her vantage on the balcony overlooking the great hall. Gendra had already been dressed when she arrived at Ordnung—having flown there in hummingbird form and showing off her shapeshifting skills by returning to human form wearing the gorgeous indigo ballgown—but she'd joined Lena and Zeph for wine and gossip while they changed clothes after the journey. Stella hadn't been able to pop in as she'd hoped, sadly too busy playing hostess with Astar. "You didn't mention that tidbit before."

Zeph nodded. "It's true. Even if a few birdies hadn't over-heard—and it was apparently a *loud* argument—Rhy got drunk afterward and bitched to all his buddies about his mother running his life."

"Oh, please. When is he going to grow up?" Lena conveniently set aside the fact that she'd had a similar argument with her own mother, and welcomed the exasperation that helped defuse the heart-tripping dizziness of seeing Rhyian again. He'd only gotten better looking over the years. How was that fair?

"Speaking of growing up, Astar is looking fine tonight," Zeph murmured, licking her crimson lips. "That boy has seriously filled out."

Gendra and Lena exchanged glances. "Astar *always* looks fine," Lena said, though he did seem to have added bulk. "I hear Harlan has him working with a broadsword now. That will build some muscle."

"And I'm sure it helps to be the son of the most beautiful woman in the Thirteen Kingdoms," Gendra added. "Though, really, he looks just like his father, the late Prince Hugh. I saw a portrait of him at Castle Windroven."

Astar was handsome, it was true, fair with golden hair, and eyes the color of the summer sky. He was also the high queen's heir, and the responsibility, along with his innate honor, lent him an air of nobility. Over the years, Astar had taken on the role of leader of their group of friends, and he was the sun they orbited around. To Lena, though, Astar's sweet sunniness couldn't compare to the dark, languid, and wicked appeal of Rhyian. Not that she was going to let him break her heart again. "Fool me once," she murmured.

"What was that?" Gendra asked with concern.

"I'm going to seduce Astar tonight," Zeph, completely oblivious to Lena's angst, announced in the same breath, sparing Lena from answering. Zeph tossed back her long hair, which fell nearly to the hem of her scarlet gown in a glossy blue-black waterfall. If Astar was their sun and Rhyian the dark star, Zeph was the beauty of the four girls, with her mother's exotic Dasnarian bone structure and her father's Tala coloring—and his flirtatious nature. She licked her perfect lips again as Astar and Stella escorted Rhyian off somewhere. Astar wore powder blue with gold trim, and even Lena had to admit he cut a fine and truly princely figure.

"Look at that ass," Zeph mused, nearly salivating. "Makes your mouth water. Do you think he's still a virgin?"

Gendra had a hand clapped over her eyes. "Noooo... Don't say things like that."

"Don't be silly," Zeph scoffed. "Astar isn't our cousin. We can lust."

Gendra dropped her hand, her eyes fixed on the trio as they disappeared from view. Lena wasn't sure if Gendra's longing gaze lingered on Astar or Rhyian. Or Stella, for that matter. Unlike the rest of them, Gendra hadn't dabbled in romance much, keeping to herself, spending much of her time in one animal form or another. Always practicing her skills. Of course, Lena wasn't much better. Since Rhyian, she'd buried herself in her work—and she was happier for it.

"Astar is just honorable enough to be a virgin," Lena said. "He probably has some idea of saving himself for whichever princess they marry him off to."

"Yes," Gendra agreed vehemently, "which is why you should not mess with his head, Zeph."

"His head isn't the part I want to mess with," Zeph purred.

"Zephyr!" Lena and Gendra exclaimed in one voice.

"What?" She pouted, managing to look utterly gorgeous doing it. "His being so noble and honorable makes me want to seduce him just that much more." She narrowed her sapphire eyes in the direction he'd gone. "He's a big boy now, and I think I'm just the girl to drag him to the dark side."

Lena closed her eyes in dread. "We have to keep them apart," she said to Gendra.

"Absolutely. For the sake of the Thirteen Kingdoms," Gendra agreed.

Zeph glared at them. "Why, you traitors? I thought you loved me and wanted me to be happy."

"We do," Lena said.

"But we also love Astar and want him to be happy," Gendra added.

"I could make him happy," Zeph said, truly sulking now. "That's entirely the point of seducing him."

"Astar is to be high king," Lena explained patiently, "which means a marriage of state for him someday."

"I don't want to *marry* him," Zeph replied in a petulant tone. Then she grinned wickedly. "Just deflower, despoil, and thoroughly debauch him."

"Are there any 'de's' left after that?" Gendra wondered.

"I'm just saying," Zeph continued, fully warmed to her subject, "if our darling Willy has to be saddled with some ice-hearted, baby-making mossback princess someday, I can at least tutor him in all the delightful perversions he'll be missing. That's just being a good friend," she added loftily, not fooling anyone.

"Odds are his future queen will be Dasnarian," Lena pointed out, "which means she could be better tutored in the sensual arts than you are."

Zeph gave her an arch look. "My mother is a Dasnarian princess, don't forget, and—"

Lena and Gendra groaned. "How could we forget?" Lena asked.

"You remind us daily," Gendra agreed.

"—*and*," Zeph plowed on, "she taught me as she was taught." She smiled smugly. "Plus, I've been practicing. Did I tell you about the two—"

Gendra held up her hands in surrender, stepping away from them. "I'm crying uncle on this conversation."

Lena had to agree. Combining her mother's sensual Dasnarian education with her father's Tala flirtatiousness had been like putting oil on a fire in producing Zeph. She'd already cut a swath through Annfwn, and Lena was only thankful that Zeph hadn't seduced Rhyian. So far as she knew, anyway. If Zeph had, she wouldn't want to hurt Lena by saying so and, of course, Rhyian didn't speak to her at all.

"Naughty Zeph. What did you say to scare our sweet Gendra?" an arch voice inquired.

All three young women spun and squealed, launching themselves into Jak's arms. Laughing, he managed to embrace them all at once, kissing their cheeks and foreheads. Zeph managed to plant an enthusiastic kiss on Jak's mouth, but he shook a finger at her. "I'm wise to your ways, shapeshifter. You won't be witching me."

Zeph gave him a saucy smile, swishing her scarlet gown, which glittered with crystal beads. "But you dressed to match me."

Jak threw back his head and laughed, then struck a pose. "You like?"

"I didn't know this was supposed to be a costume party,"

Lena remarked, eyeing the high glossy boots and long crimson coat. He even had a cutlass hanging from his belt. "Are you supposed to be a pirate?"

Jak scowled at her. "So cruel, fair Lena." He plucked up her hand and kissed it, bowing with a dramatic flourish. "I bought this in Jofarstyrr and thought it would be perfect for tonight."

"It *is* perfect," Gendra assured him with perfect sincerity—and giving Lena a reproving glare. "You look very handsome."

"Ah, sweet Gendra!" Jak whirled her into his arms and spun her in a few steps of a waltz. "And you look dazzlingly lovely tonight. Say you'll save every dance for me."

She giggled, and Zeph made a face. "Except for when you're dancing with us," she called.

"Bah." Jak didn't even pause, spinning Gendra faster. "I know how this goes. *You* will be drooling over Astar, and Lena will be mooning after Rhy. A plain sailor like me doesn't stand a chance."

"And Stella won't notice Jak is alive," Zeph murmured to Lena, who agreed with a rueful smile. Jak had his Dasnarian father's height, but his loose-limbed and agile bone structure was all from his mother, Jepp. He had her keen dark eyes, dusky skin, and brown hair, too—and all of her zesty lack of restraint.

"But I forget!" Jak whirled Gendra to an abrupt halt, kissing her hand, too. "I am commanded to escort you ladies to the private salon Astar arranged for our merry crew. I was sent to seek you out. Now that I have, you are my prisoners, and you must face the censure of your king." He winked. "Or the high king in waiting, which as good as the likes of us will get."

That was where Astar and Stella had taken Rhyian. And where Jak intended to take them. Lena's heart jammed in her throat, choking her breath away, and she felt abruptly far too warm. "I... have to go check in with my parents," she stammered. "Tell me where, and I'll join you. Later."

The look all three gave her was far too knowing.

"Don't be absurd, lovely Lena." Jak hooked her arm firmly over his. "The kings and queens are not thinking of us—for once in our lives—and we have toasts to make. The seven of us, together again. This will be a night to remember."

Lena dragged her feet, but Zeph poked her in the back, she and Gendra falling in behind them to prevent escape. "The Feast of Moranu is a night for forgiveness and renewal," Gendra reminded her.

"You can't forgive someone who isn't sorry," Lena retorted over her shoulder.

"Of course you can," Jak replied cheerfully. "People forgive me all the time, and I've never once been sorry."

"Besides," Zeph said, "how do you know he isn't sorry?"

"The tiny fact that he's never said so," Lena muttered.

"He can't apologize if you won't speak to him," Gendra put in.

"I've never *not* been speaking to him," Lena protested.

All three very loudly said nothing.

"I've been busy," she added into their accusing silence. "In the Aerron Desert."

"Yes, darling Lena." Jak patted her hand on his arm, as if that made up for the vise grip she had on him. "We *know*." Before she could open her mouth to say anything else, he darted in to kiss her cheek. "And we love you. Let's all just set aside any differences and have fun tonight."

"Bless Moranu, yes," Zeph agreed fervently.

Neatly trapped, Lena turned with them into the small salon, where Astar, Stella, and Rhyian sat in a conversation circle of ornately upholstered chairs and sofas. Rhyian's cobalt-blue eyes immediately fastened on hers—immobilizing her like a snake strike to the heart.

A ND THERE SHE was. Salena. Looking like she'd stepped
out of his fantasies. Rhy couldn't look away. He was
dimly aware he sat riveted to the spot, frozen like an idiot,
holding a goblet of truly excellent Branlian whiskey in his
hand, but he seemed unable to do anything about it.

Of course he'd known that she'd grow up in the intervening years, but Salena had truly become a woman as formidable
as her namesake's reputation. With the wide, angled cheekbones of the Nahanauns, bronze skin and a full, generous
mouth, Salena's face had matured from the pretty blossom of
her teens into mesmerizing beauty. Her gleaming hair was the
color of rich caramel kissed by the sun, and her thick, dark
lashes framed her Tala blue eyes, full of magic and sharp
intelligence. She wore white—an unfair reminder, there—
lavishly embroidered with pearls and small crystals, which
caught the light and scattered it again. The gown left her
shoulders bare, showing off her gracefully muscled arms and
an entrancing amount of cleavage.

She was staring back at him, standing frozen in the doorway, her arm looped through Jak's. Zeph and Gendra eased quietly into the room on either side of them. Rhy realized all their friends were holding their breath, avidly awaiting whatever came next. Jak even smirked pointedly, knowing full well how painful this was for Rhy—and making it clear the next move was up to him.

Faithless, treacherous louts, every one of them.

All except for Stella. The tense undercurrents must be nearly unbearable for her because she put her left hand to her lips, inserting the tips of the prettily enameled nails of the littlest fingers. It was an old habit of hers, to suck on those two fingers, and when they were kids, Stella's mother had been forever after her to stop, bemoaning the eternally shriveled state of those fingers. Even shapeshifting back to human form restored them only so much. Stella hadn't much cared, though she was careful to hide the habit around her mother, but Rhy remembered that summer in Annfwn when Stella had suddenly started to care—and how Salena had helped her break the habit.

It had been the same summer that he'd noticed Salena as more than a friend.

Shaking that memory away, Rhy pulled himself together, if only for Stella's sake. These days, she only reverted to nibbling those two fingertips under stress—and him and Lena not being adults about dealing with each other was a stupid reason to upset their sensitive Nilly.

He stood, grateful for the shapeshifter heritage that at least guaranteed his balance and maybe a modicum of grace. The way he felt, pulse pounding in his skull, he'd otherwise pitch over face first. Finding he was clutching his goblet hard enough to dent the ornamental metal, he lifted it in a toast. "To old friends," he said, impressed with himself that he sounded reasonably poised.

Jak gave him a disgusted look, but Astar came to his rescue, standing also. He offered his twin a hand up, gently tugging her fingers from her lips. "To enduring friendships," Astar said, lifting his own goblet, Stella joining him.

After a moment's hesitation, Rhy affirmed the toast and drank, watching over the rim of the goblet as Salena looked everywhere but at him.

"But I'm a terrible host," Astar exclaimed. "We can hardly have a toast when not everyone has drinks." Releasing Stella's hand—though not before giving her a searching look to make sure she was all right—Astar strode over to embrace Salena. "Princess Salena Nakoa KauPo, you look ravishing," he said, releasing her to take her hand and kiss it. "We hear daily about your brilliant work in Aerron—and the High Throne thanks you—but I can't say how happy I am to have your sun-kissed self here with us tonight."

Salena laughed, a throaty sound that Rhy would recognize anywhere, though he'd long since given up hoping to elicit it himself. "Why, Prince Astar," she replied with warm affection, "I do believe you've been practicing your courtly charm."

Rhy gulped some whiskey. Coming tonight had been the second-stupidest thing he'd ever done, and he'd done more than his share of stupid things. It only figured that the top two—possibly more—had to do with Salena.

"Don't be sad." Stella touched Rhy's arm, her healing magic flowing into him with green light that chased his dark thoughts into hiding.

"I'm not," he assured her. "Don't waste your magic on me."

"You're not a waste, Rhy," she replied gravely, her eyes softly gray, like fog. "You're too hard on yourself."

He smiled at her, feeling the wistfulness in it. "I think you're the only person who isn't hard on me." Then he kicked himself for sounding like a self-pitying gruntling and produced a grin. "Too bad we're first cousins, otherwise you'd be the perfect woman for me."

"*Every* woman is the perfect woman for you," Zeph informed him archly, draping herself against him. She had the whiskey carafe and refilled his goblet. "At least for the five minutes she's in your bed," she added with a smirk.

He feigned an outraged expression. "I beg your pardon! It's at least ten minutes—sometimes fifteen."

Zeph laughed lustily and kissed his cheek. "Happy Feast of Moranu, Rhy. I'm glad you came tonight, even if you had to be hog-tied."

He clinked his goblet to hers. "Just a bit of emotional leverage and a royal command. No ropes involved."

"More's the pity," she purred. "But this is a family celebration, so we must resign ourselves."

Rhy laughed at Zeph's flirtatious remarks, enjoying her easy ways and outrageous loveliness. Across the room, Salena glanced over, a set expression on her face, before she looked back at Astar and Jak, pasting on a patently fake smile for them.

Rhy knew all of Salena's smiles, and that one was her I'm-pretending-I'm-not-really-upset smile.

"Tonight is hard for her, too," Stella said, tapping the two littlest fingers of her left hand against the goblet. "She doesn't want to be here either."

"She doesn't?" Maybe Rhy didn't know her as well as he'd thought. Salena had seemed to be eating up the attention from Astar and Jak. And that dress...

"Dafne didn't have to make it a royal command," Zeph agreed with a flutter of black lashes, "but I hear it was a near thing. Lena is here under protest, too. A pity, as I'd think you two would love the rest of us enough to *want* to attend. We're never together anymore."

"I see you and Gendra all the time," he protested, then tugged on one of Stella's dark curls. "And Willy and Nilly here nearly as often." It was only Jak and Salena he hadn't seen as much. "I can't help it if Jak and Lena are always off adventuring."

"Maybe. Maybe not," Stella replied, eyes darkening and magic making her hair coil around his fingers as she focused on him. Rhy knew that sorcerous look well from his mother and had to resist backing up from it. "I'd like a gift from you tonight."

"I didn't think to bring gifts," he admitted. Tala just weren't that great with *things*, but that was an excuse. He hadn't been thinking about his friends much at all—he'd been trying so hard not to think about the past. And Salena.

Stella huffed at him. "Moranu is the goddess of the intangible. Even mossback tradition recognizes that, so we give gifts of promises and favors."

Ah. That explained all the scrolls. Now that he thought about it, his mother had tried to explain that to him, but he'd been too annoyed with her to listen. "I'm an idiot," he told Stella with a smile, mentally apologizing to his mother, too. Something he'd never do aloud. "What would you ask of me, cousin?"

"You can make it easy for us to be together, Rhy. This group has always followed your lead, and that's where I want you to take us. That's the gift I ask of you tonight."

Zeph, who'd been uncharacteristically silent till now, smothered a laugh and quickly drank from her goblet, but her blue eyes sparkled with amusement at his expense. He scowled at her, then smoothed his annoyance to turn back to Stella. "This group follows Astar's lead." He gestured with his mug at the golden prince, holding forth with expansive gestures as he told some tale that had Salena, Jak, and Gendra laughing uproariously. "As it should be."

Stella gave him a pitying look. "I love you, Rhy, but you can be very thick skulled."

Zeph actually choked on her whiskey, so Rhy pounded her on the back, much harder than was helpful. She escaped him by briefly becoming a black cat—who clawed his wrist with a brisk swipe before she manifested again, perfectly coiffed and in the same crimson gown and matching jewels. Just figured she'd mastered that trick, too. Nursing his bleeding wrist, he gave her a warning glare.

"Will you do it?" Stella prompted, gazing at him with earnest entreaty.

"I will do my best," he promised her. It was impossible to refuse Stella anything.

She beamed, happiness lighting her eyes to a silver as bright as her gown. "That's all any of us asks of you, Rhy. Not the impossible. Just your best."

He'd opened his mouth to reply when Astar called out for everyone to gather at the fireplace. Dutifully, they all obeyed— Stella was crazy to suggest that anyone but Astar led their group—and they made a circle around a black-draped table set with pieces of paper, crystal-tipped quills, and elegant short glasses.

"We're going to have our own ceremony," Astar informed them. "And a special toast."

"For a special toast, we should open the mjed," Jak said, surveying the setup. He punched Rhy on the shoulder. "Help me out, Rhy."

Though they were speaking Common Tongue, Rhy heard the command sense from his half-Dasnarian friend anyway. "Have you gotten so puny that you need my shapeshifter strength?" he taunted.

Jak grinned. "Yeah, that's it."

The four women stood together on one side of the table, their soft laughter twining through their animated conversation like flowers blooming on lush vines. Salena had her back to him, and he wondered what they were discussing. Hoped it wasn't him.

Astar frowned at Jak. "I can call for footmen to bring it, if this cask is too heavy," he offered.

Jak looked affronted. "The day a man can't carry his own

cask of mjed is a sad day indeed."

"Oh, good," Rhy said blandly, "then you don't need my help after all."

Jak poked him in the chest, hard enough to hurt. "Too good to help a common guy with a menial task, Prince Rhyian?"

"Not really a prince," Rhy muttered under Astar's booming laugh.

Astar clapped him on the shoulder. "Jak got us there, cousin. Let's see this enormous cask."

It *was* enormous. Astar and Rhy stood back, surveying the man-sized barrel in one of the outer courtyards near a service gate. Rhy coughed into his fist. "Ah, Jak, *why* under Moranu's gaze did you bring a cask this huge?"

"It's a big party." Jak gestured at the looming edifice, its towers white against the night sky.

"What I want to know is how you got it here." Astar scanned the courtyard as if an answer might present itself.

"A wagon," Jak replied. "It's this device with wheels that common people use to cart heavy things around when you don't have footmen to do it."

Astar and Rhy exchanged glances. "Why didn't you leave the wagon here?" Rhy asked.

"Or at least bring the cask inside?" Astar added.

Jak gave him a look of exaggerated patience. "Because, you royal ass, the wagon had other stuff to deliver, and I told my folks that we could handle it between the three of us. I didn't know you guys had gone soft."

"Can we just get this done?" Rhy asked. "It's colder than

Danu's tits out here." Though it was still early in the evening, no light remained in the sky, and the wind bit even harder, the rivets holding the banners rattling on the battlements high above.

"It's going to have to be in human form," Astar said, eyeing the cask. "Too bad, as my bear form could probably hold it, but I can't return to human form and still be wearing these clothes. Still can't do that trick."

He looked so mournful that Rhy shrugged in solidarity. "Neither can I."

"And some of us can't shapeshift at all," Jak declared, then flexed his muscles. "But I bet I'm as strong as either of you. We can lift it."

Astar tried wrapping his big arms around it, barely reaching halfway around. Grunting and straining, he hardly budged it. "There's no good leverage."

"Idiots. We all three have to lift, which will work better with it sideways." Jak grinned at them. "Teamwork. Rhy, stand there and be ready to catch it when I tip it toward you."

Rhy studied the giant—and heavy—cask with a jaundiced eye. "No."

"I'm calling the footmen," Astar said.

"An army of them," Rhy advised.

"You two give up too easily," Jak said in exasperation. "Stand aside, then, and I'll show you. I can carry this by myself." He shrugged out of his scarlet coat, unbuckled the sword belt, then climbed the cask like a monkey, clipping on some straps.

"All right." Rhy put his hands on his hips and stood well

back. "Let's see this."

"Wait," Astar said, holding up placating hands. "That thing is seriously heavy. We don't want—"

"Jak says he can do this," Rhy replied blandly. "Are you impugning his Dasnarian manhood?"

"Right." Jak scowled. "Watch this."

"I'm watching all right," Rhy called cheerfully.

"*You* are a troublemaker," Astar muttered.

Rhy grinned at him. "Love you, too, cuz."

Jak put his back against the cask, looped his arms in the straps, and leaned. Slowly, improbably, he lifted the thing. He balanced there with the cask on his back, grunting, breath puffing out white in the torchlight...

Until his legs gave.

Jak managed to drop the cask to the side, so it didn't come straight down to crush him. The cask hit the courtyard stones—fortunately buffered with snowdrifts—then rolled down the slope of icy snow, whipping Jak helplessly toward the sky as it went. With a shout, Astar and Rhy leapt to stop its roll before it smashed Jak beneath its considerable weight. Serendipitously, with a loud *crack*, the cask fetched up against the stone-well housing in the center of the courtyard—with Jak still trapped in the straps facing upward, kicking like a squashed bug. Rhy burst out laughing at the sight.

"You all right, man?" Astar called, then glared at Rhy. "Don't laugh, he could be hurt."

"Get me down from here!" Jak yelled, thrashing at the straps so that Rhy—who'd really tried to manfully swallow his laughter—cracked up all over again. He pointed at Jak, arms and legs flailing as he tried to get loose, but couldn't get words past the wheezing laughter.

A smile cracked through Astar's concern before he squashed it into seriousness. "We have to get him down," he said.

Unable to speak, Rhy clutched an arm around his gut and nodded. Astar tried to look disgusted, but a snicker escaped him, snorting out his nose. He tried to stifle the laugh, but that only made it worse. Astar's face tightened and swelled with suppressed laughter until he looked like a bloated jellyfish about to pop, which only made Rhy laugh harder. Finally Astar lost the battle, his booming laugh ringing out, both he and Rhy leaning against the barrel to keep themselves upright.

"Fuck you guys!" Jak yelled with renewed frenzy. He went on, but in Dasnarian, the few words Rhy recognized increasingly filthy.

"All right, all right," Rhy managed, finally mastering himself. "Hang on. We'll get you down."

Astar stood with his butt against the cask, bent over with his hands on his knees as he wheezed. "I'm sorry, Jak," he managed to say. "Really, I am. But the way you look—" He choked on another laugh and cleared his throat. "How are we getting him free?"

Rhy began resolutely stripping off his clothes. "I have an idea."

Astar eyed him. "I take it this idea doesn't involve calling footmen?"

"Not for us manly men," Rhy agreed with a thin smile.

"We could call the girls to help."

"We are not calling the girls!" Jak yelled at the sky.

For once, Rhy agreed. "Strip, Astar, and do the bear thing. Jak can carry our clothes."

~ 4 ~

"**W**HAT IS TAKING them so long?" Gendra frowned at the door the three guys had gone through.

"Hopefully we won't have to stage a rescue," Zeph said, tossing back the last of her whiskey. Lena was nursing hers, as she was not a shapeshifter and lacked the hearty metabolism that kept them from getting drunk without serious effort. If Zeph's story was true—and there was no reason for her to lie or exaggerate—that Rhyian had gotten drunk following his mother's edict that he attend the party, then he'd had to work at it. Certainly said something about his feelings for her. As if he hadn't demonstrated that clearly enough with the *incident*.

"I could go spy on them," Zeph offered. "I have a bat form that would work. They'll never see me."

"Never mind them," Stella said. "They can handle it, and their absence lets us talk. Lena, how are you feeling?"

"I'm having a great time," Lena lied through her teeth. Being in the same room with Rhyian was sheer torture. He kept staring at her with intense, broody eyes over the rim of his goblet, like she wouldn't notice. And he had yet to speak to her directly. She wished everyone could just get it through their heads that she and Rhyian did much better with a desert and a mountain range between them.

"You don't have to stay if it's too difficult for you," Stella persisted.

"Yes, she does so have to stay," Zeph insisted, sliding a long arm around Lena's waist and hugging her like she meant to keep her from running.

Stella's soulful eyes searched Lena's face. "It's painful for them, Zeph. Don't be cruel. You weren't there for the *incident*."

Stella had been there. She'd been the one to sit with her while Lena cried—and to witness Lena's vow that she'd never shed another tear over Rhyian. Stella had also promised never to tell anyone what had happened, and she never had. Not even Astar, unless she had told her twin and he'd kept it to himself, too, which was possible.

"No, I wasn't there for whatever happened," Zeph said, sharpening. "Isn't it time you told us?"

"No," said Lena decisively.

"It's good to talk about these things," Zeph persisted. "Isn't that right, Gendra?"

Gendra's indigo eyes widened, and she choked on her whiskey. "Leave me out of it. Rhy is my friend, too. Whatever terrible thing he did, I don't want to know."

"How do you know it was Rhy who was terrible?" Zeph demanded.

"Because he feels so guilty," Gendra retorted.

"He does?" That surprised Lena. Rhyian had never demonstrated a hint of remorse. Quite the opposite. The way he'd smiled when she discovered him, sly and smug and shameless... She clenched her teeth to force the memory away.

Gendra met her gaze with sincere concern. "He does feel guilty, Lena. He's never gotten over it, whatever happened between you. I'm not saying you have to forgive him, but at least talk to him."

Just then, the doors to the salon opened, music and the roar of the party crowd spilling in, along with Astar in huge grizzly-bear form, Rhyian as a black bear beside him, both of them upright on hind legs as they rolled an enormous cask into the room. Jak followed them, red-faced, hair mussed, walking slowly and stiffly as he carried a stack of clothing.

The four women stared at the sight. "Do we even *want* to know?" Lena said into the silence.

The two bears wrestled the cask upright to stand on one end, then the black bear vanished, becoming Rhyian in his basic black pants and loose shirt, the simple outfit he'd drilled in since childhood so he wouldn't return to human form naked. He met Lena's gaze with a crooked grin. "Suffice to say that Jak is an idiot."

"We knew *that*," Lena replied lightly, excruciatingly aware that these were the first words she and Rhyian had exchanged in seven years.

Rhyian smirked, his eyes still on hers. "You have no idea. Once we get dressed, we'll tell you the whole story."

He snatched his clothes and boots from Jak, who scowled. "Hey! You promised you wouldn't tell."

"In your dreams," Rhyian retorted, prowling to the other side of a high-backed sofa and stripping off his shirt. His leanly muscled chest and back gleamed golden in the light of the many candles, their glow lovingly caressing the planes and angles of his long, gorgeous body.

Astar had returned to human form, too, his clothes a basic white tunic and blue pants. He shook his golden head. "If you ladies would please turn around?"

"Of course," Zeph replied sweetly. The four women fanned out for the best view, watching steadfastly and sipping their drinks.

Astar gave Stella a pleading look. "I'm your brother, for Moranu's sake."

"Rhy isn't," she pointed out placidly. "And the Tala don't worry much about modesty."

"Then why is Rhy hiding behind the sofa?" Astar retorted, stalking that way to join him.

Rhyian shook back his hair as he straightened—clearly naked now, though Lena couldn't see past the sofa any lower than the carved bones of his narrow hips. He slanted the women a wicked grin. "I don't want the sight of my glorious nudity to make them faint," he said. "We have a lot of drinking yet to do. Witness that enormous cask we nearly killed ourselves to bring in here."

"I'm the one with the strained back," Jak muttered.

"Whose fault is that?" Rhyian shot back, bending to work the tight black velvet pants up his long legs. Was her mouth watering? Lena was definitely feeling warm. Astar was also swiftly changing clothes, but he was mostly a golden blur compared to Rhyian's crisply dazzling darkness.

"Let me help your back," Stella said, going to Jak. His crimson clothes bore wet patches and smears of mud. "Between my brother and my cousin, it's true that the show doesn't do much for me."

Jak blew her a soft kiss. "You are a true friend, Nilly. Marry me and be my love forever."

Stella blushed lightly. "Don't tease, Jak."

"I feel I should point out that I'm not blood-related to anyone here," Zeph announced.

"Me neither," Gendra put in, with unusual boldness for her. The two toasted each other.

"Not that it matters," Lena put in with some irritation, finally managing to wrench her gaze from Rhyian's brilliant masculine beauty, "as none of us are here tonight for sex."

They all turned and looked at her, even Astar, who'd just poked his head through the opening of his shirt. Zeph snorted, unapologetic gaze fastened on Astar's bare abdomen. "Speak for yourself, Lena," she purred.

Astar yanked his shirt down and pulled on his powder-blue velvet coat. "Lena is right. Tonight is for celebrating our enduring friendships, not indulging in lustful flirtation."

"You were the ones putting on the naked man show," Zeph pointed out.

"Out of necessity," Astar replied tersely, then glared at Jak, who held his hands up in innocence—the gesture completely ruined by his roguish smile. Apparently restored to his usual agile fettle, he returned to busying himself with tapping the cask.

"I, for one," Rhyian put in, gaze lingering on Lena as he pulled on his glossy boots, "would be perfectly willing to be a gentleman and entertain some turnabout, if the ladies care to put on a show for us."

"Hear, hear!" Jak toasted with a goblet freshly filled with mjed, dark eyes going to Stella.

"Absolutely not," Astar nearly growled, glaring at both Rhy and Jak as he fastidiously buttoned up his jacket. He leveled the glare on Stella, who blinked in surprise. "You're keeping your clothes on."

She made a face at him. "Sheesh, Willy—I grew out of that phase by the time I was five."

"Six," he corrected.

"Don't be such a prude, Willy," Rhyian agreed with a sly smile, prowling over to swipe two of the elegant glasses from the table by the fire, taking them to Jak to fill with mjed. "I miss the days when Nilly ran naked through the halls, sending the fancy mossback ladies into palpitations."

"I'm sorry I missed it," Jak said warmly, winking at Stella.

She rolled her eyes. "I was a child."

"One who hated having to return to human form dressed," Rhyian said. "It's natural—nothing to be embarrassed about."

"I'm not embarrassed," Stella replied, lifting her chin.

"Good for you," Rhyian murmured with a smile.

Astar, once again more or less perfectly attired, cleared his throat. "Let's try this again. If everyone would fill their glasses and gather around the table, please."

Lena moved to get a glass, but Rhyian intercepted her with smooth grace and shapeshifter speed. She managed not to gasp at the sight of him suddenly in front of her, so lethally gorgeous, his hair no longer sleeked back, but tumbling wildly around his face. He held out one of the glasses. "This one is for you, Salena." When she hesitated—more out of sheer surprise than anything—his lips quirked in a half smile. "Unless you refuse to accept even this much from me."

Stung, she plucked the glass from his fingers, being careful not to touch him. "That's unfair. I never refused you. *Anything*," she added with a hiss, which she immediately regretted.

He didn't take the easy opening, however, instead regarding her seriously. Surely that wasn't regret in his deep blue eyes. "You refused to talk to me."

Her stomach dropped and her head swam. Oh no. This was exactly the confrontation she hadn't wanted. She'd begun to relax, believing that he didn't want to revisit the bad old days either. "I did not. You weren't exactly available for conversation," she replied coolly, congratulating herself for her poise. "Besides, there was nothing to discuss. You made yourself very clear through your actions."

"I know," he admitted. "But you left before we could sort it out."

"You didn't exactly chase after me," she bit out, then kicked herself. *Gah.* Why was she still talking?

Rhyian was searching her face. "Was I supposed to chase after you? I didn't know I'd made that mistake."

"You made a *lot* of mistakes, Rhyian." The bitter heartbreak of that time felt excruciatingly fresh and raw. "We both did."

"Salena, I..." He trailed off, pressing his lips together.

Those lips that had caressed her skin with such intimate delight. She'd once thought she'd give anything to have those lips on her—and then she'd given too much.

"We were young," she said, gentling the old bitterness. She didn't—couldn't—forgive him, but it had been a long time ago. "We didn't know what we were doing."

He dipped his chin ruefully, his gaze catching on her bosom, then rising to meet hers, the blue fulgent with desire she remembered all too well, lips curved in a sensual smile. "We did *some* things right."

She couldn't help an answering smile. That summer had been the best of her life, regardless of how painfully it had ended. "We did," she conceded.

Rhyian gave her a more serious look. "Could we—"

"Are you two joining us or what?" Astar called out, then grunted as if in pain.

"Shut *up*," Zeph chastised the hunched Astar, who'd apparently taken a sharp elbow to the gut. "Are you completely oblivious, you oaf?"

Gendra and Stella gave Lena rueful smiles, while Jak tossed off a little salute from where he leaned against the fireplace. Lena's face heated with embarrassment. She'd been so intent on Rhyian that she'd forgotten about their audience. "Don't be silly," she said brightly. "We were being rude." She moved to join their waiting friends, but Rhyian caught her hand.

His fingers lightly tangled with hers, his touch scalding, bringing back so many memories. Rhyian holding her hand as they walked on the beach at Annfwn. The first time he kissed her sensitive fingertips, his eyes heated as he savored her shivering response. When he laced their fingers together on either side of her head as he lay against her... She couldn't breathe. "Rhyian..." she said helplessly.

"Dance with me later," he said with dark intensity. "Please."

Rhyian never said please or thank you. At least, the Rhyian she'd known hadn't. He'd disdained mossback manners, along with rules of all kinds, and she'd once found that exciting about him. She'd also suffered because of it. Extracting her fingers, she folded them into her palm, where they burned with longing. "I don't think that's a good idea."

"I don't get why you're all so upset with me," Astar's voice rose in the background, Stella and Zeph hushing him.

Rhyian's gaze didn't even flicker in their direction. They held hers fast, the blue drowning deep in his wildly beautiful face. "One dance. Isn't it a night for letting go of the past, for new beginnings?"

"So I've been informed," she answered drily. "Repeatedly." Her little sister, Bethany, had babbled on at length on how the crystalline moon made it the perfect night for falling in love. Well, Lena had fallen in love once and still had the bruises to show for that brutal fall. Never again. Certainly not with Rhyian, who'd been the one to shove her off the cliff.

"One chance is all I ask," he said with hushed intensity. "Just for tonight. Can we pretend to be friends again?"

"It would still be a pretense," she warned, absurdly tempted to say yes. But then Rhyian had always been able to tempt her into going against her better judgment.

He smiled, slight and more than a little wicked, as if he

knew the effect he had on her. "I'll take whatever I can get."

"One dance," she breathed. It didn't have to be about love or the past. Just friends. And in the morning she'd be gone, back to her desert and her work, where he'd never follow.

"One dance—with potential for more," he qualified, smile widening.

And there he was, the old Rhyian in fine style, teasing and pushing for just a little bit more than she wanted to give. Well, she'd learned her lesson. She hoped. "We'll see," she replied loftily, and turned her back on him.

~ 5 ~

R HY WATCHED SALENA glide away, her caramel hair falling down her back like an inverted flame, emphasizing her narrow waist and the graceful curve of her hips. His mouth had gone dry, and he didn't have any idea what had possessed him to say any of that to her. Except that he felt like a lust-filled and awkward lad again, which had come as quite a shock. Tossing back the mjed, he sent an earnest prayer to Moranu— something he was normally careful never to do, as he didn't care to awaken the goddess's interest in him—to keep him from making the biggest mistake of his life.

Or at least, not one to knock all the others out of the top ten.

"Rhy," Astar complained, "you were supposed to wait to drink until we all toasted, to seal the good luck and the goddess's blessing."

"A pointless superstition, Willy, my boy," he replied easily. "Especially when, thanks to Jak's delusions of grandeur, we have a cask big enough to fill the glasses of everyone in

Ordnung for a week. Anyone else need a refill?" he asked as he went to the cask.

"I do," Jak and Zeph chimed together, coming to join him.

Zeph kissed him on the cheek while she waited. "Well done," she whispered. "We have your back."

"Don't meddle, Zephyr," he muttered under his breath, sliding a look to Salena, who watched them with that serious, pensive look she got when she was thinking about rules instead of fun.

"What meddling?" Zeph widened her eyes in shocked innocence. "I have no idea what you mean."

"Uh-huh."

Jak handed Zeph her refilled glass. "It's not delusions of grandeur when you deliver," he pointed out.

"Seems to me like Astar and I delivered, while you acted as our valet," Rhy taunted him.

"Please come do Astar's ceremony," Gendra called, "or we'll *never* get out of this room."

"It's tradition," Astar protested, "not *my* ceremony."

The three of them returned to the group at the table, making a loose ring around it and setting their full glasses down.

Astar, happy that they were all finally going along with his plan, beamed at them. "I wanted us all to have a private ceremony before the main one at midnight. You each have two pieces of paper, one for the past and one for the future. Once you've all written down your own regrets and wishes, we'll have a toast to each other, to ask Moranu to set Her hand on our friendships to endure."

An uneasy feeling crept down Rhy's spine, one that came

of invoking the goddess. Across the table from him, Salena watched him with a speculative expression, as if she could read his apprehension. She was one of the few people who knew how heavily Moranu's hand sat on him. When the heroic Queen Andromeda had eliminated the scourge of Deyrr from the world, his mother had done it partly by making a bargain with the goddess, pledging her unborn child to Moranu's service in exchange for Her help. That unborn child being him. A hell of an onus to be born under. Moranu hadn't called him to Her service yet, but it was only a matter of time.

"What, exactly, are we writing down?" Rhy asked, trying not to sound as tense as he felt.

They all looked at him. "Haven't you ever done this ritual?" Gendra asked.

"Nope." He shrugged in the extravagant Tala style to remind them. "This is my first Feast of Moranu outside Annfwn, and the Tala don't do this." He wiggled a dubious finger at the quills and paper.

"True," Salena said drily. "We're lucky if the Tala write anything down at all."

He eyed her. "Not everyone worships libraries, Princess."

She narrowed her eyes and opened her mouth, but Astar put a hand on her arm. "It's good to remind us all," he said, looking around the table. "For the past, we write down a regret we'd like to leave behind. For the future, we write down a promise, wish, or hope for ourselves or for someone else."

"Isn't the past already behind us?" Rhy asked.

Salena's gorgeous lips quirked in an appreciative smile. "That *is* the definition of the past, after all."

Gendra groaned and thunked her forehead on the table. "Why did we want them to start talking to each other again? I'm never going to make it to the dancing. Never."

"The past," Stella said, not raising her voice, but silencing everyone immediately with her gravity and the resonance of magic, "is only behind us if we make an effort to leave it behind." She leveled her storm-gray gaze on Rhy, then on Salena. "Past mistakes and regrets can be like stones we tied around our necks of our own free will. They weigh us down, chains to the past that prevent us from moving into the future. If we are forever dragging those weights, they stunt our growth. This is an opportunity to break those chains and drop those stones of remorse, leaving them here to burn cleanly in the fire, so that we can move into the new year unfettered by past mistakes, free to grow into better people."

A hush settled, and they all looked at each other. Rhy started to drink his mjed, but Gendra, beside him, put a hand on his forearm to lock it in place, giving him a pleading look. Right. No more delays.

Astar cleared his throat. "On that note, you all should have an idea of what to write down. Past first."

They all bent over the task, quiet filling the room, the fire crackling and the wind roaring distantly among the high towers. A few of them were already scratching words down. Show-offs. Rhy stared at the blank paper, about a hundred possibilities flying through his mind of mistakes and regrets he'd love to never think about again.

"What if my paper isn't big enough?" he said into the quiet. Five heads snapped up to level unamused glares on him, while

Jak tossed him a jaunty salute.

"Pick *one*," Salena suggested in a lethal tone. "If you like, I can make a list for you."

"That's the problem, isn't it?" he replied. "The list is so long. How to choose?"

"Rhy," Stella said, not without sympathy, "no one but you and Moranu will know what you write down. It can be anything at all."

"Yes, well, Moranu is not that fond of me," he retorted. "I try not to let Her into my head."

Stella cocked her head, looking *through* him in that sorcerous way his mother did, and nodded to herself.

"It doesn't even have to be real," Gendra snapped at him, folding her paper several times into a tiny square. "Write down the color blue for all I care, just write something and burn it."

He followed as she strode to the fireplace and pitched in her note. "But then I wouldn't have your pretty blue eyes in my life," he teased, stepping back in surprise when she whirled on him.

"Fine," she hissed. "Don't take this seriously. But do try not to ruin it for the rest of us."

"Why are you pissed at me?" he asked, genuinely taken aback. Gendra never got mad at him—unlike everyone else—and was always staunchly on his team.

"I'm not." She sighed, relenting and putting a hand on his arm. "You know I love you like a brother, Rhy, but it would be nice if, for once in your life, you thought about how someone else feels." She walked away, leaving him gaping after her.

"Burrrrnnn," Zeph whispered in his ear as she leaned past

him to toss her paper in the fire.

He narrowed his eyes at her. "What did you tell Gendra?"

"Me?" Zeph patted his cheek. "Not a thing. Go write something down so Astar will let us leave the Room of Doom, all right?"

Beyond irritated, he stalked back to the table and dashed off one word—using a Tala rune just in case any of them peeked—crumpled it in his fist, and threw it in the fire. The flames caught it, burning slowly as the pungent smoke coiled up. The runes seemed to glow, taunting him.

"Put a lot of thought into that, did you?" Salena teased as she tossed her crumpled paper into the fire.

"What is this, everyone yell at Rhyian night?" he grumbled, and Salena paused, giving him a considering look. He'd forgotten about that, how she couldn't let a question go unanswered. She took every one seriously, and he'd used to love to tease her by asking questions she couldn't possibly know the answer to, just to wind her up.

But this time she did. She really had changed. "Just play along for a bit longer, and then you can be free," she suggested.

"Not hardly," he replied in a sour tone. "I'm trapped in mossbackland until dawn. On the longest night of the year."

"I'm sure you'll find a way to cope," she replied, walking with him back toward the table. "You can drown your sorrows in one—or several—of the hundreds of women out there waiting to enjoy the longest night with you."

He caught her hand again, partly to stop her harsh words—all the harsher because he knew he deserved them—and partly because he needed to touch her again. The glide of her clever fingers against his skin reminded him of so much. Why should he want to forget the past? It had been far better than his recent present. Salena raised an inquiring brow at him, and he released her hand before he made some declaration in the impulse of the moment that his future self would never be able to live up to.

"Do we get to drink now?" he asked Astar somewhat desperately, gazing at his temptingly full glass of mjed.

"Not yet." Astar gave him a stern look. "Now we write down a wish, hope, or promise for the future, to keep or to give to someone else."

"Yeah, yeah," Rhy sighed. "I remember that part." Catching the edge of Gendra's glare, he pasted on a happy smile. "This is so fun and meaningful!"

"Oh, for Moranu's sake," Gendra muttered, writing rapidly.

"You could wish for me to be a better person," he murmured to her, hoping to make her smile.

"I'm not wasting any more of my wishes on you, Rhy," she replied crisply.

"I'm done," Zeph declared, folding her paper and making a show of tucking it in Astar's breast pocket, giving him a sultry look as she did it. Salena and Gendra exchanged looks, and Rhy wondered if he'd missed this development. Stella looked on calmly, her mind possibly somewhere else, as it often was.

Astar, always well-mannered, took Zeph's hand and bent over it. "Thank you, my lady. Should I read it now?"

Gendra groaned under her breath, and Salena closed her

eyes as if in pain. Zeph smiled, bringing Astar's hand close enough to brush it with her breast. "Later," she said as Astar jerked and turned bright red, "when we're alone."

"Shall we toast?" Gendra said, much too loudly, and everyone seized on the moment.

"Rhyian isn't done with his," Salena said, giving him a lethal smile.

"Yes, I am," he told her, writing down another single rune, then folding the paper and putting it in his pocket. He picked up his glass and looked to Astar. "What is the toast, Your Highness, Crown Prince Astar?"

As Rhy had hoped, the words shook Astar out of his flustered embarrassment. Salena flashed him a grateful look, and Gendra squeezed his forearm. There. A hero to his favorite women in the world. Who said he was a *total* shit?

Astar lifted his glass, holding it up, once again secure as leader of their small cadre. "I offer this toast, in the name of Moranu, on this, Her most blessed night, to the people I love best in all the world." His summer-blue eyes lit on each of them in turn. "We've grown up together, traveled apart, and come together again." With his other hand, he turned over his piece of paper and slid it to the center of the table. "This is my hope, my wish, and my promise to all of you: that we shall be friends all our lives. May Moranu make it so."

They all lifted their glasses, repeating "May Moranu make it so," though the words threatened to stick in Rhy's throat. Hopefully far too many people were appealing to Moranu tonight for Her to pick out his insincere voice. Salena's gaze lingered on him, her thoughts dark behind them, and it occurred to him that she might not feel enthusiastic about Astar's vow either. At least not where he was concerned.

Well, he'd done his best to set her free before, and after their one dance tonight, he'd do his best to send her on her way again. Tipping his glass at her as he fingered the paper in his pocket, he caught her eye and smiled. Then drank to seal the promise.

~ 6 ~

"THANK MORANU!" GENDRA moaned in Lena's ear as they spilled into the corridor, the two of them arm in arm. "I thought Astar would never let us leave and I'd spend the entire ball in that tiny room."

Rhyian ambled up on Lena's other side, leaning around her to grin at Gendra. "So many walls, right? I don't get how Astar stands it, even being more than half-mossback."

"Maybe even mostly mossback," Gendra agreed, "as Stella got the lion's share of the Tala magic, along with the mark. Astar really only has First Form and that's it."

"Really? Just the bear still? Huh." Rhyian ruminated on that.

"Didn't he have a cat form when he was little?" Lena asked. "There's that story about him shredding the curtains at Lianore during that Feast of Moranu."

"Could be." Rhyian tipped his head for the vagaries of shapeshifting. "Kids sometimes manifest forms once or twice and never again."

Gendra nodded. "Getting a form once is no guarantee. Being able to do it consistently is the real accomplishment. It takes assiduous practice."

"You sound like your mother," Rhyian growled. "There's no shame in having only a few forms—or even just First Form."

"I never said there was," Gendra returned evenly.

Tired of having them argue across her, Salena snorted at them both, flashing them a disgusted look. "Oh, come on, you two. You know you multiform shapeshifters are totally snobby about those of you who have only one form—and you're even worse about those of us who can't shapeshift at all."

"Not at all," Rhyian said easily, then leisurely dropped his gaze to her abundantly displayed cleavage. She went hot, as if he'd caressed her there, her nipples tightening, and she could only hope he couldn't see her response with his sharp eyes. Lifting his gaze to hers, he grinned. "I like your *one* form very much."

She set her teeth. "Don't flirt with me, Rhyian."

"Why not? I thought we declared a truce for the one night."

"Is that what we decided?" She gave him a sidelong look, and Gendra squeezed her arm, in warning or comfort, she wasn't sure. It had been a mistake to agree to give him a chance tonight, to promise him even the one dance. Just by having that initial conversation with him, she'd opened a door she'd fought hard to close and lock forever, and now all the old feelings poured through, drowning her good sense and better judgment.

Rhyian just gave her that wicked smile, the one that had always made her melt, and she firmly changed the subject. "What are we going to do about Zeph?" she said to Gendra.

"What's up there?" Rhyian asked. "Are they lovers? Nobody told me."

"No," Gendra and Lena said in one voice, and Rhyian blinked at them.

"Oh-ho, it's like that, huh?" He chuckled.

"Like what?" Gendra demanded, leaning around Lena.

Rhyian managed an elaborate shrug, even with his hands in his pockets. He still looked impeccably beautiful, not the least bit rumpled—or rather, he was mussed exactly the way he was after sex. Lena shoved that thought—and painful memory—down deep. That was what she should've written down and burned.

"You all right?" Rhyian asked, deep blue eyes full of concern, or the pretense of it. Rhyian was very good at pretending to show what she wanted to see, and she had to remember that.

"Yes, why?"

"You made a sound, like you hurt yourself."

"These shoes pinch. And I'm with Gendra. Why do you say 'oh-ho, it's like that' with Astar and Zeph?"

He gave them a pitying look. "Obviously Zeph has finally decided to seduce our noble and innocent Willy."

"Then he *is* a virgin," Lena murmured to herself, and Rhyian flashed her an amused smile.

"Sadly, yes. But with Zeph on the job, he won't last out the night."

"He has to!" Gendra exclaimed. "Rhy, you have to help us keep her away from him."

Rhyian looked genuinely surprised. "Why? It's past time for him, and he could do far worse than Zeph."

"No, he couldn't," Gendra argued. "Zeph is the worst possible choice. She's way too much for him. She's been with half of Annfwn."

"At least," he agreed. "And all of them very happy for the experience."

"Including you?" Lena asked, regretting it instantly.

Rhy gave her an opaque look and an enigmatic smile. "Zeph is my friend, so I'm not going to dignify that with an answer. But to address Gendra's point, Astar is a grown man. If he wants to sample Zeph's charms—as she so clearly wishes to sample his—then more power to them both. It's not like they'd be hurting anyone."

"They would," Gendra insisted, tears in her eyes, and Lena put her hand over Gendra's on her arm. "Sex changes everything, Rhy!" Gendra spat, seeming not to notice Lena's touch. "Only a few moments ago, we vowed to be friends forever, and you should know better than anyone what two of us pairing off does to the rest. It's wrong and unfair."

They'd all come to a halt just shy of the ballroom. Rhyian glanced at Lena ruefully, and she shared the discomfort. Gendra, clearly regretting her outburst, looked between them. "I mean, I..."

"It's all right, Gen," Lena said, patting her friend's hand. "Rhyian and I handled things badly, not thinking about how it would affect all of you. We've already decided to do better—

and be *only* friends in the future."

"Is that what we decided?" Rhyian murmured, throwing her words back at her with a smile that didn't reach his hot blue eyes.

"Yes," she told him decisively, meaning it.

"Oh," Gendra huffed in exasperation. "Why am I even saying this to you two? I'm wasting my breath, *and* valuable dancing time."

Lena frowned, turning to take Gendra's hands. She'd been so busy with her job in the desert that she couldn't recall the last time they'd had a heart-to-heart conversation. "What's going on, honey?"

Gendra yanked her hands away and glared at both of them. "Neither of you could possibly understand. I'm off to find someone to dance with."

"Hey," Rhyian called after her, "I thought you promised me a dance."

She flung a rude gesture over her shoulder. "*Not* one of my supposed friends." And she plunged into the whirl of dancers.

Lena rounded on Rhyian. "What was *that* all about?"

He considered her, leaning languidly against the archway. The garland of moonflowers dripping with crystals and pearls framed his dark and seductive self, a rivetingly masculine version of Moranu, the avatar of all the deepest night offered—unseen dangers, and also delights never beheld in the light of day. "How should I know?" he purred.

She had to drag her thoughts back to the conversation. "You should know because you're Gendra's best friend, and you see her every day."

"Not every day," he mused. "At least, not lately."

"Far more than I do," she insisted.

"What's stopping you?"

"I've been in Aerron. Gendra rarely leaves Annfwn," she retorted, "and I—" She skidded to a mental halt, abruptly aware of the treacherous ground she found herself treading.

"And you never come to Annfwn," he finished for her, his eyes fastened on hers, sparking with annoyance. "Are you claiming that's my fault?"

Lena faltered, breathless as she felt her toes on the edge of the precipice of the chasm between them. "I don't want to have this conversation," she whispered.

He straightened from his indolent slouch. "Well, we're in the middle of it now. Annfwn is a big place. Did you really never visit Gendra all these years because of me?"

"No." *Yes.* "I've been busy," she added, far too defensively.

Smiling slightly, he shook his head. "It's been a long time, Salena, but I haven't forgotten how to read you. You ran away to avoid me—and have avoided me for seven years."

"You knew where to find me," she shot back, her face hot with embarrassment.

He inclined his head. "I was a coward, too. I couldn't face you at first. Then, after a while, it was just… easier to not think about it. About you."

"Yes." The word hissed out of her on a sigh full of regret and so much more. Gendra was right—she'd let the bad blood with Rhyian affect all of her relationships. "I don't like to think of myself as a coward," she admitted.

"That was maybe harsh," he said with a self-deprecating

smile. "I was the coward—among my many failings—and you were rightfully wary of having anything to do with me."

Her heart had tumbled over so many times this night that she'd grown dizzy from it. "Rhyian... I don't know what to say."

He grinned and held out a hand. "Then don't. Less talking. More dancing."

She found herself smiling back. "The Tala solution to everything."

Since she hadn't yet placed her hand in his, he snagged it and drew her closer. "Always," he breathed. "Do you remember—"

"Prince Rhyian!" Bethany's shriek scraped over Lena's nerves, a pained response echoing in Rhyian's face as the girl ran up to them, curtseying deeply. "Happy Feast of Moranu."

"Bethany," Rhy said smoothly, dropping Lena's hand to offer it to help Bethany up. "You look ravishing."

Bethany giggled, doing a pirouette to show off her gown, which seemed to be made entirely of black lace and obsidian crystals. Lena wondered if their mother knew the gown Bethany had worked on in secret was so very... adult. "We match!" she crowed. "Do you see?"

"Indeed we do." Rhyian seemed bemused, but he also smiled on Lena's sister with apparently genuine affection. Another surprise, as Lena hadn't realized the two even knew each other. She'd have known if Rhyian ever visited Nahanau, whether she was there or not. "But how did you guess?" he asked.

"Silly." Bethany leaned on Rhyian's arm, swanning in close

to him. "You always wear black," she breathed.

Lena raised a brow at Rhyian, and he had the grace to look chagrined. So far as she knew, Rhyian had last seen Bethany when she was five or six years old. And Bethany had been going on earlier about falling in love and the crystalline moon. *Oh, Rhyian had better not!*

"I've been looking for you *everywhere*," Bethany scolded, flashing an angry look at Lena, as if she'd been holding Rhyian captive. "I've been practicing the dance steps you showed me. Now you must dance with me for real."

"Of course." Rhyian patted her hand where she leaned on him, peeled it off his arm, then bent over it to brush a kiss over it. "As soon as this set ends, I'll meet you on the floor."

"But—" Bethany began, giving Lena another suspicious look.

"I must take care of something first," he said, winking at her. "Even shapeshifters are only human."

"Oh!" Bethany blushed prettily, then nodded knowingly. "See you in a bit. Don't be late." Casting Lena one more smile, this one decidedly impudent, she trotted off to where a group of her friends waited, all bursting into giggles at her arrival.

Rhyian shook his head, turning back to Lena with a smile. "Now, where—"

"Bethany has been coming to Annfwn?" Lena asked, cutting him off.

His expression cooled. "You're not the only one with friends in Annfwn, Salena."

"And she's been spending time with you." Fury—and maybe a bit of jealousy—burned acid through her stomach.

"*Dance lessons?*" She made the words scathing.

"Yes, if you must know," he bit out.

"Is that a euphemism?" she asked with bitter scorn. She hadn't been much older than Bethany when she'd fallen under Rhyian's seductive spell.

"What? No, I—"

She didn't want his excuses. "You stay away from my little sister, Rhyian." Her voice shook with anger. "She is too young for you."

Matching fury lit his eyes to cobalt, and he stuck a finger in her face. "Don't you dare accuse me of something like that. I would *never.*"

"No? That's not how I remember things."

His expression froze, skin smooth and eyes fulgent. "Oh, Salena," he said on a hush. "That seems terribly cruel. It was different between you and me."

It had been cruel, unfairly so. "You're right. I apologize. It just... took me by surprise, that you even know Bethany. That you and she... She's so young, Rhyian."

He drew back, a world of pain in his eyes, though his face remained icily composed. "She sought me out. She's a sweet girl, and I like talking to her."

"I can't imagine what you'd talk about."

"She tells me what you're doing."

Lena stared at him in shock, once again at a loss for words. He smiled without humor, cocking his head. "The set is ending. I'd best meet her before she tracks me down. Again."

She nodded, numb from the onslaught of conflicting emotions. Rhyian paused, then picked up her hand once more, holding it in both of his, running his thumb thoughtfully over the back, lifting a black-winged brow. "She's like my little sister, too, Salena," he said softly. "And I only tolerated her because of you."

Lena nodded, feeling stiff and awkward—and like a total idiot. "I'll see if I can find Gendra. Talk to her."

"You're a good friend. I didn't mean to imply otherwise." He bowed, his lips whispering over her skin in sensual promise and memory. "The next dance is ours," he said, and strode off, a lethal sword of darkness slicing through the crowd.

~ 7 ~

"**Y**OU LOOK SO handsome tonight, Prince Rhyian," Bethany cooed breathlessly. Only the fact that she kept craning her neck to see if her friends were watching them kept Rhy from escaping the girl's clutches to go find Salena again.

Salena, who hadn't changed at all and who'd changed entirely. It was as if they'd been together only that morning and as if she was someone he'd never met at the same time. Fascinating, infuriating, endlessly seductive. The person who could both call him on his shit and make him laugh. How had he managed all these years without her in his life?

"Prince Rhyian?"

"You know I'm not really a prince," he chided. "The Tala don't have a hereditary monarchy." Most of the time that didn't bother him. Rhy's parents were hale and hearty—and more than capable of ruling Annfwn. But having mossbacks call him "prince" only reminded him of how truly pointless his life was. All of his friends had goals and fine aspirations, and he had... nothing of note. No wonder Salena found him so contemptible.

"I think you aren't listening to me at all."

He looked down to find Bethany pouting, and gave her a charming grin that wouldn't fool Salena for a moment. "So much noise and so many walls. It's hard on us Tala, you know."

Her brown eyes sparkled, and she gave him a coy look from under her dark lashes. "Then let's get you out of this noise and go somewhere we can be *alone*," she breathed.

Uh-oh. Far too late, he realized he was being well and truly stalked. He'd been so offended by Salena's accusations that he hadn't given credence to her warning. Also, he had no idea how to handle this, especially when he spotted King Nakoa KauPo—darling Bethany's truly terrifying father—searching the dancers and pinning Rhy with his menacing gaze. The crowd parted as the king strode toward them, and Rhy turned Bethany in the dance so she could see. "I think someone is looking for you," he said.

Bethany blanched, chewing her lip in girlish dismay. "Oh no! What do I do? He told me I'm too young to dance with men yet, but I'm *not*!"

Internally, Rhy sighed. Surely he could've avoided this somehow. *Maybe by listening to Salena,* an internal voice whispered. "I'll handle this," he told her, wondering when he'd become the adult and responsible one.

He danced her toward the sidelines, in Nakoa's direction so the king wouldn't take alarm thinking they meant to dodge him, then halted. He bowed gallantly to Bethany, waiting until

Nakoa reached them to say, "Thank you for rescuing me, Princess Bethany Nakoa KauPo. I know you said you couldn't dance, but you did so beautifully. Greetings, Your Highness." Rhy transferred the bow to the king, certain he heard a low rumble of thunderous displeasure.

"Your devoted mother seeks your pleasant company, kiki," Nakoa said, barely sparing the girl a glance as he stared down Rhy. *Down* being the operative word, as the King of Nahanau stood a good head taller than Rhy, who was far from short. Nakoa also outweighed Rhy by a considerable amount. If the man were a barrel, Rhy could fit himself inside. And Nakoa was an accomplished warrior besides. Rhy's only hope of surviving a fight with the man would be to shapeshift—and then his parents would kill him for causing a diplomatic incident. There was no win here.

"Yes, Muku," Bethany squeaked, abandoning Rhy to disappear into the crush with impressive agility and a noteworthy absence of concern for Rhy.

Rhy bowed to Nakoa, holding the pose a moment to show respect—he hoped—then straightened. "Happy Feast of Moranu, Your Highness."

King Nakoa KauPo studied him with a stern expression, one as thunderous as the storms he could summon with a thought. Then he grunted, nodded once, and strode off.

"You got lucky," a throaty voice purred in Rhy's ear, and he spun, surprised anyone had managed to sneak up on him. Salena grinned at him, clearly pleased with herself. "Actually, Muku is a pussycat compared to Mom, but I was still ready to step in to defend your honor."

He gazed back at her, rather astonished. He'd figured her for avoiding him the rest of the night, not coming to his aid. "I'm touched," he said, then worried that it sounded too flip. "I know you have no reason to defend me, and plenty of reasons not to."

She sobered, giving him a thoughtful look. "I never wished you ill, Rhyian. Well," she amended, giving him a grin, "not beyond a few fantasies of your painful demise."

He laughed. "I deserved that and more." Taking the chance, he held out a hand. "Shall we have our dance?"

This time she placed her hand in his, and he deftly slipped them into a space between whirling dancers. She moved with sensual grace, and the way his hand settled into the narrow of her waist felt far too familiar, reminding him sharply of those long-gone days. But those watchful eyes held little of the wide-eyed wonder she'd had in that first blush of womanhood. Salena the girl had embraced everything life had to offer with uninhibited joy and delight. Now the deep blue, bordered by a fine line of deepest storm gray, regarded him with a mixture of cynicism and uncertainty. She was waiting for him to hurt her again, and honestly, he was expecting that eventually, too.

"I'm sorry I said that about Bethany. It was cruel and wrong."

He shrugged a little. "You had reason to think it. We both know I'm far from faultless that way."

She was quiet for a bit, and he savored the feel of her against him. They fit still—possibly even better—after all this time. She had a hand on his shoulder, her gaze focusing there for a moment as she brushed something away. "It was kind of you," she finally said, and he suspected it wasn't what she'd been thinking about saying. "Considerate, of Bethany's feelings to dance with her, with all of her friends watching. I realize that now. I just... didn't expect that from you."

No, of course she wouldn't. He'd been far from kind and considerate back then. "It *has* been seven years. I've grown up since then." He had to smile at her dubious expression. "Some," he qualified. "Not entirely."

"Yes, I've heard the stories," she quipped with a saucy smile that faded at the edges as she looked away, realizing what she'd revealed.

That slip, however, more than anything else, gave him some hope that she might not have so thoroughly cut him out of her life as she'd like it to seem. Slipping his hand more to the center of the small of her back, he eased her just a little closer, dropping his mouth to near her temple. She smelled of distant rain, of sweet skin and nostalgia. Of moonlit nights and the flowers of Annfwn. Of his own innocence, and a time he hadn't loathed himself. "Tell me the truth, Salena—have you been seeking out stories about me?"

She made a small sound, of distress or desire, he wasn't sure. "No," she said, her voice firm and breathless at once. Her breasts, so temptingly displayed in that luscious gown, rose and fell, brushing against him in a way that threatened to make him lose his mind. "But," she said on a light gasp, "one can't help hearing things, can one? The more salacious, the more people love to chatter on."

Daring more, he brushed her temple with his lips. Not quite a kiss, but terribly, agonizingly close to one. "Tell me what you've heard," he purred against the delicate shell of her ear. "The most salacious tidbit."

She laughed, throaty and sensual. "Oh no, I don't think so. Your enormous ego needs no further stroking."

"Maybe that's not the enormous part of me that *does* need stroking." Needing to taste her, he licked just that little curve of her ear, and she shivered in his arms.

"I've seen your 'part,' remember," she replied, pulling back to establish more formal distance between them, narrowing her eyes, "and it is *not* enormous."

"You wound me cruelly," he said. "I was a barely more than a boy. I told you, I've grown." He lowered his voice to tempt her closer. "*And* I've been practicing my selective shapeshifting."

Her lips parted in shock at his wickedness, and he enjoyed the glimmer of interest in her eyes—until she punched him in the shoulder. "Liar. You have not," she scolded.

"You don't know," he protested, but laughed, spinning her so she had to use her hand on his shoulder to steady herself instead of punching him again.

"I do know," she replied, almost primly, when he slowed them again. "Even this ignorant mossback knows that selective shapeshifting requires painstaking practice and that only the most talented—" She broke off, a furious blush crowning her cheekbones. "I didn't mean…"

"That's all right," he replied, making sure to sound bored, which was easy since he'd become essentially numb to any references to his lack of talent and inexcusable refusal to apply himself. "You are far from the first or only person to make note of my startling lack of shapeshifting ability."

"Gendra and Zeph both say it's not lack of ability," Salena continued, blithely poking at the sore spot. "Even I can see Moranu's hand on you. You're Her chosen. If you'd just apply your—"

"Salena," he broke in, cutting off her words ruthlessly, "if I want a lecture on my laziness and feckless ways, there are any number of people I can go to for that."

"I didn't mean to upset you," she said quietly, after a few moments of fraught silence.

"You didn't," he said with deliberate lightness, sending her into a twirl and snagging her back closer than before. "You'd have to work much harder to match the casual gossip and direct remarks from my nearest and dearest that I hear on any given day."

"Oh, Rhyian…" Salena searched his face, sympathy in hers. Now *that* stung.

"Feeling sorry for me?" he asked coolly, layering in haughty disdain. "Don't. At least I *can* shapeshift." As soon as the words escaped his lips, he wished them back. But it was too late. Salena's expression chilled.

"Was that supposed to hurt?" she asked evenly. "I'd forgotten how well you do that, go from charming to cruel in an instant. Thank you for reminding me." She stopped, yanking her hands from his.

Moranu curse his stupid tongue. "Salena, listen—"

"No," she flung over her shoulder as she plowed a path through the dancers. "I'm done listening to you."

He caught her arm but continued on the same trajectory.

"I don't see how that's possible," he said through his teeth, "as you've avoided any real conversation with me for seven years."

"There's a reason for that," she shot back, face set in furious lines. "Fool me once, shame on you. Fool me twice, shame on me."

"What does that even mean?" Spotting a small salon off the main hall, Rhy poked his head in, verified it was empty, and dragged Salena inside.

"Stop dragging me around," she spat as he closed and locked the door.

"Stop running away from me," he snapped back. "Either that or stop blaming me for not chasing after you."

She pulled up short, her fury cooling. "You have a good point. Just leave me alone, Rhyian," she said wearily.

"I did," he said simply. "Didn't we both do that? We left each other alone for seven years, and it didn't fix anything."

She sat heavily on a plush chair by the fire, holding out her hands to its warmth. "Maybe some things are too broken to fix," she said in a quiet voice to the cheerful flames.

"Your heart?" he asked, not sure if he wanted to ask sincerely or make a joke to lighten the mood, so his words came out somewhere in between, uneven and raw.

Salena looked up at him, no poise in her face, only sorrow, blue eyes glimmering with unshed tears. "Don't laugh at me. You know you broke my heart. You did it on purpose."

He raked his hand through his hair, deeply regretting he'd forced this conversation. This was why he hadn't gone after her to begin with. But, as always happened when Salena was near, he couldn't seem to resist her siren call. "It wasn't like that," he said, knowing it sounded weak and cowardly as he spoke the words.

"What *was* it like, Rhyian?" she asked. "Here's your big chance to explain."

He opened his mouth, but no words came out. Sometimes he didn't even understand why he'd done what he had.

"Let me tickle your memory," she said in a quietly lethal tone, standing and stalking toward him. If Salena were a shapeshifter, her First Form would be a predator for sure. Probably a wolf. "I gave you my virginity. After months of spending every moment together—as best friends and more. We were lovers in every sense but that. Intimate in every way."

"I remember," he said. He remembered those heady days all too well.

"You were so romantic, so attentive, you made my head spin. I thought you loved me." Her voice cracked as the tears spilled over, and Rhy, wracked with guilt, stepped toward her. She stopped him with an upraised hand and a ferocious glare. "I know you never said it, but I thought 'Oh, Rhyian, he's just not expressive that way. It's the Tala nature.' I made all the excuses for you, so you didn't have to. No, don't say anything yet."

Her fury had returned, building as she finally said every-thing she hadn't before. Rhy sat, burying his face in his hands, telling himself he'd asked to hear this. That he deserved having his heart cracked open and fed to the fire.

"You *showed* me love, Rhyian," she continued, the words

burning. "In countless small ways. I thought I didn't need the words, but that maybe you did. So I told you that night. Do you remember that night?"

It was seared into his memory. Lifting his head, he made himself meet her fulminous gaze, the sense of a distant storm gathering. Lightning about to strike. She had her hands clenched into fists. "I will never forget that night," he said, more or less evenly. "It meant something to me, too." He took a deep breath and made himself give her the truth. "Because I *was* in love with you."

L ENA STARED AT him, beyond infuriated that he could say those words—the ones she'd ached to hear and convinced herself she never would—and that he could say them *now*, in the past tense, with such cool remove. The emotions of the past blended with those of the present, and she wanted to simultaneously weep and rage. Worst of all, she hadn't learned. Some foolish, self-destructive part of her hoped—actually *hoped*—that Rhyian might love her still.

Rhyian could always do that to her, lure her in with his sensual teasing and flattering attention. When he looked at her, she felt like the most beautiful woman in the world. The intensity of his regard had always turned her head, sweeping everything else away until she lost all of her good sense and only wanted. *Well, you can't want Rhyian,* she told herself firmly. She'd had him before, and she'd paid the price. He was like a dragon, so beautiful and enticing with his jeweled scales, that seductive dark magic in him shimmering, luring her to warm herself in the heat of his unwavering regard—until some little thing annoyed him and he turned her to ash with a cruel remark that breathed fire.

"How can you say that to me?" she demanded, but it came out as a broken plea. "I don't want or need your lies."

He stood, raking a hand through his hair again, more agitated than she'd ever seen him. Starting to reach for her, he jammed his hands into his pockets instead. "I'm not lying."

"Then why did you—" She'd thought it would do her good to say the words, to make them both relive that terrible morning. How she'd awakened in his bed full of bliss, transcendent with happiness. Rhyian had been gone, but she'd lingered, happily anticipating his return with the Nahanaun coffee she loved and pastries they could feed each other in bed. It was the first time they'd spent the night together—and the first time they'd made love all the way—but they'd stayed up until dawn plenty of times, cuddling and sharing those intimate breakfasts.

And after a while, her joy had chilled as his spot on the bed cooled, an ice of dread forming on the edges. Even then, she'd known, though she'd denied it. Just as she'd denied everything she understood about Rhyian and didn't want to. When she dressed and went to find him, she'd tried to hope she was wrong.

"Why did I go from your arms to someone else's?" he asked, the words bitter, his shoulders rigid.

"Yes." She wiped the tears from her cheeks, amazed that she could still cry over it, over him. "You wanted me to find you."

He met her gaze, his eyes deep blue with turbulent emotion, his face ravaged. "Yes."

And there it was, the admission she'd craved and dreaded. "Why?"

He took a deep breath. "I don't know."

She gaped at him, cleansing rage rushing in to displace the old, festering hurt. Launching herself at him, she shoved him hard. He staggered back, eyes flying wide in surprise. "Don't you dare!" she shrieked at him. "Don't you stand there and snigger at me and say you were in love with me but don't know why you did the one thing certain to break my heart and drive me away."

"It worked, didn't it?" he shouted back. "I was stupid and I was terrified. You said you loved me and I-I panicked." He raked a hand again through his already wild hair. "I knew it was the worst thing I could do to you. And when you found us…" He turned away to stare into the fire. "I'll never forget the look on your face. And when I heard you'd left Annfwn, I was…" Blowing out a harsh breath, he met her accusing gaze. "I was relieved."

She huffed out a bitter laugh, reliving that rending pain, the betrayal. "A relief to be rid of me, I'm sure."

"No." He shook his head. "Relieved that I didn't have to face you, to justify actions that couldn't be justified." Dragging his hands from his pockets, he swept her an elaborate bow. "And thus the feckless bastard before you was born: lazy, useless, loathed by one and all."

Staring at him, she found herself dry eyed at last, shaking her head slowly from side to side. "I'm not going to feel sorry for you."

"Good," he said, jamming hands back in his pockets. "Because I don't deserve any sympathy, least of all from you—the one person I cared about most and the one person I've hurt the worst." He took a deep breath. "But I want to apologize to you. I don't expect you to forgive me, and certainly not to forget, but I am sorry, Salena. I'm so very sorry for how I hurt you and betrayed your trust."

Her heart turned over, a painful wrench that made her dizzy. "You never apologize," she said faintly.

"Yes, well, I saved them all up for this." He gazed at her, longing in it. "I only wish I could do or say something that means more."

"Do you know what I threw in the fire?" she asked, the question jumping from her lips.

He assessed her cautiously. "I'm afraid to find out."

"You," she said bluntly, rather enjoying his flinch. "I wrote down your name and burned it, because I just want to be done with you, Rhyian. With this." She flapped a hand between them.

"Fair enough," he replied. "Do you think it worked?"

"Obviously not," she ground out, "or I wouldn't be locked in this room with you, rehashing the worst experience of my life."

"Maybe we have to wait for midnight," he suggested, "when Moranu will magically wipe the slate clean."

It seemed absolutely impossible that she wanted to laugh at that. But that was Rhyian, too—irreverent and cynical in all the same ways that she was.

"Amusingly enough, I burned something similar. A rune,"

he explained when she raised a brow, "representing the past self and all its myriad flaws. I'm fully confident that sunrise will see me as an entirely new person."

"I'm pretty sure it doesn't work that way," she commented drily.

"No? Alas for that. I doubt that anything less than divine intervention could make me into a worthy person at this point."

She considered him, taken aback by the level of self-loathing in his words. He wasn't being flippant, either, but brutally honest. "The goddesses can't change us, Rhy," she said gently. "We have to do the hard work to change ourselves."

"Ah. Hard work," he replied in the same tone. "Also not my forte."

"It could be, if you want it enough."

"Hmm." Moving slowly, he edged closer to her. "Maybe if there's a tempting reward?"

She didn't step back—couldn't make herself—but she stopped his approach with a hand on his lean chest. "I can't be your reward. That's all in the past. I can't... go through that again."

He grimaced, then searched her face. "But we both burned the past. It's gone. What we have is the present. Tonight. Right now."

"I—" She hated how she faltered, how she so wanted to hope. How foolish it would be to let him hurt her again.

"I have something for you," he said, drawing a folded piece of paper from his pocket. Taking her hand, he placed the square in her palm and closed her fingers over it, holding her gaze all the while. "I can't change the past, Salena, but I *can* try to change the future."

With shaking fingers, she opened the tightly folded square, the Tala rune shimmering with promise. "The moon?"

He quirked a smile. "I always forget you know every-thing."

"When your mother is a proficient linguist and practically lives in the library…" she commented with a smile. "You're giving me the moon?"

Breathing a laugh, he touched her cheek. "It's my wish for the future. It's you. Your name means the moon. It was the only thing I could think of that I want, that I felt was worth wishing for. I know I don't deserve your love or regard—I never did, and that was part of the problem—but I wish that…" He trailed off, sounding so wistful that she couldn't help moving into his touch. "I'd like to give you some joy and pleasure, Salena. To at least leave things in a better place between us. Instead of ending as we did. Would you let me try?"

She shouldn't want this. She couldn't seem to refuse him.

"How about just tonight?" she breathed. "One night when we forget the past."

"I would love that," he answered, long fingers trailing over her jaw. His eyes focused on her mouth, and he tilted his head, slowly closing the distance. Lena held her breath, anticipating.

Outside the door, trumpets blared, announcing the advent of the high queen. *Saved by a well-timed fanfare,* Lena thought wryly to herself. And she was a fool to have needed saving. Firmly, she stepped away from temptation. "I have to go."

"Can I come with you?" Rhy asked, uncertain, searching her face.

She laughed, feeling the release of a burden she'd carried for far too long, and seized his hand, pulling him to the door. "Yes. We must hear Her Majesty's speech."

"Oh, joy," he commented, sounding so much more like his usual self that she giggled, heady with relief that they'd finally put the hurt and heartbreak behind them. *And he'd been in love with her.* It didn't change anything, but knowing that helped. At least she hadn't been a total fool.

Lena found them a spot below the balcony where she'd watched the ball earlier with Gendra and Zeph, a good position to see and hear the queens.

"Salena," Rhy breathed in her ear as he settled his hands on her waist, his body hot against her back. "What if we—"

Another fanfare drowned out his words. "Shh," she hissed.

Everyone had fallen silent, turning expectant faces upward. A third, longer fanfare echoed, and into the ensuing quiet, a herald called. "All hail the High Queen of the Thirteen Kingdoms, Her Majesty High Queen Ursula."

The crowd broke into frenzied cheering—except for Rhyian, still pressed against her—so she elbowed him hard in the gut.

"Ow!" he yelped.

"Cheer," she tossed over her shoulder, glaring at him.

"Whee," he said, perfectly deadpan. "Ooh. Ah. Look, it's Danu made flesh."

She successfully suppressed a laugh, turning her back on him to see Ursula arrive at the balustrade, waving to the people below. A lean blade of a woman, she wore a simple sheath of white-gold, bright as the midday sun—high noon belonging to the goddess Danu—and Salena recalled her mother saying that Queen Amelia had insisted on dressing Ursula and Andi. Ursula wore her deep-auburn hair coiled against her head, topped by the tri-point crown of the Thirteen Kingdoms that paid homage to the three sister goddesses. She smiled, thin as a sword's edge, her steely gaze that of a warrior queen.

"And Queen Andromeda of Annfwn and Queen Amelia of Avonlidgh," the herald declared as Ursula's sisters joined her.

Ami had clearly run with the theme, dressing herself in palest pink to honor Glorianna, goddess of love and beauty. Elaborately beaded with tiny crystals, the dress caught the light, glowing like dawn, though dim compared to Ami's own radiant beauty. The poets fell out evenly on whether her rose-gold hair, tumbling in glossy curls to her waist, resembled sunset or sunrise, though all agreed her eyes were the violet of twilight—intense enough to be visible at this distance.

On Ursula's other flank, Queen Andromeda wore a gown of stunning black, though crafted of a shining material that shimmered with silver like the moon. Andi wore her hair loose in the Tala style, a cloak of night that gleamed with bloodred highlights, and her magic shifted around her like an unseen fog.

The three daughters of the old high king had long been likened to the avatars of the sister goddesses, and Salena had never seen the truth of that so clearly before this moment.

"Mother looks quite impressive," Rhyian whispered in her

ear, managing to sound impertinent despite the innocuous words.

"People of the Thirteen Kingdoms," Ursula called out to silence the cheering crowd, "I have no wish to observe formalities tonight. My sisters and I have gathered here, in our childhood home, together with our families, to celebrate the Feast of Moranu and Her crystalline moon. We welcome you all—regardless of age, wealth or station—to celebrate with us. Danu confers her bright sword to allow us to gather in justice and peace." She glanced to Ami.

"And Glorianna bestows her unconditional love," Queen Amelia declared in her angelic voice, "so that we may set aside old hurts and past conflicts, to gather with joy."

"But tonight belongs to Moranu," Ursula continued, "so I yield to her avatar, Queen Andromeda of Annfwn."

This time, Rhyian cheered with real enthusiasm, and Lena thought Andi noticed, picking her son out of the crowd and giving him a grateful smile as she took point position at the front of the balcony. Unlike her sister, she didn't silence the crowd, but waited in quiet for them to settle. The magic that had been shimmering darkly around her began to expand, flowing outward, the black mist shooting with sparks of light no longer tightly contained, but billowing as it grew.

"Moranu is the goddess of night," she intoned in a quiet voice, the crowd falling to a hush to better hear. "The goddess of the moon, of mutability, of the intangible and the shadows that shift, waxing and waning, to hide and reveal. She of the many faces embraces all of you tonight, you in all your multitudes, your dark faces and your bright ones. Unlike Danu,

Moranu has no interest in the division of lines—She will not judge you. Unlike Glorianna, Moranu doesn't ask for your beauty—She embraces the darkness in you, the parts you would keep in shadow and hide from the light of day."

Lena didn't think she imagined that Andi's gaze lingered on Rhyian as she said those words, and Lena felt his stillness behind her. As Andi spoke, the room filled with the glittering black mist, the formerly bright light dimming, and it seemed night shadows flowed from the corners, nocturnal creatures softly calling. Looking down, Lena realized a lightless fog had shrouded the floor to knee height, heightening the feel of otherworldliness. It was as if the castle had receded and they'd truly stepped into the mind of Moranu, full of tenebrous mystery.

"We have two hours until the stroke of midnight," Andi said into the hush. "Until then, we shall keep the fires burning, though night will continue to deepen Her sway. Use this time to reflect on your shadows, to offer the detritus of your soul to the cleansing flame, and set down your intentions, your hopes, and promises for the new year."

"Didn't we already do this?" Rhy muttered in her ear, clearly recovered and neatly dodging her elbow this time.

"As midnight draws nigh, we shall gather on the battlements," Andi continued, smiling as the crowd muttered in dismay. "I promise you will be warm, that you will be sheltered from the cruel winter winds—and that we will see Moranu's crystalline moon. For now, discard your old hurts and angers. Leave them in the fire, and make your way to the battlements, where we will greet the new year with the light of the crystalline moon."

"That's my cue," Lena told Rhyian, extracting herself from his hands as the crowd broke up into excited murmurs, people streaming toward the scribes' tables or lining up at the bins with blank scrolls.

"Wait," he said, clever hands simply finding a new purchase on her waist as she turned. "Where are you going?" In the magical dimness, Rhyian's eyes seemed to catch the sparks of light, like distant stars glittering in a midnight sky. Shadows clung lovingly to the gorgeous planes of his face, his black hair falling loosely around it, reminding her of how he'd looked after kissing her senseless, when he'd been naked against her, skin to skin and—

"I have a job to do." And focusing on that job would help her to remember that making up with Rhyian didn't—and shouldn't—mean anything more.

"At a party? I thought we were taking tonight to enjoy. Please, let me try to do better."

Softening—truly unable to resist him when he spoke honestly—she caressed his cheek, catching her breath when he turned his face to brush his mouth over her fingertips. "I mean I really can't, Rhy," she breathed. "I have to go clear the sky and make it warm."

He stared at her, arrested. "You can do that?"

She found herself grinning, delighted by his astonished admiration. "I can. Unlike some people, I *have* been practicing my skills."

Rhy clapped a hand over his heart, gasping as if mortally wounded. "So unkind, fair Salena."

She shook her head at his histrionics and untangled herself from his hands once again. "I will see you later, after my work is done."

"Can I come with you?" he asked, striding beside her as she wended her way through the crowd.

Giving him a sidelong look, she raised a brow. "It will be cold up there, summer boy."

"But I have a weather witch to keep me warm," he replied, making her laugh. "Also a cloak, if we can stop to grab it."

"All right, then." Her smile so wide it threatened to crack her cheeks. She treasured the headiness of his company. And maybe the opportunity to show off for him a little. "Come see this."

W HILE A FOOTMAN retrieved their cold-weather gear,
Rhy seized the opportunity to snag a carafe of Jak's
mjed and a couple of glasses. *You were so romantic you made my
head spin,* Salena had said, reminding him of how it had been
back then, when making her smile was everything. "In case
you're not quite enough to keep me warm," he teased when
she raised a questioning brow.

The footman led them up the grand stairs to the next level,
then through various corridors lit with more white candles in
silver candelabras and decorated with more crystal-studded
moonflower garlands. The decorations highlighted various
paths to the battlements for the guests, but the footman soon
diverged, taking them up a more practically lit back staircase.

"This is where Her Majesty has designated for the showing, Your Highnesses," the young man said with a bow,
opening a door to an icy blast of wind and a group of guards
huddled around a brazier. "It's the most-sheltered spot."

"I'd hate to experience the less-sheltered spots," Rhy complained, pulling his black fur cloak tighter around himself.

"You don't have to stay," Salena replied with a droll look. "I'm sure you can think up more regrets to offer the fires."

"You have no idea," he muttered. "But I'm not missing this."

"Welcome to the Castle Ordnung battlements, Princess Salena Nakoa KauPo." Prince Harlan, the high queen's husband, strode up to them in full dress regalia and saluted.

With a squeal, Salena launched herself at the big Dasnarian, giving him a hug.

"Nephew Rhyian, it's a pleasure, as always."

Rhy clasped forearms with his uncle, who he'd always liked. Harlan was one of the few who never nagged him about making something of himself. Also a former imperial prince who'd renounced his hated title, Harlan never forgot that Rhy hated being called "prince" himself. "I wondered where you were, Uncle Harlan."

"I've been up here most of the evening," Harlan replied. "Essla can handle the crowd inside, and I feel better keeping an eye on the battlements with so many personages gathered here tonight."

"Surely you don't expect trouble?" Rhy asked.

"It never pays to be complacent, Rhy. We've had peace, yes, but there's always trouble brewing in the world. That's the nature of trouble, and of the world we live in. There will be time enough after midnight, with everyone safely tucked back inside, to dance with my lovely wife." He winked at them. "What do you need from us, Lena?"

"I simply need to see the sky."

"Of course, though it's bitter cold out there with this storm."

"Not for long," she promised.

He grinned. "I'm looking forward to seeing this. I'll accompany you, for your safety. Unless you need to be alone?"

"Not at all," Lena assured him, to his obvious relief.

Harlan led the way, and Rhy followed them out of the guard hut into the truly bitter blizzard.

"This will work," Salena said, pausing in a semi-sheltered corner where a square tower cut the wind somewhat. Down below, the township of Ordnung blazed with light, distant music wafting in occasional bursts with the blustery wind. The sky roiled overhead, the overcast thicker than ever.

Harlan paced a short distance away and turned his back on them, gaze focused outward. Salena raised her hands, palms upward, her magic gathering palpably around them as she sent it toward the sky. She'd never looked more beautiful to Rhy than in that moment. With her hands raised to the black and storming sky, the bitter wind whipping her hair like a banner of gleaming bronze, she tipped her head back, magic lighting her from within.

"Can I ask you questions?" Rhy asked quietly, leaning against the wall where he could watch her. "Or do you need to concentrate?"

She slid him a look. "If I did, you'd have already broken that concentration."

"Sorry." He should know better. Moranu knew it took all of *his* concentration to shapeshift into anything but his raven First Form.

Salena made a choking sound. "Did the determinedly unapologetic Rhyian actually apologize *again*—or am I dreaming?"

"Ha-ha," he huffed. "I've apologized to people before."

"You *have* changed," she replied in a voice heavy with sarcasm.

He was glad it seemed that way, but he wondered if he really had. *She embraces the darkness in you, the parts you would keep in shadow and hide from the light of day.* Had his mother directed those words at him? It had been a relief to finally talk about what happened with Salena, but he knew the confession hadn't absolved him. Probably nothing could.

"You can talk to me," Salena said after a few moments. "This isn't all that difficult."

"Dispersing a storm is easy, really?" He pounced on the offered topic with enthusiasm, not only because it drew him out of his dark thoughts, but because he was fascinated. She fascinated him—as always and more than ever.

"Really," she said, casting him a smile. She loved doing this, he realized, sheer joy in her proficiency lighting her up as nothing that evening so far had done. "Part of it is that I'm not actually dispersing the storm. I'm simply sending the greatest intensity to other parts of the storm, and it's a large one covering a wide area, so there's lots of room to absorb a small amount over just this area. As I move the moisture and cloud cover away, I'm warming the air, which is again pretty straightforward because I only need to invert the extreme cold." She glanced at him again. "This is really boring, right?"

"Not even a little," he replied sincerely, utterly enchanted by her. The wind had already dropped, and he felt certain the air around them had warmed. The sky might be brighter, too.

She smiled at that, the way she used to smile at him, full of love he hadn't deserved. It warmed his lonely heart—and chilled him to the bone. They'd finally had it out between them, but he didn't expect that she would love him again. She couldn't. If she did... Sudden terror filled him that he'd only break that love into pieces again.

"Also," she continued, oblivious to his angst, "I'm only creating a change of a couple of hours. It's not like my work in Aerron, where I'm having to fight entrenched weather patterns to reverse the encroachment of the desert and bring life to the region again. There I'm having to work with all kinds of atmospheric energy to gradually move in moisture and create conditions where rain can form. There's a lot of intricate manipulations involved that have to be handled with precision and delicacy, or it all goes out of whack—and the cascading backlash can be vicious. Compared to that, this is child's play. Have your eyes glazed over yet?"

Only blinded by her. "You're amazing," he said, his voice full of unabashed wonder.

She looked up at the sky, maybe blushing, though it was difficult to tell. "You should maybe come visit me in Aerron sometime," she offered hesitantly. "The changes are what's amazing. They're really something to see."

"I would like that," he said, an odd pain in his chest. Was that hope or fear? Either way, a world in which he simply visited Salena in Aerron like she was just another friend seemed impossible.

"I've learned a lot from that work," she said reflectively.

"Studying with Andi taught me so much, but there's nothing like actually doing the thing, day in and day out, to make you learn it, to force you to grow in your abilities."

He knew she was musing on her own changes, and didn't intend a double edge to her words, but he felt the slice of them anyway. Salena had spent the last seven years becoming an adept sorceress who found making summer from winter for a few hours "child's play," and he'd spent them doing... what? Sulking, avoiding Moranu's attention, and trying to forget what a colossal ass he was. No wonder everyone called him lazy and feckless.

"Is that why your father isn't doing this?" he asked. "You're better than he is now."

She glanced at him, eyes wide. It was definitely brighter out. "Nooo... I am not better than Muku by a long shot. But I *am* different. He brings storms—over incredible distances and with such astonishing power to them, I think I'll never match his prowess—*and* he can sustain them. When he stalled the Dasnarian navy during the Deyrr War, he summoned that storm from Annfwn and held it there, at full power, for *five days*, with an eye of calm for our ships."

"I've heard the story," Rhy commented drily. Countless times. Their parents loved to tell the tales of their heroism in the glory days. Talk about something that could be burnt in the fire and consigned to the past. He was almost too warm now in his heavy cloak, and shrugged it open to hang down his back.

"I don't know how he did it." Salena shook her head, moonlight rippling over the long fall of her hair, no longer blowing in any wind. Above them, the pennants lay limp against their tethers, and silvering clouds scudded across a black sky, fleeing in all directions as if banished. She lowered her arms, studying the sky. "It will take a bit more to clear," she said, more to herself than to anyone, Rhy thought, "but that will do it. Harlan?"

"Yes, Princess?" Harlan rejoined them, saying Salena's title like an affectionate nickname. Like Rhy, he'd shrugged back his heavy cloak. Smiling broadly, he gestured at the limp pennants. "It's like a miracle."

Salena smiled with genuine pleasure. "You can tell Her Majesty that we are on schedule. I'll keep the clouds over the moon until midnight and the relighting."

He beamed and bowed. "I'll go inform Essla, and we'll allow the guests to begin to ascend. Will you two be all right on your own until I return? I can send out a guard, but I'm working with a skeleton crew tonight, and I rather keep them in other, key positions."

Rhy rolled his eyes, but only Salena saw it, giving him a narrow glare. "Yes, we'll be fine. Thank you." She hugged him again and he departed, leaving them alone.

~ 10 ~

"A LONE AT LAST," Rhyian said, just a hint of his wicked smile showing as he retrieved the carafe of mjed and filled their glasses. He handed her one and held his up in a toast. "To you, Salena, the most extraordinary woman I know."

She felt her face heat, the keen pleasure of his praise almost more than she could bear. Rhyian's opinion had always mattered to her. It had mattered *too* much, which was one part of why his casual dismissal of her and what they'd shared had been so devastating. Knowing now that he *had* been in love with her... She accepted the toast and drank, the mjed burning on its way down.

Rhy smiled at her, then cast his gaze to the clearing sky. The magic tugged at her, holding steady for now, though it would get more difficult to hold the artificial bubble around them as time passed. "I don't see this famous crystalline moon," he said, frowning at the bright quadrant of the sky where the moon's silver rays streamed, silhouetting the boiling black clouds.

"I'm keeping that cloud bank in place until the relighting," she explained, "then I'll pull it back for a grand reveal at midnight."

"What is this relighting?" he asked, and she paused in surprise. Of course the Tala observances differed from theirs. And even in Nahanau, they didn't celebrate the light from darkness as people did in the colder, darker regions.

"You'll see," she replied with a coy smile. "It's a better surprise to experience it for the first time."

"True of many things," he said in a low, warm voice, edging closer to her. She didn't have much room to evade him in that corner between the tower wall and the parapet—nor did she have the willpower to do so. Temptation, thy name is Rhyian. He slid his fingers down a lock of her hair as if savoring the texture, then wound it loosely around his finger. "Have I told you that you're more beautiful now than ever?"

"No," she breathed. He meant it, too. One thing about Rhyian—he didn't flatter idly. If anything, he was too honest about his feelings, both the delightful and the cruel. This was dangerous, and yet she couldn't make herself put a stop to it. She'd missed him. Despite everything, she *missed* him. And this.

He took the glass from her and set it beside his on the parapet. Turning back to her, he slipped both hands into her hair, combing it back from her face, his gaze rapt. "You are," he said, almost in wonder. "You were always so vivid, so lovely as a girl, but now..." His gaze wandered over her face. "You're extraordinary. Wise. Magical. Incredibly gorgeous."

Salena couldn't breathe. Couldn't seem to summon any sense. Rhyian's hands in her hair brought back visceral memories of how he'd made her moan and plead for more, exploring together those first sweet pleasures of the flesh. His mouth shaped the seductive words, tempting her to taste them. She'd been with men since him—a few men, none of them so darkly alluring—and not one had kissed her like Rhyian. Something that had infuriated her. Now, she only craved one more taste. Gently, he tugged her hair, tipping her head back slightly, his expression enthralling as he looked at her.

"I can't stop looking at you," he murmured.

He was going to kiss her, and she couldn't put two thoughts together to decide what that would mean. *Just tonight. One night when we forget...* She wanted that. "Would you like to see the moon?" she whispered.

"What I would love is to see *you* in the moonlight," he purred, stirring that tenderness deep inside her. "Salena, my moon."

Shivering and steaming at once, she sent a tendril of magic to pull the clouds away, unveiling the crystalline moon. The darkness around them fled, chased by light nearly as bright as day. The enormous moon, crystal clear and luminously silver, hovered just over their heads, seeming close enough to touch. Even Rhyian had no words, staring with a reverence at odds with his usual flippant self. "It's beautiful," he breathed, then turned his gaze to hers. "Thank you."

"Just for us," she told him. "Just for tonight."

"Is there no future?" he asked.

She nearly said he'd been the one to decide that, but she didn't want to lose this moment. "I can only offer you now."

"I'll take now." His eyes, catching the moonlight, glowed from within. Moranu's dark and silvered fingers loving on her chosen, stirred his gleaming hair, highlighting his gorgeous face. "A kiss?"

"Rhyian..." Her chest felt too tight, her heart too hopeful, too afraid.

"Please," he murmured, gaze going to her mouth. "One kiss."

"Yes." The word escaped her, a plea from the unthinking part of her that yearned for him still, after all this time, against all reason.

"Yes," he echoed with a crooked smile, once again that sweet-hearted lover of her youth, the one who'd shown her everything of himself with artless honesty.

She'd expected him to swoop in, to seize the kiss, but he moved slowly, one hand in her hair still, cupping her head, the other sliding down her back to embrace and support her. He brushed his lips over hers, a light taste, like butterfly wings, and she almost whimpered in protest at that being all there was to it.

But it was only a beginning. His lips lingered on hers, never breaking contact, gradually deepening and intensifying the kiss, his tongue brushing the tender inside of her upper lip, extracting a bone-deep sigh from her. She clung to his shoulders, but all the rest of her melted, yielding in bliss to the feeling of being against her beloved again. He gathered her up, supporting her with his easy shapeshifter strength, bowing her back over his arm and holding her head as he plundered her mouth. He drank from her like a starving man, and she shuddered in primal need, wanting to give him everything, needing to take everything.

The moon shone with silvery intensity, haloing his dark head, and she dug her fingers through his hair, his body humming against hers like a storm building and about to break. She moaned as his hand left her head to trail down her throat, tracing the curve of her breast and then dipping inside her bodice to brush her nipple. She cried out at the shock of intense pleasure, and he swallowed it, echoing with a low groan of his own. "Salena, my love," he murmured into her mouth. A sharp and chilly breeze caught his hair, tossing it wildly.

"Oh!" She pushed him away, rapidly restoring the magic to wall out the wind and heat the air around her. Pulling the cloud cover over the moon again, she reinforced the circle of overcast, ensuring clear skies overhead. Fortunately, her work had only frayed a little around the edges. Rhyian still held her in his arms but had his head tipped back to watch the sky, the line of his jaw fine as cut glass, the long column of his throat so enticing she wanted to kiss him there.

As if sensing her desire, he lowered his face, smiling at her. "I thought you didn't need to concentrate," he said with silky satisfaction. His gaze trailed lower, and she realized her breasts were still exposed.

With a groan of frustrated exasperation, she wriggled free of him and adjusted her gown.

"Do you need help?" Rhy asked, widening his eyes in innocence when she glared at him.

"I thought we said one kiss," she hissed at him.

"Not to be pedantic," he replied smoothly, "but it was *one*, very long kiss. And you didn't seem to mind a moment ago."

No, because she'd lost her head, as she always had with him. She gazed back at him helplessly. "Rhyian, I..."

The guard hut door burst open, and a cascade of festively dressed people poured through, light and laughter flowing with them. Everywhere on the battlements, torches blazed, showing rivers of people taking their places. The three queens, Andromeda at the lead, glided in their direction. Maybe Lena imagined Andi's keen attention on them, but she tugged her hand free of Rhyian's anyway.

"Later," she said. "It's showtime."

"All of tonight," he insisted, oddly serious.

"Until dawn," she promised, feeling reckless. She'd likely regret this, but for now she couldn't seem to think about the future.

"Until dawn, at least," he agreed, snagging her hand to kiss it before stepping aside.

"Lena," Queen Andromeda said, opening her arms. "It's been so long."

"Too long," she agreed, embracing her with fervent delight. She'd let her estrangement with Rhyian keep her away from too many people she loved.

Andi released her, gazing on her fondly, then glanced at Rhyian behind her, giving him a warm smile. "It's so good to see all of you together tonight. Are you ready?"

"Yes," Lena agreed. "I'll follow your cues."

~ 11 ~

R HY'S MOTHER STEPPED to the edge of the parapet, magic tossing her hair, though the warm bubble of air Salena had created for them silenced the natural winds. He drew Salena back against him, wrapping an arm around her waist. "Shouldn't you be up there?" he asked in her ear, letting his lips brush the delicious curves. Having Salena quivering in his arms again, so sweetly lush and shimmering with unleashed power, had been almost more than he could bear, and now he couldn't stop touching her.

"I'm fine here," she replied, sounding breathless. "This is Queen Andromeda's show. I'm just the backstage help."

He chuckled at that. "I think you—"

"Shh. Watch. Last chance to release any of the old."

Rhy didn't want to think about the past anymore. This was now, and this was good. Dawn would come all too soon.

"If you have anything left to burn, do it now." His mother's velvet voice, thrumming with the presence of the goddess and magically amplified, spread over the battlements like a mist. Salena pulled out of his arms, dug something from her pocket, and took it to a moonflower-patterned basin set on the parapet nearby. Pausing a moment, her profile illuminated by the crackling flames, she looked to be praying, though his old Salena had never had much patience for "superstition," as she called it. She tossed the paper in the fire, then turned around resolutely, returning to him and—to his intense pleasure and satisfaction—once more leaned against him. When he slipped his arms around her waist, she sighed, sounding content.

All around on the brilliantly lit battlements, people were doing the same, hurrying to burn their last-minute regrets.

"I am Moranu," his mother's voice rang out, the bell-like tones dense as the goddess channeled Her words. The presence of the numinous prickled at his skin, the many-faced goddess of shadows casting her cloak over them all. "And I give you the night."

At once, every flame went out. Even in the township below, every light was extinguished in the same moment by his mother's sorcery. As if their very selves had been stilled at the same instant, everyone went silent. No strains of music. Not even the sough of the wind broke the silence inside Salena's circle of magic. Above them, the sky grew black and brilliant with stars as full darkness descended.

A bell began tolling the hour of midnight.

Heavy and sonorous, it rang in slow measures. Rhy found himself counting along, surprising himself that he cared. Suspended in the blackest night, though, it seemed entirely possible to the frightened animal part of himself that the light might never come again.

Ten.

Eleven.

Twelve.

The last note rang out and held, rolling and building, a wave crashing over them.

"And in even the darkest night," Moranu's voice rang out, blending with the last eternal toll of the bell, "I also give you light. Behold My crystalline moon."

Salena barely twitched in his arms, but he sensed the bright streak of her magic. The clouds covering the moon rolled back, and once again the moon shone forth, pearlescent and achingly magical. The people gasped as one, then broke into wild cheers of delight, more cheers echoing distantly from the township below. As he watched, a torch on the tallest tower of Ordnung sprang into life, the flame leaping from one torch to the next, spiraling down in a cascade of light, spilling to illuminate the entire castle, then running down the roads leading away, to reach the township and outlying farms, and farther down the valley to the horizon.

"That was incredible." He hadn't meant to say it aloud, but the words escaped him. Somehow all his jaded cynicism had fallen away, and he felt renewed. With Salena in his arms, it was as if he was that youth again, unafraid of loving her, wanting nothing but to revel in the light after darkness.

"Yes," she said, equally hushed. And when she turned in his arms, her eyes glistened with tears.

"Are you crying?" he asked, feeling so raw, so open that he almost understood.

"Not from sorrow." She put her arms around him and

leaned in to kiss him. "This was good."

"This *is* good," he corrected, and she smiled.

"Do you have a wish to offer the new year?" she asked.

"Already done."

"Me too." She looked so mysterious, so sensual and full of joy, that he wondered what her wish had been.

"What next?" he asked.

"Food," she replied with a dazzling smile. "I'm starving. And this is a good opportunity to fill our plates, while everyone else is moongazing."

She had a point, as the crowds lingered on the battlements, faces turned upward, pointing, their voices rising with laughter and awe. Some sang songs, arms looped together as they swayed. Others offered toasts to uproarious response. "And we already had our private showing," he said, kissing her again.

"Our own private crystalline moon," she agreed, returning for another kiss, her lips beyond sweet against his.

He realized in that moment that even the longest night would never be long enough.

~ 12 ~

L ENA TOOK RHYIAN'S hand and tugged him along behind
her, wending through the crowd fairly easily, since
everyone else was focused on the moon and toasting each
other, embracing and kissing. They made it inside and ran
down the winding staircase like kids, laughing breathlessly. She
felt like a girl again, lighter than she had in years. The halls of
the castle were nearly deserted, as they almost never were,
with even the servants outside. A few lone guards nodded to
them, and occasional laughing couples and groups lingered in
alcoves, enjoying their own private observances.

The long tables laden with food were theirs for the moment, and Lena loaded her plate with all her favorites, Rhyian
following along and imitating most of her choices. When they
reached the fountain pouring white-gold sparkling wine over
an ice sculpture replica of Castle Ordnung, Rhyian winced. "I
forgot the mjed upstairs," he groaned.

"I'm sure it won't go to waste," she told him, feeling giddy
from his company and the expenditure of so much magic.

"Moranu knows, Jak made sure there's plenty of the stuff."

"That's the truth. Say, where did the others get off to?"

"I don't know. I never did find Gendra. Do you want to go look for them?"

"Honestly?" He handed her a glass flute of the sparkling wine and filled one for himself, clinking it against hers. "Right now I just want to be with you."

She tipped up her mouth, and he accepted the invitation, kissing her with lingering tenderness. "That sounds good to me," she whispered when their lips parted.

"Ha!" Zeph crowed. "I knew it. The crystalline moon wrought a miracle."

Rhyian groaned and tipped his forehead against hers. "I hate her. I hate them all."

She grinned at him, then turned to face Zeph. "What did you think?"

Zeph slipped deftly between Lena's full flute and fuller plate, kissing her on each cheek. "It was brilliant. Extraordinary show. Everyone is agog. Even Jak thought so."

"Why do you say 'even Jak?'" Jak wanted to know, coming up behind Zeph with Stella, Gendra on Astar's arm behind them.

"Because nothing impresses you," Stella told him with a serious smile.

"That's not true. I think *you* are scary impressive."

Stella shook her head. "You forget I can feel it when you lie like that."

"It isn't a lie," he protested.

Lena gave Gendra a questioning look, and her friend

shrugged slightly with a rueful grimace, then patted Astar's arm. He smiled at her sunnily, apparently saved from Zeph's clutches for the moment.

As if reading the thought, Zeph leaned in to whisper in Lena's ear. "I haven't given up. There's still half the long night left, and sometimes the better strategy is to *appear* to retreat."

Salena just shook her head, laughing at her incorrigible friend. Stella and Gendra joined them, while Rhyian stepped a short distance away to talk with Jak and Astar. "Soo...." Gendra said, eyes sparkling. "You and Rhy?"

"We talked it out," Lena told them. "We agreed to enjoy tonight."

"And after that?" Stella asked, her keen gray eyes looking *through* Lena, possibly glimpsing the future. "How will you deal with each other in the days to come?"

"Very carefully," Lena quipped and sipped her sparkling wine, the bubbles like bursts of joy. Rhyian glanced at her, giving her a secret, ever-so-slightly wicked smile. "I'll go back to Aerron tomorrow, so there's no need to make any hard and fast decisions now. We can just see how things go."

"No, you won't go back to Aerron tomorrow," Stella said, all three women stilling at the sound of foresight in her voice. "Not anytime soon."

"What are you saying?" Zeph asked, and Gendra wrapped her arms around herself, shivering.

"Our lives are about to change," Stella told them. "And challenges lie ahead. Nothing will ever be the same."

"Your Highnesses, lords and ladies," a footman gasped, running up to them. "Her Majesty summons you. A most urgent matter."

Zeph plucked the flute from Lena's hand and drained it. "Happy Feast of Moranu, all."

Heirs of Magic will continue in
The Golden Gryphon and the Bear Prince.
Coming December 2020

Titles by Jeffe Kennedy

FANTASY ROMANCES

HEIRS OF MAGIC
The Long Night of the Crystalline Moon
(in *Under a Winter Sky*)
The Golden Gryphon and the Bear Prince

A COVENANT OF THORNS
Rogue's Pawn
Rogue's Possession
Rogue's Paradise

THE TWELVE KINGDOMS
Negotiation
The Mark of the Tala
The Tears of the Rose
The Talon of the Hawk
Heart's Blood
The Crown of the Queen

THE UNCHARTED REALMS
The Pages of the Mind
The Edge of the Blade
The Snows of Windroven
The Shift of the Tide

The Arrows of the Heart
The Dragons of Summer
The Fate of the Tala
The Lost Princess Returns

THE CHRONICLES OF DASNARIA
Prisoner of the Crown
Exile of the Seas
Warrior of the World

SORCEROUS MOONS
Lonen's War
Oria's Gambit
The Tides of Bára
The Forests of Dru
Oria's Enchantment
Lonen's Reign

THE FORGOTTEN EMPIRES
The Orchid Throne
The Fiery Crown
The Promised Queen

CONTEMPORARY ROMANCES

Shooting Star

MISSED CONNECTIONS
Last Dance
With a Prince
Since Last Christmas

CONTEMPORARY EROTIC ROMANCES

Exact Warm Unholy
The Devil's Doorbell

FACETS OF PASSION
Sapphire
Platinum
Ruby
Five Golden Rings

FALLING UNDER
Going Under
Under His Touch
Under Contract

EROTIC PARANORMAL

MASTER OF THE OPERA E-SERIAL
Master of the Opera, Act 1: Passionate Overture
Master of the Opera, Act 2: Ghost Aria
Master of the Opera, Act 3: Phantom Serenade
Master of the Opera, Act 4: Dark Interlude
Master of the Opera, Act 5: A Haunting Duet
Master of the Opera, Act 6: Crescendo
Master of the Opera

BLOOD CURRENCY
Blood Currency

BDSM FAIRYTALE ROMANCE

Petals and Thorns

OTHER WORKS

Birdwoman
Hopeful Monsters
Teeth, Long and Sharp

Thank you for reading!

About Jeffe Kennedy

Jeffe Kennedy is an award-winning author whose works include novels, nonfiction, poetry, and short fiction. She has won the prestigious RITA® Award from Romance Writers of America (RWA), has been a finalist twice, been a Ucross Foundation Fellow, received the Wyoming Arts Council Fellowship for Poetry, and was awarded a Frank Nelson Doubleday Memorial Award. She serves on the Board of Directors for the Science Fiction and Fantasy Writers of America (SFWA) as a Director at Large.

Her award-winning fantasy romance trilogy *The Twelve Kingdoms* hit the shelves starting in May 2014. Book One, *The Mark of the Tala*, received a starred Library Journal review and was nominated for the RT Book of the Year, while the sequel, *The Tears of the Rose*, received a Top Pick Gold and was nominated for the RT Reviewers' Choice Best Fantasy Romance of 2014. The third book, *The Talon of the Hawk*, won the RT Reviewers' Choice Best Fantasy Romance of 2015. Two more books followed in this world, beginning the spin-off series *The Uncharted Realms*. Book One in that series, *The Pages of the Mind*, was nominated for the RT Reviewer's Choice Best Fantasy Romance of 2016 and won RWA's 2017 RITA Award. The second book, *The Edge of the Blade*, released December 27,

2016, and was a PRISM finalist, along with *The Pages of the Mind*. The final book in the series, *The Fate of the Tala*, released in February 2020. A high fantasy trilogy, The Chronicles of Dasnaria, taking place in *The Twelve Kingdoms* world, began releasing from Rebel Base books in 2018. The novella, *The Dragons of Summer*, first appearing in the *Seasons of Sorcery* anthology, finaled for the 2019 RITA Award.

Kennedy also introduced a new fantasy romance series, *Sorcerous Moons*, which includes *Lonen's War*, *Oria's Gambit*, *The Tides of Bàra*, *The Forests of Dru*, *Oria's Enchantment*, and *Lonen's Reign*. And she released a contemporary erotic romance series, *Missed Connections*, which started with *Last Dance* and continues in *With a Prince* and *Since Last Christmas*.

In September 2019, St. Martins Press released *The Orchid Throne*, the first book in a new romantic fantasy series, *The Forgotten Empires*. The sequel, *The Fiery Crown*, followed in May 2020, and culminates in *The Promised Queen* in 2021.

Kennedy's other works include a number of fiction series: the fantasy romance novels of *A Covenant of Thorns*; the contemporary BDSM novellas of the *Facets of Passion*; an erotic contemporary serial novel, *Master of the Opera*; and the erotic romance trilogy, Falling Under, which includes *Going Under*, *Under His Touch*, and *Under Contract*.

She lives in Santa Fe, New Mexico, with two Maine coon cats, plentiful free-range lizards, and a very handsome Doctor of Oriental Medicine.

Jeffe can be found online at her website: JeffeKennedy.com, every Sunday at the popular SFF Seven blog, on Facebook, on Goodreads, and pretty much constantly on

Twitter @jeffekennedy. She is represented by Sarah Younger of Nancy Yost Literary Agency.

jeffekennedy.com
facebook.com/Author.Jeffe.Kennedy
twitter.com/jeffekennedy
goodreads.com/author/show/1014374.Jeffe_Kennedy

Sign up for her newsletter here.
www.jeffekennedy.com/sign-up-for-my-newsletter

Blood Martinis & Mistletoe: A Faery Bargains Novella

by

Melissa Marr

Half-dead witch Geneviève Crowe makes her living beheading the dead—and spends her free time trying not to get too attached to her business partner, Eli Stonecroft, a faery prince in self-imposed exile in New Orleans.

After a faery bargain gone wrong, a walking-dead relative and a deadly but well-paying job make juggling the holidays, romance, and work a lot more complicated than anyone needs.

With a killer at her throat and a blood martini in her hand, Geneviève accepts what seems like a straight-forward faery bargain. Eli's terms might make the holidays a little more bearable, but if she can't figure out a way to escape *this* faery bargain, she'll be planning a wedding after the holidays.

Acknowledgments

Thank you to the rattlesnake. If you hadn't rolled under my kayak with me, the series wouldn't exist. Realizing you have a rattlesnake in your hair? Bad. Getting bitten when you shove it away from your face? *Monkey Balls, Son of Weasel,* **ouch.** (Seriously, it's a special sort of pain.)

So these books are entirely the fault of a rattlesnake...and Molly Harper and Jeaniene Frost and Kelley Armstrong who thought my hillbilly accent and rural sass were fair game for a book. I grew up barefoot country, and while a pistol isn't offered at birth it's sort of an implied I.O.U. So Gen and Eli are the characters I wanted to write for *years.* (Thank you to all of you for the love I'm getting on their first book, too!)

Thanks, Jeffe and Leslye, for inviting and welcoming me, and thank you, Kelley, for . . . more things than I have space to say. From organizing tours and conferences to standing at my side for a memorial, you are a once-in-a-million friend.

And thank you to the readers, the writers, and the booksellers and librarians who have recommended my books, cheered and wept with me, and made me feel so much love. I will continue to try not to let you down.

~ 1 ~

GIANT ALUMINUM BALLS hung around me even though I was standing in the cemetery not long before dawn. I didn't know who hung the balls, but I wasn't too bothered.

Winter in New Orleans was festive. We might have *draugr* and a higher than reasonable crime rate, but damn it, we had festivities for every possible occasion. Gold, silver, red, blue, purple, and green balls hung from the tree. Samhain had passed, and it was time to ramp up for the winter holidays.

November—the month after Samhain—was uncommonly active for necromancy calls. Unfortunately, a certain sort of person thought it was festive to summon the body and spirit of Dear Uncle Phil or Aunt Marie. Sometimes the relatives were maudlin, and sometimes they were thinking about the afterlife.

Now, the dead don't tell tales about the things after death. They can't. I warn folks, but they don't believe me. They pay me a fair amount to summon their dead, so I always stress that the "what happens after we die" questions are forbidden. Few people believe me.

Tonight, I had summoned Alphard Cormier to speak to his widow and assorted relatives or friends who accompanied her. I didn't ask who they were. One proven relation was all I needed. Family wasn't always just the folks who shared your blood.

Case in point, the faery beside me. Eli of Stonecroft was one of the people I trusted most in this world—or in any other. I closed my eyes for a moment, which I could do because he was at my side. I was tired constantly, so much so that only willpower kept me upright.

"Bonbon," Eli whispered. His worried tone made clear that a question or three hid in that absurd pet name.

Was I going to be able to control my magic? Did he need to brace for *draugr* inbound? Were we good on time?

"It's good." I opened my eyes, muffled a yawn, and met his gaze. "I'm still fine."

Eli nodded, but he still scanned the graves. He was increasingly cautious since my near-brush-with-death a couple months ago.

My partner stood at my side as we waited in the cemetery while the widow, her daughter, and two men spoke to their reanimated relative. Mr. Alphard Cormier was wearing a suit that was in fashion sometime in the last thirty years.

Why rouse him now? I didn't know and wasn't asking.

"Twenty minutes," I called out. I could feel the sun coming; I'd always been able to do so—call it in an internal sundial, or call it bad genes. Either way, my body was attuned to the rising and falling of the sun.

"When he is entombed, we could—"

"No." I couldn't force myself to glance at him again.

I was bone-tired, which made me more affectionate, and Eli was my weakness. Cut-glass features, bee-stung lips, and enough strength to fight at my side, even against *draugar*, Eli was built for fantasy. His ability to destroy my self-control was remarkable—and no, it wasn't because he was fae.

That part *was* why I wasn't going home with him. Trusting him, wanting him, caring for him, none of that was enough to overcome the complications of falling into his bed. Sleeping with a faery prince had a list of complications that no amount of lust or affection overcame.

"I won't get married," I reminded him.

"Are you sure that's a good idea?" Mr. Cormier asked, voice carrying over the soft sobbing women.

The man with them handed Cormier something metallic.

I felt as much as saw the dead man look my way, and then his arm raised with a gun in hand. The relatives parted, and there was a dead man with a gun aimed at me.

"Fuck a duck. Move!" I darted to the side.

Eli was already beside me, hand holding his pretty bronze-coated sword that I hadn't even known he owned until the last month. "Geneviève?"

"On it." I jerked the magic away from Mr. Comier.

It was my magic that made him stand, so I wasn't going to let him stand and shoot me.

REST, I ordered the dead man.

"I'm sorry, ma'am. They made me. Threatened my Suzette if I didn't . . ." His words faded as my shove of magic sent him back to his tomb.

I could hear the widow, presumably Suzette, sobbing.

"I do not believe those gentlemen are Mr. Cormier's relations." Eli glared in the direction of the men who had hired me to raise a dead man to kill me. They'd grabbed the two women and ducked behind mausoleums.

"Why?"

"They seem to want you dead, buttercream," Eli said. "If they were his family, that's an odd response."

A bullet hit the stone across from me. Shards of gravestone pelted me. Oddly the adrenaline surge was welcome, even if the bullets weren't. Nothing like a shot of rage to get the sleepiness out.

"Not why *that*." I nodded toward the men who were staying crouched behind graves. "Why go through the hassle? Why not simply shoot me themselves?"

"Dearest, can we ponder that *after* they are not shooting at you?"

I felt my eyes change. As my rage boiled over, my eyes reflected it. They were my father's reptilian eyes, *draugr* eyes. The only useful thing he'd ever done was accidentally augment the magic I inherited from my mother. Unfortunately, the extra juice came with a foul temper—one that was even worse the last few weeks. After I'd been injected by venom, my moods were increasingly intense.

I wanted to rip limbs off.

I wanted to shove my thumbs into their eye sockets and keep going until I felt brain matter.

Before the urges were more than images, I was moving from one spot to the next.

I could *flow* like a *draugr*. I could move quickly enough that to the mortal eye it looked like teleportation. I *flowed* to the side of the shooter and grabbed his wrist.

Eli was not far behind. He didn't *flow*, but he was used to my movements and impulses. He had his sword to the shooter's throat a moment after I jerked the gun away from the man.

"Dearest?" Eli said, his voice tethering me sanity.

I concentrated on his voice, his calm, and I punched the other shooter rather than removing his eyes. Then I let out a scream of frustration and shoved my magic into the soil like a seismic force.

The dead answered.

Dozens of voices answered my call. Hands reknitted. Flesh was regrown from the magic that flowed from my body into the graves. Mouths reformed, as if I was a sculptor of man.

"You do *not* wake the dead without reason," I growled at the now-unarmed man who dared to try to shoot me.

Here, of all places. He tried to spill my blood into these graves.

I stepped over the man I'd punched and ignored the cringing, sobbing widow and the other woman who was trying to convince her mother to leave.

And I stalked toward the shooter in Eli's grip.

"Bonbon, you have a scratch." Eli nodded toward my throat.

"Shit." I felt my neck where Eli had indicated. Blood slid into my collar.

I stepped closer to the shooter. "What were you thinking,

Weasel Nuts?"

"Would you mind *covering* the wound?" Eli asked, forcing me to focus again.

His voice was calm, but we both knew that I could not shed blood in a space where graves were so plentiful. I'd accidentally bound two *draugr* so far, and blood was a binding agent in necromancy. Unless I wanted to bring home a few reanimated servants, my blood couldn't spill here.

I had to focus. And I didn't need an army of undead soldiers.

"Take this." Eli pulled off his shirt with one hand, switching the hilt between hands to keep the sword to Weasel Nuts' throat.

I stared. *Not the time.*

Eli's lips quirked in a half-smile, and then he pressed the blade just a bit. "And, I believe you need to answer my lady."

I shot Eli a look—his *lady*? What year did he think this was?—but I pressed his shirt against my throat. I did not, absolutely did *not*, take a deep breath because the shirt smelled like Eli.

Eli smiled as I took another quick extra breath.

"Thou shalt not suffer a witch to live." Weasel Nuts spat in my direction. "Foul thing."

I opened my mouth to reply, but Eli removed his sword blade and in a blink turned it so he could bash the pommel into the man's mouth.

Weasel Nuts dropped to his knees, and this time when he spat, he spat out his own teeth and blood.

If I were the swooning sort, this would be such a moment.

Something about defending me always did good things to my libido.

"Geneviève, would you be so kind as to call the police?" Eli motioned toward the women. "And escort the ladies away from this unpleasant man?"

It sounded chivalrous—or chauvinistic—but it was actually an excuse. I needed to get my ass outside the cemetery before I dripped blood. Eli had provided a way to do so gracefully.

"Ladies?" Eli said, louder now. "Ms. Crowe will walk you toward the street."

The women came over, and the widow flinched when my gaze met hers. My *draugr* eyes unnerved people.

But then she straightened her shoulders and stared right into my reptilian eyes as if they were normal. "I do apologize, Ms. Crowe. They have an accomplice who is holding my grandson as a hostage. We had to cooperate."

My simmering temper spiked, keeping my exhaustion away and my focus sharp.

I stared at the women. With my grave sight, I saw trails of energy, the whispers of deaths, and the auras of anything living. These women were afraid, but not evil. They were worried.

The older woman grabbed the fallen gun and ordered, "Walk."

For a moment, I thought I'd been wrong, but she pointed the barrel at the man who had shot at me. "You. Get up."

Her daughter smiled. "Would you mind helping us, Ms. Crowe?"

Eli and I exchanged a look. We were in accord, as usual.

He bowed his head at them, and then scooped the unconscious man up.

In a strange group, we walked toward the exit.

As we were putting the unconscious attacker in the trunk of the Cadillac the women had arrived in, the sun rose, tinting the sky as if it were a watercolor painting.

I paused, wincing. Sunlight wasn't my friend. I wasn't a *draugr*—luckily, because sunlight trapped young *draugr*—but my genetics meant daylight made my head throb if I was out in too much of it. I slid on the dark sunglasses I carried for emergencies.

"It was nice to see Daddy," the younger woman said quietly to her mother. "I wish it had been closer to Christmas, but still . . . it was nice."

The widow motioned for the other prisoner to get into the trunk. Once he did, Eli slammed the trunk, and the widow squeezed her daughter's hand. "It was."

The daughter handed Eli the keys. She was shaken by the shooting, and I was bleeding from the shattering stone. Neither of us was in great shape to drive. However, it wasn't great for Eli to be trapped in a hulking steel machine. Faeries and steel weren't a good mix.

"I'll drive my car," he said, popping the trunk and grabbing a clean shirt. Working with me meant carrying an assortment of practical goods—clean clothes, duct tape, a sword, zip ties, and first aid supplies.

I tried not to sigh that he was now dressed fully again. Don't get me wrong. I respect him, but that didn't mean I wasn't prone to lustful gazes in his direction. If he minded, I'd stop.

He walked to the passenger door and opened it. "Come on, my peach pie."

The widow drove her Caddy away as I slid into the luxurious little convertible that had been fae-modified for Eli.

"Are you well enough to do this?" Eli asked as he steered us into the morning light.

"One human." I kept my eyes closed behind my sunglasses, grateful for the extra dark tint of his windows. I rarely needed sleep for most of my life, but lately I was always ready for a nap. Not yet, though.

I assured Eli, "I'm fine to deal with this."

So we set out to retrieve the young hostage. We didn't discuss my near constant exhaustion. We didn't talk about the fear that my near-death event had left lingering issues for my health. We would have to, but . . . not now.

We arrived at a townhouse, and I *flowed* to where the captor held a smallish boy. *Flowing* wasn't a thing I typically did around regular folk, but there were exceptions.

The boy was duct taped to a chair by his ankles.

The captor, another man about the age of the two in the trunk, was laughing at something on the television. If not for the gun in his lap and the duct tape on the boy's ankles, the whole thing wouldn't seem peculiar.

When the man saw us, he scrambled for his gun.

So, I punched the captor and broke the wrist of his gun-holding arm.

Eli freed the boy, who ran to his family as soon as they came into the house.

The whole thing took less time than brewing coffee.

"Best not to mention Ms. Crowe's speed," Eli said to the women as we were leaving.

The younger one nodded, but she was mostly caught up in holding her son.

The widow looked at me.

"Not all witches are wicked, dear." She patted my cheek, opened her handbag and pulled out a stack of folded bills. "For your time."

"The raising was already paid," I protested.

"I took it from them," she said proudly. She shook it at me insistently. "Might as well go to you. Here."

Eli accepted a portion of the money on my behalf. He understood when it was an insult not to and when to refuse because the client couldn't afford my fees.

Honestly, I felt guilty getting paid sometimes. Shouldn't I work for my city? Shouldn't I help people? Shouldn't good come of these skills?

But good intentions didn't buy groceries or pay for my medical supplies. That's as much what Eli handled as having my back when bullets or unwelcome dead things started to pop up.

After we walked out and shoved the third prisoner in the trunk of the Cadillac, Mrs. Cormier said, "I'll call the police to retrieve them. Do you mind waiting?"

"I will wait," Eli agreed, not lying by saying we "didn't mind" because *of course* we minded. I was leaning on the car for support, and Eli was worrying over my injury. If he had his way, he'd have me at his home, resting and cared for, but I was lousy at that.

It was on the long list of reasons I couldn't marry him. Some girls dreamed of a faery tale romance, a prince, pretty dresses. I dreamed of kicking ass. I'd be a lousy faery tale queen.

But I still had feelings for a faery prince—and no, I was *not* labeling them.

So rather head than home, I leaned on the side of the Cadillac, partly because it was that or sway in exhaustion. "I'll stay with you."

Once the widow went inside, Eli walked away and grabbed a first aid kit from his car. I swear he bought them in bulk lately. "Let me see your throat."

"I'm fine." Dried blood made me look a little garish, but I could feel that it wasn't oozing much now.

Eli opened the kit, tore open a pouch of sani-wipes, and stared at me.

"Just tired. Sunlight." I gestured at the bright ball of pain in the sky. Midwinter might be coming, but the sun was still too bright for my comfort.

"Geneviève . . ." He held up a wipe. "May I?"

I sighed and took off my jacket. "It's not necessary."

"I disagree." He used sani-wipes to wipe away my blood as I leaned on the Cadillac, ignoring the looks we were getting from pedestrians. Maybe it was that he was cleaning up my blood, or that he was fae—or maybe it was that there were people yelling from the trunk.

Either way, I wasn't going to look away from Eli. I couldn't.

Obviously, I knew it should not be arousing to have him clean a cut in my neck from grave shards because someone was firing bullets at me, but . . . having his hands on me at all made my heart speed.

"Would you like to take the car and leave?" Eli was closer than he needed to be, hips close enough that it would be easier to pull him closer than push him away.

"And go where?"

He brushed my hair back, checking for more injuries. The result was that I could feel his breath on my neck. "Drive to my home and draw a bath or shower. I'll stay here and . . ."

"Tempting," I admitted with a laugh.

He had both a marble rainfall shower and the largest tub I'd ever seen. It came complete with a small waterfall. I admitted, "I've had fantasies about that waterfall."

"As have I."

I pressed myself against him, kissed his throat, and asked, "Ready to call off the engagement?"

He kissed me, hand tangled in my hair, holding me as if I would run.

I'd sell my own soul for an eternity of Eli's kisses if I believed in such bargains, but I wouldn't destroy him. Being with me wasn't what was best for him.

When he pulled back from our kiss, he stated, "Geneviève . . ."

I kissed him softly. I could say more with my touch than with words. I paused and whispered, "You can have my body *or* this engagement. Not both."

He sighed, but he stepped back. "You are impossible, Genevieve Crowe."

I caught his hand. "It doesn't have to be impossible. We're safely out of *Elphame* now. We could just end the enga—"

"I am fae, love. I don't lie. I don't break my word." He squeezed my hand gently. "I gave you my promise to wed. In front of my king and family. I *cannot* end this engagement."

We stood in silence for several moments. Then he held out his keys, and I took them.

"Meet me at my place. Maybe we can spar," I offered.

Eli pulled me in closer, kissed both of my cheeks, and said, "I will accept any excuse to get sweaty with you."

"Same." I hated that this was where we were, but I wasn't able to change who or what I was. Neither was Eli. He had a future that I wanted no part of, and I felt a duty to my city and friends. We had no future option that would suit both of us. I'd be here, beheading *draugr* and trying not to become more of a monster, and he would return to his homeland. There was no good compromise.

AFTER THE WEIRDNESS of handling the Cormier situation, life resumed normalcy. I was still unnaturally tired, still engaged, and still not getting any loving.

What passed for normalcy in my life was overrated.

The work part, at least, was a welcome lull. This was an annual tradition. I tended to think of it as the pre-holiday calm. By January, it would be hectic. Mid-Winter was always when I had the most downtime, but during the end of year holiday people would start deciding death was overrated and hunting down *draugr* for a shot at eternal life on Earth instead of natural deaths. I wasn't sure if it was depression, greed, or sentimental holiday moods.

Mine was an odd job, but I didn't ever want to give it up. I wasn't immune to *draugr* venom, but I was stronger than humans and could *flow* as fast as the *draugr* could. I had advantages, and I felt duty-bound to make use of them.

Tonight, I was enjoying a night out with my closest friends. *Draugr* weren't all trapped by sunlight, but the newly-infected, bite-first-think-never ones were. I tended to think that was a good excuse to stay in the bar until dawn's light.

"Yule? Chanukah? Christmas?" Sera was holding up pictures of formal dresses. "Did you discuss it? Which are you celebrating in *Elphame*? I know Mama Lauren has usually had dibs on Chanukah. Do we call one? Or do we wait on Eli?"

Jesse and Christy said nothing. They exchange a look that spoke volumes. No one expected my first holiday season as the future queen of *Elphame* to go smoothly.

Running away to *Elphame* as if I could be fae wasn't an option for more reasons than just my issues with Eli—which was why I was livid when I received a beautiful handwritten summons to celebrate "the holiday" with the king of the faeries. Eli's uncle seemed to think there was *one* holiday. As a Jewish witch with Christian friends, I could guarantee that there were at least three of them on my social schedule.

The four of us were enjoying a night off at Eli's bar, the oddly named Bill's Tavern. No one called Bill had ever owned or been employed here, but whenever I asked "who is Bill," Eli simply laughed.

Fae humor confused me sometimes.

I still had my weapons, but that was like saying I still had on trousers. It would be weird and uncomfortable to go out for the night without them. One sword, two guns, and a dagger if I needed to draw my blood. It might seem odd, but my blood was my best weapon. One loyal army of the dead trumped most conventional weapons.

Christy, whose job was mostly pool-hustling—often here—wasn't working tonight either. She and Jesse were sort of hand holding, but not being all couple-y in an obnoxious way. Sera was scheduling our lives. It was her thing. One of them, at least. She was why we were out tonight, too. She was our glue.

"I have received a summons from the king," I said.

"You'll need another dress," Sera said, as if dresses were the priority not the fact that some old dude had summoned me like I was his subject.

"That's what you got out of this?" I met Sera's gaze.

"Maybe we should get a couple of them."

"Or not," Jesse muttered.

"She cannot go before the king of *Elphame* in jeans." Sera gave us all a look, one that meant she was debating smacking one of us upside our heads. "Which holiday did he invite you for?"

"*The* holiday, as if there is only one." I was starting a list of grievances against the faery king—starting with the fact that he insisted on referring to me as "death" or "death maiden" and rolling right up to the moment. Honestly, the only thing I liked about him was his nephew, Eli.

Sera sighed.

In a game of chess, she'd be the king—maybe the queen. It varied. Christy was a bishop, influential and strong. She was impervious to Sera's quelling look and spoke her mind. Jesse was the Rook, the castle. He was *home*. Steady in whatever way we needed. And I was either a knight or a pawn, depending on the moment. I'd like to be a knight, but lately I felt like I was being played.

I just couldn't decide whether the player was someone I knew already or not.

I looked up and met Eli's gaze. If you asked him, he'd claim that he wasn't on the chess board at all. I had trouble believing that a faery prince was so innocent—and Eli was *the* faery prince, as a matter of fact. He failed to share that tidbit with me at first. Right up to the point where he'd spirited me away to his homeland to save my life, I thought he was just a guy: a very hot, infuriating, loyal, fae guy. So, maybe I was still pissy over the whole my friend is an exiled faery prince thing.

Now that we were accidentally engaged because of it, I was starting to think that he was the hand in the sky. Was Eli the chess player toying with my life? Had he always planned to trap me?

But based on the way my life had gone of late, he was far from the only one moving pieces. His uncle, the king I might have to wear a dress to meet again, and the dead lady I thought might be an ancestor or mine . . . and some unknown figure who hired a *human* to murder me a few months ago. The shooting at Cormier's raising was weird, too. The police had no answers, and all three of the men were suddenly dead. Too many people were trying to play with my life, and I was fed up.

I couldn't do anything about that murder-attempts thing, but I could handle the holidays. I was still me: half-witch, half-*draugr*. I wasn't a fae princess, no matter what the King of *Elphame* thought, and I wasn't pleased to be summoned as if his laws applied to me.

"Which holiday do *you* want us to celebrate?" I asked my friends. "Cocktails. Friends. Maybe we can do a formal meal. You want dresses, Sera? Fuck it. We do dresses."

Jesse and Christy both looked at me like I'd suggested we

knock over a bank or gnaw on a witch's house.

"Gen, you can't just ignore the king," Jesse said. "You're engaged to—"

"Not on purpose! For an honorary brother, you're awfully calm. Eli is trying to *marry me*. Besmirch me." My voice was loud enough that several people looked our way.

"You like besmirching," Jesse said. Then he met my gaze and added, "And you're obviously not *besmirched* yet because you're surlier than usual lately."

I shot a glare at Eli. It took effort to glare at him, though. Logic meant I was still angry that he wouldn't free me from our engagement, but logic was a weak defense against him. I wanted Eli the way witches crave nature, the way the starving crave food.

And I was in definite need of being besmirched, preferably by Eli. Repeatedly. I'd been ready to ignore the risk to our friendship, tired of resisting our chemistry, over all of the very sound reasons not to lock the doors and get gloriously naked with Eli.

But then someone tried to kill me.

And Eli had to save me.

And in the mess that followed we ended up accidentally betrothed—which meant no sex for me. Fae rules of love and matrimony meant that if I banged him while we experienced true love, we were *de facto* married.

"Both holidays," I said, louder than necessary. "We'll celebrate twice. Fuck him."

"Oh, I do wish you would," Sera muttered.

Christy snorted.

Sera squeezed my hand fondly. "Eli is not without his charms. You're engaged—and please don't take this wrong, sweetie—but you need to burn up some sheets or something. You're on edge."

"Understatement," Jesse said with a shrug.

When I made a crude gesture at my friends, Sera held up her hands. "Fine. Eli is hotter than Satan's knickers are in the summer, and Geneviève is as tense as a kitten in a room of rocking chairs and Rottweilers." She took a long drink of her bourbon, and then she added, "The point, Gen, is that you *like* him, and he obviously loves you. Why not give it a go?"

Sera pursed her lips at me when I tried to interrupt.

"And he was willing to do whatever it took to keep you safe," she continued. "For the fae, that's a *lot*. So, go to dinner with the king, and try to be a little kinder to Eli. His greatest crime—as far as I can see—is that he wants *you*."

My temper fizzled. She was right. Hell, they all were. I wanted to give in to Eli, but he *needed* to have a child. That child had to be carried by his wife, or his line of the fae would wither. He—literally—carried his ancestral memory in his blood. A child of the blood was required to pass on the living memory of his family.

He had to have a kid.

And I would never ever be a mother. Some people just weren't meant to be parents, and that *should* be okay. Freedom of choice ought to mean freedom to choose not to breed.

Eli, however, had to have a kid. There wasn't really a compromise there.

It wasn't even that fae law was unreasonable. There were

exemption options for infertility or if a person was gay or lesbian—or if they had a sibling who was able to pass on the family memories. *Elphame* Law addressed most concerns. There were even Temple partners who were magical enough to have multiple children. That enabled the exceptional cases— gay, lesbian, or second children—to pass on their genes.

Eli was neither gay nor a second son.

I'd be asking Eli to sacrifice his ancestors if he was with me. I wouldn't do that to anyone I liked even a little, much less someone I trusted and respected as I did with him.

"It's complicated," I said quietly.

I didn't have consent to share the fae secret of ancestry. I couldn't explain why I was refusing him. And no one quite understood my aversion to parenthood. It wasn't *just* that I didn't want to pass on my fucked up genetic soup. That was a huge factor, but when Eli explained how we could avoid that . . . I still didn't want to be a parent. I wanted my life. My mission in my city. I *liked* what I had.

The only thing I'd change was . . . adding Eli.

He'd always been the flame that drew me. His glamour hadn't ever worked on me—either because of my witch blood or maybe my *other* blood. I wasn't sure what he looked like to others, but he'd always been perfect to me.

If not for the whole royal requirement and duty to pass on his ancestral lineage, I'd be naked with him by now.

Without quite meaning to, I looked over and met his gaze again, and this time, he walked over to the table. I guess a guy could only ignore being stared at so long.

"Christy. Sera. Jesse." He nodded at each of my friends.

Then he looked at me. "Geneviève."

My insides turned to mush, and I realized I was *still* staring at him. It had been forty-three days since I'd thought we could be together. Forty-three days that we had been engaged. Two weeks since the last job together when we kissed and sparred. For the first time in my life, I couldn't even pretend to want anyone else. I'd never been monogamous, but something about Eli had me embracing monogamy—without the sex that should go with it. It was baffling.

I licked my lips unconsciously, and then blushed at his responding smile.

"What?"

"I said 'Would you accompany me?'" he asked, eyes twinkling as if he was aware that I'd completely failed to hear him the first time. He added, "To meet Lady Beatrice."

"Beatrice?" I echoed.

Eli nodded. "Indeed."

I had been avoiding the *draugr* queen since she's saved my life. I was being ungrateful, but I had complicated feelings. I was, awkwardly, related to her, and as best as I understood, she was my maternal ancestor—but she was a *draugr*. My job was killing her kind. So, yeah, it was complicated. "I'm not sure I—"

"She has requested my presence, and I am unable to visit her alone."

I startled. Eli was the strongest person I knew—other than Beatrice—and they had no discord. She knew who he was and had no desire to start a war with the fae. And while Eli had no great love for her, they'd spoken almost cordially.

"It would be inappropriate to see her without you with me. A fae who has pledged devotion must not meet unchaperoned with anyone sexually mature." His voice was level; he always had the same calm tone when I was panicking or about to lose my temper.

"Like you can't see her because you might be overcome and marry her instead?" I stopped short of saying that would be fine. It wasn't—and everyone who knew me knew it. I might not be interested in making his babies, or a future in *Elphame*, but I was exceedingly interested in Eli.

"Geneviève—"

"Monkey balls. This is that whole faux engagement that—"

"Not faux," Eli interjected. "My hand is already yours, sugar cookie." He gave me the sort of look that could melt knickers. "This was a formal invitation, Geneviève, which means I cannot visit her without accompaniment of my intended, a relative, or a male friend."

"I can go, Gen," Jesse offered.

Eli smiled. "Your offer of friendship is cherished."

"Faeries are weird," Christy said when Jesse's mouth gaped open—presumably at the realization that he'd called Eli a friend. They'd been at odds before my almost-dying-thing.

At that Eli bowed his head to her and to Sera and added, "It means much to have your regard."

Christy toasted him. They had a strange dynamic. Their friendship was natural, equal regard but not sexual tension. Sometimes I envied them.

Sera opened her mouth, but before she could say anything, I blurted, "Let's go, Eli."

We said our goodbyes, and I walked away with Eli. In some ways it was less awkward than trying to talk to him and my friends. They had turned to his side when he saved my life, risked his freedom to do so, and now, I was left with no defense other than "I don't want to." It was weak—because I couldn't spill his secrets *and* because they were a lot more accepting of my *draugr* heritage than I was.

We made it halfway to the bar door before I told him, "Your uncle sent an invitation."

"I know. He has commissioned six gowns so far in hopes that one will please you." Eli had the carefully calm tone again.

"Six *gowns?*"

"Did the invitation mention the presentation of the future queen?" He tucked my hand into the fold of his arm. "It's traditional."

I stopped walking. "Presenting the future qu—... you mean *me?* The event is about presenting me?"

Eli nudged me forward. "I suggested he order you a sword or three to assuage your ill mood in his direction. Not that I'll give him all the answers, Geneviève, but in this case, I thought weapons might interest you more than gowns. The armory has been working on several pieces."

"Flaming monkey balls."

"Geneviève, there are laws. You are my intended. I cannot change that," he said, again.

I glanced back at my friends. I was to be out tonight enjoying life. Not off to see a *draugr* queen or navigate Yule plans with the fae king. I mouthed, "Help?"

Sera gave me an encouraging gesture, and Jesse smiled.

Christy mouthed back, "Get some."

"I do like Christy." Eli chuckled at seeing her. "Smart woman. Wise. Perhaps you should listen to her advice."

"If only it were that easy." I leaned in and kissed him quickly, just a butterfly brush of lips. "There ought to be perks to this clusterfuck, and you naked under me sounds like an excellent idea."

"Indeed, bonbon." He growled a little.

I shivered at the desire that little noise sparked.

Smiling, Eli open the door for me. "What do you say to a faery bargain, Geneviève Crowe?"

The last faery bargain was for a kiss, and that had led to this engagement. Was I fool enough to make a bargain with Eli? When he stepped outside, his hand pressed against my low back, and my fracturing resolve grew even weaker.

"What are your terms?" I was pretty sure that Eve had felt this same flutter in a long-ago garden.

"Ones that include pleasure."

"Tell me more," I encouraged.

He smiled. There were a million sins in that look, and I wanted to commit every one of them twice.

ELI'S CAR WAS waiting for us. He opened the passenger door, and I slid into the little blue convertible. If my hand brushed his stomach as I did so, it was purely accidentally, as was the way I looked up at him.

"Temptress."

I grinned. "Says the faery who just offered me my greatest desire."

He closed the door and was silent as he entered the driver's side of the car and eased us into the nighttime traffic.

Once we were zipping through the ever-busy night streets of New Orleans, Eli finally said, "If I could avoid the traditional presentation of the queen, I would."

"I know."

Eli added, "And if I wasn't who I am—"

"A bar owner? A liar?"

"Geneviève, I do not lie," he stated.

It was true in a manner of speaking. The fae never lie. Omit? Distract? Trick? Those are a kind of mistruth, too, but they are not what the fae consider a lie.

"A man who desperately wants to tell my world and yours to go burn while I lock us away and start to slake the needs we have," he said, as casually as anything.

"Oh . . . So, this bargain—"

"I would have picked a fiancé from the women there if I could have," Eli continued. "That was too much of a lie to do, though. I want none of them. No one in *Elphame* or here. Just you."

"So, we're really discussing this, then?" I glanced over at him. "No longer avoiding it?"

Eli sighed. "The fae are not renowned for being *direct* without reason."

"What's your reason?"

"A bargain, love. I want to propose a deal with you." His voice was somehow even more alluring here in the dark as we zipped through the city. "Are you clever enough to make a bargain with me, Geneviève?"

It would be wrong to throw caution away while he was driving, but his voice did things to my body that some men couldn't accomplish with their mouths.

"I'm listening," I said. It was the most I could offer without destroying the peace we were building.

Inside the car, this small bubble of safety where the monsters were unable to get to us, where our issues were tucked away as we rushed off to jobs or meetings, I felt like we could exist outside of time. I wanted that desperately, to ignore the reasons we couldn't be more. I wanted a simple world. And I suspected I wasn't alone in that.

The city was alive with too many decorations already. Oak trees draped in cheap balls and tinsel. Mardi Gras beads repurposed as Christmas beads. There was a defiance to the way the city approached festivity.

That defiance made sense to me.

Eli added, "We will go to *Elphame*. We will present ourselves to my family and world. . . unless you can tell me you don't feel the same. Do you care for me?"

"Obviously." I sighed loudly. "But some people are not meant to have children. I am n—"

"Did I ask that of you?"

"No but—"

"So, shall I tell His Majesty that we will be there for Yule? Or am I wrong about your regard for me? I can sever our tie, return there, and allow my uncle to select my future bride." He sounded calm, but I heard the trickle of fear in his voice. "Or you can make a bargain with me."

The thought of it, of Eli bedding and wedding another person, made my jaw clench. I couldn't, wouldn't send him away. "We are a terrible idea, Eli."

"Do I go home alone or do you feel as I do?"

"You're . . . not wrong about my feelings," I admitted. I was the least romantic, least appropriate choice for a man like Eli, but for reasons that I didn't understand, he *liked* that he had my heart. "A wiser man would leave me."

"I've never claimed wisdom, my dear Devil's Cake." He reached out and took my hand, and I knew that he was relieved. He sounded happier as he added, "I like danger, passion, a foul temper, talent for violence, fierce loyalty. I prefer warriors."

"My sword is yours," I swore. "You have that. No matter the future, you will always have that."

"Then I'll wait for the rest. Your heart. Your body. All of you, love. I want all of you."

I shivered again. We both knew he had a lot of my heart, and the only reason he didn't have my body was this damned engagement. The trouble with faeries, I was discovering, is that they have the patience to go along with their longevity.

I twined my fingers through his, keeping hold of his hand, even though I felt like a child for wanting to hold hands. My reaction to this touch was far from childlike, though. Touching Eli made me flush and my heart race. We'd kissed and had the sort of heated admissions that ought to be headier. This, though, was about my heart. His heart. Admitting that we wanted to find a way to be . . . more. That was scarier than sex or lust ever could be.

"So"—I cleared my throat—"what's this bargain?"

He laughed, and the sheer wickedness in that sound had my thighs clenching against the instinctive urge to yell, "Take me now." Instead I took a steadying breath and said, "Eli . . ."

"Date me."

"What?"

"Date me until Twelfth Night, and you will earn a favor," he said. "Anything you ask of me. One request. Whatever you most desire on that day. I won't say no."

I rolled it over in my mind. Anything? I could end the engagement. It seemed so simple. I stared at him and said, "Faery bargains are never this simple."

"Maybe this one is. All you need to do is truly date me," he said. "Not think about forever. Just . . . date me as if the rest wasn't a factor."

Part of me knew what he was implying. Most of me thought I could manage it. No rules, no strings, meant that we could revel in the thing between us.

"So, no rules? Just no holding back. We . . . date."

"And on the sixth of January, you have one favor," he clarified.

I paused, rolling it over in my mind. Twelfth Night, the Masquerade Ball that started Carnival season, was on January sixth. That was roughly a month from now. Between now and then, however, were a lot of events. Chanukah began in ten days. Yule and Christmas were roughly ten days later, and then New Year's Eve in six *more* days, and then the Twelfth Night Masquerade Ball six days later.

"Why are you offering so many details?" I asked. The last bargain he'd offered me was without much clarity.

"Because, Geneviève, I want you to understand the terms." He steered us onto the bridge, taking us out of the city into the ghost zone.

Something about the ghost zone, what was once the suburbs of most cities, was eerie. It was simply a ghost town of sorts, one that existed beside most cities. If you were brave enough or foolish enough, you could scavenge there; those who left their homes there, did so without taking most of their possessions. But the risk of *draugr* encounters in the ghost zone was high.

After the ghost zone was the Outs. I grew up there. Nature. People with more guns than sense. That was where Jesse and I met, neighbors in the Outs. My mother, Mama Lauren, was still there. I thought briefly about Chanukah. I'd have to take Eli to meet my mother if I agreed to this.

"Date, as in I play nice at the Yule presentation and you are at my side for *any* event during those weeks," I clarified.

"More or less. I want you to be yourself, but without thought or discussion of the future," Eli added.

"But any event?" I pressed. "You mean you'd meet my mother?"

"I would like that." His hand tightened on the steering wheel. "That, however, is not my primary goal. I just want . . . to be in the now with you."

I glanced at him, enjoying the moonlight on his profile. There was something about those cheekbones that just made me want to touch. Something about Eli that I barely resisted. My voice felt too loud even though I was whispering when I said, "If I didn't think about the future, we'd already have been naked, *bonbon*. . ."

He grinned at my use of one of his pet names for me and said, "All the more reason to date me."

I sighed.

Eli glanced at me then. "Give me these days. Let me be in your life. We were so close to progress, and then this"—he gestured between us—"engagement stalled us. I want us to be as we were."

My throat was parched with the wave of need he brought to the forefront of my every nerve, but I still had to add, "Whatever happens is not precedent-setting. When January sixth comes, we . . . reset."

He chuckled. "Expected, and accepted."

"Agreed, then," I said shakily. "I agree to your terms, Eli. We will date."

"I look forward to courting you," he said in that damnably calm tone, which meant that he was hiding his emotions.

I knew for sure then that I was fucked somehow, but the deal was done. I was going to let Eli into my life.

I swallowed hard and tried to sound just as calm. "For tonight, let's see what disaster awaits us at Beatrice's door."

~ 4 ~

A LITTLE LATER when we arrived in The Outs, the region that was once called Slidell, I had to concentrate not to send out a summons to the dead. I was on edge, and my magic was akin to a malformed pipe lately. Sometimes, I tried for a trickle and ended up with a flood. Sometimes, I tried for a stream and received a few droplets.

If I let my magic out tonight, I would wake the dead.

Or beckon the again-walking.

My affinity with death was an affront to some people—the faery king included—and I couldn't entirely blame them. I had a pheromone that meant the not-living found me irresistible. Not in a weird lets-get-naked way . . . okay, sometimes that way, too. Mostly, though, that response was because I was powerful, and power gets many a motor revving.

"What do you feel?" Eli asked, his tiny little convertible was bouncing along a road that seemed to be cobblestone.

"At least twenty *draugr*," I said, feeling the minds of those re-animated dead notice me. "Scattered bones."

Even if I tried not to reach out with magic, I would still feel death, absences in pockets of space. Graves. *Draugr.* My sense of the dead was simply there, like hearing or sight. Near me now was a man. Recently dead. I let the magic roll out in several directions. Three woman in the bayou. Six more men in the ground closer to the house. A child in a grave.

And a tangle of bones in a field . . . sixty. . . maybe up to eighty bodies.

"The ground is filled," I said, the horror of so many dead trying to connect with me slid into my voice. I knew without doubt that Beatrice had summoned Eli in order to make me come here. I didn't know why, but this much I knew.

Eli stopped the car under a willow that looked like it was here before the Civil War. The trunk was thick and old, and the wind through the branches felt like a song. Nature. Soil. Plant. Sky. These were the parts that called to my maternal heritage, and they were the parts of this world that also beckoned Eli.

The fae have an affinity for nature that makes it atypical for them to come to our pollution filled world, but despite the parts of the human world that were flawed, the Outs were like that. Without people, the land there was increasingly pure. Alligators, raccoons, feral pigs, snakes, life thrived and blossomed now that most people had to retreat to the cities. Nature was where people *visited*, but to live out here meant to know that there were Alpha Predators that looked like you but thought you were more of a snack than a friend.

I stood, feeling the humid air and listening to night birds sing and mosquitoes buzz. I'd give a lot for more time surrounded by this. I grew up out here, and if I could, I'd have stayed here.

"Lady Beatrice will join you in the courtyard," a well-dressed, once-human girl said. She was young in appearance, maybe fifteen upon her death, and she was dressed as if we were at an expensive Renaissance festival.

She'd *flowed* in the way of most *draugr*. She, I would presume, had been at the door, but now she was at my side.

"The house is . . . unusual," I murmured as we approached what appeared to be a small castle. As far as unusual Southern homes went, this might be the winner for ostentatiousness. It was vaguely modernized—no drawbridge—but there was a long stone bridge between parking and the massive front doors.

As we were walking toward it, I could see that that the bridge was over a moat. Under the moat were resting alligators.

"The Lady Beatrice had a canal put in. That way the bayou waters come closer and the water dragons can swim around her home."

"Dragons?" Eli echoed.

The girl pointed toward the one enormous alligator. "We didn't have these in the forest at home. Sir George is always here. The others come and go, but Sir George is my lady's pet."

"Of course she has a pet alligator."

"Do you mean the dragon?" the girl asked.

Eli motioned us forward. "Are there more dragons in the courtyard?"

The girl giggled and led us to the main doors. Wide enough to walk an elephant into the castle, and tall enough to allow a giraffe with minor stooping. Wooden. Medieval. The doors opened with minimal noise at our approach, as if by magic, but in reality, there were two women there. One had obviously pulled each door open, and when we stepped into the foyer, they marched the doors shut.

No one else was visible.

To the foolish, the house would seem to be the possession of an eccentric and her all-woman staff. The two very muscular women at the door were human. The *draugr* escort spoke so clearly she had to be at least two centuries old. Young *draugr* were never so articulate. They were all Caucasian, female, and I was glad to see that the Southern tendency toward racism in staffing was not at play here. There were plenty of places in the South where things had begun to change in the years before the cities put up walls. New Orleans was a leader in that change.

But New Orleans was a city that had a rich history of finding its own path, so no one who knew the city was surprised when we led the way.

"Are there any men here?" I asked as we crossed the foyer to exit into a small passageway that was stone-lined and lit by honest-to-Pete sconces.

Our guide gave a smile that was disturbing on such a young face. "If we have use of them, we send out for them."

Eli laughed, but all he said was, "As I was summoned, I am glad I chose to bring my fiancé with me tonight, then. I have no desire to be besieged."

"You *are* a fine specimen." The girl nodded at me, though, not him as she opened another door. This door was average-sized, although there was a salt line across it.

The girl met my gaze. "If you must keep a man, the fae are a good choice."

Before I could ask what in the name of duck dongles *that* meant, she was gone. Her giggles echoed in the hallway, but Eli and I were alone. A part of me, a surly not-interested-in-bullshit part of me that was typically my largest deciding factor, wanted to *flow* after her and demand answers. The less reasonable sort wanted to simply leave.

"Candy apple," Eli began, his hand already reaching for mine as if he knew that I might bolt. "We are here to meet with Beatrice."

I sighed. "I know. No beheading the hostess' staff."

It pained me to admit, but this was not a new conversation. Sometimes clients for my job—which was typically only beheading *draugr* or summoning dead relatives to answer a few lingering questions—were about as charming as angry weasels. My witchy genetics should lend me calm, but I guess that was countered by the *draugr* side.

"Is she coming outside or intending to chase after Eleanor?" Beatrice's voice rang out, sounding amused.

"Geneviève?" Eli prompted.

"I am here," I murmured.

I stepped out before Eli did so, bracing myself for something wretched. Instead I was met with the only other witch-*draugr* I'd known of. I didn't know if she had been born *draugr* and witch, or if she'd been made so.

Right now, she was standing beside two feral pigs.

"Son of Stonecroft," Beatrice said with a moderately deep bow in Eli's direction. Then she met my gaze. "*You* have been avoiding me, Geneviève."

I shrugged.

Beatrice looked at the pigs and made a sweeping gesture. I could swear they bowed their heads before leaving.

"Are those regular pigs?" I asked.

"What else would they be?" Beatrice was dressed in the most normal thing I'd seen to date, a simple black linen pantsuit. Her feet were bare. "Do I look like Circe to you?"

"Witch with feral pigs who bow to her? Yeah. A bit," I admitted.

Beatrice's expression twitched like she was trying not to laugh. I couldn't decide if it was a laugh that I was *right* or laugh that I was wrong.

I glanced away. Her courtyard, where we were currently standing, reminded me of my childhood home because of the nature, and for a brief moment, I could swear that I'd met her before this past year. I stared at her. I would've known, right? Mama Lauren wouldn't have . . . I chased that thought away.

"What do you want?"

"To catch a killer," she said.

"Lydia was—"

"A pawn. I want to know who held her marionette strings." Beatrice motioned to me. "And why something of *mine* was targeted."

"I am not one of your feral pigs."

This time she did laugh. "You must realize that there are

those who are unhappy with my rise to power, Geneviève. I am a *woman*. Most *draugr* of any importance are centuries old, and you may not be surprised to hear that the transition was not bestowed on many women. We were food or playthings or servants. Not equals."

"Okay but . . . what does that have to do with me? Why would being pissed at you mean I get injected?"

She shrugged. "I trust you know that answer."

I steadfastly ignored that question. I had enough clues to have a theory but I wasn't quite ready to address it. "What do you want from us?"

Beatrice straightened in a way that was less casual, more regal, and said, "I need a small favor from the *bougie-man* that makes *draugr* quake"

"No," Eli said. "Miss Crowe is quite busy over the holidays."

"I can pay for your work or I can be in your debt, Geneviève," Beatrice said, as if Eli hadn't spoken. "A substantial amount."

I was busy, and I had just agreed to date Eli—but both Beatrice's money and her help had been of use to me lately. Her payments for my investigation into the *draugr* venom murders added up to the equivalent of several years of work, and her assistance had been immeasurably helpful when I was injected with venom.

"Someone shot at me a few weeks ago," I said. "Figure out who, *and* cut me a check for my help, and I'll help you."

Beatrice pressed her lips together tightly. "It may be connected, but either way I would investigate *that* without a favor owed. You are too important to me for that offense to go unanswered."

I squirmed, and Eli gave me a searching look. Apparently my attempts to ignore this topic were about to be thwarted.

"Did she not mention our familial tie, young prince?" Beatrice said lightly. "I would cross even the boundary to your lands for my granddaughter's safety."

Eli didn't reveal his feelings on that matter—or answer the implied threat—and I wasn't about to follow that topic if it was possible to ignore it.

So, I tried to steer the conversation back to the job she had, "What do you need?"

"I'll have a gathering." Beatrice motioned, and a fire started blazing. The courtyard was medieval in style, giving the fire more of a pyre feeling than I liked. "You will come and see what you can glean from the minds of the guests. I simply need you to read their minds, find threats, determine loyalty. I can read humans, but not fae or *draugr.*"

"So, the guests are. . . all dead?" I prompted.

"Except you and your escort."

Eli, my likeliest escort, looked at me. The flickering of flames made him look ominous; at least, I hoped it was the firelight that cast such shadows in his expression. I didn't want to ask if it was the party, the risk, my continued exhaustion, or the relationship to the dead lady that had him looking so irritated.

"I find it fascinating that you can read one of the fae, granddaughter. I'd imagine it's too intense to read him without fornicating," Beatrice offered, possibly trying to be helpful.

"That much magic must be difficult to engage with clothing impeding you."

I swallowed. Energy was woven into Eli's very fiber. As a witch, it called to me. Touching him was nearly addictive, and admittedly, sometimes I wanted to intrude on his mind as I could with the dead, but the few times I'd done so were sheer accident.

"Reading Eli gives me a blinding headache," I confessed.

Then I looked at him and added, "The only time it didn't was when you invited me. I don't *try* to, I swear."

"But can you read me if you want to do so now?" he prompted.

He'd invited me to do so, but this was not about that. What he wanted to know was if I could do so without his consent. I hadn't tried. It felt wrong.

I shrugged. "Stray thoughts about me or us."

"More often now?"

I nodded. "It's like you left a door open."

"I see," Eli said, calmer than before.

I, however, did not see what he had realized. Something had been answered for him, possibly for Beatrice, too. Now was not the time or place to ask him, though.

I looked at Beatrice, who was smiling at us. "I have tried with my friends. They get headaches. I can read the dead as if they are speaking aloud, though."

"Most *draugr* cannot do that. Nor can witches. Lauren would never have mated with Darius if she could have read him." Beatrice frowned. "Had I known he was targeting my granddaughter, I—"

"Explain the granddaughter thing," I interrupted.

"I had a child when I was a human. She mated with a human. That child grew to adulthood. She mated, as well." Beatrice pressed her lips together and shook her head. "It's blurry. Centuries pass. Humans age, mate, age more, die." She turned to meet my gaze. "Eventually, there was Lauren. Darius found her, and he decided to procreate with her. Now, there is you."

Eli took my hand, and I realized I was trembling. Both my witch and *draugr* genetics were standing before me. She was my ancestor, and I needed no necromancy to ask her questions.

"So, Darius knew about my mother because of you," I clarified. "Because you were a witch."

"I am still a witch, Geneviève." Beatrice sighed. "Sometimes when you're powerful, people want that power or simply want to end your life because of it, more so if you are a woman. More so when you are a Jew. Their hatred of us has changed over time, but only slowly."

I didn't ask if by "us" she meant hatred of witches, women, or Jews. Historically—and now—all three earned violence for the sheer act of living. We were scapegoated, murdered, and despised. Adding *draugr* to the list probably had changed very little for Beatrice—or for me.

"I don't like you," I pointed out. "But not because of any of those things."

"You dislike me because I am a *draugr*." Beatrice shrugged. "How is it different than hating me for the other things?"

"I don't *hate* you," I stressed. "I just don't like anything that tries to bite me."

"I shall remember that next time I am called to save your life." Her voice held all the laughter she didn't show in her expression. "But I do doubt that Lauren would agree that you ought to hate me for such a thing."

Beatrice walked away, staring into the edge of her moat, and I was left with very few options. Did I apologize to my dead ancestor? Or did I simply acknowledge my bias?

I hated being an adult.

I released Eli's hand and followed her.

"I may have . . . issues with *draugr* because of my father." I stood beside her and stared at the alligator filled canal. There were a lot of gators there. "He wanted to, err, breed me to as many *draugr* as he could. Use me . . . whether or not I consented."

She nodded. "They attempted that with me several centuries ago. It was how I died."

Her voice was calm, but she let me see inside her mind. A human Beatrice. A captive Beatrice. A group of *draugr*. She fought them—and lost.

"I killed them slowly," she said, shrugging as if it was no significant feat. "When I regained my senses, I killed every one of them." She shrugged again. "And now I am queen."

I thought she was insanely fucking strong to turn her rage into power. Beatrice was old; the sort of old that meant my bones ached at the chill she radiated. When she died, dust and air would be all that remained of her, so her assault was longer ago than I could fathom. Her rage was still vibrant, and her pride at avenging herself was burning bright.

I met her eyes and said, "Fine. I like you some."

And she laughed, peals of joyous laughter as we stared at the alligators.

Then she leaned in and whispered, "The pigs were men once, granddaughter. I tolerate no man injuring me or what's mine." She glanced behind us to where Eli stood calmly watching the fire and us. Then Beatrice said, "He seems to care deeply for you. Fae blood is more nourishing, but if he hurts you . . . I will not forgive that. Had you not killed Darius, I would have. Once I discovered what he'd done, I was not pleased. I did not live here then. If I had . . ."

Just to be clear, I said, "You came here because of my mother."

"And you."

In a tone as close to Eli's calm as I could manage, I said, "Eli is mine, Beatrice. To hurt him is to enrage *me*." I touched her wrist. "Blood matters. I am grateful that you care for Mama Lauren, but . . . do not ever threaten my family or friends, or I will find a way to sever your head."

Beatrice kissed my forehead. "I am grateful to know you, granddaughter." Then she *flowed* toward her castle. Her voice drifted back, filling the courtyard in an echoing sound. "There will be a dinner to celebrate my granddaughter's betrothal to the crown price of *Elphame*. Hear and be welcome."

I shuddered at the realization that her magic was undoubtedly carrying that invitation to *draugr* in her queendom.

Eli looked at me and said, "This job of hers will complicate things, Geneviève."

And my few weeks of relative calm ended. I felt it as surely as a warning knell. I was engaged to the heir of *Elphame*'s throne, with whom I'd made a faery bargain, and now declared family to the queen of the *draugr*, for whom I was ferreting out a threat. The holidays were no longer simply about irritation over dresses and random witch-haters who shot at me.

"Probably," I admitted. "But complication is what we do. Nothing is ever simple."

I took his arm and walked through the passageway of Beatrice's castle. No one stopped us. No one did anything other than open doors and bow deeply. Now that Beatrice had made her little proclamation, all eyes were going to be watching us.

~ 5 ~

I N THE SPAN of one night, I'd agreed to a Yule Ball in *Elphame* and an "early Yule" party with the *draugr* queen.

Eli was silent as we drove back to the city, and I decided to simply wait to speak.

Finally, Eli parked alongside at a building in the Garden District that looked like it could have been one of the first in the city. A fence, stone not iron, that surrounded his house. The house was almost so plain as to be unnoticed—which required a lot of magic. There was neither balcony nor gallery, neither porch nor Ionic columns, just a nondescript house in a very expensive area.

His home.

When we were standing at the door, Eli bowed to me. "You are eternally welcome in my home, Genèvieve Crowe. I offer you my hearth and lintel. May you find shelter."

"That's some formal sounding stuff," I hedged. "I was here before and—"

"I cannot answer the questions you have right now." He

held out his hand. "You will have the answer on Twelfth Night."

"You're making me nervous." I didn't take his hand, and he didn't lower it. Whispers rose up from some knowledge older than the stone that protected this house or the magic that flowed in my veins. "What does it mean if I take your hand right now?"

"That you accept my protection, my shelter. That you willingly enter this house." Eli stood, waiting.

Some part of me thought he'd been waiting longer than I knew, longer than I wanted to know.

He stayed there, hand outstretched, and said, "Come into my home, and let me shelter you, love."

"Is this how you normally treat dates?" I tried for lighter tone, for avoiding this tension that was in the air like magic between us.

"I've never dated." Eli shrugged slightly: elegant and utterly telling all at once. It was often to avoid discussions—usually for my benefit. Tonight, that was not the case. He felt embarrassed or awkward.

My staring at him all agog probably didn't help matters.

"You will be the first," he added.

"*What?*"

"I've fucked. I've had sex. I've spent time clothed and naked with friends and acquaintances, but dating is only done with intent among the fae."

My mouth was drier than the desert. "Oh. . . *fuck*. What if we didn't—"

"You agreed to date me, Genèvieve. Are you reneging on a

bargain with one of the fae?"

No matter how much I'd thought I understood, once more, I was fucked by my own hubris. Every human in history who had made a bargain with a fae believed they were clever enough to outsmart the fae. That *never* happened. Ever. And yet, I'd tried it twice.

"So dating, to you, is a precursor to . . ."

"Matrimony."

I sputtered, "It's not what it is to me, Eli."

He smiled. "You are bound in promise to the fae, which means fae law applies to you. You've even agreed to a date for the end of our courtship."

I stepped away from him. "This is not how to seduce me, Eli."

"You have a month to find a way to end our courtship," he reminded me. "And I have a month to make you accept the inevitable. You said 'I agree to your terms, Eli. We will date.' So, I do believe, my Divinity, that you now must either date me or break our bargain."

"What happens if I break the bargain?"

"The king of *Elphame* would determine your fate, as he is chief in my familial line." Eli shrugged again. "So, I ask again, will you date me or do you break our bargain?"

"Fine." I took his hand.

He lifted me into his arms bridal style. The smile he gave me would probably incinerate knickers in at least a three-mile radius.

My voice was squeakier than it had ever been as I asked, "Eli?"

"You are eternally welcome in my home, Genèvieve Crowe. I offer you my hearth and lintel. May you find shelter." He stood under the keystone of the doorway. "In this world and my home, you are mine to safeguard."

I felt magic swirl around us, as if we were in center of a firestorm. Each spark of magic brushed against us with butterfly wings. Whatever vow he'd made was one my body accepted—loudly. Desire surged like lava in my veins, and a moan of need escaped my lips.

I wasn't sure I could stand if I tried.

Arms around his neck, I pressed my lips to his. I wasn't sure if it was magic or lust driving us, but I *flowed*, carrying us both into the house. I'd never moved a second person this way, but I did. In a heartbeat or three, we were inside, upstairs, and somehow entangled on the floor.

"Genèvieve." Eli pulled back and stared at me. His already bee-stung lips looked thoroughly kissed. "How did you . . .?"

"You're not the only magic creature here." I removed my shirt. It was too much of a barrier. "Please?"

He looked at me like he'd never seen my half-naked body. He'd stitched enough of me that I wasn't sure I had many secrets, but the way his gaze burned me up now, I thought I might be wrong.

Our gaze was only interrupted by the removal of his shirt.

"Rules?" he asked.

"Touch me."

He laughed, low and full of the same needs I was feeling. "That's a demand, Genèvieve, not a rule."

My hands were on his skin already. Muscle under silk.

Magic under flesh. I wanted all of it, all of him—but I wasn't going to end up married.

I kissed his chest, his shoulders, his throat.

"*Genèvieve,*" he said. "Rules?"

"No intercourse," I said between kisses. I couldn't call it fucking because it wouldn't be, and I couldn't call it making love because I was afraid to say that. If a faery made love, truly made love, to a person who reciprocated that love, they were wed. It was that simple. "No intercourse. No . . . I want to, but I won't end up accidentally wed."

He looked unsurprised by my demand, but disappointed.

I knew damn well that he wasn't going to remind me of that rule, but I wasn't going to forget it. There were other options.

"What do you want, Genèvieve?"

"Touch me. Kiss me." I stepped closer. "Please?"

Maybe it was the please, or maybe he simply understood me better than anyone else ever had. Eli took my hand and led me to a bedroom.

He leaned down and kissed me speechless. Then he ordered, "Stay right here. Strip. No jeans. No shoes. Nothing."

When he returned, I was naked. I don't know what I expected. Ravishing? Hurried grasping? I ought to have known better. Eli was fae—which meant he had the patience of nature.

In his hand, he had a bowl. "Turn onto your stomach, love."

I rolled over, and soon I felt the hot drizzle of oil. The room smelled of the clean nature of *Elphame*, so whatever oil it was, it was fae in origin.

At a word in his language, the room became completely dark.

I could see nothing. "Eli?"

"You asked for touch," he said, voice low and rough. "No intercourse. Merely touch."

I felt him place my hands along my sides, arrange my body as if I was clay in his hands. Then I felt him touch me. Slowly, steadily, hard, teasing, he rubbed and caressed *almost* everything in some fashion.

Time seemed to freeze. I could see nothing. The world was reduced to touch, scent, and sound. His murmured words, sighed, groaned as he explored my body. It didn't matter whether he was caressing sensitive spots or mundane. Under Eli's touch, everything was erotic. My feet, my calves, my hips. He was leaning his weight onto me, his forearms and muscular chest brushed my body as his rubbed along my spine.

And I realized he was atop me.

Straddling me.

Naked.

Eli was naked.

I felt the hard length of him nestled between my thighs. Unconsciously, I parted my legs further, and he leaned down so his chest was flat against my back and his lips were by my ear. "No intercourse, Genèvieve," he taunted.

Goddess help me, I whimpered. "We can't, but this is . . . nice."

"Nice?" he echoed. He was a voice and pleasure in the dark, and I was certain that no one had ever made me so desperate so quickly.

He thrust his hips against me, groaning. Not entering me, merely taunting me with what I was refusing.

"Still just nice?" he asked.

I moaned and admitted, "More than nice."

By the time he had me roll over, exposing my naked chest and hips to his touch, I was wishing I could find a loophole in the no intercourse clause.

He parted my legs further. "Shall I be thorough, Genèvieve?"

"Please. *Please.*"

His hands danced between my legs, but only for a moment, sliding along my most delicate skin, and then they were gone. In the dark, he plucked my nipples, massaging my thighs, my belly.

I could only feel and beg. "More, Eli. Please. *More.*"

In that moment if he'd asked me again, I'm not sure I'd have refused intercourse. Damn the consequences, I was shaking in need. Maybe he knew that, and it was why he didn't ask.

Instead he asked, "Is it so horrible to date me, bonbon?"

"No." I took several breaths. "Not horrible."

He was quiet, breathing as needy as mine. I heard the strain in his voice as he asked, "Would you still only like touch or would you like a kiss? Or more?"

I knew what would happen if I agreed to *more*, and as much as I wanted his mouth on my body, I wanted to *see* him when we burned that bridge. So, I reached out into the darkness and trailed my hand over his hip. The oil from where his naked body had been against mine made my hand glide over skin and muscle.

"Touch," I asked, demanded, begged.

"Yes."

So, I stroked him as he touched me. We were nothing but hands and skin and moans in the darkness. I wanted more, but I wasn't sure I could endure it.

~ 6 ~

I'D SLIPPED OUT of Eli's house in the night. I slid away from his embrace and fled. He said I was to be myself, and well, my self wasn't great at the softer side of dating. My world was tilted by the intimacy we'd shared—and in my usual way, I ran from emotions.

Honestly, sometimes I felt sorry for anyone who tried to date me.

I liked Eli more than I'd cared for anyone, and I suspected most of our conflicts boiled down to my innate panic at feeling tender things in his direction. Some girls had pretend-weddings as children, fantasies of gowns as teens, and thought about the future as young women. Me? I thought about monsters. I dreamed of swords or trips. I fantasized about the sort of sex that made grown men blush.

The odds of finding anyone who found my messed-up brain and monster-tainted body appealing were so thin that I never really expected to deal with it. I'd always been the person that nice boys and girls took for a spin before settling down. I was the mid-life crisis car, the thrill-ride, and not the sort anyone wanted to marry. I chose that. I highlighted my traits that kept me firmly in the "makes a great mistress, not a wife" box.

So, I was not prepared to wake up the next evening to a gift-wrapped faery-wrought dagger and antique bottle of the same oil Eli had rubbed all over me. I sniffed the bottle and couldn't help but smile.

The post also delivered a piece of parchment with elegantly written instructions for a "celebratory holiday gathering" hosted by the dead-chick-in-charge of the *draugr*. The dinner at Beatrice's castle was later that week.

No rest for the dead, or half-dead, I supposed.

BY THE TIME the gala rolled around, I'd procured a total of three dresses, contacted my mother to tell her that I'd be bringing an extra guest the next week for our holiday dinner, and managed to not feel completely overwhelmed by my fiancé.

The latter took a lot of effort. Eli sent gifts each day: a brooch, a poison ring and pendant set, a scarf with a beautiful wire embroidery that was perfect to garrote someone. When he saw me—a brief moment here or there—he bent me into a dip and kissed me, or he pulled me into a hallway and pulled me tightly to his always aroused body.

Every embrace he whispered, "No intercourse?"

My resolve was not . . . weakening. I would not be married

because my needs were spiking so intensely. I was stronger than that.

By the time the night of the gala was upon us, I was ready to torment him until he was as maddened with need as I had become. I chose not one of the reasonable holiday dresses I'd planned, but an ivy column gown. My throat was covered by a high collar, and my arms were bare. The back had a teardrop cut-out, the bottom of which was scandalously low. The left slit exposed a long thin dagger—Eli's gift—strapped onto my thigh.

If I stood perfectly still, I was as covered as a matron. Only my arms were bared. If I walked or turned my back to him, bare flesh and weapons glinted at him. And if the light was bright, most of the dress was nearly translucent.

Eli met me at my home—and the light was, indeed, bright enough that his eyes dilated in desire. "You are radiant, Ms. Crowe."

I twirled, and yes, I'd practiced to get that twirl just right. My leg with the dagger practically winked at him, and the hair pins that he'd gifted me that day were holding my tumble of blue hair in place. Tiny little sheathed throwing knives with jewels at the top held my masses of hair in an elegant up-do that had taken Sera and I an hour to create. The effect was, mostly, to expose my back, but it also let me wear his gifts.

"Winter at her finest looks less lovely than you," Eli said, voice nearing reverence.

In fairness, my escort was gorgeous. Eli had elected to dress to his heritage. No glamour. No mortal attire. He was wearing leggings that made clear that his legs were all muscle, tunic, vest, and a circlet crown. The most unusual item was a codpiece that matched the crown. Although the codpiece was barely visible under the tunic, the glint of jewels made it challenging not to look.

"You test my resolve," I admitted.

"I *do* try, Geneviève." He looked me over. "Your loveliness and strength would shame the queens that came before you."

There was no reply that seemed suitable, so I brushed my lips over his gently and prompted, "Shall we?"

ARRIVING AT THE castle again was different. Everything felt different, tonight. This would be our first official outing as an engaged couple. A couple. The mere thought made my stomach twist in anxiety.

"You have been busy," I said as we parked.

Eli met my gaze. "I wanted to show you that I have no need to take up *all* of your time, peach pie." He offered me his arm, and we approached the massive doors. "Being with me will not consume your freedom."

I nodded.

"It's not you," I reminded him. "Any woman would be lucky to be chosen by you."

He stilled briefly, not quite bringing us to a stumbling halt, but slowing us. "I would remind you that we have a bargain, Geneviève Crowe."

I winced.

"You are not to be thinking of the future." He began to

walk, and I stayed in step—even when he added, "If I have not satisfied you with my touch or my gifts, you will tell me, so I might correct my errors."

I blushed despite myself. "You have not failed to satisfy me."

"You left without word. One might find that worrisome," he said lightly.

I laughed. "It was that or fear that I'd fail in my own resolve. You are a very thorough lover. Already. Even with . . . not . . ."

The look he gave me was enough to make me well aware of my lack of knickers.

"You are remarkable as well, Geneviève."

Then we reached the door and followed Eleanor to a ballroom, where we were swept into Beatrice's soiree. Her attention was drawn to us as if she could sense our arrival. Perhaps, however, that was the ripple of whispers that carried through the ballroom.

I let Eli handle the speaking and mingling. I followed his lead as we danced. I meekly stayed at his side to enjoy hors d'oeuvres—and I slid in and out of the minds of the well-dressed corpses walking around the ballroom. Only about fifty people were present, so the search and scan wasn't terrible. I was as uncomfortable as a lamb invited to the side door of a restaurant.

"You are a wolf," Beatrice said, her voice a reminder that she could read me, too.

I didn't flip her off, but I thought the visual at her and felt her answering laughter.

"Hunt our enemies for me, wolf."

I hated to admit it, but I was mollified by her faith.

As I let my magic roll out, sliding in and over the cacophony of voices, I thought that this was not that dissimilar to reading the dead in the graveyard. I'd expected minds like the *draugr* I usually encountered. They were nothing but feral needs.

Unlike the disjointed minds of the newly walking, however, these were orderly minds. Pretentious. Bored. Judgmental. There were thoughts of hunger, but it was more often hunger for power. These were not the *draugr* who would be found on the streets of the city. They struck me as the sort who had chefs or delivery or whatever service posh dead folk used for their food.

"I would drink her dry."

"Why do we need to allow his sort here?"

"Vintage fae juice. What a lovely pet he'd make."

"Stupid bitch."

"When Guarin was in charge, we weren't so burdened by rules."

The last one was the first that felt angry in ways that were alarming. I reached out with my magic until I found the speaker. He was tall, and from the look of him, he'd died before reaching full maturity. His face was soft, and he lacked the tell-tale texture of facial hair. He was trying to compensate for his physical appearance of youth with austere dress. His only concession to holiday frivolity was an ostentatious medallion-broach-thingy. A ruby as big as my thumb-nail was surrounded by emeralds.

"Thou shalt not suffer a witch." He glanced at Beatrice, at

me, and then he started toward me.

"Harold," Beatrice said, *flowing* to my side as if she had intended to be there all along. She stood in front of me. Her assistant, servant, whatever-she-was Eleanor arrived with two more women.

The room felt charged, and the thoughts were weirdly gleeful.

"How charming!"

"Entertainment!"

"Is it vulgar to accidentally cut the faery for a sip of blood?"

I glared at that one, a rather regal looking woman who had been grandmotherly upon death, and growled. "Mine."

"Witch." Harold tried to push passed Beatrice. "We have no use for witches."

Simultaneously, Beatrice said, "Back up."

Harold drew a respectable-sized blade and tried for Beatrice's throat. Her guards were there, but I was literally inches from her, so I pulled her backward to safety.

Harold's knife sliced my arm from shoulder to near my elbow.

"Witches have no right—"

"Duck fucking weasel." I kicked Harold and snatched his machete. "I'm getting sick of hearing that nonsense."

It was too much of a coincidence to ignore. Harold was somehow tied to Weasel Nuts shooting at me. I pushed that thought at Beatrice, who transformed from elegant to feral in less time that it took to blink.

"Take her out of here," Beatrice said.

Eli had my hand, but we were jerked apart as Eleanor

moved me further away from Harold. Then in a little more than a heartbeat, Eli and I were both outside.

"You are a gift," Eleanor said. "Her Majesty will dispatch with the vermin."

Then she was gone, and I was swaying precariously over ground that was filled with bodies, outside a castle where there were ancient *draugr* I very much didn't want to adopt.

~ 7 ~

I F I WASN'T mistaken, there was a poinsettia petal in my cleavage. It was hard to tell because I was losing blood faster than the average tourist losing their dinner after midnight. It could have been blood, but I thought it was a petal.

Admittedly, it was a toss-up between bleeding and vomiting on my "things I dislike" list, but in this particular moment, I was thinking I'd have preferred puking.

"Are you well enough to stand?" Eli was at my side, looking more warrior than prince. He looked fierce, even as he stepped over the already-rotting corpse.

"I'm good." I nodded. I was standing. Well, I was leaning on a cooperative oak tree outside Beatrice's castle, but that was *like* standing.

"How bad?"

"I'm upright." I shrugged, clutching my new blade as if I'd be any use against the sort of *draugr* inside the castle.

"I want you to get me inside the car before my blood spills

onto the ground."

So far, I'd held my arm so the gash was angled upward, so nothing had dripped to the soil.

Yet.

"I give it about ninety seconds." I shoved off the oak's trunk.

Eli scooped me up and all but ran to open the passenger door on his little blue convertible. I was ready to leave, not argue with whatever Thom, Rick, or Marie I summoned if I bled on soil.

Inside the safety of the car, Eli said, "Lower your arm, cupcake."

"Can't. I'll ruin the seats." Blood wasn't great for Eli's butter-soft leather seats. They weren't going to come to life, but I still had no desire to bleed on them.

If my magic wasn't fucked sideways lately, I wouldn't be bleeding. Trying to avoid the *draugr* meant I'd been careless. My temper was lousy.

"Least I got a new toy." I patted the machete in my lap. "And Beatrice owes me."

"You could have died."

I don't know if I replied. I was sleepy, the sort of sleepy that only seemed to come with massive blood loss. I closed my eyes for just a moment, but somehow my moment was almost an hour.

When I opened my eyes, Eli was driving through the city with the sort of speed that came of fae reflexes and arrogance. I was in far more danger from my average week than his driving though, so I just let myself relax as much as could.

When he scraped the undercarriage to park directly in front of the door, blocking the side walk, I didn't argue.

And I didn't argue when he half lifted me out of the car. All I knew was that we were on the sidewalk and then inside. No blood on the soil. No dead summoned to me. That was a victory.

Machete loosely in my hand, I leaned against the building while Eli rolled up the steel doors that protected the building. Mostly it was for thieves, but sometimes the newly-dead were apt to crawl into a person's home. No one liked that. Finding out that a biter was watching you was creepy. Hell, dead or not, it was creepy. I like some weird, but stalkers are another thing entirely.

My eyes were drifting closed with all these thoughts of sleep.

"Plum pudding?" Eli's voice was falsely cheery.

So, I made a rude gesture.

"I'd prefer you be awake when we consummate our love," he said.

I opened my eyes. *"Our what?"*

Rather than answer, he opened the door and ushered me inside the bar. We were, obviously, late enough that the bar was closed, and for that I was grateful. Eli's bar staff was alternately tense and mothering with me. No one was outright unpleasant, but I think they worried that I was about to get their boss killed.

That was how I'd first ended up cozying up to him. No human was strong enough to fight again-walkers. Eli was. I was . . . and *that* was how I ended up here. Again. Tonight was to be a simple dinner, but somehow, I was bleeding.

"My pretty dress," I said.

Eli set the locks and rolled the steel. "You look gorgeous, buttercream, even with the blood. A warrior goddess."

I grabbed a bar towel. They were clean, bleached, and absorbent. It wasn't the worst bandage ever.

"Let me get the kit so I can st—"

"Absolutely not." I dropped the new blade on a table. Now that we were secure, I could be unarmed.

I wound the bar towel around my arm. I wouldn't wake anything here, but I'd still rather contain my blood.

We were alone in the bar. Just me, Eli, and my weapons. I glanced at my dagger. It needed wiped down, and with one arm holding my cotton bar towel on the other, I was in no shape to do it.

"My stitching is excellent," Eli said, as if he was insulted. For all I knew, he was.

"Did I say otherwise?" I walked behind the bar, putting the long expanse between us.

Eli stared at me, as if his fae bullshit was going to work. It wouldn't, although that smile of his was a sort of magic. "Geneviève Crowe, you are being unreasonable. Sit down and let me stitch—"

"Using my full name would only work if I was a faerie." I poured a drink for each of us. Shaky, but mostly in the glasses.

"Are we calling out species, delectable witch of mine?" His tone was falsely light—which meant I'd probably violated one of the eight hundred and thirty-seven rules of dealing with faeries.

Okay, admittedly, I didn't know how many rules there really were. I gave up counting somewhere around eighty. I tried, legitimately tried to have peace with Eli, but we had a complicated relationship.

"I'm not *really* yours," I muttered, stepped closer with both drinks in my working hand.

"You're dripping on the wood." He gestured to the floor.

When I looked down, he moved closer. It was the sort of speed neither of us usually used in front of the other. He hid his; I hid mine. We're complicated.

The blue-tint from humming bar lights that were still on even though the bar was closed cast an ethereal glow over him, highlighting his inhuman beauty. No human was as striking as even the least of the fae, and after our brief trip to *Elphame*, I discovered that no faery was as beautiful as Eli.

Not because he was fae.

Not because witches were susceptible to them or anything so convenient.

It was just Eli.

Or maybe I still had a lot of pent-up feelings in his general direction. Our one encounter that led to orgasms wasn't enough. Maybe we just had too much unresolved lust and it made him somehow *more* attractive—which, incidentally, was fucking horrifying because he was already stunning.

He took his drink, tossed it back, and waited for me to do the same.

"Just give it a minute," I said, peering at the gash on my arm.

"Why are you being difficult, Geneviève? Do I stitch you

poorly? Have I caused undue pain?" His hand was alongside my cheek, hovering in that sliver of space where if I sighed, he'd be touching me. "You are seeping blood."

"'s not *you*. I want to know how fas' I'll heal now. This is an oppur. . . *oppurtuney*."

He gave me an incredulous stare. "Not even *you* are this brash, love."

Silently, I removed the now scarlet-red cloth from my arm. The bleeding was slowing some. Congealing. That was new. As I watched the edges of the ten-inch cut on my upper arm were straining, as if they could touch.

It was, in truth, a bit horrible to see my skin seeming to reach out. It was, well, not what human flesh did, not what witches' skin did. This was a result of my paternal heritage. Creepy arm thing? Gift from doubly-dead dad.

He was dead when he fathered me, but his status was revised to permanently dead at my hand. But as any Southern-born person knows, the sins of the father don't end at death—even two deaths. I was a freak of nature, neither dead nor alive. And after an awkward attempted murder that didn't take, I was changing.

"Geneviève?"

I looked up.

"You have lost too much blood. You are drifting." Eli gestured at me, and I could see the spectral shape seeping out of my body, as if my shadow had taken on life.

"Well, that's no good." I realized I had slid down the wall right about when Eli caught me. Propped in his arms, I took a good long drink of the bottle of white liquor he held out.

Tequila.

Life was always better with tequila. Eli and I were better with tequila. Hell, everything was probably better with tequila. War? Famine? Plague?

"Fucking tequila heals everything."

"Of course, it does, plum pudding. One more," Eli urged, tilting the bottle for me as my hands were feeling less than grippy.

"Is grippy a word?"

Eli shook his head, but I wasn't sure if that was disapproval or disagreement with my choice of "grippy" as a word.

"I'm stitching that cut, Geneviève."

"Pro'lly good plan after all, muffin."

He laughed. "Muffin?"

"'s what you call me. Stupid pas'ry words." I closed my eyes.

"You like it," he whispered, kissing my forehead as he settled my head gently on the bar floor. "And you like me."

I did, of course, but I wasn't dazed enough to admit *that*.

~ 8 ~

WHEN WE WERE alone, I allowed myself to nestle into Eli's arms. It was the sort of thing that I ought to avoid, a vulnerability that I seemed only able to share with him. Sometimes, I felt like it was what I needed most in the world, though, a safe place to rest. I was stitched and had consumed two bottles of liquor. I wasn't feeling my best, but I was coherent again.

Eli held me so that my cheek was on his chest, and he stroked my hair. It was soothing to be held, to be safe, and to feel cherished.

"Dating you is more stressful than I expected," Eli murmured.

I looked up at him. "This is me. What I do. Who I am."

He sighed. "Geneviève, I *know* these things, but I had hoped that dating during your seasonal lull would include more romance and fewer stitches. Is it so much to ask for some time where we can dance and avoid bleeding?"

A flash of guilt rolled over me. "I wore a pretty dress for

you. Seductive, and wore gifts you bought to show my regard." I turned my head and kissed his chest. "We danced."

Eli looked at me so intently that I squirmed in embarrassment. "You read about fae customs. You wore my gifts because you *researched* my people."

"There *are* a lot of rules. I got one right, but I get a lot wrong."

"You *researched*," he repeated in a voice filled with wonder.

"Fine. Maybe I read everything I could find on fae rules over the last few years," I hedged. "I felt like I offended you often, and I just . . . you matter to me, Eli."

He held me in silence for several moments. "Enough to take no more jobs for the next three weeks?"

I thought about it. In terms of the things he asked of me over the last year, it was perhaps the easiest request so far. I nodded. "You have my word: no more jobs between Yule and Twelfth Night. We'll call it a witch bargain."

He chuckled. "Terms for this 'Witch Bargain'?"

"No talk of weddings."

"Done."

"Nothing that happens as a result of festivities is precedent-setting," I tried to sound calm, but Eli's slow smile said that he knew exactly what I was saying. Festivities often involved desserts, some of which left me as drunk as a human with a fifth of whisky.

"Of course, my crème brûlée." His voice sent welcome shivers over me. "I cannot change the law of intercourse for my people, but . . . I can touch you as often as you allow."

If I wasn't fighting to keep my eyes open, I'd be ready for

that. The combination of blood loss and daylight wasn't doing great things for me. I was drifting in and out of sleep until evening came. Eli was asleep finally, so when I woke, I started to slip out of bed.

Eli, half-asleep, caught my hand. "If you need space, stay here in the guest room. I'll go to my room."

I paused. "I'm feeling better now. I could go h—"

"I want you here, Geneviève." Eli met my gaze. "Will you stay with me?"

The way he said it didn't feel like he meant just for the night, but that was all I could offer in the moment. No sharing a lover's bed. No letting them stay in mine. It was frightening to stay, but I trusted Eli with my life regularly. Surely, I could trust him with my heart for a few weeks, too.

I crawled closer to him and nestled against his side.

"So, dating you involves sleep-overs?" I asked, voice as light as I could manage.

"I'd like it to," Eli said. "I know it's not your preference, but let me have today."

"And tomorrow?" I asked.

Eli knew me well, which he proved by adding, "This is a guest bed, Geneviève. It's not *my* bed. You are simply staying in my guest room. Say the word, and I'll go to my bed. Alone."

Maybe that wasn't romantic for most people, but it made me want to swoon. Instead I kissed him. "I'll stay."

"I'll get you breakfast," he said.

Within moments, Eli held out a steaming coffee cup of vodka with a dash of grenadine and a couple cherries. Liquor was magical with my biology. Bring on the booze. It was a key part of what kept my biologically-irrational body running.

"You're smarter than anyone that attractive ought to be," I grumbled as I reached for the mug.

Eli laughed and helped me sit up. "A little fruit for the pain?"

"Yes." I reached out further, but we could both see my arm shake. Fruit, unlike liquor, made me tipsy, but after my failed experiment, I could stand a little tipsy in my—. . . I glanced at the wall clock.

He steadied the cup as I wrapped my hands around it and drank.

"Do you know how worried I was, Geneviève?" Eli asked, voice heavy. Worse yet, he was using my real name instead of whatever pastry or dessert he chose to use as a term of endearment.

I'd rather be called food stuffs than my name—especially when it sounded so ominous. "I suggested I go out without you, so—"

"Endangering yourself alone is no better." Eli walked away. He sounded increasingly calm as he added, "Beatrice sent word while you were recovering. Harold has ceased."

"Ceased?"

"Existing," Eli clarified. "She also sent a suggestion."

"A suggestion?"

"For an elixir that might aid your recovery," he said evasively. "I procured the supplies."

Then he left, and I was too damn weak to pursue him. Honestly, I hadn't intended to let some dead guy practice his subpar threshing skills on me. I hadn't meant to get injured, but was it so bad that I took advantage of my bad luck to see if my healing had changed since my semi-murder earlier that year?

It really *wasn't* my worst idea the last year.

"Eli?" I started, but it wasn't Eli in the doorway this time.

Alice Chaddock stood there. "Good morning, grumpy!"

"Alice, why are you h—"

"Oh you poor thing!" She leaned down to fluff my pillows, giving me an awkward up-close look at her cleavage. "You look even worse than normal."

"Thanks."

"I *felt* that you needed me," she continued in her cheery breathy voice. "I'm sure of it."

"Alice, you're *human*."

"We bonded, though. Witch thing." She waved her hand around.

I didn't think I could bond humans, but I'd accidentally bonded two *draugr* to me. Honestly, I really had no idea if bonding a regular human was possible, but on the off chance that Alice was my responsibility, I kept her around.

That, and the queen of the *draugr* was likely to kill her if I didn't, and I'd feel guilty. I hate feeling guilty.

"Fine. You are the best servant ever." I grinned up at Alice.

She rolled her eyes at the thought of being a servant. Alice could probably buy the whole block my building was on—and not dent her bank account too much.

"Now, *go away*," I muttered.

Alice laughed. She was growing on me, although last week she'd tried to be helpful and used steel wool on one of my knives. I'd explained that I liked the guy who sold me my last sword more than her. I certainly liked my actual friends better, but Alice waved all of those facts away.

"I'm going to do your face." She opened her bag, designer and expensive, and started pulling out her torture devices. "I was afraid you'd look terrible for the party."

"The party was last night," I admitted. Then I closed my eyes, pretended not to be able to think of all the ways my life could be better if I simply stabbed Alice. She took more energy than anyone had a right to do, but my choices were either kill her or keep an eye on her.

Only one of those was *actually* an option.

"I don't understand what Eli sees in you," Alice said, staring at me as if I had become a math problem she might could solve. "Let's at least get some eyeliner and rouge—"

"Alice, I was injured. I lost a lot of blood and—"

"That's why you look so pale!" She thrust her wrist between my lips, scraped the skin on my teeth. "Here. Top off."

I shoved her away, hard enough that she stumbled, even as my teeth descended to bite. "Stop that. I don't need the taste of your perfume in my mouth."

My so-called best friend pouted. Perfectly outlined, perfectly painted, smudge free lips jutted out like a child denied a treat.

"I'd be sad if you died, you know?" Alice flopped onto the bed beside my feet. "Tres gets impatient with me. And Beatrice is scary. And"—she darted a guilty look toward the doorway—"I don't think Eli even *likes* me."

"You belonged to a hate group opposed to *him*," I pointed

out once my teeth retracted. "And you tried to kill me. He likes me."

"I said I was sorry!" Alice sounded genuinely upset. "And no one told me SAFARI was a hate group."

"It's called the Society Against Fae and Reanimated Individuals. That wasn't a clue?"

Alice patted my feet through the duvet. "I wasn't enlightened then. I am now. . . but Eli is still so grumpy with me. I like you, now."

"Alice, honey," I said, keeping my voice very level. "You tried to kill me just a few months ago. To a faery, that was yesterday."

She stared, blinked, and finally whispered, "He *time* travels?"

I opened my mouth, and then I closed it without saying a word. What was there to say? If she wasn't really as gullible as she appeared, this was the longest con ever. Her stepson, Tres, swore she'd been exactly the same since they were in school together.

Yeah. She went to the same college with him and then married his dad. Of course, my own parents were a special sort of wrong, too. My deadbeat dad wasn't even alive, much less anywhere within range of my mother's age, when I was conceived.

Alice wandered away while I was thinking. Honestly, I wasn't recovered enough to deal with her. I could hear her, presumably washing her wrist from the sounds of the bathroom sink.

"She's willing to help you," Eli said when he walked in. "I

had her delivered here—"

"She's not a take-out meal."

He leaned in the doorway, giving me enough space that I figured I must be looking less like death. He was polite when I was healing, pushy when I was well or bleeding.

"Do we even know that blood would help?" I tried to stand, not quite pushing to my feet but sitting upright and swinging my feet to the floor. I was preparing.

Eli came to my side as I stood, not infantilizing me but near enough to catch me when I tumbled—which I would've if he wasn't there. He'd swept me into his arms, cradling me for a moment. "You are the least obedient patient I've met, Geneviève."

"I waited for you before trying to stand." I rested my head on his shoulder.

He said nothing, and we stayed there listening to singing from elsewhere in the house. Eli and I exchanged a surprised look. It was the sort of voice that should be immortalized, twangy enough to burn up country music charts and soulful enough to make sinners repent.

"That's *Alice?*"

"I had no idea."

We stayed there, listening. Perhaps it sounded a little better because the acoustics were so phenomenal here, but either way, she could sing. I enjoyed it. Eli obviously did, too. He began to waltz, as if we were at a ball.

"Can we *not* experiment on you? And can we avoid death, excessive bleeding, or dismemberment until the new year?"

"Yes . . . ?"

Eli smiled and added, "And what if we just put a little of Alice's blood in a martini? Beatrice suggested that it might aid your health."

I scowled at him. "Fine."

"Alice?" Eli called. "Could you bring Ms. Crowe's breakfast?"

A moment later, she came into the bedroom with a beautiful glass of pink vodka. There was a lemon twist and cherry. I guessed the cherry was to hide the real source of the pink. Alice was as clever as she was bouncy.

In a chipper tone, she announced, "I made it myself!"

I held out a hand. I knew that the pink tint to my martini was a result of additives she took from her vein.

Truth be told, I'd considered trying blood, but it felt wrong. I had moral qualms about drinking from anyone, and I was fairly sure I shouldn't have to do so. I'd existed for most of my twenty-nine years with a mix of vodka, green smoothies, and assorted herbs. Never sick. Rarely tired. Since the venom injections, I was always tired, and no amount of liquor made me feel satisfied.

I took a tentative sip of my blood-tini. "This tastes different."

Alice looked at Eli. "I made it *just* the way he said to."

"Hmmm." I drank half of it. "It's good. Spicy, though."

She folded her arms and looked at Eli before blurting, "That's the blood. He made me. I wasn't going to lie, but—"

"Okay." I drank the rest.

Eli rolled his eyes at me, and Alice stared at me in surprise. It was sweet that her loyalty to me made her unable to lie.

Honestly, it didn't have much taste. Vodka. Touch of spice. My blood martini was surprisingly unexciting, despite the anxiety that I'd felt even considering it. The reality was far less exciting than my fears, and I felt like my stress was washing away—or maybe that was my hunger fading.

I wanted to be normal, whatever *that* was. I wouldn't ever be human, so *my* normal was a little different. I didn't mind the witch part, mostly didn't even mind necromancy. I minded my paternal DNA. A lot. I was terrified of being a *draugr*. I grew up as the equivalent of a rose garden to every bee in range—but instead of bees, I attracted the dead. They were drawn to me, and I responded as well as anyone would when dead things popped up everywhere.

I killed them.

What did it mean if I was *like* them? If my genetic soup was more dead than witch? Necromancy worked by pressing life into the dead, and apparently, it worked on *draugr*, too. I shoved life into them, and suddenly, they functioned as if they were a century old. Coherent. No longer slavering toddlers. What would happen if I was changing? Would I be unable to kill them? Would I be unable to heal? To summon the natural dead? Maybe it wasn't that I wanted normal. Maybe I wanted to control who I was, what I was. Define myself.

"How do you feel?" Eli took the glass, unfolding my fingers from the stem, and I realized I'd licked up the last drops of my blood martini.

"Embarrassed." I paused. "Better though. Energized."

Alice tossed herself at me. "You do need me! I knew it. Like it's our *destiny!*"

"I . . . umm . . ."

She straightened up. "It has to be fresh, but I'll be *right here* whenever you need me."

It had to be fresh? That was news, and not the good sort. Questions popped around like manic bunnies in my brain. How fresh? How often? How much? Was it all the same? Should we test the theory?

But Alice was already gone, and I doubted she had the answers I needed. I glanced at Eli.

"We'll figure it out," he said, undoubtedly seeing my worries and questions. Obviously, the answers weren't ones he knew or he'd tell me.

I swallowed my panic and nodded. One crisis at a time.

When Alice returned, she had a cocktail shaker in her hand. "I made more. Just in case."

Eli held out my glass, and Alice filled it. "I'll mix up another batch before I go."

She gave me a little finger wave like she was in a parade, and then she was gone again.

"Hey, Alice?" I called after her. "I like your singing."

Her squeal, presumably a happy noise, was all the answer I got. Okay, maybe she *was* growing on me. The whole attempted murder thing was still a factor, but she was so damnably cheerful that I couldn't entirely resist.

"We're friends, aren't we? Alice and I are friends," I whispered to Eli. "I . . . *like* Alice."

"You were too hungry to think clearly," he offered. "Like a duckling imprinting on a food provider . . ."

Alice's voice rang out, louder this time, as she presumably

was mixing up another batch of blood and vodka for me. She was singing an old blues song, again managing to make it sound like it ought to be on a stage.

"I'm doomed if she keeps feeding me *and* singing."

Eli laughed. "Drink up, butter cream. You sound more like yourself already."

I hated how right he was, but I felt alert. I felt focused. Alice had just rescued me.

Although Eli didn't point out that I'd been off since my attempted-murder, we both knew it. And it wasn't just the appearance of fangs now and then or the weird energy. My necromancy had been erratic before I was injected with *draugr* venom. Since then, it was all over. Some days, my blood was calm. Other days, I could feel it thrumming inside me like war drums. I could summon anything. I felt sure of it.

But energy required balance. Magic always had a cost. And I wasn't sure what the fee was—or if I was ready to pay it.

~ *9* ~

B Y EVENING, I was feeling more alive than I had since my attempted murder in the fall. I vacillated between thinking that there was something energizing about blood and that my heritage had finally caught up with me. Either way, my cocktail hours throughout the day were revitalizing.

By the end of the week, though, blood martinis, murdering "best" friends, and machete-wielding dead men were the least of my troubles. I'd started to suspect that without regular blood I was going to flag. Eli and I set out to see Mama Lauren, closely followed by Jesse, Christy, Sera, and for reasons I'd never admit, Alice. Chanukah wasn't a *major* holiday for Jews, not a high holy day despite the fact that it was one of the only ones Christians knew we had. Still, my mother was keen on any excuse to cook for my friends.

It was a topic we rarely addressed, but my peculiar diet was a challenge for her. I was fairly liquid based, and the few solid things I ate were a choice not a need. Honestly, it was a testament to her cleverness that she discovered that I needed alcohol of all things. To her, I was a hummingbird, existing on some sort of water with additives.

Technically, we were there for the holiday, lighting a candle and sharing prayers and food, but in truth, I also needed maternal insight on what was wrong with me. She could tell. She had always been able to tell what I needed, as far as I knew, so if anyone in the world had answers, it would be Mama Lauren.

In some ways, driving into the Outs for this was not that different than driving to see Beatrice. The primary distinction was that I rarely had the chance to do this of late.

The Outs were dangerous for me in a way that they weren't for most people. I was tempting to the dead, and my childhood included waking too often to desperate monsters trying to peel off the rolldowns.

Mama Lauren coped, but she always just shrugged and asked what else was she to do? The sort of people who lived here were peculiar. The cities were where folks clustered, and the immediate space outside that—the ghost zones—were where *draugr* gathered. The Outs were their own thing. No utility services. No sheriff. No law. A special sort of madness drew folks to live out in nature.

Your energy was via solar or wind power, and your liquids were well water, septic, and leach fields. Law? Well, that was a combination of firepower and the judicious use of roll-downs for every window, door, chicken coop, and greenhouse on her farm. In the Outs, you didn't go outside once the sun set— which made the sunset candle lighting a challenge.

We'd always made do. Our "sunset" was noon for the

purposes of holidays with friends. The alternative was staying over, and that was complicated sometimes with the way I beckoned to dead things. Mama Lauren could cope, but I didn't want my friends to wake up to *draugr* clawing at the walls to get in.

We crawled down the pitted lane, and Eli's steering managed to avoid pits that seemed likely to swallow his car whole. Maybe it was nerves, but I wasn't feeling like talking. I clung to the "oh shit" handle on the door as we bounced along.

Mama Lauren was expecting me, so she stood outside watching for us. Her hair was starting to gray, and she'd pulled it back into a long braid for a change. It was almost always tied up in a knot, but today it was bound in a braid that reached past her hips. My tresses might be blue-dyed, but the thick coils were obviously from her genes.

She had on her usual tall boots, dress, and a pair of pistols holstered at her hips. Today an apron covered the dress. Her hand rested on the butt of one of those guns until she saw me step out of Eli's car.

I *flowed* toward her before anyone else was out of the cars.

"Eli's here," I said. "Alice, too. Please, don't hex either of them."

Mama Lauren laughed and swept me into a hug that reminded me that she was strong for her age. Honestly, she was strong for *my* age. "You worry too much, bubeleh."

Then she was off to greet my friends. "No Yule log, my darlings! I do have the menorah in the window, but..." I tuned her out and watched Eli.

I think she enjoyed the confusion her mix of Yiddish, Hebrew, and pagan terms caused a lot of people, but honestly, none of my friends blinked at it today. I'm not sure they ever did.

I wondered, though, what Eli would think.

He waited until everyone had greeted her, and then he bowed so deeply you'd think she was royalty. "It is my honor to meet you. I am not nor will I be worthy of the gift that is your daughter's attention."

"True." Mama Lauren nodded at him. "Not even a prince is worthy of Geneviève. She says you are helpful, though."

Jesse snorted in laughter.

"I do attempt to be of use," Eli said with not a hint of laughter in his voice.

Then, my mother patted his cheeks. "That's all any of us can do." She looked over at Jesse and swatted him. "You! You haven't visited your family."

"Yes, Mama Lauren," he said, laughter vanishing. Jesse had been my childhood bestie, so he was well aware of my mother's temper—and her stinging hexes.

But then my mother looked down at Jesse's hand, holding on to Christy's. "At least you figured that out."

She shooed us into the house, where she'd set a table that no city restaurant could match. That was the not-so-secret truth of life in the Outs: there were things aplenty that might kill you, but there were also benefits. For someone so bound to the soil, someone who grew her own food and herbs, there was no contest.

Later, when I had fewer witnesses I'd ask my mother about the blood. For now, I simply asked for a "pick-me-up" and downed whatever concoctions she handed me during our visit. I wasn't typically this compliant, but I wasn't ready for my mother or friends to discover how much I needed the blood martinis that Alice made me.

And Alice was, for all her cheery remarks, looking tired. So, I was without my martinis for a few days. Maybe I lied to her that I was fine, but I wasn't going to leech away her energy when she was clearly donating too much.

We all tucked into our odd version of a holiday, knowing that I would much rather stay for several days, and no one remarked on the way that Sera and Christy both kept track of the time. Holiday or not, the *draugr* would come if I was out here after hours—and after my run-in with Harold, I'd really rather have a *draugr* free event.

~ 10 ~

SOMETIMES I THOUGHT that every single time I believed things might go well, there ought to be a laugh track in my life to remind me that was never the case. I'd been shot at for being a witch, had my arm flayed open by a pissy *draugr*, discovered a need for blood, and accidentally entered a courtship that was supposed to result in marriage in a matter of weeks.

I might have managed to avoid the conversation, and loudly argued that we weren't actually getting married, but fae customs were better understood as laws than traditions.

The only thing that had gone well was introducing Eli to my mother. Our trip to the Outs was good, and it drew me closer to him.

Okay and dating Eli as a whole. That was going really well.

And so was my resolve at the not-having-intercourse with Eli. Honestly I tried not to think about it, but Eli was as damnably perfect for me. I felt treasured, but also satisfied. It was enough to make a rational woman beg to marry him. A lifetime of that? *Yes, please.*

Unfortunately for both of us, I like Eli far too much to marry him.

I spent a few hours resisting the urge to see him, but I failed over and over—which is why I was sitting at the bar watching Christy free a tourist of the burden of his bank roll. Honestly, if he hadn't been flashing it around, she would've gone easy on him, but flash a thick roll of twenties, and someone will have it by the end of the night. At least Christy's method wouldn't involve bloodshed.

When I received a festively-decorated package that was delivered to the bar on ice, I had the good sense to carry it into the back room. Maybe it was fine. Maybe it was edible. But it was delivered by a *draugr*.

When I saw that it was from Beatrice, I had my doubts that anything good would come of it.

"Butterdrop?" Eli asked.

"*Draugr* delivery."

We closed the door and exchanged a look. I held up an envelope. That was easier to make sense of: cash. Beatrice paid me well for my services. I set it aside. I knew it was more than I'd charge, but I wasn't too proud to accept it. No one else could do the things I did. Sometimes people who realized that paid extra—which meant that when they needed me again, I'd make time for them.

I plopped the silver foil-wrapped box on the counter and untied the bold blue ribbons. "Maybe it's a toaster or pressure cooker? Rare liquor?"

Eli gave me a look. "And maybe you'll take up macramé."

"It could happen. I have hidden depths." I loosened the lid, not quite ready to face the contents. Nothing involving Beatrice was ever simple.

"You're stalling." Eli pointed at the box on the wooden table beside us. It looked festive, and whatever it was, I doubted that it would explode or injure us.

Tentatively, I opened the box. To exactly no one's surprise, there was no pressure cooker, salad bowls, or even macramé supplies. There, surrounded by ice packs, was the head of Weasel Nuts, the man who'd shot at me at the Cormier job. On top of his severed head, jabbed into the meat of his forehead, was Harold's ornate broach.

"There's a letter." Eli unfolded the paper that had been in the envelope and read: "'Hunters ought to be rewarded. Harold employed miscreants to discover your abilities. This human expired before sharing further knowledge.'"

"Is it me or are there a lot more brushes with death lately?"

"It is far more frequent than I'd like." Eli tucked the cash and letter in a pocket.

We'd long ago realized that I'd misplaced far too many things for me to be the one handling deposits. Eli, along with being my partner in the field, had begun to handle my accounting. I trusted him more than myself on this.

"Do you know what to *do* with that?" I nodded at the garish jewels jabbed in Weasel Nuts' forehead.

"Sell or store it." Eli shrugged. "Antique, obviously."

I wasn't squeamish often, but unpinning the broach from the dead man's head was not terribly appealing. I put the lid back on it for now.

"I have a woman who handles gems. I brought a cache with me when I moved here," Eli said in that uniquely Eli way that was somehow downplaying his connections and wealth. "They covered the bills of a life here—until I established the tavern—and then I sell one now and again."

He looked at me and stressed, "Bonbon, I would suspect the ruby alone will be between six and thirty thousand, simply due to size and clarity."

I swallowed. Who in their right mind wore jewels like that? And who pinned them to the head of dead men?

Obviously, Beatrice was not wanting for funds, but her proclamation of familial ties was said so carelessly. I was starting to think my dear, dead, many-times-great-gran truly liked me. It was, in truth, a bit disconcerting.

I shuddered. "Do whatever you think best with it."

"Shall I dispose of . . . the contents as well?"

"I have no use for the head of Weasel Nuts, and re-gifting that would probably lead to awkward questions." I shoved the box slightly toward him.

"You never bore me, my dear plum pudding. For someone with eternity ahead, that is a treasure."

I THOUGHT MORE than a little about Eternity as I prepared for the trip to *Elphame*. Unlike my visits to Beatrice or my mother, this trip was a multi-day affair. Oddly, perhaps, time between the worlds was uneven. My first stay there had been a month, but in New Orleans a mere three hours passed.

Going there did not mean I missed anything at home. My city was not left unpatrolled, and it wasn't as if the police did nothing. New Orleans had reconfigured their entire force. They protected the city, watched for the *draugr* and aided the citizens.

Still I was, for reasons that I was not pleased to admit, anxious.

Witches from the Outs were not a good fit for royal courts. I mean, sure I coped with the *draugr* queen's soiree but that was because I figured I'd get to threaten or stab someone. Eli repeatedly stressed that neither of those were advisable at the Yule celebration with his uncle, the king of the fae.

Tonight, though, Eli and I were having a "date-night." A few hours locked away in my home, surrounded by fight dummies and weapons. It wasn't as romantic as his place, but it was my home. It was important to both of us that we spend time here, too.

I wasn't the world's best date, though, much to my frustration. My nerves were frayed, and it was making me filter-free. "What if I glare at him? Is that—"

"A terrible idea?" Eli said. "Yes, it is."

"Can I hex him?"

"No."

"Make a bargain?"

"No!" Eli gave me a look that everyone in my life did from time to time. It usually meant I was a lousy patient, but . . .

"I'm *hungry*." I was both pleased to realize why I felt surlier than usual and surlier because I had the distinct feeling that a good bottle of gin wasn't going to fix this.

Alice wasn't there, and the martini shaker was still empty. Draining her energy had me on restriction, and I still couldn't bring myself to ask anyone else. I knew my friends would tap a vein for me, but I just . . . couldn't.

"I swore I'd die before I become like a *draugr*," I said, admitting the thing that had been plaguing me more and more. I'd survived an attempt on my life a few times, bad luck, pretending to be more human than I was, but the injection of venom a few months ago was life-changing.

Eli walked out of my apartment without a word.

When he returned, he had a bag with the top of a dusty bottle of whisky sticking out.

He pulled the bottle out and put it on my coffee table with more force than he would've if he were calm. Then, he looked at me.

"What?"

"If I didn't know how hard this was for you, I'd accuse you of trying to avoid my home country," he started. He opened a bag again and pulled out two glasses.

When I opened my mouth to object, he caught my hand. "You are impossible, Geneviève Crowe. Difficult to get to know. Fierce to the point of recklessness. But you are not a *draugr*. You are not monstrous, by any definition."

I nodded because what could I say? I knew he believed it, but sometimes I felt monstrous. I had *draugr* eyes, and I could *flow*. I was the only one of my kind, and the dead came to me at my will. The faery king called me things like "death" or "dead witch," and more than a few people thought I ought to be dead *because* of being a witch.

I didn't exactly *feel* loveable.

He poured whisky into both glasses.

Then Eli reached in the bag again, and when I saw what he held I was standing on the other side of the room. A small, gleaming knife. Mother of pearl handle. Thin blade. Watching me the whole time, he pushed up his sleeve and slid the blade over his forearm.

He turned his arm so the cut was over a glass. Still holding my gaze, he said, "Given freely."

"Eli . . ." My mind said no, but my teeth were there to remind me that I was less witch than I used to be.

I shook my head no even as I stepped closer, watching blood—*his* blood, fae blood—drip into my glass.

"My life is yours, Geneviève Crowe." He took a bandage from the bag and pressed it to his arm. "I would shed every drop for your safety, your health, your happiness."

"Eli . . ."

He held out the glass of blood and whisky. "The fae date with eternity in our minds, dearest. Everything I am is yours, including my body inside and out."

I took the glass with a shaking hand, and he lifted his blood-free drink.

"To eternity," he said.

I clinked my glass to his and echoed, "To eternity."

~ 11 ~

After Eli's blood gift, there was nothing to do but behave as I hoped would win the favor of the fae. His blood and his words made his seriousness exceptionally clear. No person could ask for a better partner than Eli. I didn't deserve him, and I never would. Of that, I was sure—but I was damn sure that I would do my absolute best to try to be an asset as we stepped into *Elphame* a few days later.

We were arriving an hour before the Yule Ball. He was no more interested in a longer stay than I was. Eli was subtle about it, but he'd made clear when we were here the first time that he had no desire to assume the throne. Eli liked my world, *our* world. Maybe he wouldn't always feel that way, but right now, he was opposed to becoming a king.

Luckily, the king was young enough that we weren't yet at that crossroads.

When we arrived, we were greeted by a contingent of royals and the king himself. I still didn't know what to call him. The fae were not free with their names. Maiden, lady, lord, or a false name were often used. I knew that.

They, of course, knew my name. I'd given it freely as a sign of trust.

The royals that met us, exactly six lords and six ladies as well as five guards, were spanned out from the king in a formation that would allow weapons. I smiled at that. The thought of training with fae warriors was more tempting than any ball could be.

"Welcome, Geneviève of Crowe." The king looked at me with an implacable expression.

But I felt the others judge me, eyes lingering on the Renaissance-meets-function dress I wore. Soft blue with silver-shot designs, it was as festive as I ever was.

The king, to his credit, made note of the colors and knew enough about me to say, "We are honored that you would join us during the festival of Chanukah. *Chag Urim Sameach.*"

I could tell that he'd practiced his words, and it made me feel a little warmer.

"Blessed Yule, and *Chag Urim Sameach,*" I said with a deep curtsey.

And yes, I'd practiced *that.* I had never in my life curtsied before, but if I bowed, the faery king and his entourage were going to be staring into my cleavage. That seemed a bit awkward, so curtsey it was.

The king, to his credit, didn't comment on my willingness to observe protocol. I gave him a genuine smile when I straightened. The ruler of *Elphame* was striking and raw in his beauty, more warrior in appearance than nobility. He was draped in a white-fur-lined cloak, and a simple circlet of silver with green gems sat atop his hair. He did not look any older than Eli, but that could mean he was anywhere from forty to four hundred.

There was no queen at his side.

I realized then that he'd never wed. Faeries' lifelines were bound together, so by staying unwed, the king had not risked dying because his partner did. It said something about his priorities and independence. In this, he and his brother—Eli's father—were very dissimilar. It was also a thing *I* understood.

Eli offered me his arm, and we walked to the king's side, and without a word, we walked in a procession from the gateway to an open field. There under the boughs of a beautiful oak tree, the fae king went to his throne. It looked as if the earth herself had crafted the chair.

Beside the throne was a silver menorah. There, in Elphame, the king of the fae motioned me forward.

"I do not find it is my place to say the words you'd need," he said. "Light your candles, and know that you are welcome here, Geneviève of Crowe."

I whispered my prayers, and I lit the candles.

Then, the king walked to that stone and wood throne.

Eli took my hand. He led me to the exact center of the field, knelt to remove my shoes and whispered, "I would offer you everything I possess in both worlds if you were here willingly."

When he stood, I sighed and slid my hand into his as we prepared to dance. "I am willing, Eli, more so than is good for either of us."

Maybe it was the amount of Eli's blood that still rolling

through my veins, or maybe it was the holiday. Or perhaps, despite every ounce of willpower, the act of dating this man had been wearing down my defenses. I still was not going to doom him by marrying him, but more and more I was wishing I could.

We danced, feet bare on the earth, and when the first song ended, the field filled with fae couples. Fireflies and stars lit the night, and candles and bonfires burned. There was peace here, among the people of the wood and air. There was acceptance here, more than I allowed myself.

And when the king greeted the dawn's light with a deep bow to me, I barely flinched.

"I present to you Geneviève of Crowe. Betrothed of my nephew. Born of magic. Giver of life and death. Future queen of *Elphame*."

The faeries bowed, curtsied, or knelt. Swords and gowns were brought before me. I winced at the whole thing, but on the outside, I smiled and replied, "It is an honor to be made welcome by the people of earth and air."

It was not an acceptance, but it was more than I thought I'd be able to muster. Eli kissed me soundly, and for a flicker of a moment, I let myself imagine a future here with him. Nature unbound. Acceptance. Love. There was much to treasure.

But I was not made for ruling. I was a warrior first, a creature that summoned the dead, and a woman utterly unsuited to motherhood. No amount of wishing would change that. My womb would not create life, not even for Eli.

THE FOLLOWING AFTERNOON, I was sleeping outside on a mossy hill with Eli beside me. Well, half under me. I was held against his side, my head resting on his chest, and we were both pillowed by thick moss.

He may not have napped; I wasn't sure. What I did know was that we needed to address matters.

"We have a bargain, and I do not seek to break that," I said, treading carefully. "I fear that it was entirely to my benefit, and for that I am grateful, but nonetheless . . . I need to ask you to let me speak of the future in general."

He sighed. "I know."

"I won't speak of our future," I hedged. I'd been thinking of ways around the rules because well, *of course I had*. I was not as clever as the fae, but I had spent a lot of time researching faery bargains.

Eli smiled, although it looked sad when he did.

"Courtship . . . dating . . ." I started, awkwardly fumbling forward despite knowing that danger was ahead. "I need to understand this, Eli. It's not fair to expect me to know things when this is not my culture."

"Do you think of the fae as fair, Geneviève?" His hand trailed over my back, fingertips tracing my spine.

"Eli . . ."

He sighed. "At the end of the courtship, one must accept the betrothal with an exchange of vows, or one must forsake the betrothed."

My heart thudded at that.

"That is traditional." Eli paused, and I knew he was trying to impart some wisdom to me. "There are no other options, traditionally. Matrimony or division. A date was set, and without an extenuating event, there are only no further options."

I weighed the things he admitted, pondering options. "So, that means that on Twelfth Night I have to commit or quit."

He looked at me. "We may not discuss our future, Geneviève. There are laws. The *terms of a bargain* overrule every other tradition for my people."

"If I quit?"

"Then I will never speak to you again," he said, voice tight. "Not as friends or partners. Nothing."

"But I'm not ready to marry anyone," I exclaimed. I sat up, glaring down at him. "And I can't lose you. I . . . have *feelings* for you."

Eli took my hand. "I am aware of all of this."

"But I can ask for anything?"

"That is our deal." Eli stared at me, and I let myself read the images he was trying to will to me.

"*I would wait,*" he said. "*I am in no rush, Geneviève. I have no desire for a wife unless you are that wife.*"

"If I ask for our engagement to end? As my request?" I prompted. "End but you not forsake me as a . . . friend and partner?"

"I could never touch you intimately."

I realized then what options he'd offered me with this bargain. I could not end it without losing him, and he could not end it at all. So, my options were marriage in about two weeks, or to ask for a request that was so carefully worded that I would have time. We would still court, but with no intent—

on my part—to marry.

"It's exhausting, dealing with the nuances of the fae," I muttered before pushing him down and snuggling into his arms. "I like dating you, though."

Eli laughed. "There is much to be said for dating."

"I could do it for a very, *very* long time," I whispered.

"Indeed." He kissed my forehead. "I do enjoy our dates." He paused and in a low voice asked, "Where do witches stand on orgasms outside?"

"Pro. Some witches, in fact, are distinctively in favor of this. Was there one in particular witch you were asking about?"

He rolled me onto my back as he moved over me. "Mine."

I'm not sure I'd have objected to the possessive tone in his voice, but it didn't matter because he covered my mouth with his and kissed away any words I might have had.

~ 12 ~

WHEN I RETURNED to New Orleans, I was worn out, weary, and ready to ask for a time-out on my life—as much as I was ready for the next week to pass so I could test my plan on my faery bargain.

I'm pretty used to drama, and the holidays are full of it for most folks. Between the three types of beings in my life—human, *draugr*, and fae—I was ready to propose a time share for future holidays. One species per year. Of course, *my* humans included my witchy mother and friends, so given my wish, I'd stick with just them.

Still the money, wisdom, and favor from Beatrice were useful.

And maybe the swords from the faery king were nice.

But I was ready for a nap after dealing with everyone's agendas—which was why I was anything but charming when Beatrice *flowed* to my table at Bill's Tavern.

"Really? Don't you have a daytime nap or something to attend? Beauty sleep? Minions to frighten?"

"Invite me to be seated."

"You need an invitation?" I perked up. *Draugr* rules were as hard to find as rooster's teeth.

"No, Geneviève." Beatrice's pale lips curved in a mimicry of a smile. "I simply have manners."

I sighed and gestured to a chair across from me. Beatrice, ever the cooperative dead lady, sat next to me.

"There are those who would wish you dead no matter what," she started.

"You must be a riot at parties."

"The last party included beheading vermin." She met my gaze. "Did you receive my gifts?"

I nodded. What exactly was the protocol for a box with the head of man? Or the antique jewels from a man who undoubtedly became dust and ash? I figured I'd go for subtle and said, "It was a very you"—I made air quotes—"gift."

Beatrice smiled. "I have another gift, Geneviève."

She slid a book to me. It felt heavy with magic, and I knew that it was a grimoire of some sort.

"I understand from your friend's shop that the buyer for this would be you," she said. "I've supplied others you or Lauren sought, but this is not one you could afford even with Harold's jewelry."

I couldn't even joke that I had nothing to give her. There were gifts, and then there were *gifts*.

"Why?" I managed to ask.

For a moment, Beatrice appeared centuries old; not that she suddenly amassed wrinkles, but that she looked weary in a way that reminded me that bitch though she could be, she was a woman in a man's world—and had been for centuries.

"I have removed threats, but there are those vile men or *draugr* every generation that seek my descendants out. You, Geneviève, are more of a target than most. You are witch and mine, but you carry other traits."

I swallowed.

"Threats will come. They are a storm, waves pounding as if they will wear us down in time." Her eyes were glimmering with a light that was eerie to behold. "I do not lose. I will not. And you, daughter of my daughters' daughter, are the last of my line. They will come, and you will be able to win." She tapped the book with a finger. "Learn."

Then the *draugr* queen stood to go.

Before I could think too long on it, I asked, "Would you want to have dinner with Mama Lauren and me? I mean sometime . . . maybe not dinner, but—"

"I will"—she smiled wickedly—"BYOB, as they say. Bring my own blood."

I laughed, more at her delivery than her bad sense of humor. "And we could talk. I think my mother would like that. I would, too."

I WAS STILL sitting there with my book in silence several hours later when Eli joined me. "Frosting?"

I looked up.

"Are you well?"

"Beatrice brought me a book." I stroked the cover again. I

wasn't prepared to open it yet, and certainly not here.

"I see . . ." He sat beside me. "Alice had this sent by courier."

The hot pink canteen he handed me looked more practical than I would typically have thought of when thinking of Alice, but when I opened it, I recognized the scent. I'd already begun to be able to tell the owner of cocktail by the scent. My body had changed.

A server brought us both mugs of what appeared to be tea for Eli and vodka for me. It made a weird sense. Alice's blood worked well with clear liquor; Eli's was more suited to whisky.

I poured a generous shot from my hot pink canteen into my mug of vodka. I tossed the whole thing back and looked at him. "I am ready to claim the request at the end of our bargain."

"It's still December and—"

"I know." I stared at him, and I saw the anxiety there. Did he doubt me so much that he thought I would give up what we shared? I wasn't easy to love, but I suspected he loved me. I wasn't going to lose that.

Carefully, I explained, "I'm already exhausted. I feel like there are disasters at every turn, and faery bargains are hard, so I want to do this while I *think* I can say it right."

"Geneviève, please, don't—"

"I do not forsake you," I said. "I do not agree to enter a marriage *on that date.* By the terms of this bargain, I can make a request. Eli of Stonehaven, my request of you is that the courtship we have begun here continue until such time as we both agree that marriage must and should happen. To each other or you to another."

He was smiling as he took my hand. "At this time, I understand that you will not release me from my pledge to you, but neither will you enter marriage."

"This is my request."

"And so the rules of courtship shall continue between us, and you have willingly entered this courtship with me," Eli added.

"I have."

"Your request is granted, Geneviève Crowe," Eli whispered. "My betrothed."

"So, mote it be."

Somehow, it felt as if nothing and everything had changed. We were still engaged, and I was still masquerading as a viable partner, but by way of a faery bargain we had secured a modification to that betrothal that not even the king could overrule.

It wasn't perfect, but the holiday season had turned out far better than ever I had hoped. Sure, there were more gatherings, bleeding out, and the addition of blood martinis to my diet, but all said, it wasn't terrible.

"I'm fairly sure that courtship includes kissing," I teased. "There's even mistletoe over the doorway."

"We're nowhere near that doorway." Eli was smiling when he leaned in to kiss me, though, and everything felt just about perfect in that moment.

Death threats, *draugr*, and drama with relatives were undoubtedly in our future, but for today, I'd enjoy my blood martini and mistletoe kisses.

Also by Melissa Marr

Signed Copies:

To order signed copies of my books, go to
melissamarrbooks.com

RECENT WORK:

Cold Iron Heart: A Wicked Lovely Novel (2020)
The Wicked & The Dead: A Faery Bargains Novel (2020)
Cursed by Death: A Graveminder Novel (2020)

Audible Original

Pretty Broken Things (2020)

BACKLIST:

YA Faery (Harper)

Wicked Lovely (2007)
Ink Exchange (2008)
Fragile Eternity (2009)
Radiant Shadows (2010)
Darkest Mercy (2011)
Wicked Lovely: Desert Tales (2012)
Seven Black Diamonds (2015)
One Blood Ruby (2016)

YA Thriller (Harper)

Made for You (2013)

Adult Fantasy for HarperCollins/Wm Morrow
Graveminder (2011)
The Arrivals (2012)

All Ages Fantasy for Penguin
The Hidden Knife (2021)

Coauthored with K. L. Armstrong (Little, Brown)
Loki's Wolves (2012)
Odin's Ravens (2013)
Thor's Serpents (2014)

Co-Edited with Kelley Armstrong (HarperTeen)
Enthralled
Shards & Ashes

Co-Edited with Tim Pratt (Little, Brown)
Rags & Bones

ECHOES OF ASH & TEARS

AN EARTHSINGER CHRONICLES NOVELLA

by L. Penelope

Brought to live among the Cavefolk as an infant, Mooriah has long sought to secure her place in the clan and lose her outsider status. She's a powerful blood mage, and when the chieftain's son asks for help securing the safety of the clan, she agrees. But though she's long been drawn to the warrior, any relationship between the two is forbidden. The arrival of a mysterious stranger with a tempting offer tests her loyalties, and when betrayal looms, will Mooriah's secrets and hidden power put the future she's dreamed of—and her adopted home—in jeopardy?

~ 1 ~

Shield of Strength: To harden the body and mind against attack from within or without.

Add equal parts ground bitterleaf, blue ginger, and silent barbshell. Also have the ingredients for the Cleansing of Scales on hand in case a bony shell appears on the recipient's skin.

—WISDOM OF THE FOLK

WITH A STEADY drumbeat pumping in his veins, Ember wiped the sweat from his brow and regarded his opponent. The man across from him in the brawling circle, Divot, breathed heavily, but no other evidence of strain tensed his broad features. Ceremonial paint ran in rivulets down his neck and chest mixed with his sweat, but his eyes were bright. His waistcloth, however, was no longer pristine, but dingy with dirt. Evidence of the fierceness of the match so far. Ember grinned. This would be a good bout.

The two challengers circled one another, stepping lightly. The glow of firerocks illuminated the large cave, nearly all the way to its high ceiling and the tiny circle of daylight barely visible above. They were deep in the interior of the Mountain Mother, on neutral territory belonging to no clan. Whispers rising from the surrounding crowd reminded Ember of their presence, but he pushed the observers from his mind. He needed to stay focused to win this match—the blade of his father's intense scrutiny threatened to pierce his skin. Not only was his own honor on the line, but that of the Night Snow clan as well.

Ember and Divot were well matched as warriors. And though the other man had a few knots of height on him and was a bit broader about the chest and shoulders, Ember had been training nearly since birth. If not formally, then informally as a result of his brother's constant attempts to best him.

He rushed the larger man, grabbing him around the waist and sweeping his legs from underneath him, using well-practiced technique to bring him to the ground. Grappling eliminated Divot's height advantage and longer arm-reach. The men wrestled, Ember trying to get his opponent into a submission hold, but Divot evaded and executed an impressive reversal, throwing Ember on his back. While Divot applied his weight to Ember's bent knee, attempting to press him further into the ground and pin him, Ember's other leg was free for a sweeping kick to the head. It knocked Divot back to allow Ember to escape the hold.

He jumped to his feet while Divot rose slowly. When the

man faced him, a shiver of revulsion rippled through Ember. The kick had split Divot's lip; he spat blood onto the sand underfoot.

Ember's stomach roiled. He'd eaten no breakfast that morning, for this reason. Shame brought the noise of the crowd rushing to his ears. The scent of sweat and blood and dirt assaulted him, shattering his concentration. With the aid of a lifetime of practice, he clamped down an unforgiving manacle on his body's reactions and his emotions.

A Cavefolk could not hate the sight of blood. It was absurd.

He steeled himself, not looking at the man's red-tinged smile, instead staring aggressively into his eyes before ramming his shoulder into Divot's chest. Soon they were caught in a clinch, arms locked together as they directed knee and elbow strikes. This close, the coppery scent of blood filled Ember's nostrils. It tickled his gag reflex and caused his gorge to rise. All involuntary reactions he had long ago learned to smother with ruthless desperation. But wrangling his body under control distracted him for a fraction of an eye-blink. Long enough to fall victim to a knee directed at his ribs. The breath flew from Ember's body. Divot took him to the ground hard, their momentum moving them right out of the sparring circle and into the spectators.

Cries of feminine shock and pain rang out. Hands pushed at him, and Ember rose to his feet. A chime sounded, indicating the end of the first round. Divot had recovered quickly and now stood in the circle, wearing a smug, ruby grin. Ember glared, his pulse racing in his ears, as the man laughed. Pushing him into the spectators was a sign of disrespect. He turned to see what damage had been wrought.

Several women were righting themselves, brushing dirt from their waistcloths, but one was still sprawled on the ground. She had taken the brunt of the force of him crashing into her and was a petite creature, with hair like midnight cascading down her back, loosed from the tight braid in which she usually kept it. If her skin tone hadn't identified her, the hair would have—clan women kept their heads shaved, preferring instead to decorate their bare scalps with paint as a sign of beauty. The hair of the unclanned was kept long, never cut until their initiation.

"My apologies, Mooriah," he said gravely. He bowed deeply and held out a hand to her.

"It is nothing. I am unharmed." Her voice was like the gentle rhythm of a drum. It soothed whatever remained of his disquiet. She blinked up at him then extended her hand in return. He held his breath.

His calloused hand enveloped her soft skin. He gripped her gently, swallowing down the fireflies that had taken flight within him. Her weight was light, and she was back on her feet in no time. She blinked rapidly, staring at their joined hands for a moment before slipping out of his grasp.

Though he had known her all his life, never before had he touched her skin. Its rich shade was a deep contrast to his—to all of the Folk, who shared similar features. But she had been born Outside, the daughter of sorcerers, and brought to the live in the caves as a baby. The two of them did not run in the same circles, and since she was as yet unclanned, their interaction was prohibited.

She caught sight of something behind him and scowled. He turned to find Divot leering at them from his position across the circle.

"Ember," Mooriah whispered. He spun back to face her. "Show that beast what the Night Snow clan is made of." She flashed him a smile that hit him harder than any fist ever had. He nearly stumbled backward but managed to nod.

He had enough time to towel off and rinse his mouth with water before the break between rounds was over. Then he cracked his neck and fingers, trying to concentrate on his opponent and ignore the scent of cinderberry that had clung to her skin. He flushed, willing away the feeling of fluttering wings the interaction with Mooriah had left inside him and reached for his focus.

The chime rang, and the fighters circled one another. "Your discourtesy to women shows what manner of vermin you and Iron Water are," Ember taunted.

Divot shrugged. "What courtesy do the low-ranked and unclanned deserve? Unlike Night Snow, we do not offer clan membership to Outsiders."

"And your clan's inferiority is well known throughout the mountain." He lowered his head and charged.

Ember did not generally use anger to fuel him as his brother and father did. Though his temper was not a vicious fire like theirs, it still scared him sometimes. But he did use it to focus himself, to home in on his opponent's weaknesses and exploit them.

Divot was a skilled fighter indeed, but Ember had much more to lose than just a bout. Expectation and the future of the clan were bound up in what was, on the surface, a simple game. He could not afford a loss today, and with Mooriah's whispered words spurring him on, he fought with renewed vigor and drive. He was fully in the zone, blind to the rest of the world, and emerged minutes later to the ringing of the final gong.

Cheers went up, and the official stepped forward to drape him with ribbons and declare him the victor. The shaman of Night Snow, an ancient man called Oval, stood next to the chieftain of the clan, Ember's father Crimson, both looking just as morose as always, as though the match had ended in defeat.

Crimson's voice rose to echo against the cave walls. "Once again, Night Snow shows its superiority. Let all the clans be on alert, we will take on all challengers and prove to them that we cannot be bested!"

Cheers from Night Snow were joined by grumbles and jeers from the other clans gathered. Divot stood with the Iron Water chieftain, head lowered, no doubt being chastised for losing the match. Ember felt a twinge of sympathy for him. With the First Frost Festival coming up in just a week, this match was the pre-qualifier for the largest competition of the year for each clan.

Tensions between Night Snow and Iron Water, the two largest clans, were high and these nonlethal games were meant to diffuse it, though Ember wasn't certain it was working. He'd certainly rather show his proficiency in the circle than have their people embroiled in a deadly war. He could only hope that his performance, and the opportunity these games gave for the chieftains to work out their differences, would be the key to peace.

As Crimson and Oval left the center of the circle, his father motioned for him to follow. Ember shot a glance at the section of the audience he'd fallen into but couldn't glimpse Mooriah through the crowd.

Once ensconced in the side cavern that Crimson had at his disposal, his father whirled on him. "Your victory was solid, but how in the Mother's name did he manage to roll you out of bounds? You lost your focus, and it could have cost you the match! Do not let it happen again."

"Of course not, Father." Ember dropped his head. The scent of blood still lingered in his nose, and he waged a constant battle to ignore it.

The echo of heavy footsteps entered the small cavern. That particular stomp could only belong to one person. "Well done, brother," Rumble said, insincerity dripping from his voice. "It looks like it will be you and me facing one another in the festival."

Ember met his brother's cool gaze. Eyes of pale gold regarded him with barely concealed hatred. They were the same age, born in the same month to two different mothers. As the son of the Lady of the Clan, Crimson's first wife, by tradition Ember should have been the heir, but Rumble's mother effectively lobbied for consideration for her son. Had Ember's mother been alive, she might have objected, but as it was, Crimson had kept the two in competition all their lives, holding the promise of heir to the chieftain's seat over them.

"I look forward to besting you in battle," Ember said.

Rumble raised a brow. "I do as well."

Crimson grunted. "Come, we have matters requiring our attention. Try not embarrass me or the clan." Rumble smirked before following their father out.

Ember grit his teeth. A match against his brother was what he'd expected, and victory would offer more than just bragging rights. Both men suspected that this, their twenty-fifth year, would be the year Crimson made his choice between them.

Ember needed to win, not for his own sake, but for the sake of the clan. The Mother only knew what horrors a chieftain such as his brother would bring down upon them.

~ 2 ~

Sanctification of Amity: To ensure a good rapport between rivals.

Combine generous pinches of star root and funeral bane along with a dram of natalus ichor. Do not inhale the fumes. In the case of reluctant participants, sprinkle ash of mercy.

—WISDOM OF THE FOLK

MOORIAH ONLY GOT a glimpse of Ember through the throngs of people after the match concluded. She still couldn't believe that the chieftain's son had helped her up after he'd crashed into her. It had taken quite a while to slow the beating of her heart, only to have it start racing again—this time with annoyance—when Glister's grating voice sounded behind her.

"Oval has summoned us."

Composing her face into a brittle smile, Mooriah turned to face the other young woman. "Of course," she said through gritted teeth. "I'll be right there." Glister narrowed her eyes, then turned on her heel and left. With a last, longing look at the circle but no further sight of the victorious warrior, Mooriah grabbed her satchel and followed.

They wended their way through the crowds to find the Night Snow shaman waiting at the entrance to a narrow tunnel. He was an ancient man, his skin leeched of all hue in the way of elderly Cavefolk, the effects of many generations spent inside the Mother Mountain with little access to the rays of the sun. Not just pale, like the younger Folk, but edging toward translucent, the bluish-green veins already easily visible all over.

Oval stood with Murmur, the clan prophet. Murmur was younger, still an elder, but his often dreamy gaze, which saw so much, gave him a more cheerful manner. Oval called his two apprentices over, and Mooriah and Glister hurried to the men's side and away from the crush of bodies.

"I hope you both enjoyed the festivities. To close out these events, and as a show of good faith between clans, we will join with Iron Water in the Sanctification of Amity." Oval's voice was low and creaked with advanced age. "We will seek the blessing of the Breath Father for continued peace between us and mutual advancement."

Anticipation grew within Mooriah at the pronouncement. For the past three years, she had worked diligently as apprentice shaman, studying hard and completing the duties she'd been tasked without complaint. At the end of her training, if she were promoted to assistant, then her place in Night Snow would be assured. She would no longer be unclanned, an Outsider, and though she would still be recognizably different in appearance, the slights and snubs that came with her current status would plague her no more. This chance to seal the peace with their old adversary was another opportunity to prove herself.

The elders led the way through the narrow tunnels to the location where they would complete the ritual. Firerocks embedded in the walls lit the way, shining with the bright blue cast shared by the glow worms living in the innermost caves.

She was surprised when the path led them to the Origin, the holiest place for the Folk. It was neutral ground, though not a place where ceremonies were generally done. However, they did not enter the sacred cavern, but stopped just outside of it in a chamber where a large, flat altar rock lay, its height reaching her knees. It was oblong and of a size to fit a dozen people seated around it.

Footsteps sounded from one of the other entrances to the chamber, and the Iron Water contingent appeared. Their shaman was a younger man, perhaps only in his thirties. His chest, bare like all men's, was decorated in the black painted markings of his clan, his head bald and gleaming. Two male apprentices followed him, looking to be in their early twenties—of an age with Mooriah and Glister. The shaman bowed at Oval, who returned the gesture.

Beyond that no one moved, but Mooriah knew enough not to question it. Her apprenticeship had been composed of much waiting, listening, and figuring things out on her own. Murmur was helpful in private, away from Oval's piercing intensity, but the elder shaman's style of instruction consisted mostly of allowing his apprentices to shadow him, observe, and work things out for themselves.

Now, they waited in silence. Several minutes later, the Iron Water clan chief arrived with his daughter. Moments afterward, Crimson stepped into the chamber, followed by Ember and Rumble.

Many of the rituals required a chieftain's presence, though only the most sacred required that of his or her blood kin. In the years of her apprenticeship, she had never witnessed one. She called to mind the steps and requirements for the Sanctification of Amity. It was, indeed, strengthened by the blood of the chieftain's descendants.

As the eldest present, Oval began the proceedings. He led them in a prayer to the Mountain Mother and the Breath Father. All lifted their heads to the sky in reverence as he spoke.

"Hallowed Mother and Divine Father, givers of blood and life. We come to you in humility, grateful for all you have bestowed. Cleanse our spirits and anoint us with your care. Sustain us with your power and absolve us with your shadow and your light. Hear the pleas of your servants and accept our honor and praise. We revere you with the blood of our bodies, *umlah.*"

After a few moments of silence to allow the words to penetrate the air and rock, Oval turned to his apprentices. "Let us begin the ritual. I will require the activating agents for the invocation."

Mooriah swallowed, running through the list in her mind. Funeral bane, star root, ash of mercy, natalus ichor. She reached into the hessian satchel strapped around her, which she carried for this very purpose. Glister did the same, though her bag was made of fine lizard skin from one of the master crafters. They raced one another to provide the necessary ingredients enclosed in tiny vials and leather packets.

A stricken look crossed Glister's face. She'd hurriedly produced everything but the natalus ichor, a foul-smelling substance that was difficult to procure. Obtaining the materials necessary for the spells and rituals was another of the apprentices' duties. Mooriah had spent three sleepless nights tracking a colony of bats and didn't want to dwell on what it had taken to retrieve this particular animal secretion now stored in the tiny vial she retrieved from her bag.

She set it on the altar next to the others. Murmur winked at her. Glister's stormy expression was its own reward. Mooriah couldn't imagine the girl going to the same lengths to acquire such a substance. Oval merely nodded, not letting on whether he'd noticed which apprentice had contributed which item.

The Iron Water shaman spoke up, his tone thin and high-pitched. "Since we are all gathered, I humbly request we also complete the Binding of the Wretched."

Murmur frowned. "That is quite an arcane rite. I cannot recall it having been done for generations."

The young shaman nodded. "It is my belief that it has been too long. In these trying times, it would be wise to revisit it. If you agree."

Mooriah scanned her memory for the ritual in question. She had studied everything, no matter how old or rarely used.

Glister hailed from a high-ranking family, well-connected with the clan elite. She was talented and ambitious and offered strong competition. But unlike the pretty and popular young woman, Mooriah had no family commitments, no social engagements, nothing but the drive that propelled her.

Glister's dejection was evident on her face. She had no idea what the binding entailed. When Oval nodded his agreement to include the ritual and looked to his apprentices expectantly, Glister swallowed nervously.

Mooriah quickly produced the powdered featherblade and bitterleaf packets from her satchel and placed them on the altar. Oval's hairless brows rose slightly, the only indication that he was impressed. Her heart thumped a stalwart rhythm. It wasn't proper to smile, but light wanted to pour from her.

Then she glimpsed Ember, standing just a few paces from her. He appeared troubled. The Binding of the Wretched was also strengthened with the blood of the chieftain's kin, specifically his heir. Since one had not yet been chosen for Night Snow, both Rumble's and Ember's would be used— though he probably had no knowledge of that. It was unlikely he spent much time studying obscure customs.

Murmur lit the censer of incense, and fragrant smoke soon filled the space. Oval freed the white bone knife from its sheath at his side. He also loosed the simple clay bowl which hung from its handle on a loop on the belt around his waistcloth. The bowl spanned two hand-widths and was unadorned with decoration or markings. It was said to have been made from the same red clay and water with which the Breath Father initially made his own physical form.

The Iron Water shaman looked upon it longingly. No other clan had such a treasure and Night Snow's possession of it had been the cause of more than one war over the generations. But now they were invoking peace. Hopefully lasting peace, though a glimpse of Crimson's and Rumble's faces was not encouraging. As Murmur expertly measured out the various ingredients into the bowl and intoned the opening words of the chant, the chieftain and his son appeared bored. Was this ceremony all for show?

Crimson's hot temper was legendary. Mooriah's youth had been marked with the protracted war he had led against two smaller clans. Eventually, those people had been absorbed into Night Snow. First as unclanned, which some still were, but others had been accepted and initiated.

Oval's voice rose and fell with Murmur's, vocalizing the various chants and obsecrations required. Then it was time to seal the ceremony with blood. The Iron Water shaman gripped his own bone knife in a long-fingered hand. Oval set the clay bowl before him on the altar and motioned for them all to kneel. On the Night Snow side, Murmur was to the right of the shaman, then Glister, Mooriah, Ember, Crimson, and Rumble.

Oval made a shallow cut into his palm and allowed his blood to drip into the clay bowl. He whispered the words of the blood magic spell to close his wound then passed the bowl and knife to Murmur, who repeated the practice as they all would.

Glister followed, then Mooriah. When she passed the bowl

and knife to Ember, his hands shook slightly upon accepting, before his grip firmed. He hunched over the altar to make his cut and then passed everything on to his father.

Mooriah noticed that Ember didn't mutter the healing spell. But perhaps such a small cut on such a strong warrior was of little matter. Mages needed to preserve their blood, but fighters spilled it all the time.

Once the bowl had made its way around the altar and was once again with Oval, he spoke the words of completion— another spell, this one transformed the contents of the bowl. The mixture of ingredients congealed and hardened into a small, jewel-like stone the color of blood. It rose into the air, hovering above the altar for pregnant moments.

Oval and the other shamans chanted, their voices harmonizing and growing louder and louder. The red stone—a caldera, or holder of magic—shimmered with a glittering shine and then continued to rise far above them, out of sight of the firerocks lining the walls, to the roof of the chamber, invisible in the darkness overhead.

Mooriah sagged with relief. Though she had not been leading the ceremony, as one of the blood mages the spell pulled energy from her for its efficacy. For some reason, the others never seemed as affected by the magic as she did. She supposed, being an Outsider, she was just weaker—or it could be because of the other thing that made her different from the Folk. The reason that she had been sent to live with them in the first place.

Not wanting to dwell on that, she took a deep breath and pulled herself together. Fortunately, the Binding of the

Wretched was a simpler undertaking. Similar, but with different chants and ingredients designed to protect those who had left the safety of the Mother and sought lives Outside. With each generation, the population of the Cavefolk became more and more depleted, the lure of the Outside increasingly enticing. It did not tempt Mooriah, for life Outside was notoriously dangerous.

Oval surprised her by calling her name.

"Yes, Exemplar?"

"Lead us in the binding."

Shock did not begin to describe her reaction. But she held it all inside and merely nodded her assent. "Certainly, Exemplar."

She cleared her throat and took the clay bowl that Glister passed her, not missing the fact that the other woman's hands vibrated with barely leashed anger.

Mooriah mixed pinches of the powders together and retrieved her own bone instrument for use in the ceremony. Unlike the sanctification, the binding required only a drop of blood from those gathered, taken from the fourth finger of the left hand, the one that, according to belief, held the artery which led to the heart. As all shamans were blood mages, they carried a variety of utensils for piercing the skin; Mooriah pulled out a sliver of bone as long as her index finger, its tip needle-sharp.

Chanting the words of the ceremony, she pricked her fourth finger and allowed just one drop of blood to fall into the clay bowl. She passed the bowl and needle to the left, back to Glister. As each person contributed their blood, their voice joined the chant. Soon a chorus had risen with power vibrating the air.

Last in the circle was Ember. He took the bowl and needle from his father, placed the bowl on the altar, and held his left hand over it. His hand was definitely shaking. So was the hand holding the pin.

He brought the sharp edge to the pad of his finger and paused. The shaking intensified. Around the circle the chants went on. Ember's face was rigid, his eyes wide. He was terrified. She checked on the others, but most had their eyes closed and hadn't noticed.

Ember's gaze met hers. He blinked rapidly, looking paler than normal. She didn't understand what was happening. His hands went to his waistcloth and fumbled at his belt. A small bladder hung hidden there, too small to be a canteen. He opened the stopper and a splash of blood leaked onto his hand; he visibly flinched. Then his body hardened, each muscle practically turning to stone.

Did Ember carry blood with him so he would not have to pierce his flesh? Mooriah nearly lost the rhythm of the chant in her surprise.

Whatever his reasoning, that technique would not work. This old ritual was specific, only a drop must be used, and he would not be able to get such an amount onto the point of the pin, not without piercing the bladder and leaving blood streaming down his leg.

She forced her face to remain calm and realized that now attention was on him. The Iron Water assistants as well as their chief's daughter had their eyes open. This ritual could not be corrupted—it was Mooriah's chance to show Oval and the others her true worth. Her opportunity to advance and prove herself. Plus, she had no desire to show weakness in front of Iron Water.

She made the decision in a split second. Raising her voice, she began to practically shout the chant, startling several around the circle. Now the attention was on her instead of Ember. In the breath between repetitions, she invoked a blood spell to conceal her movements for the next few seconds. Even Oval would not be able to see what she did. Those watching would only see her as she'd been the moment she'd uttered the spell.

She grabbed Ember's hand, wiping the blood away and grabbing the pin. She pricked his finger and, ignoring his flinch, added a drop of his blood to the bowl. Then she took the bowl from him.

The brief concealment spell petered out, and she finished the ritual like nothing had happened. The new caldera rose into the air like the others, an offering to the Breath Father and Mountain Mother. Beside her, Ember looked dazed, but held his peace.

After a few minutes of forced pleasantries between clan chiefs, Iron Water retreated. Ember and his family left as well. Mooriah glimpsed him trying to catch her eye, but she studiously ignored him.

Once the others had left, Oval turned to her, face stony as ever. "A thorough, if enthusiastic performance, Mooriah."

She lowered her head. "Many of the old rituals mention that additional fervency in our pleas gratifies the Breath

Father."

"Hmm," was his only utterance before he turned away with Glister on his heels. The other apprentice hadn't looked directly at Mooriah since Oval had made his choice.

Murmur eyed her strangely as she cleaned up, putting away her materials.

"Do you think I will get marked down for too much exuberance?" she whispered.

He considered Oval's retreating form. "You could have gotten through it faster and perhaps quieter, but given the Exemplar's penchant for a snail-like pace, I would not worry overmuch." He smiled kindly and patted her shoulder.

Her triumph was somewhat dimmed by the oddness with Ember, and she hoped that helping him had not hurt her chances of joining the clan.

Charm of Entanglement: To confirm an agreement between non-rivals to work together for mutual benefit.

Mix sapphire basil and crushed mammoth bone until well blended. Phantom rosemary may be substituted if the basil is overly fragrant but be mindful of its tendency to cause hiccups.

—WISDOM OF THE FOLK

F OR TWO DAYS, Ember searched the city for Mooriah. When he wasn't training or studying, he was finding reasons to be near the shaman's cave. He caught glimpses of the old man coming and going, but never the woman he sought. And he couldn't just ask one of the elders because they would doubtless want to know why he was looking for her, and he couldn't really lie to them. It was said that elder blood mages could suss out truth without even piercing your skin.

Having no idea where she lived, he wandered the criss-crossing paths which stretched across the open cavern of the city, hoping to run into her. Silly, since such a thing had never happened before.

There were so many levels and tunnels and honeycombed chambers within the Night Snow mountain home. Endless staircases and bridges led to dwellings and businesses tucked away in caverns cut out of the rock. Moriah was not in the farming grottos on the bottom level, where firerocks shined bright as the moon and stooped farmers tended their plots. She was not with the fishers in the streams which circumnavigated the city or with the tanners or the masons.

He entered the teeming marketplace, wincing at the ca-cophony of voices echoing on the stone. Vendors shouted from stalls sectioned off with colored rope. The scents of stews and skewered meat wafted over, but did not entice Ember, preoccupied as he was. He was despairing of ever finding her as he turned a corner and ran, nearly headfirst, into Glister.

"Ember," she said, smiling brilliantly. "You nearly mowed me down." Her shaved head was painted with delicate artistry in the clan colors of white and gold. The nightworm silk chestcloth and waistcloth she wore were more expensive than all his possessions combined. Her family cultivated the creatures and harvested the fiber and even the chieftain only had a few bits of clothing made of the valuable fabric.

"Forgive me." He bowed in apology. "I was not paying attention. I hope you are well."

"Better now." She stepped closer until they were nearly

chest to chest. "Where are you going in such a hurry?"

"I'm looking for someone. Actually, it's Mooriah. Have you seen her?"

Her flirtatious grin turned into a scowl. "Why would you be looking for *her*?"

"Clan business," he said brusquely. She flinched, narrowing her eyes. Ember wasn't certain what sort of clan business he could manufacture if she questioned him further, but fortunately, she did not.

"Well, I haven't any idea where she is. You could, of course, summon her."

She pulled out a pin from her pocket and pierced her finger before Ember could do anything to stop it. He doubled over in a fake coughing fit to hide his horrified reaction. What must it be like to shed your own blood with so little care?

Glister muttered a summoning spell. Ember vaguely heard her mentioning his name but was using every faculty he had to keep the contents of his stomach in place. During a match or a ritual, he was prepared for the sight of blood, but this took him completely by surprise. He straightened, still fake coughing, and a nearby vendor handed him a cup of herb water, which he accepted gratefully. After drinking down the cool, sweet liquid, he faced Glister again.

"She should be here in a few moments."

"Thank you."

"You're welcome. I'm always here for you, for anything you may need." Her fingers grazed his arm. He wasn't sure if she hadn't closed her wound, or just hadn't bothered to wipe off the blood, for a trace of it lingered on his skin.

Two of her friends, whom he recognized from their days in school, waited for her a few steps away. She sauntered toward them, looking back at him saucily, while his arm burned. Logic told him a trace of blood couldn't possibly sear his skin, but such was the nature of his affliction. It was not logical, and he could not control it. Neither could he control the shame it brought him.

He stared at his arm, unsure of what to do. Beside him, someone cleared their throat.

When he didn't respond, they did it again. "Ember? You required my presence?" Mooriah sounded annoyed.

He shook himself and wiped his forearm on his hip, transferring the stain to the side of his waistcloth. "Thank you for coming."

"I didn't have much of a choice. Your summoning spell made me feel an all over itch until I complied."

His gaze shot to her, surprise lifting his brows. "I'm sorry. It wasn't my spell. I ran into Glister and apparently made the mistake of telling her I was looking for you."

Mooriah snorted. "Well, that explains it. I'm not her favorite person."

"Is this one bothering you, sir?" the vendor asked, stepping out from his stall. His wares included boots and clothing made of some kind of animal hide, one of the small rodents that made the caves their home. Mooriah's eyes narrowed, and she took a step away from Ember.

"No, she's not. Thank you for your concern." He gazed around the nearby crowd to find many eyes upon them. "We should speak elsewhere," he said in a low voice. "Will you come with me?"

She sighed, looking resigned and not at all pleased about it. A weight settled upon his heart. On top of the burden of the peoples' attitudes regarding the unclanned, he was adding an additional load, something he hadn't considered.

He led her away from the market and onto a wide avenue. "Were you busy? I didn't even ask Glister to do the summoning. I definitely wouldn't have if I knew it would be so forceful."

"Not busy, not really. Just studying. Practicing. That's mostly all I do." Her voice was matter of fact, but the statement was sad. Ember could relate. Fight training, strategy, and history lessons took up almost all of his day. If he became chieftain, he wanted to be a better one than his father. And even if he didn't, he would become an advisor to Rumble—not that he expected his brother to take any of his advice.

They headed to one of the upper tiers of the city, crossing a series of angled bridges, which took them higher into the domain of the upper classes of the clan. However, some levels were entirely abandoned as more and more had left the mountain for the Outside.

One of Ember's suggestions to his father had been to consolidate living quarters so that everyone was closer together and more defensible. Crimson had taken umbrage to the suggestion, seeing little cause to live so near to those he felt were beneath him.

After a few minutes of silent walking, they arrived at an empty chamber, one he knew quite well as it had once belonged to his nanny. The woman had passed on to become one with the Mother, but he had never found more comfort than he had between these walls. He kept the place clean and stocked with food since he often came to clear his head or just to be alone. The chambers all around were also vacant, so there was little fear of being overheard or discovered.

He invited Mooriah to sit on the mat while he stoked a small fire in the pit. The upper caves were cooler, especially now that winter was upon them. Smoke disappeared into the vent in the ceiling once the fire caught hold.

"Can I offer you some tea? I have jerky."

"No, I'm fine. Thank you."

She was patient as he settled himself and ordered the words in his mind. "I wanted to thank you for your help the other day at the ceremony. I... I don't know what I would have done without it."

Mooriah swallowed. "Of course. It was the first time for you, and the ancient rituals are a bit unusual. I understand the nerves, I felt them too."

He smiled sadly, both touched and shamed by her kindness. "We both know it wasn't nerves. I... I have never been able to, that is..." He took a deep breath. "I hate the blood."

She tilted her head in surprise.

"I've never been able to stand the sight of it. It makes me queasy. And the idea of cutting myself on purpose." He shivered. "I can't bring myself to do it."

Mooriah frowned. He could practically see the wheels turning in her head. "But how?"

He shrugged. "The chieftain's son has servants. They do the spells, charge the firerocks, put protection wards on everything."

"But your own personal protection." She looked at him wide-eyed. "Against danger. Against the sorcerers. Against me." She spoke the last words in a hush.

From the time they reached adolescence, all the Folk set yearly wards on their person against magic and curses. Parents did so for their smaller children. The wards also protected against the natural magic so many of the Outsiders were born with.

"You know what I am, right? Why my father brought me to be raised here?" she asked.

"The Outsider sorcerers' magic is called Earthsong—it's fueled by life energy. Your magic is different, right? You control death."

She nodded, her expression grave. "My father is a powerful Earthsinger. Apparently, my mother was too. But I was born different. I can't turn a seed into a plant in an instant, I can't control the weather or heal with a thought, the way they do, but I can kill with one. It's only safe for me to live in Night Snow because of the wards in place to protect the Folk."

Ember firmed his lips. He had not been warded since he was a youth. His shoulders sagged under her scrutiny.

"Does no one know about your... problem?"

He shook his head. "What do you think my father would do? Or my brother?" He snorted. "I've hidden my affliction for my entire life. Mother knew, and she told me I would grow out of it. But I'm grown now, and it's still here. It's paralyz-ing—I've tried so many things to get over it. In battle or in a match, blood is often drawn. It bothers me, but I can hide my reaction to it. However, my body shuts down when I try to spill my own blood."

She leaned forward. "What if you become chief? How will you...?"

Their eyes met. So much of Cavefolk society and culture revolved around blood magic. While the shamans were true mages, all the Folk used the magic for a variety of everyday tasks: a snick here to call a child back home for dinner, a scratch there to ensure a fair price at the market. But the chief used the blood for more important tasks—rituals to protect the harvest, for the health of the people, for their security and welfare.

"I need your help, Mooriah. Everyone knows how skilled a blood mage you are. Glister got her apprenticeship through favors and family ties, but you earned yours—unheard of for the unclanned. You can teach me, find some way to help me get over this disability. If I succeed my father as chieftain, the future of the clan will be in my hands."

Mooriah ran her hands over her face. "Forgive me for saying this, but perhaps you should not be chief then, given this... issue."

He stood and began to pace. "Believe me, I've thought of that. But what do you think life under Rumble's leadership would be like? He is more bellicose than even Father. The only way for the Folk to survive is to eventually combine the clans. Otherwise we will continue losing more and more each year to the Outside until we are too weak to go on. But all Crimson and Rumble are concerned with are war and supremacy. Our people have fought enough. Another war would decimate us.

We need peace. We need to get the people on board with the idea of uniting the clans under one banner, in one city. Share resources and survive for as long as possible."

She sat back, staring up at him. He stopped his pacing and stood straighter under her perusal. "It is your desire to become clan?" he asked.

She nodded. "This is my home. For all its flaws, I love it here. I want to be shaman, and I want to be clan."

Her earnestness and straightforwardness were endearing. "And do I speak false?"

Her eyes were heavy. She shook her head. "We lose craftsmen and farmers year after year. And soldiers, too. Another war would be devastating. Uniting the Folk is sensible." She stood and crossed over to him. "Very well, I will try my best to help you overcome this difficulty. I suspect you will have to work very hard."

"I am no stranger to hard work," he replied gruffly.

"No, you are not. I am not certain that you will succeed, but I vow to try. For the sake of the clan."

"For Night Snow," he replied, thumping his chest.

Mooriah bowed respectfully. "We can start tomorrow after my studies. Would you like to meet here?"

"Yes. This place is safe from prying eyes."

Her eyes roamed him up and down, an assessing gaze so different from Glister's possessive one which had left him feeling like a slab of meat. Mooriah's held worry. For her or him, he wasn't sure. But he was drawn to her face over and over again. Her cheeks were round and her eyes slightly slanted. They were so dark, the color of shadows and mystery.

He felt that he could disappear in their depths and never be found again.

She blinked and looked away. "All right. We will meet here tomorrow after the dinner hour."

"Thank you, Mooriah."

She shook her head. "Don't thank me yet."

~ 4 ~

Binding of the Wretched: A protection to those who have sought their fortunes beyond the reach of the Mountain Mother.

Half a handful each of featherblade and bitterleaf. When seeking to strengthen, add no more than a bead of the blood of the chieftain and his or her heir, else participants may be struck with a cold plague.

—WISDOM OF THE FOLK

M OORIAH SAT IN the cave that had been assigned to her for practice, far away from the business of the city. It was not located on the upper levels, like Ember's hidden place, but in the depths, muggy and warm where no one would want to go. Here, none could unintentionally stumble upon her while she trained with her unique ability.

Though the Folk were warded against her, and she would

not be able to kill any of them accidentally, she could still cause harm. The power she wielded was mighty and required a tight rein. Which was why, when she wasn't attending to her apprentice duties or studying, she was here practicing. Learning the fine-tuned control she needed to keep the others safe.

Often Murmur helped her, for while the Cavefolk had no inborn magic, they had long ago mastered the magic of the blood. Nethersong was death and spirit combined, and as such, shared properties with blood. She'd often wondered if she'd taken to wielding blood magic so easily because of her Nethersong abilities. Death was the power Mooriah controlled, one she was born with and would die with, but was determined not to kill others with.

On the Outside, she would have been murdered at birth, even a baby Nethersinger was deadly. But her father had sought to spare her and so had brought her here, to be raised under the watchful eye of the shamans who could control her if needed, and the prophet who would guide her in how to use her birthright.

Her thoughts turned to Ember, to his unique problem. She did not know if one could ward another adult—children were easy and pliable, but someone of his mental strength would be difficult. There was a reason why adolescents had to learn how to protect themselves. She would have to research the matter when she was done here.

She released thoughts of the chieftain's son to focus on the task at hand. Allowing her gaze to go soft, she relaxed enough to accept the embrace of the Mother. Her sense of her own body left her, freeing her consciousness. Her power awakened inside her, and she found herself in the heart of the Mother—another plane of existence where she could practice her deadly skills without fear.

She stood in a dark place where she was lit from within. An obstacle course of sorts manifested before her. Focusing her will and intention, she felt for the death energy all around. She sensed the decay from insects and organisms and life-forms too tiny to ever see—things that lived and died in the blink of an eye.

Her inner Song unfurled with a dancer's agility and grace. She controlled it tightly as it always seemed like it wanted to escape her grip, to fly free like a bird soaring overhead.

She stretched her senses through the mountain, seeking death energy farther and farther away. Her awareness traveled through the veins of stone. To the freshly dead bodies in the morgue—elders who'd passed on in their sleep, to the blood flowing from a butcher's kill.

Echoes resonated from the ancient blood of the Folk from generations past, ones who had performed the human sacrifices that were far rarer now. Blood had coated the walls to create protection spells from Outsiders—from people like Mooriah's parents. But she was of the Folk now. She knew nothing of Outside and had dedicated herself to the future of the clan. She would be one of them.

A curious sensation reached for her, something new and different—not quite definable. She was just beginning to investigate it when a message reached her. This spell was a summons, not nearly as harsh as the one Glister had used the day before. A simple message from Oval to meet him at the detention chambers.

Her mind and spirit left the liminal space and returned to her body, then she hurried to follow the Exemplar's instructions. When she arrived at the prison area, she found Oval speaking with the guards.

They quickly left, and he turned to her. "An Outsider was found trespassing. He tried to steal a piece of the Mother and suffered Her wrath."

Mooriah gasped and peeked into the darkened cave behind him. On the ground lay a prone man, but all she could see of him was that he was covered in blood. "What happened to him?"

"The Mother has safeguards in place. An avalanche of rocks kept him from escaping. It took some time for our patrol to find him and dig him out. It seems he'd been there for several days."

She shook her head in disbelief and reached into her satchel. "I'll gather the healing supplies." But Oval held out a hand to stop her.

"This is part of his punishment."

She peered back at the prisoner whose head was turned away from her. His chest rose and fell with labored breath. It certainly appeared as though some of his bones were crushed, and he must be bleeding internally. Everything she could see was battered and bloody. He was gravely injured.

Still attuned to Nethersong, she felt it pulling at her. His death energy was potent. Without healing, this man would surely die.

"He will be interrogated shortly," Oval said. "Prepare the necessary elements for the Binding of Truth." She nodded obediently.

Oval went to confer with the guards again, and Mooriah knelt and dug through her satchel, organizing its contents so that she had easy access to everything she needed. As she did so, keeping Oval in view in the corner of her eye, she mentally scanned the death energy ravaging the prisoner's body.

Certainly he had committed a crime, but he was an Outsider and had no knowledge of the Mother's rules. Whatever he'd done, he could be punished for, but not like this. Not with a slow, agonizing death. With her Song, she pulled Nethersong from the man's body, taking the energy into herself. It invigorated her, filling her with vitality and staving off the man's death.

But it put him into a kind of limbo; he was not dead, but neither would he get better. She could not heal the way her father and the other Earthsingers could. Her Song could prevent death or give it. That was all.

However, she was also blood mage. Once Oval and the guards moved off down the hall, she crept into the darkened cave, approaching the prisoner's body. Since so much of his blood was present, she could use it for the spell. Softly, so no one would hear, she began the incantation that would set his bones.

It was a difficult working, forbidden for use by all but the shaman. If done incorrectly, it would do more harm than good. But having done little else but study and practice for years, she was confident in her abilities and focused all her will and intent on saving the man's life.

The blood allowed her to knit his bones back together and inflate his collapsed lung. It stopped the bleeding inside of him. She could not afford to heal him too much, else she would be discovered, but at least now he was no longer on the cusp. He would live—at least until his interrogation.

She sat back on her haunches and took a closer look at him. He shifted, his head rolling toward her, giving her a good look at his face. High cheekbones and skin a shade somewhere between the coloring of the Cavefolk and her own hue. His hair was coiled in thick, dark locks, and his eyes fluttered and slowly opened.

She sucked in a shocked breath. Gold and copper swirls moved inside his irises. She'd never seen eyes like that. They transfixed her so that she couldn't look away.

"Who are you?" he asked, his voice a rich honey. He spoke the language of her father, not the tongue of the Folk.

"My name is Mooriah, who are you?"

"I am Fenix." He looked around, then tried to sit up only to groan in pain and lay back down. "Where am I?"

"You trespassed in the mountain and disturbed a stone from the sacred Mother. Our guards found you and brought you here to await sentence by the chieftain."

A strange look crossed his face. "Another prison." He huffed a humorless laugh. "You are one of them? You don't look like the others."

Her back straightened. As if she hadn't heard that enough. "I was not born of the Folk, but they are my people. I have lived here my entire life." She stood and prepared to leave.

"Wait—I, I'm sorry. I didn't mean to offend you."

She froze at the sincerity in his voice. She was being over-sensitive. He wasn't from here, and it was a perfectly reasonable question.

Vibrations shook the floor. "Someone's coming. Please don't tell anyone I helped you."

He frowned. "You weren't supposed to. Why did you then?"

These were her people, but she still didn't understand or agree with some of the rules. She turned away, stepping to the entrance to the chamber. "The penalty for your crime is death. I probably shouldn't have bothered, but it should be swift, not slow and full of suffering."

The footsteps drew nearer. When the guards arrived again, she was pulling out the ingredients that Oval would need to aid in the man's questioning. The guards loaded Fenix onto a litter and carried him away. As he passed, he looked upon her with his golden swirling eyes, making Mooriah's breath catch.

They were so strange—he was so strange. She followed behind him, hoping once again that her impulsiveness would not come back to bite her.

~ 5 ~

Binding of Truth: To aid in determining lie from truth.

Best enhanced with doe herb and the scent of funeral bane. To be undertaken only by those well versed in communing with the Mother. The strength of the blood of the recipient will determine the spell's efficacy.

—WISDOM OF THE FOLK

"WHO ARE YOU?" Coal, the clan's Protector, asked, his voice thunderous. Mooriah stifled a wince. She'd never liked the man who used his fists liberally for even the most benign of offenses. Crimson, Ember, and Rumble stood in a line next to him, standing over Fenix. The chieftain had included both of his potential heirs in this interrogation, probably to evaluate their leadership styles.

Mooriah and Glister were seated next the prisoner who lay

upon the ground in the justice chamber, unable to sit upright. Mooriah held the censer of incense and a fan, wafting the smoke over to him, Glister sprinkled him with herb water every few minutes. Both were used to keep the prisoner calm, as the Binding of Truth often agitated people.

Oval sat cross-legged at Fenix's head, deep in meditation with the Mother to monitor the man's answers. An incision made just above his lip was part of a spell that had transferred the knowledge of the speech of the Folk to Fenix so that he could speak and understand them.

"I am a visitor," Fenix replied. Fortunately, his eyes were closed, and Mooriah did not have to worry about becoming distracted by their odd shade.

"A visitor from where?" Coal questioned.

"Far away." He sounded wistful.

Crimson grunted and crossed well-muscled arms. "Were you sent here to steal from us? To plunder our valuables and take them back with you? Speak, Outsider!"

"I was sent to observe. I found myself in a cave and saw the jewels embedded in the wall. I did not realize it would be considered stealing to take one."

"Hmph." Crimson was not satisfied in the least.

"What were you sent to observe?" Ember asked, voice soft.

Fenix rolled over and groaned. Mooriah suspected he was acting a bit, playing up his pain and injuries. She appreciated the performance. "Why does my power not work in these caves? I should be able to heal myself, but I cannot."

"So you are a sorcerer?" Coal's voice rose. "We are protected from your magic here."

If he was an Earthsinger, he was an unusual one. Though Mooriah had only ever seen her father on his rare visits, she knew that the Singers bore similar features—quite different to Fenix's. She wished he'd answered Ember's question, what *was* he supposed to be observing?

Crimson let out an annoyed sigh. "This interloper from the Outside has nothing of interest to relay. He is sentenced to death. We will have no one desecrating the Mother in such a manner, ignorant or not."

Next to him, Rumble smiled while Ember's expression stayed carefully blank. But his gaze flashed to hers for a moment, and she recognized sorrow there. She pressed her lips, keeping her own emotions in check. Why did either of them care what happened to a stranger? She could do nothing to stop it. She just hoped his death would be speedy and painless.

Swift footsteps raced down the tunnel towards the chamber. A messenger stopped there, bowing low. "Forgive me, Chieftain, but the sorcerer has arrived." The young boy's gaze flitted to Mooriah, and her breath caught. "He wouldn't wait, he said he needs to speak with you immediately."

Emerging from the darkness behind him was a hooded figure. His brown cloak hid his features, but Mooriah recognized the walk. He stepped into the chamber, moving past the messenger and bowing before the chieftain, before removing his hood.

"I'm sorry to interrupt, but this is urgent," he said, voice gravelly. "I must speak with my daughter."

She swallowed the lump in her throat. "Hello, Father."

SEATED ACROSS THE fire from him in the chieftain's quarters, Mooriah studied her father, Yllis. It had been close to eight years since she'd last seen him. His hair was coiled in thick, silver locs, which cascaded down his back. The coloring was that of an old man, but he was only in his mid-forties. His face was still unlined, but stress and strain had changed his hair color too early.

Over the years, he had visited to check in on her at seemingly at random intervals. Always he asked how her studies were progressing, how her control of her Song had improved. He showed a detached sort of interest in her life but nothing of the love and care she saw between other fathers and daughters. He did not hug her or murmur endearments. Once he'd stroked her face and looked at her mournfully before leaving.

Now, seated next to Crimson, he sipped tea. Oval and Murmur were there as well, both remaining quiet. Ember and Rumble sat just behind their father, not included exactly, but observing. Soaking up knowledge for the day one of them would become chief.

"Why have you come, sorcerer?" Crimson asked gruffly.

Yllis was solemn. "I bring news of the war to you."

Crimson waved an arm. "We care nothing for your war. Whether you Outsiders annihilate yourselves or not means little to us."

"Even if many of those killed are your kin?"

Crimson sniffed and sipped from his drinking bowl.

"We are all kin when it comes down to it," Yllis said softly, staring into the fire. Ember frowned, but no one else acknowledged his statement.

"Father, what of the war? I thought there was peace now because of the Mantle. Why are you here?"

Yllis's eyes had deep circles beneath them. He looked haggard, as if he'd gone many nights without proper rest. He took a deep breath. "I came for you."

All the breath left her body. She tensed, childish hopes living entire lives within her.

"I need your help."

She struggled to keep the disappointment at bay. Of course he had not come to take her away with him, to be a real father. She was far too old for that anyway—she was a woman grown. What need did she have for a father? Ember's gaze upon her was like a physical touch, but she kept her attention on her father's face. His skin was so like hers. Familiar, but foreign.

"You need my help with what?" she croaked out.

"The Mantle separates the two lands and has paused the conflict between the Earthsingers and the Silent—those with magic and those without. This is true. It protects us from one another, but in the east, on the side with the Singers, there is still strife. The fighting has changed, it's now more clandestine. The man who caused the war, who calls himself the True Father, has an uncontrollable lust for power. He steals it from the people, draining their Songs and taking them for himself. The Mantle keeps him trapped, locked in a land full of Earthsingers who fall victim to him."

Misery suffused his face. "There are those in the east who oppose him and who are willing to fight. I am helping them, but the True Father has begun looking for ways to destroy the Mantle and unleash himself upon the world. The barrier is strong but could be stronger. I have been endeavoring to reinforce it at its most vulnerable point, its cornerstone, but the working requires something I do not have."

Understanding dawned and Mooriah's eyes widened. "Nethersong?"

He nodded, grave. "Yes, daughter. I know the strife of the Outside means little to you all down here. The Folk exist beyond the complications of what we go through, but this is still important. The True Father is trapped in a web of his own making, but I fear what it would mean if he were freed to roam the world with his stolen Songs. It could very well impact the Folk."

"But how could Nethersong help?"

"I have long studied ways to combine the magics. We have successfully mixed Earthsong and blood magic and caused it to do things impossible with just one or the other. I have discovered that adding Nethersong can be quite potent. It can help form an additional layer of protection, one which I hope will not be necessary—my goal is still to defeat him—but I want to ensure there is a failsafe."

Mooriah chewed on her lip. "I will help if I can."

"It must not interfere with her studies," Oval spoke up. "When you brought her to us all those years ago, it was for good reason. We accepted her on certain conditions."

Mooriah bristled, her face growing hot.

"It is vital for her to master control of her Song, for the good of all, I know," Yllis replied evenly. "This task will only aid in her study. It will give her hands-on application, not mere practice."

Murmur swayed in his seat, eyes closed. His breathing was shaky, like it was when he received a vision. After a moment, he held up a hand and opened his eyes. "Something is coming, but I cannot see it yet." He sighed heavily. "It will come in its time, but your father is right. Your control is admirable, but you must better understand the use of your Song."

Oval huffed. "True, but that work is of a lifetime. She has also made a commitment to her apprenticeship that cannot be shirked."

"I'm quite certain I can do both, Exemplar."

His heavy-lidded eyes displayed some skepticism, but he merely nodded. "See that you do, else your position will be forfeited." Along with her hopes of becoming a clan member.

She should tell her father no, reject him the way he had always rejected her, but she could not bring herself to do it. Silently cursing her weakness, she grit her teeth.

Murmur peered at Yllis and stroked his chin. "Your work on the Mantle's cornerstone, would it benefit from the help of another Earthsinger?"

Yllis frowned. "Certainly, but none can cross the Mantle save me. All the others are locked in the east."

"Not all," Murmur said, looking at Oval significantly.

The elder shaman shook his head. "You speak of the Outsider? He has desecrated the Mother and must be punished."

"His work on this would benefit the Mother, protecting Her from a scourge of sorcerers from the Outside descending upon Her. It would offer restitution for his crime that his mere death would not."

Oval shrugged. "It is for the chieftain to decide."

Mooriah held her breath as everyone looked to Crimson. The chieftain turned to his sons, seeking their input. Rumble spoke up first.

"The penalty for his action is death, we must hold fast to justice." He crossed his arms, eyes flashing.

Ember tilted his head. "I believe that the prisoner's blood would sully the Mother. Better he offer a redress and benefit Her in some way and then be exiled with the knowledge that if he ever returns, he will be killed."

Crimson tapped his chin, considering. "Impure blood such as his should not be further spilled inside the sacred Mother. I will leave him in your custody, sorcerer. And you," he motioned to Ember, "ensure that he never returns."

Mooriah held back the sigh of relief. She shot Ember a grateful look. He gave an almost imperceptible nod. Though she was taking on this new task, she still had to find the time to meet with him and help him. It was more obvious than ever that he would be the far better choice for chieftain.

She turned to her father. "When should we begin?"

"As quickly as possible."

~ 6 ~

Ritual of Banishment: Prevents the unwanted from entering protected ground.

The blood of the banished is sufficient. Attempting to use any other activating agents is unwise. The focus of sincere intention will prevent unwanted consequences, but any distraction or confusion may exile those you do not intend.

—WISDOM OF THE FOLK

Y EARS HAD PASSED since Mooriah had been outside of the Mountain Mother. The only sunlight she saw usually came from far overhead from the vents and airholes in various caves. The streaming light up ahead at the end of the tunnel through which she followed her father was beginning to give her a headache. She used the bone needle in her pocket to pierce her finger, then murmured the words of a blood spell to help her adjust to the brightness.

Behind them, two guards carried Fenix on his litter. Ember brought up the rear of the party to carry out his father's command and ensure the Outsider was properly exiled and forbidden from returning.

They emerged on a plateau, with paths leading down either side of the peak on which they stood. She shivered as a sharp wind blew across her skin. Though there were no seasons inside the Mother, evidence of the weather still reached them. They celebrated the upcoming First Frost Festival every year, along with the Celebration of the First Bud, when the plants in the farming caves sprouted in the spring.

Once on the plateau, Yllis set down his pack and retrieved a heavy cloak from within, as well as a pair of boots then handed them to Mooriah. She accepted them gratefully, for her teeth were chattering. The boots were a bit too large but served to protect her bare feet from the weather.

The guards set Fenix's pallet on the ground, but he stood up at once, flexing his arms and legs. Out of the reach of the wards embedded within the rock walls, he had healed himself almost instantly. The bruises were gone, and the blood still encrusted on his limbs disappeared. His tunic and trousers were still stained, but the rest of him was whole and hale.

Holding their arms at their sides, the guards retreated without another word. That left Ember alone in the entrance to the tunnel, squinting at the land beyond. His eyes were also unused to the brightness of day, though, with a warrior's stoicism, he showed no sign of the effects of the cold on his bare chest and legs.

He turned to Mooriah, his eyes still narrowed against the light. "The Ritual of Banishment," he said, speaking low. She nodded. She would not need anything from her satchel, just her knife and the blood.

Ember eyed her warily but stood his ground. The wind ruffled his waistcloth, revealing more of his well-muscled thigh. A shiver raced through him, uncontrollably, and she rushed to perform the ritual so that he could return to the warmth.

"Your hand," she said to Fenix. He looked at her curiously then extended his hand.

She sliced a shallow cut in his palm and allowed his blood to spill into her clay bowl. She did the same to her own palm before looking to Ember whose jaw was clenched. "This is the first lesson," she whispered to him. "Close your eyes."

He did so and held out his hand. She made the tiniest cut she could. His muscles were rigid as stone as she collected drops of blood into the bowl. Then with a whisper, she bound hers and Ember's wounds. Fenix's healed on its own a moment after she'd sliced him.

Mooriah closed her eyes and invoked the spell, banishing Fenix from entering the Mother again. To her surprise, Ember added to it, including words to banish all his kind. Her eyes opened in shock. Would that mean her father could not enter as well? He was an Earthsinger, too. But Ember spoke the words of closing and the blood in the bowl shimmered and hardened, forming a caldera which floated up and then back toward the tunnel entrance. It would embed itself in the rock there and become a permanent part of the mountain.

"It is done," she said.

Ember nodded and turned to Fenix. "Safe travels to you." He bowed.

Fenix raised a brow, a smile playing at his lips. He seemed amused by Ember's stiff formality.

Ember nodded at Yllis before turning to Mooriah. "I will see you later?"

"Yes, I will find you when I return."

His gaze held hers for a long moment as if he was trying to communicate something, though she wasn't sure what. Then he turned and walked back to the tunnel. She watched him until he disappeared into the darkness, then found Fenix looking at her, his golden eyes swirling. His skin also had taken on more than just a healthy glow. It seemed to be shining with some kind of inner light.

It was such a strange effect that she stared for several moments. "Did you know that you are..." She motioned to his body. "...radiating?"

He looked down and smiled ruefully. His skin dimmed somewhat but was still oddly luminous. "I still have not grown used to holding this form."

She blinked rapidly. "What form do you usually hold?"

He grinned before his body practically exploded into light. She stumbled backward and her father caught her as Fenix transformed. He was like a star come to life. He bobbed and weaved and then took on a human form again. This time, the tunic and trousers he wore were spotless. She noticed now they were of a material she'd never seen before. Had he manifested them with his power?

"You are not an Earthsinger," she said, awe in her voice.

"I use Earthsong, but I am not a Singer in the way that those born here are."

Yllis still had his arm around her. He peered at Fenix, tilting his head. "You are an observer? Sent from the remnant of the Founders' people?"

Fenix nodded.

"The Founders?" Mooriah asked.

"Do you recall the stories I told you of the origin of the Earthsingers?" Yllis asked.

She had listened to every word her father had ever spoken on his rare visits, committing them to memory. "A magical Lord and Lady from a distant land arrived here. They had great power and transformed the desert into farmland. They had nine children who found husbands and wives among the first of the Folk who left the Mother."

"My great-grandmother was one of those nine."

His family tree—hers as well—was of great interest to her. The children of the unions between the nine children of the Founders and the Cavefolk were born either Singers or Silent—one sibling could have magic while another would not. And these differences were the root cause of the war that had raged before her birth.

She could understand the jealousy of those who could not wield Earthsong. Any of them could learn to use blood magic if they chose, but after the Folk left the Mother to become Outsiders, they lost the old ways for the most part. And so they fought the sorcerers—sometimes their own brothers and sisters. Meanwhile, inside the mountain, clans fought for far pettier reasons.

"What were you sent here to observe?" Mooriah asked. "You never said."

Fenix spread his arms. "This land. Your ancestors settled here from my world and found safety and hospitality. There are those where I'm from who keep track of such things in case a need for another exodus comes to pass. Our world was destroyed, and our people scattered. If any of us find ourselves displaced once again, victims of another calamity, it is helpful to know where we might find refuge."

"Another calamity? What happened?"

His all over glow dimmed even further. "That is a long, sad story. One for another time."

Mooriah nodded. Curious as she was, she had no desire for a sad tale. The wind picked up again, ruffling her braid. She turned to her father who was pensive.

"How long will you be here?" Yllis asked.

"I am not certain," he said, gazing at Mooriah speculatively. "Until my task is complete, I suppose."

She didn't know how long observing took or if there were special requirements or perhaps a report he had to compile, and she sensed Fenix was being vague on purpose. They had explained what Yllis was planning on the trip out of the mountain, when Fenix was still playing at being gravely injured. "Well, will you help us?" she asked.

"Certainly. It seems I owe you a debt for saving my life from those vile, pale creatures in the caves."

She set her jaw. "You are lucky that some of those vile,

pale creatures are kind and generous."

Fenix quirked his lip, which only served to stoke her ire. He took very little seriously. "I consider myself lucky, indeed." His tone edged toward flirtatious, which flustered Mooriah, but also had the effect of cooling her anger. He gazed so directly at her with eyes of liquid gold. They were almost hypnotizing.

"We have a long walk to the cornerstone," Yllis announced, breaking the strange effect she'd been under. "I will explain more on the way."

As they trekked across the mountain paths, Mooriah slowly grew used to the cold. The cloak her father had given her was lined with fur and provided adequate warmth, and she could always do a blood spell to further warm herself but decided to hold off. Part of her wanted to feel such a foreign sensation. The slight stinging of the wind on her cheeks was something new, something she wanted to investigate.

Yllis told Fenix of the war between Singer and Silent, of how the man who called himself the True Father was slowly draining the Earthsingers of their magic and how the Mantle kept him hemmed into his side of the mountain.

"So this Mantle, it's only above the mountains correct?" Fenix asked.

"Yes, you can pass through the mountain if you know the way," Mooriah said. "However, several million kilometers of tunnels and thousands of angry Cavefolk make that a nearly impossible proposition."

"Could they not be bribed to help?"

She laughed. "Doubtful. And even if you found someone

brave or foolish or desperate enough, they would be discovered by others. Superstitions are intense among the Folk, and Outsiders are not welcome. As you've experienced."

"Hmm. So why do you live there?" Fenix asked. "Are you not a Singer?"

Mooriah fell silent, an old ache taking hold of her throat.

"Are you familiar with Nethersong?" Yllis replied.

Fenix stumbled and caught himself on a boulder. She wanted to laugh, but it really wasn't funny. He looked at her apprehensively for the first time. She swallowed her disappointment.

"My daughter was born a Nethersinger and would have been killed, or killed many people, had she not been properly trained. However, there was no one to train her except the blood mages. I had little choice but to allow her to grow up there."

She had always understood this reality, but it didn't make the sting of his rejection burn any less. She stared defiantly at Fenix, who now looked apologetic.

"Those with death magic are quite rare where I come from as well," he said. "Though as far as I know, in all the places settled by the refugees, the power has not manifested. I wonder why here?" His gaze was now alight with curiosity. "Are you proficient?"

"Yes."

A grin took over his face. "You are a rare creature indeed. Kind and powerful."

She felt flushed and looked away.

"We're close now," Yllis announced. "Watch your step."

They had crested a high ridge and were about to descend a steep incline. The cornerstone was well hidden in this section of the range. She questioned whether she would be able to find it again without her father's help.

"Perhaps we should create some sort of map," she mused, stepping carefully down the path.

"The whole point is for it to remain hidden, dear."

"Yes, but there may be cases in which someone will need to find it in the future. You are reinforcing it now. Such a thing might once again be necessary. We should be ready for all eventualities."

Yllis shook his head. "A paper map is too dangerous. Too easy to copy and distribute. And if it fell into the wrong hands…"

"No, not paper. I was thinking of something more substantial. But you're right, the cornerstone itself needs strong protections. The True Father knows it's here, does he not?"

"He does, though for now it's safe on this side of the Mantle, where he can't access it."

A caldera could be created holding the memory of the route to the cornerstone. It would serve as a map for those who would one day need to find this place. Her mind raced, considering what would be needed to create both the map and some kind of protection spell.

She was so focused on her thoughts that she barely noticed they had arrived until she nearly ran into a stone pillar. She backed up to find a ring of such pillars, towering high in the air—each one must be as tall as five levels of steps back in the cave city. They were spaced about ten paces apart. In the center of the ring of stone was a caldera, an enormous one in the shape of an obelisk. It was blood red in color and rose even higher than the columns surrounding it.

"It's magnificent," she whispered, her head tilted up.

"How is it made?" Fenix asked, staring in awe.

"Blood magic and Earthsong. I built this here so that the Mantle could stretch the entire length of the mountain range. It is my life's work." Yllis placed his hand on one of the outer pillars. "I know of no other spell like it."

"I have not heard of its like." Fenix's voice was hushed.

Blood magic and Earthsong. Her father had combined the magic in some way. The sheer size of the obelisk was beyond impressive—how much blood had it taken to create? She shivered, but not from the cold. A spell of this magnitude, one that could create a barrier so strong, it must have taken quite a lot of power. If Earthsong had not been present, she would have estimated this caldera would have required the blood of thousands, maybe more.

She tore her gaze away from the remarkable stone to view her father's face. The Mantle had stood since before she was born and she was afraid to ask how many people had sacrificed their blood to create this. Plus, the most powerful calderas required death to activate. Did she even want to know?

Yllis caught her eye, noticing her fearful expression. His face softened. "We were at war. There was quite enough blood to use without my having to shed a drop from anyone. The erection of the Mantle changed the war. Now the True Father can only terrorize those on his side of it."

Fenix had his eyes closed, both palms on the nearest stone

pillar. "This is a clever spell. It fuels itself with Earthsong from all around, reaching deep into the earth and from the surrounding region."

Yllis nodded approvingly.

"So what will Nethersong do?" Mooriah asked.

"Nethersong, Earthsong, and blood magic are needed for a defensive spell. Something to protect the cornerstone and reinforce it. Though creating this was a singular achievement, it is not infallible. And I have no illusions that it cannot be destroyed. I will tell you my theory on combining the magics, and then we will find a way to protect this place. The Mantle has stood for twenty-three years. I don't know how much longer it will be needed, but it must not fall."

"I understand, Father. I will do all I can."

He smiled at her and her heart broke a little. He looked so tired, so worn. She had no idea of the burdens he'd taken on. When he'd built the Mantle all those years ago, he'd inadvertently become the only Singer left to the west of the mountains. He felt responsible for the actions of the True Father for reasons she never quite understood. But if this was the only way she could spend time with him, get to know him, she would do it. And protect his world in the process.

She just hoped it would not also serve to disconnect her from her own. Pulled in two different directions—family versus community, the man who'd abandoned her versus the people who never quite accepted her. She settled down to work wishing that her life could be easier. Wishing for something that could never be.

~ 7 ~

Fortitude Seals: A series of wards against true death by various means.

Absolute precision is needed, else failure is assured. The spell may be enhanced by the consumption of water blossoms or blister seeds—but only by those well acquainted with their side effects.

—WISDOM OF THE FOLK

EMBER PACED THE floor of his hideaway. The dinner hour had long ended and Mooriah had still not arrived. He had so much to tell her and beyond that, he just wanted to see her again.

Something about how she'd looked outside the walls of the Mother had made his heart stutter. Her hair blowing in the raw wind, her skin glowing in the light of the overhead sun, it made him wonder if she would ever return to the Folk at all, when she could take her place Outside where she had been born.

The prisoner had also given him pause. Ember had not thought the man's life should be forfeit for the mistake he had made. Yet on that ledge he had gazed upon Mooriah in a proprietary way. He was also a powerful sorcerer like her father. Though his skin and eyes were strange, perhaps they were more alike than they were different. Perhaps she would not come back at all.

Ember shivered and knelt to stoke the fire in the pit. His thoughts had grown maudlin and worse: fearful. But he had so much pent up energy within, he didn't know what to do with it.

He didn't hear any soft footsteps but all the same he became aware of her presence just as she slipped through the entrance. She looked tired.

He rose, worried. "Are you all right?"

"Yes, I'm fine. Just wanted to make sure no one saw me."

He winced, although he knew what she did was appropriate. "I made food, I wasn't sure if you would have eaten."

Her stomach growled then, and she smiled ruefully. "Thank you, I haven't."

He opened the pot of stew warming over the fire pit and she moaned at the aroma wafting from it. Turning away from her to hide his suddenly flushed face, he scooped some of the steaming vegetables into a bowl and handed it to her. Their fingers brushed; hers were cold. She still wore the voluminous, fur-lined cloak her father had given her, but shrugged it off seating herself on the cushion before the fire.

"This should warm you," he said, grateful as she dug into the meal.

He could not tear his eyes away from her as she wolfed down her food. When her bowl was empty, he gave her some more.

"Sorry to eat like such a beast," she said, grimacing. "The work my father has me doing, it triggers my appetite."

"The mage work?"

She nodded. "For some reason working a blood spell affects me more than it does Oval or Murmur or even Glister. I think it's because of my..." she waved a hand around, "...differences."

It seemed she was uncomfortable talking about her sorcery. Which made sense. The Folk hated sorcerers of any kind. Most here had probably forgotten that she held strange natural magic, since she was so adept with the blood.

"Anyway," she said, putting her bowl down at last. "I've been thinking about where we should begin."

"Before we start, I should tell you that something has happened."

She looked at him warily, her brow lowered. Ember took a deep breath. "Crimson has made it official. The victor in the match at the Frost Festival will be the heir to the chieftaincy."

Her frown deepened. "That's ridiculous. How can he base such a decision on the outcome of a game? What about leadership? Honor? Good sense?"

He smiled, pleased by her disgust. "For him, it is only the strongest who matters. Brute force is weighed far more heavily on his scales than any other quality. Only one who embodies the quality of victory may lead Night Snow."

"What a foolish man." She looked up suddenly, chagrined. "I'm sorry. He's your father and I shouldn't have—"

"No, it's fine. In this, we agree. He and I don't see eye to eye on many things." The apprehension which had filled his heart when Crimson had first shared the news came back full force. Ember was capable in the ring. He was more than a match for Rumble—if the fighting was fair.

"Well, the only good news is that Crimson's choice won't be based on you completing a ritual or ceremony." Her hopeful expression slayed him.

"The bout will be to the short death."

Her warm skin grew ashen, and her jaw dropped.

"We are to use wards to protect against a killing strike. But to win, we must land a death blow. Rumble is already warded against death by knife blade and strangulation. I must do so as well to survive."

His stomach had turned into a bottomless pit. Warding against danger, curses, and sorcery was part of Cavefolk life. Generations ago, fights to the short death were more common as a way to raise the stakes, entertain the audience, and truly practice for real battle. However, such practices had fallen out of favor.

"The festival is in one week's time," Mooriah said. "You will have to learn the Fortitude Seals by then?" Her voice evoked her disbelief that such a thing was possible. "This type of spell is difficult and layered. That is one of the reasons why brawlers do not do it any longer. One mistake and the spell will not work."

"I know." His body felt like it was made of lead. "My father has said that a chief should be able to do it. He is right."

She firmed her lips and nodded. "All right. That is our goal then. I will do my best to help you."

"I know you will."

She studied him for a long moment before pivoting to face him directly. He did the same, so they sat cross-legged, knees nearly touching.

"Give me your hands," she said.

His throat tightened as he considered her long, elegant fingers extending toward him. He rested his palms atop hers lightly, shivering at the contact.

She closed her eyes, giving him the opportunity to study her. Lit by firelight, her skin was smooth and unmarred. Her full lips formed perfect bows, and her lashes grazed her cheeks. He tried to clamp down his body's response to her closeness, to the feel of her skin but he could not. Then she stroked his palms gently, and it was as if the rod holding up his spine had been removed. He nearly collapsed like an empty balloon.

She smiled. "That's it. Release the tension you carry, Ember. You need to relax. Now, can you tell me what it's like when you try to pierce your skin?"

A shiver went through him and the tension returned, but he focused on the softness of her palms. All his awareness was on the place where they touched. It was innocent, but sensual. Her scent came to him, incense mixed with lavender today— fragrant and lovely, just as she was.

She'd asked him a question, what was it? Oh yes, his bane. He swallowed before answering. "I'm just paralyzed. It's not the pain, that is negligible. But to cut into myself... The blade against my skin..." He shivered. "I cannot make my hands move. My mind is telling my body to act, but it will not."

He clamped his lips shut, embarrassed that he'd revealed so much.

"It's all right. It sounds like you cannot control it. Some people have these things."

"Weakness."

Her eyes snapped open. "Not weakness. Your strength is within. You've bested every challenger in the circle. You show compassion and wisdom and good leadership. You are not weak, Ember."

Her glare was fierce. She believed every word. "Repeat it."

He lifted his brows. She stared at him until he complied. "I am not weak."

"Again. Louder."

He smiled. "I am not weak."

"Good." She squeezed his hands then released him. "I'd like to see you try to just prick yourself with this pin."

She held out a bone shard in her hand, the thinnest, tiniest one he'd ever seen. He took it from her, the thing was almost too small and delicate to hold in his thick fingers. He might just snap it in two.

"Try to pierce the meaty part of your palm," she said, her voice low and comforting.

He placed the edge of the pin against his skin until it indented the pale flesh of his palm. All he had to do was apply the slightest amount of pressure. She was asking for just a single drop of blood.

He held the pin there, willing himself to do it. But he couldn't.

He exhaled, realizing he'd been holding his breath. "I'm sorry, I can't."

"What happens when you try?"

He shook his head. "I'm not sure. My muscles lock up. They refuse to obey me. I feel like I'm not in control of my body any longer. It's… impossible." The weight of reality set upon him, and he wanted to give up. He would never be chief, and Night Snow would be embroiled in constant war.

"Nothing is impossible," she hissed, her voice steely. "I think we need to take another tack." She rummaged in her sack and pulled out a packet, which she opened and sprinkled over the fire.

"Lie down, close your eyes," she commanded. He did as she asked, lying across several cushions with his head at her knees.

She placed her hands on either side of his head, and his eyes popped open. She smiled down at him. "Keep them closed."

He did and she began massaging his temples. Whatever she'd sprinkled on the fire smelled sweet and a little cloying. He was going to fall asleep at this rate. Her fingers gently kneading his head was more delightful than he could have imagined. He focused on that sensation until everything else dropped away.

EMBER'S EYES OPENED and he was standing, not in his old nanny's dwelling, but in a dark place. Apprehension sparked, but then Mooriah flickered in place next to him.

"We are in the heart of the Mother," she said in a calming tone. "This is where I go to practice with my power. Your form here is not real, or I should say it exists only in your mind. Your body is still in front of the fire."

She held out the tiny bone shard. "Try again."

He swallowed and took it, surprised at how substantial she looked and felt when their fingers brushed again. He placed the pin against his palm again.

This time when his mind told his body to pierce his skin, it did so. A single drop of red welled against his skin.

His gaze shot to her, wide-eyed. Her smile broadened, illuminating the dark, ethereal cave in which they stood.

"That's the first step. You can get over this, Ember. I know you can."

He nodded slowly, trying to wrap his mind around what had just happened. He stared at the dot of red on his palm and wanted to cry with joy.

Effusion of Hardiness: Reinforces sturdy good health and robustness of body.

Two parts wolf fungus, one part jade bite, and three drams of salamander ink. Excessive yawning and a loss of taste may occur in some cases. The recipient should avoid ingesting fish or sea fowl for at least three moons.

—WISDOM OF THE FOLK

M OORIAH STOOD WITH her hands pressed against the red surface of the cornerstone caldera, searching for something—anything—within.

"What are you hoping to find?"

She startled at Fenix's voice behind her and spun around. "I'm not sure." She shook her head. "It's foolish."

He tilted his head, those eyes peering deep inside her. "I

doubt that."

"Both of my parents were powerful Earthsingers—but my Song calls to death instead. Shouldn't there be something of them inside of me?"

He frowned then looked up at the obelisk's great height. "Unfortunately, that's not how it works. Would you rather be an Earthsinger?"

"I don't know. Sometimes. It would be easier for Father. I wouldn't have been sent away." The pain of the admission settled across her fiercely. She knew that Yllis had done it to save her life, but still...

"Do you enjoy living inside those dreary caverns?"

"They're not dreary," she protested. "They're beautiful. I wish you could see them as I do. Each wall is embedded with generations of history going back to the very beginning of the mountain. You can walk for days and learn the tales of people who lived long before you. And the firerocks illuminate the patterns hidden in the stone, they tell their own story in images—you just have to know what you're looking for. The Mother is truly wondrous."

She smiled, thinking of her home. "There are gardens with plants that only bloom under the firerocks, with flowers more colorful and impressive than anything above ground, I'm sure of it. And the lakes—all around the city there are lakes, places where you can go and meditate and be at peace."

"And swim?" His brows were raised, and his mouth quirked in a smile. *That* was what he had focused on?

"Well, yes, you can swim." She frowned.

"That, at least, sounds like fun." A grin ate up his face, and she sighed.

Fenix seemed good natured, but he also lacked the ability to take anything seriously. His constant smirk was beginning to grate her nerves. "We had better get back to work. I'd like to finish today, if possible."

He sucked in a deep breath of frigid air. "Helping your father is a great deal easier than what I was sent here to do. Observe the people, make reports, take a census. Boring." He rolled his eyes.

She stiffened. "But that's the assignment you signed up for, isn't it? Don't your people need the reports?"

He shrugged. "Need is a strong word. They desire them, but they'll just send someone else along if I don't complete the job. I only took this on because I wanted to travel. And I had old debts to repay. But what they don't know won't hurt them. I'd much rather be here with you." His smile was bright and charming, enhanced perhaps by his natural glow which he no longer bothered to dampen.

Looking at him was almost painful—he was beautiful, to be sure, and so different to anyone else she'd ever met. But his carefree nature and indifference to duty rubbed her the wrong way.

"Well, the faster you're done here, the faster you can leave and continue your travels," she said.

"Oh, but I like it here."

"On the top of this cold mountain?" She raised her brows.

"There are very pleasing things to look at."

Mooriah turned away, flushing at the compliment he obviously intended. "Well, I need to finish. So I can go back."

She had brought a large pot with her today and used it to combine the ingredients for the spell she was working on. Blood magic could, of course, be done without all the additional elements stored in her satchel, blood and intent were all that were needed, but generations of shamans had come up with formulas to focus and amplify the spells. The ingredients, properly used, brought a level of refinement to the magic, which it did not have on its own.

She'd added star root for longevity, featherblade to measure a person's heart, salt bronze as a calming agent for those who would trigger the spell. She was finally doing something she'd been longing to for her whole apprenticeship—creating a new spell. Putting her years of studying to the test was oddly gratifying, and it somewhat made up for the fact that her father was just as distant as ever.

An hour ago, he'd pronounced his Song drained and had gone off to his campsite nearby to rest. An Earthsinger's power needed to regenerate after heavy usage. Mooriah wasn't sure if hers did as well or if she'd just never used her Song for long enough to exhaust it.

She'd tried telling Yllis about her spell, explaining how novel and original it was. But he'd just smiled absently and given the verbal equivalent of a pat on the head. She willed herself to not let it bother her. Later, when she returned to Night Snow, she would tell Murmur and he would be appropriately impressed.

As her thoughts veered back to her working of blood magic, Fenix interrupted again. "Pretty lighting and calm lakes can't be the only reason you stay locked away down there.

They have all that and more out here."

She shook her head, focusing on her work—the mixture had to be right or it would not work as intended. "It's my home. I like it there."

"Even though the people barely accept you. They consider you an Outsider, isn't that right?"

She pursed her lips. "For now. But once I'm initiated into the clan, things will change."

"Just like that?" She looked up to find his gaze intense. For once, the smirk gone from his lips. "Do you truly think you'll ever be one of them? That they'll ever really accept you for who you are?"

That gave her pause. But the other unclanned who had become full members enjoyed all the rights and privileges that every other Night Snow member did. No cutting remarks or stares. That would be her too, she was sure of it.

"I realize that you were eager to leave your home, Fenix, but not everyone is like you."

He shrugged. "Home is tedious. You should come with me and explore. See what this world has to offer."

She grit her teeth. "Have you forgotten why my father brought me there in the first place? My Song is dangerous to those not warded against it."

He scoffed and her temper rose at the sound. He wasn't listening to her. Not only was he irresponsible, he was self-centered.

He opened his mouth to reply and then froze, tilting his head. Then he jumped to his feet. "Your father is in trouble."

"What?" She leapt up as well.

"Follow me."

They raced down the trail leading to the plateau where Yllis had set up his camp. He had not yet had enough time for his Song to restore itself. If there was some danger, he would not be able to defend himself.

Fenix raced ahead of her and stopped. She reached his side and her heart froze. Yllis stood with his back to them as a mountain lion prowled just a dozen steps away. It was a male, and the biggest one she'd ever seen, easily twice her father's weight. Cool green eyes never left Yllis's still form.

A long dagger lay on the ground just out of her father's reach. The cat paused, sniffing, then bent its forelegs and haunches, settling into a pounce position, its gaze narrowing.

Mooriah clenched her fist and reached for her Song. Her power arrowed around her father and settled on the cat—a strong and healthy specimen with little Nethersong to latch onto. Little, but enough. With pinpoint accuracy, she multiplied the Nether, increasing the death energy until it spread throughout the creature's entire body.

"Mooriah, no!" she vaguely heard her father say, but it was too late. She manipulated the energy of the animal until it seized and fell over, its large green pupils filling with black.

When it was done, she released her Song and breathed heavily. Unlike when she practiced within the Mother, she now felt exhilarated by the use of her power. The exhaustion that had chased her for the past months as she studied for longer and worked harder, melted away. It was as if she was always supposed to use this ability.

But her father and Fenix both rushed to kneel beside the

mountain lion. Yllis turned back to her. "What did you do?"

She blinked in confusion. "I saved your life. What do you mean?"

He sighed deeply, looking down, his hand on the animal's hide. "To take a life is a great burden, Mooriah. Even an animal's life."

She crossed her arms. "Do you not hunt for food?"

"Is that what you were doing?"

Disbelief made her blink rapidly. "You would have rather I let it attack you? Let it maul you to death?"

He shook his head and her frustration grew. Was she supposed to feel bad for protecting him? She took a step backward, pain filling her—not for what she did, but for how her father was reacting to her. His gaze was wary as he stared up at her.

"You've never seen me use my power before," she whispered. "Is that it?" Oh, he always asked how her control was progressing on his rare visits, but in all her years he'd never actually witnessed it. "Is it as awful as you imagined?"

"You should not use it in such a way."

Anger spiked. "So it's all right when I use it to help you, but any other usage is off limits?"

"I don't want you to become..." He searched for a word but couldn't find it. "I don't want you to live with regrets about what you've done."

She was speechless with rage and pain. Fenix's eyes were closed, his hands on the cougar's fur. They began to glow even brighter than anything she'd seen from him before. In a moment, the animal was breathing again, softly.

"It's asleep," he said, brushing off his palms and sitting back on his haunches. "We should move it away from your camp."

"You can bring life back to the dead?" Her voice was low and a little fearful.

He nodded gravely and stood. "The newly dead, at least."

"You are far more powerful than an Earthsinger," Yllis said, appearing thoughtful.

"My power overlaps in some ways but is different." He looked at Mooriah, some question in his eyes that she didn't have time to parse.

A weight had settled on her chest and was crushing her air. Stealing her ability to breathe. She could not help the power that she had been born with. She could not help her skin or her skill or her parentage. And even her father could not accept what she was.

She spun around and started back up the path.

"Mooriah!" Fenix called.

"Let her go," Yllis said.

Tears welled in her eyes, and she did not turn around.

Appeal of Discovery: To find a path to one whom you pursue.

One drop each of hairy viper venom and night-worm pigment. The mixture is quite potent and may bubble or smoke. Avoid touching it as a blister may occur. Follow the tingling of your feet until you find the one you seek.

—WISDOM OF THE FOLK

E MBER HAD WATCHED Mooriah stir the food in her bowl for five full minutes before he couldn't take it any longer. In their short acquaintance, he'd never seen her avoid a meal. "What is wrong?"

They had been practicing in the trance state for an hour before breaking for a late dinner. He had successfully pierced his skin with the pin twice more and was working with larger and larger pins, hoping he'd get to a knife soon. It was progress, though it was slow, and they still hadn't tried it outside of the Mother's meditative illusion. However, Mooriah had seemed out of sorts ever since she'd arrived. Something was obviously bothering her.

She took a deep breath and set her bowl down. "Are you afraid of my power? The Nethersong?"

He frowned. "No? Why?"

"Because I command death. Because I can kill with a thought. It's inside me—this thing that responds to what most people fear." Her hands were clenched tight in her lap, and he wanted to soothe them.

"Death is a part of life, the largest part in fact." He gave into the urge and reached for her hand, uncurling her fist to intertwine their fingers. She didn't pull away, so he continued.

"I remember crying when my mother was chosen in the lottery to be the Sacred Sacrifice. She was the last one, after her, my father insisted the shamans move away from the practice. Some of the elders protested abandoning tradition, but he truly loved her—in his way. Something inside him broke when she died. But she was proud to have been chosen. Proud to serve her community by giving her blood to the Mother. Her life reinforced our protections, and her sacrifice will go on until the Folk are no more. So, as much as I miss her and wish she was here, all life ends in death. I would have lost her eventually. We should not fear it, we must accept it for it comes regardless."

He squeezed their joined hands. "There is little point in fearing you because you wield death. You also are a powerful blood mage. I fear that more than anything." He smiled and her expression lightened.

"My father fears me," she whispered. She relayed what had happened on the mountain top with the cougar, her voice dripping with sorrow. Tears filled her eyes and overflowed.

"I don't know why I'm so upset about this. It's not as if he even knows me at all. He says he loves me, says he only wants to protect me, but he doesn't understand how his judgment is painful." She scrubbed at her cheeks.

"By not accepting your power, he's not accepting you."

Her eyes widened. "Exactly. And even Fenix had the nerve to look at me like I was made of ants after I killed that cougar."

"Fenix was there?" Ember stiffened at the mention of the sorcerer's name.

Mooriah sniffed. "Yes, he brought the cat back to life. His power is..." She shook her head.

Ember was glad that the man was banished. That sort of magic went against the will of the Mother and the Breath Father. "He should not have interfered with life and death matters."

"I did."

"You did not interfere. You defended your father. Should we not protect ourselves and those we love? If anyone, man or beast, came for someone I cared about, then their death would be assured. Bringing them back is unnatural magic. You should be careful of that sorcerer."

He wanted to tell her to be careful of Fenix for other reasons—the glint in the man's eye had shown that he admired Mooriah—but he stayed quiet on that.

She sighed deeply. "If I become clan, do you think I will ever be truly accepted? Will I ever be one of you and have my own place here—my own family?"

"When you become clan, you will need to fend off the men with one of Glister's itching spells."

She huffed a laugh. "Doubtful."

"Would you like me to do it for you?"

"Scare away all my imaginary suitors? No thank you. If I have even one, then it will be a miracle."

Her voice was light, but he froze. "Why do you say that?"

"I am not such a prize as all that. So far, the only man to show interest in me is an Outsider, an arrogant thoughtless one at that."

She tried to pull her hand from his, but he tightened his hold. "Are you certain he's the only one?" His voice had lowered without him realizing.

She stared at their hands before meeting his gaze. Their faces were very close together all of a sudden. He wasn't sure how that had happened. She swallowed, bringing his attention to her elegant neck.

Her breath brushed across his lips; she was staring at them, blinking slowly. He held his breath. Then she shook herself and sat back. Disappointment was a mallet against his chest.

"You're going to be the chief, the Mother willing. You cannot..." She scooted farther away, forcing their hands apart. "You are not even supposed to speak to the unclanned."

"You are going to be our shaman," he said, longing for the feel of her skin on his once more. But she was focusing on her bowl again, still not eating, but not looking him in the eye either.

"That's not assured."

"Oval is not a fool, Mooriah. Anyone can see that you are better, more prepared, and take your tasks more seriously than Glister does."

She shook her head but was smiling softly. He would count that as a win. However, the moment, whatever it had been, was gone, and she still had a sad air about her that Ember wanted desperately to dispel. If nothing else, he could do that for her.

He stood and held a hand out. "I know what will cheer you. Let's take a break."

"We're already taking a break," she said wryly.

"Well a slightly longer break. I'd like to show you something."

She looked at his outstretched hand and instead of taking it, stood on her own. He fisted his hand at his side, ignoring the mallet that continued hammering away at him.

They exited his hiding place and walked along the abandoned corridors of this section of the city. Some of the staircases here were already falling into disrepair; he made a mental note to have them attended to. Anything to keep his mind off what had almost happened.

"Were you raised in the orphans' home?" he asked, realizing he knew little about her life.

"At first, though when I was around six, I went to live with Murmur and his family group. He'd had a vision and was convinced to take me in."

"What does he have again, four wives? Five?"

She shook her head. "Only three—Sparkle passed on to become one with the Mother two years ago. And they added another husband, Yaw, when I was fifteen."

"The old ways seem very complicated," Ember said. "How can someone keep up with so many spouses?"

"They have their way of doing things. Though I admit, I have no desire for more than one partner in my life."

Most of the Folk under one hundred years of age or so eschewed the polyamorous lifestyle that so many of the elders participated in. There just weren't as many people around any longer.

"I agree. I'd rather focus my attention on one person. Jealousy is a poison that infects too many hearts." His mother had never shown outward jealousy of his father's other wives, but had she merely hidden it from him?

"Where are you taking me?" Mooriah asked, looking around.

"We're almost there."

She huffed irritably, and he held back a smile. It was obvious that she liked to be in control. He wisely kept to himself how adorable he found her lack of patience. They climbed up a staircase and down another, then snaked through a warren of empty halls until they finally reached the destination.

This place was high in the city, located beneath one of the Mother's taller peaks. A narrow, dark tunnel, unlit by firerocks, led to a wide cavern. Mooriah gasped as they entered the much brighter space, and Ember tried to recall what it was like to see it for the first time.

The ceiling rose high above them, nearly as tall as Night

Snow's entire city. Here, the Mother's ragged walls were not smooth like they were in so much else of the territory. This stone was unblemished by the spells which embedded memories or protections in the walls. It was just raw mountain, and on the far wall, an enormous waterfall fed a lake below. Rocks jutted up from the surface of the water, forming a rough path leading to the waterfall. The unexpectedness and majesty of the sight took Mooriah's breath away.

"Do you want to get closer?" he asked.

Her head tilted up, staring at the grand falls, she nodded mutely. With sure steps from years of practice, he showed her how to leap from rock to rock, crossing the lake in no time.

They stood on a ledge a dozen paces from the water's thunderous fall. The spray misted them as they drew closer.

"How did I not know this was here?" she said, voice raised to compete with the falling water.

"It was once a retreat for the elite who lived on the upper levels. Now no one really comes here anymore."

"You do."

He grinned as they approached the falls and stuck his hand in the spray.

"It's warm?" She laughed, splashing a little.

"There's a hot spring in a hidden mountain oasis up there somewhere. At least that's what they think. No one has ever been there, it's too high." He craned his neck to try to see the origination of the water but could not. He didn't even catch a glimpse of daylight up above. Firerocks were the only thing illuminating this cavern.

"How could there be a hot spring on the top of a mountain?"

He shrugged. "One of the many mysteries of the Mother. My own mother brought me here when I was young. It was her favorite place. I'm almost glad I don't have to share it with others anymore." He flushed and turned toward her. "I mean, I'm happy to share it with you."

She grinned, still enthralled with the feeling of the water streaming through her fingers. Her whole face was transformed with joy as she laughed, waving her arms. She accidentally splashed him, then laughed at his reaction of mock affront.

He splashed her back, and soon they were in an all-out water fight. Her solemnity of before was forgotten, and Ember was overjoyed to have put a smile on her face.

When they finally left, they were both soaked through. The fabric of Mooriah's chestcloth clung to her breasts, and her waistcloth made the curve of her wide hips impossible to ignore. Ember struggled not to stare. She didn't seem to notice though, still riding high—this place had that effect on people. In the days after his mother's death, it had been a great comfort. He didn't want to do anything to diminish her shine, and so with great force of will, he endeavored to look only at her face.

"Thank you for bringing me here," she said, still smiling as they entered the tunnel which was the only exit. At the other end she stopped, half hidden in darkness. "You truly don't care about my Song?"

"I don't."

Her gaze lowered to his chest, and he found himself holding his breath as she looked her fill. The only light was from the chamber they were about to enter. The air became charged between them, almost sizzling with a heat he was sure would dry them off in no time. When her gaze finished roaming and met his again, her eyes were heavy lidded.

She reached up to cup his cheeks and draw him down closer to her height. "I have something to tell you," she whispered.

He bent lower and lower, not resisting her pull. "What?" He wasn't certain when he'd last taken a breath, his attention was on her skin touching his, the intensity in her eyes.

"I've always wanted to do this."

This time neither of them backed away. They erased the space between them and met in the middle, pressing their lips together. The contact was like a spark on dry kindling. Ember ignited, the kiss moving from innocent and chaste to blazing in the fraction of an eye-blink.

His hands encircled her waist, and he picked her up. She wrapped her legs around him, pressing the heat of her core against his abdomen. He shuddered and broke the kiss, spinning her and bringing her back against the wall. Her arms came around his neck, and he pressed against her, causing her to gasp.

He sought her lips again, the kiss a fiery inferno of need pent up between the two of them. Her admission had surprised him. How long had she felt the pull toward him? As long as he'd felt it for her?

Their tongues danced together as she pressed tighter against him. If he could open himself up and bring her inside, he would. He settled for tumbling into the kiss, becoming consumed by it. He hitched her higher and enjoyed the feeling of her body clinging to his. The score of her nails against his back and neck. Her heat singed his stomach; he slid a hand up her thigh to explore and possibly get burned, when footsteps sounded.

Their mouths tore apart; Mooriah was wild-eyed, breathing heavily. They were at the edge of a hub where a half-dozen hallways converged. This place was obviously not as abandoned as it looked.

Ember set her down, and they swiftly straightened their drenched clothing before turning to face the person exiting a tunnel across from them. When Glister appeared, Mooriah stiffened and moved further into the darkness behind them.

"There you are," Glister said with a smile before she took note of Mooriah. Her welcoming expression turned harsh. "What are *you* doing here?"

Ember wrangled his expression, hoping he didn't look guilty or flushed or aroused or any of the other myriad things he was feeling.

Mooriah stepped to his side, though quite a distance away. "I've been looking for a new source of rubia honey. I had reason to believe a hive of cave bees was near here."

Glister frowned then turned back to Ember. "Your father is looking for you."

"Ah, okay."

"Why didn't you just summon him?" Mooriah asked, eyes narrowed.

Glister tilted her head coquettishly. "I could have, but I

wanted to find him for myself." Ember's face heated, much to his dismay. She must have used some sort of locating spell. If he could ward himself, he could prevent being found—all the more reason to train harder.

Shooting another look of disdain Mooriah's way, Glister seemed to finally notice that both of them were wet. "What happened to you?"

"The ceiling of a tunnel back there caved in," he said, quickly. "Water started pouring down. I'm going to have one of the maintainers see to it." He cleared his throat. "Could be dangerous."

Glister's smile was brilliant. "And that's why you're going to make a great chieftain. Come along, we don't want to keep Crimson waiting." She held out a hand as though she wanted him to take it.

When he did not reach for her, she grabbed him. Unlike Mooriah's, her palm felt clammy and sickeningly boneless. As Glister led him away, he looked over his shoulder back to where Mooriah stood with her arms crossed, watching them.

Her expression was shuttered, offering no clue to her feelings. Then she turned away.

This wasn't how he wanted to walk away from her—in fact, he didn't want to walk away from her. Not now or ever.

But he would go now to appease his father. He didn't want anything to make Crimson disqualify him before the match with Rumble. After that though, all bets were off. Ember would win—somehow—and then the whole clan would know how he felt about Mooriah.

~ 10 ~

Inception of Illusion: To pass a memory on to another.

A liberal mixture of salt bronze, shadow nightshade, cinderberry, and ash of mercy may be optionally used to focus those new to working this spell. The true activator must be chosen by the mage and imbued with their intention. Light-headedness and fainting are common.

—WISDOM OF THE FOLK

MOORIAH RETURNED TO the cornerstone the next day, confident she could complete her spell. Though after a fitful night tossing and turning in her bed—reliving the kiss with Ember, the way he'd felt pressed against her, and her body's reaction—she wasn't as bright and chipper as she could be.

She desperately wanted to know what would have happened if Glister hadn't interrupted them. His hand had been so close to where she longed for it to be. What would it have felt like if he'd reached his destination? Her face heated, along with other parts of her body.

She still couldn't believe Ember had taken her to a place that held so much sentimental value to him. And she had loved it. Adored being there amidst the beauty and majesty of the largest waterfall she'd ever seen or conceived of. Its strangely warm water had been comforting, and even walking back to her quarters through the tunnels soaking wet had not been a hardship.

Around Ember she felt peaceful. He wasn't judgmental. He'd never looked down on her for any reason. And though they had never been in each other's orbits before, she'd witnessed his kindness, compassion, and strength for years.

Something inside her had cracked open when their lips touched. The force of the feelings rushing out shocked her. She was so used to hiding everything, keeping everything tucked away so it wouldn't be cause for criticism, that now she felt raw and without protection. Her heart was at serious risk.

Finish, and then you can see him tonight, she told herself. Of course this day would last forever until she did.

"What has you smiling so mysteriously?" Fenix asked, cutting into her thoughts.

She startled, then with great effort, blanked her face. She'd forgotten he was there. "Nothing."

"Ah, I was hoping you'd share what put such an expression on your face. Could it be because you're here again with me?" He grinned, his lambent eyes seeking to hypnotize her. She blinked and shook her head.

"Not everything is about you, you know."

He chuckled. "No? If you say so."

She groaned at his arrogance and got back to work. Amazingly enough, Fenix did as well.

She was still feeling her way around the process of integrating Nethersong into her father's spell using the complicated weaving technique he'd described to her. Speaking of Yllis, he was nowhere to be found this morning. She squashed the pang of disappointment until it was so tiny as to almost not exist.

Mooriah flowed back into a meditative state, directing death energy around Yllis's existing spell. She could not affect the Earthsong, she could not even truly sense it, aside from a sort of emptiness where nothing else was. But that was the key to the technique, to braid a chain of energy that wrapped around what she could not see.

It was difficult but invigorating work. She was at it for half the day before falling back into her physical senses, excitement thrumming through her.

"I think I've done it!" She opened her eyes, surprised to find Fenix seated right next to her. She grinned at him. "I've finished and it's... Oh it's magnificent. I can't believe such a thing is possible. It's just—" His expression gave her pause. "Why are you looking at me like that?"

For the duration of their short acquaintance, he had generally been cheery and full of mirth. Not taking anything too seriously, except for the incident with the cougar. But now all traces of his signature smirk were missing. He reached up and touched her braided hair, freezing her in place. "It's wonderful to see such joy is all. You're so beautiful and even more so when you smile."

She swallowed and backed out of his reach. Though his face was almost grave, his body began shining bright.

"You cannot really want to stay here," he said. "Now you've completed your father's task, why would you want to retreat back into the darkness?"

"It's not all darkness. There's beauty there too." Like the waterfall and kissing Ember. Neither of which she'd share with him.

She stood and turned her back to him, her feelings a jumble. There was something intoxicating about Fenix that made it hard to concentrate with all that brightness in her eyes. She didn't want to be addled, she needed to think clearly. Which was also hard to do when he stared at her like she was some sort of jewel.

She felt him at her back and stiffened. "What do you want?"

"I want you to come with me. Leave the darkness and come out into the air and the sunshine. Explore this world and live under the blue skies every day. Maybe even..."

She looked to the side, sighting him in her periphery. "Maybe what?"

"Maybe I could even take you to my world."

Shock stole her voice.

"I'm not sure if it's possible—we'd have to find a way for you to survive the portals, but I'm willing to try."

She spun around to face him, squaring her shoulders. "Why? Why do you want me to go so badly with you? You hardly know me at all."

"Because you're a diamond trapped in a bed of coal. You deserve to shine and let the world see your light. Don't you know that you're blinding?" He glowed even brighter as he said this, making her squint. One shining hand rose to stroke her cheek, and the touch was like sparks of energy on her skin.

He leaned in farther like he was going to kiss her, but she slid away from him.

He dimmed somewhat. "I'm not imagining that there is something between us. The way you look at me sometimes."

Her stomach churned as if cave bees had taken residence within. "You are very interesting to look at."

He leveled a gaze at her, and she shook her head. "I find you intriguing. You're different to anyone I've ever known. But I don't want what you want. I want—"

"A people who will only accept you once you reach a set of criteria? Who will never truly see you as one of them?"

"And you think out here would be different for me?" she said with a dry laugh.

"Out here is real; in there is not."

Once again, his arrogance got her hackles up. "In there is just as real as anywhere else. It's my home."

But an ugly thought raised its head. Yesterday, Ember had walked away from her with hope in his eyes. But even if he became chieftain, wouldn't a woman like Glister be better for him? Someone with a good family with resources and connections?

If Mooriah succeeded in becoming clan shaman, she would have respect and a place in Cavefolk society, but it was not the same as what Glister offered.

As if he saw the doubts in her mind, Fenix came closer. "I know you are thinking about it. I'm not giving up. I will be here, waiting. I know you will change your mind."

Some of the smugness was back, but underneath she sensed real emotion. She wasn't sure how much was bravado and how much was sincerity, but her heart hurt for him.

"I don't want to hurt you Fenix. I will not be here."

She spun around and headed back down the path that led her home. As her footsteps traipsed across the trail, a voice in her head wondered if she should accept his offer. But she shook it off.

Soon she was out of the cold and back inside the warmth of the Mother. Where she belonged.

~ 11 ~

Barrier of Rivals: Forbidden, except by the elder shaman. Blocks the spells of others for short periods of time.
Can cause temporary blindness or double vision. Punishment for unauthorized usage is banishment.

—WISDOM OF THE FOLK

MOORIAH HELD HER breath as Ember sliced into his palm.
His whole body was rigid, muscles carved from stone,
but he managed it. A tiny trickle of blood trailed the route of
the thin blade. His eyes were pressed closed so he didn't see it.

"Now the incantation," she breathed, afraid too much
sound would startle him.

He intoned the words of the first Fortitude Seal, the one to
bind him against death by blade. His voice was strong, though
it cracked a few times before picking up again. And then the
deed was done.

He opened one eye and looked at her. She nodded encouragingly. She'd already closed his wound so by the time he opened his other eye there was no trace of blood left.

"I did it?" His voice was hushed.

It was the weakest ward she'd ever seen, but the fact that he'd actually accomplished it made her heart burst. She grinned and leaned over to wrap her arms around him. "You did it!"

He hooted and tightened his embrace rocking her back and forth until they fell back on the seating mats, his deep laugh filling the space and warming her. He'd taken the brunt of the fall; she lay sprawled on top of him looking down into his pale eyes.

"I'm really warded?" he asked.

She grinned up at him. "Yes." It wasn't a lie; he was protected a little. But she didn't want to dim his joy.

He rolled them over until he was on top and smiled the brightest smile she'd ever seen on him. "I can't thank you enough."

"You worked hard. I know it's still really difficult, but you can build on this."

He sobered somewhat. "Is it enough for today?"

"It will have to be."

The match began in under an hour, so there was no time for more. The ward was weak, however, Mooriah would be in the audience watching him carefully. While he may not be protected from the worst Rumble had to give, she would make sure that whatever happened, he would survive. While Ember had spent the past few days practicing basic children's spells,

Mooriah had been studying the forbidden workings for mending flesh and bones. The ones that could restore him if his own wards did not protect him.

But she did not tell him. He would need confidence to face his brother, not doubts. "You have everything you need to defeat him. Never doubt that you will win and usher our clan into an era of lasting peace and unity."

He blinked, visibly moved by her statement. "You truly believe that?"

"Of course."

"You are amazing, Mooriah."

Given their position, she thought he might kiss her again. Her breath caught and her gaze dropped to his lips.

"If I was not already nearly late for the match…" The look he gave her made her want to clench her thighs together. He was already between them. All he needed was to—

"But there isn't time for what I want to do."

"Then you'd best get off me," she said with a laugh.

He groaned and rolled away, leaving her cold without his weight on top of her. She swallowed and sat up, then took his outstretched hand and rose.

"We'll have to hurry," she said.

They raced through the pathways and down several levels to the arena. Since each clan celebrated the First Frost Festival on their own, the crowd that had gathered around the brawling circle was smaller than at Ember's last match—but still represented just about all able-bodied Night Snow members, plus the unclanned who desired to attend.

A troupe of dancers was performing the Winter Totter, a

graceful interpretation of the season. It was one of Mooriah's favorites to watch every year, perhaps if she became clan she could join the dancers one day. But today, nerves about Ember's performance kept her distracted.

They stood at the entrance to the arena, hidden in the shadows. He was so close his breath tickled her ear. "A kiss for luck?" he whispered.

She smiled, her nerves dissolved for the moment. She looked around—everyone was already inside the arena watching the dancers. No one to see their stolen kiss.

She'd intended only a peck on the cheek, but he turned his head at the last minute and their lips met. It would be so easy to shut out the rest of the world, the beating of the drums, the plucking of strings, the pounding of feet against the ground. But she knew they had to keep it short and pulled away before she fell under. Even still, she was left breathless, blinking up into his slow smile.

"Now there is no way I can lose. After the match, I need to talk to you about something."

And with that mysterious statement, he was off, jogging into the arena to prepare. Leaving her wide-eyed with a heart that had already missed several beats.

She turned around, intending to enter through another passageway and find a seat. No one was paying attention to her, but for prudence's sake it shouldn't look like they arrived at the same time. But her plans were dashed when she discovered Glister standing behind her.

A scowl marred the woman's beauty. Rage fizzed from her like steam. Her icy gaze shifted from Mooriah to the crowd beyond, where Ember had gone.

"You harlot," she spat through gritted teeth. Then she grabbed Mooriah's arm and, with her free hand, stabbed her with something small and sharp, muttering the words of a spell that made Mooriah's bones feel like they were melting. She could not resist as Glister dragged her off and away from the arena.

"You think a dalliance with him will get you anywhere?" Glister seethed. "The next chieftain will be mine. I will be Lady of the Clan."

Mooriah's mouth would not even work to protest, her tongue was heavy inside her mouth. The music from the dancers pealed and the drumbeats thrummed underfoot—they had not traveled far—when Glister stopped in an alcove cut into the stone. With her foot, she nudged at something embedded in the ground. The covering for an old maintainer's hatch. The clay lid was thick and round and protected the hatches that the maintainers used to service the plumbing lines and renew the firerocks.

Mooriah had never before been inside the warren of passageways used by the diminutive men and women who served the clan in that way. But now, Glister shifted the covering aside with her foot and then shoved Mooriah into the darkened pit.

She felt no pain when she landed, her body was still boneless and unresponsive to her commands. The shaft was as about three times her height and must have outlets, but she couldn't control her body yet to investigate. She'd landed on her back and looked up at Glister replacing the cover and leaving her in darkness before disappearing.

A few minutes later, the paralyzing spell wore off and Mooriah climbed to her feet.

"Glister! Glister! Help!"

The music from the dancers still overwhelmed all other sounds. Soon the crowd would be roaring, all keyed up for the brawl. No one could hear her. And she would not be there to protect Ember.

She slammed her hand against the rock wall and screamed in frustration. But there was no one to hear her cries.

EMBER WIPED THE sweat from his brow, never once turning from his brother's glare. Taking his eyes off his opponent would be folly. Especially when that opponent was as ruthless as Rumble.

The two were well matched in height and weight, but Rumble had one advantage—sheer meanness. He also had access to a well of ferocious fury that Ember had never been able to tap into, and it made him brutal.

The last days spent practicing blood magery instead of training did Ember no favors either, though he'd been disciplined with his exercises for two decades—a few days here or there should make little difference.

Still, the blow Rumble had just landed on Ember's jaw made his teeth rattle. He prodded one with his tongue to see if it was loose and tasted blood. He swallowed it down, imagining his stomach lined with stone. He heard Mooriah's calming words in his mind, which helped him seal away his disgust.

He longed to find her location in the crowd but was almost glad he hadn't yet—he'd want to watch her, and that was a distraction he could not afford.

The chime signaling the end of the first round sounded, and he retreated to the sidelines to swish his mouth with water. He took the time then to search for her, surprised when he couldn't spot her immediately. His gaze had always been drawn to her like a magnet, and because of her coloring and hair, she usually stood out.

Movement across the circle drew his attention from the audience. Glister was there whispering in Rumble's ear. Ember had had the feeling that she was attempting to ingratiate herself with both brothers, hedging her bets to ensure that she found favor with whomever would be the next chieftain.

Still, whatever she told him made Rumble's gaze zero in on Ember and harden. A chill went through him.

The match had already been brutal, but he got the sense his brother had been holding back. This was confirmed when Rumble spoke briefly to an assistant, who then retrieved a dagger.

In fights to the short death, the second round was when the stakes were raised. Weapons were not allowed in round one because longer matches kept the crowd more entertained. But now the blades would be drawn.

Ember sucked in a deep breath and searched for Mooriah again. Somehow, he'd expected her to be in the front row. But being unclanned, she'd probably been pushed to the back by someone eager for a better view.

As long as he won, he could ensure that she never had to face such indignities again. He palmed his own dagger, his resolve hardening as the gong sounded.

Back in the circle, they fought hard, both drawing from their long experience. Ember had been battling his brother all his life and knew his tricks. He managed to nick Rumble's shoulder, which made the man growl and retreat.

"I hear you've been spending time with the little sorceress," Rumble said as they circled one another, crouching low. "Wonder where she is now?"

Ember faked right but Rumble anticipated and was there to meet him, lashing out with the blade, but Ember was too quick and avoided the strike.

"After I win, I'll make sure she's never initiated," Rumble continued. "She'll be wandering the peaks with the nomads, reduced to eating guano before she's ever a member of Night Snow."

Ember grit his teeth, refusing to take the bait and lose focus. "You won't touch her because you'll never be chief. And she *will* be clan. She will be my wife."

Rumble snorted. "Wife? She's not good enough to even be our servant. When I'm chief there will be none of these unclanned parasites hanging around. They'll all be kicked out, left to fend for themselves in the darklands or on the Outside."

Ember shook his head and took advantage Rumble's unguarded side. In a calculated move, he slashed out and retreated, but Rumble caught his leg and flipped him. As he fell, he reached out and embedded his blade in his brother's side, just under the ribs.

His bones rattled as he hit the ground, hard, and Rumble howled in pain.

Blinking up at the ceiling high overhead, Ember's jaw dropped. He'd landed a killing blow. He had won.

Rumble was on his knees, holding the knife sticking out of him. Ember sat up, beginning to rise, when Rumble attacked and struck his own blade into Ember's belly. The move was illegal, the match was already over, but worse, the burning in his abdomen made it feel like the blade was made of pure fire.

He sputtered looking down at the blood pouring from him. It bubbled and frothed unnaturally.

Poison. He stared wide-eyed at his brother.

Ember's ward against blades would do nothing against one with a poisoned tip.

He fell back to the ground in disbelief and stared at the ceiling until the darkness welcomed him.

~ 12 ~

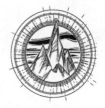

Tempest of Enmity: Inflame tensions between opponents.

A fistful of ground blue ginger, two pinches star root, sweetened with rubia honey. Blood from five incisions corresponding to the Five Doorways of Breath.

—WISDOM OF THE FOLK

T HE SOUNDS OF the crowd rose and fell as the fight went on. Mooriah had tried everything she could think of to get herself out of this pit. She'd tried climbing, but the walls were smooth and slick. The maintainers used ropes and pulleys to get in and out, and she had none. She had beaten her hands against the rock walls until they were numb, to no avail.

She found no outlets from her dark prison. No holes to crawl through or other passages leading from where she was.

Blood spells had not helped either. There was none she could think of that could make her fly or climb smooth walls. She tried to summon Oval or Murmur or one of Murmur's family group—but nothing. Could Glister have blocked her summoning in some way? Though Mooriah was the better mage, Glister was no slouch—it was certainly possible.

Everything she tried fizzled, but it was not until the crowd grew hushed that she truly became afraid. It was as if the entire audience took a collective gasp. One of the warriors had fallen, Rumble or Ember?

She cried out again, screaming in rage and pain, when light flared overhead. She looked up to find Murmur's face peering down at her. "Thank the Mother!" she cried. "Can you get me out of here?"

The elder waved a hand and murmured an incantation too softly for her to hear. The smooth stone of the walls changed and morphed into stairs which she used to climb out. She had no idea such a spell was possible and cursed her ignorance.

"Mooriah, I've been searching for you. I've had a vision—"

"I must check on Ember," she said racing past him back to the arena. She sped down the aisle to the brawling circle then stopped short.

Ember lay on his back in the center, a knife protruding from his belly. The wound was putrid, the blood foamed and was tinged with a bluish tint. She approached and dropped to her knees, horror making her movements jerky. The crowd was quiet.

This was poison. Even had Ember's wards been at normal strength, he would not have been protected from such.

Across the circle, Rumble stood with Glister. The match official had not yet awarded Rumble the winner's ribbons, but the warrior's expression was smug. Glister appeared flustered, her gaze returning again and again to Ember's motionless body and his bubbling wound.

Crimson stood at the edge of the circle, his gaze stormy. Mooriah had no idea what the chieftain was thinking or feeling as he watched his son succumb to what was obviously poison, but at the moment it didn't matter. She sank into the embrace of her Song and reached for Ember with her power.

He was nearly gone but not quite. Wanting to cry with joy, she drew away the Nethersong filling him, pulling him back from death's door. Vaguely she heard the rising voices of an argument between the match official and Rumble, and Crimson's voice intervening, but her only focus was on keeping Ember from dying.

He was no longer on the cusp, but neither was he healing. She fumbled for the blade at her waist and sliced both her palm and Ember's, mingling their blood and working a forbidden spell. The damage to his organs from the blade she could patch, but she didn't know what kind of poison Rumble had used, and it was wreaking havoc on him.

She removed the Nethersong from the substance, making it inert, but it had already worked so quickly, affecting Ember's blood. Rumble had planned well, choosing something to kill his brother that a shaman would find nearly impossible to fix. Their magic required the patient's blood, and Ember's was tainted.

She looked around wildly and found Murmur only a few

steps away. She pleaded with her gaze, but he shook his head.

"I'm sorry, child. This is not something I can undo. His blood is toxic, the blood cannot save him."

"Can we purify it?" Her mind raced for a spell that would do such, but Murmur's expression was her answer.

Her breathing became stuttered and a ringing jangled inside her head. Connected to her Song, she pulled away the Nether as it formed around Ember, but his chest had ceased to rise and fall.

Rumble's laugh drew her attention to him. Apparently tired of the arguing, he wrenched the ribbons away from the official's hand. "Enough! What does it matter what the rules say? I am alive; he is dead. I am the chieftain's heir."

He lifted a hand in the air, seeking a cheer from the crowd. A low murmur rose, but not the exuberance he seemed to want. Next to him, Glister shook with fear. Had she somehow found the blood poison and shared it with him? She seemed to be afraid of him now, but Mooriah wouldn't put it past the woman to get in deeper than she'd expected with such a character.

"Did you hear me? I am the chieftain's heir!" Both of his arms shot into the air, and the audience caught hold of his mood. More enthusiastic cheers rose all around, though the people still seemed confused.

Mooriah stood and faced him. "You will *never* be chief."

She unleashed her Song from its tether and struck Rumble down where he stood. The cheering of the crowd echoed in her ears. How dare they applaud Rumble's fraud? How dare they support this pretender?

Grief and rage took flight, and her Song swooped outward on wings of pain. Was this the clan she wanted so badly to join? One who would encourage this charlatan?

A lifetime's worth of slights and judgment exploded from her, and her Song rode this wave. It took down everyone in its path; the roar of the masses was silenced.

Everyone around her fell to the ground, taken out by her power. Even Murmur was silent and still, laying prone beside her.

She swallowed, once again leashing her Song. Tears streamed down her face, and her heart hurt. All here were warded against her, they would awaken.

But Ember, her Ember.

Nethersong could not heal him. Blood magic could not save him. He needed Earthsong.

She raced to a cart used by one of the food vendors and emptied it, then levered Ember's body into it. He was so heavy that she wasn't certain she would even accomplish it, but pure force of will drove her forward.

She pushed the cart along the pathways and toward the only person who could help her now.

SHE FOUND FENIX at the small plateau outside the tunnel. He faced away from her, staring out at the darkness beyond. Grateful that she would not have to drag Ember all the way to the cornerstone, she stopped, trying to catch her breath. Night had fallen, and a bright moon illuminated the frost, which covered not only the mountain but the farmland beyond.

"Your father has gone. He told me to tell you goodbye. You see, I knew you'd come. I..." He turned and caught sight of Ember in the cart, and the smile he wore dissolved.

She was breathing heavily and sweating from the effort of maneuvering the cart through passages that had not been designed for such. Ember was solid and probably weighed twice what she did. But she'd done it. Now she just needed Fenix to help.

She pointed to him. "He's gone. I won't allow death to take him, but he's in a sort of limbo. I need for you to bring him back."

Fenix frowned, staring down at Ember whose blood coated his abdomen and legs as well as the inside of the cart. It was becoming harder and harder to draw the Nethersong away from him without something else to fill it. But she would do it for as long as she could.

"Help him," she pleaded. Whatever force had held back her emotions up until now shattered, and she bent over the cart, tears streaming down her face. Sobs heaved themselves up from deep within. She fell to her knees, fingers gripping the edge of the cart. "Please."

Fenix's feet came into her vision; he kneeled next to her and tilted her chin up. "Of course." He gazed at her with tenderness and sorrow as she tried to stop her breath from hiccupping.

Fenix stood, then lifted Ember easily and lay him on the ground. Mooriah had forgotten her cloak, but even the bitterness of the cold or the frost at her knees didn't penetrate.

Grief, hope, desperation—the emotions were like quicksand seeking to pull her under.

With a wave of his hand, the frost melted and the ground beneath her warmed. She looked up, surprised. But of course, she knew little of the extent of Fenix's power.

He knelt at Ember's head, hands at his temples. Very quickly, a bright light enveloped Ember's body and the knife she had been too afraid to remove, pushed its way out. The blood congealing on his skin disappeared, even his stained waistcloth was now clean.

When Fenix pulled his hands away, Ember's chest rose and fell as if he was in a peaceful, deep sleep.

Mooriah gaped and sat back in a daze. "I—I—" She shook her head trying to clear it.

"He'll need to sleep for a while. When he awakens, he will be perfectly fine."

She reached for Fenix, grabbing his hand in hers and squeezing. "I don't know how to thank you. I owe you such a debt."

His smile was sad. "You owe me nothing." His gaze returned to Ember. "Is he why you will not leave?"

She swallowed, eyes drawn to the warrior's sleeping form. She stroked his cheek. "He is one reason." She set her shoulders and faced Fenix again.

She owed him a truth. "I have to admit that there is a part of me that wants to go with you. To... explore this world. I am... drawn to you. But I don't want to hurt you. Because my heart belongs to another."

Fenix sat back and looked out across the moonlit vista

again. "He is a lucky man."

She shifted, tucking her legs under her. "Perhaps in another lifetime things would have been different. Between us."

His gaze returned to her, intense, as his skin took on its signature glow. "In another lifetime, there still can be."

She tilted her head in question.

"I'm not giving up on you, Mooriah. I will return here. I will come back every ten years, at midnight on the day of the Frost Festival. I will wait for you."

Her heart clenched, and she shook her head. "Please don't. It would be a waste."

"No, it will be a hope. And sometimes hope is all you need to keep moving." He pierced her with sharp eyes that made her chest ache. She did not want him to suffer, but there was no way she could give him what he wanted.

He began to glow even brighter, shifting into his other form, the one made of light.

"Fenix?"

"Yes?" His voice came from a luminescence too bright to meet head on.

"Thank you again."

The light bobbed in acknowledgment and then raced away into the night.

~ 13 ~

Elevation of Cheer: Raises sunken spirits and provides warmth when cold.

Combine three pinches salt bronze and half a palm's worth of crushed water blossom petals. To avoid overheating, use only fresh blossoms, not dried.

—WISDOM OF THE FOLK

EMBER ROLLED OVER, pulled out of sleep by a sound he couldn't place. Memories rushed back, flooding him with vivid images and recollections of intense pain. He sat straight up with a gasp and clutched his stomach.

Only to find it whole. He ran a hand over his chest and abdomen, but the skin was perfect, unmarred. Even old scars had disappeared. His coloring was also higher, he was nearly glowing with health. A sense of wonder settled upon him.

He lay before the firepit in his nanny's old dwelling.

Movement behind made him tense, but he turned to find Mooriah, pouring steaming water into two drinking bowls. She beamed at him.

"Welcome back." She brought the bowls to him and sat beside him. "Here, drink this," she said, passing him the fragrant tea. Its scent was comforting, reminding him of his mother and being taken care of when he was sick as a child.

The bowl warmed his hands, and he focused on that as he gathered his thoughts. "What happened?"

"What is the last thing you remember?"

"The match. I struck Rumble—a killing blow. That should have been the end but... He stabbed me. There was... poison." The memory of pain assaulted him, but he pushed it back. Did he feel disappointment over his brother's betrayal? He wasn't sure, but he certainly was not surprised. He should have expected as much from him.

She nodded solemnly, blowing on her own small bowl. "The wards could not have held up against poison. Especially not a poison of the blood. There is no protection for such."

"So how am I alive?"

Instead of looking at him, it seemed that she was looking anywhere else. Why was she avoiding his gaze? He leaned closer to find tears welling in her eyes.

"I'm sorry that I failed you." She shook her head, staring at her tea. "And my chance at becoming clan is gone."

His chest tightened with disbelief. "Why would you think that?"

She swallowed and shakily told him of what Glister had done. How Mooriah had arrived in the arena to find him near death and had lashed out with her power, knocking out the entire clan.

"After this," she said, sniffing, "I am certain none will feel safe around me."

Ember set his tea down and put an arm around her, pulling her close. She buried her head against his chest, wetting it with her tears.

"You have not been back there?"

"I brought you here once Fenix healed you. I didn't want to return until you'd awakened."

At the mention of Fenix, his mouth grew dry. "The sorcerer healed me?"

"I could not let you die, Ember. I know you don't think much of his manipulating life and death, but you should not have died. It was not your time, and your blood was not in service to the Mother. I will not apologize for saving you." She pulled back to glare at him, her jaw set.

He fought a smile at her mulish expression. "I will never ask you to. I'm grateful to you. Thank you. I suppose I owe the sorcerer a debt as well." He would have to release the wariness and jealousy of the man who had saved him.

"He is gone. You owe him nothing." Her voice was carefully blank, but she'd stiffened.

"Are you... upset about him leaving?" He held his breath, unsure if he really wanted to hear her response.

Her head whipped around until she was frowning at him. "What? No. I—" She shook her head. "No."

She set her mug down and stroked his face. "I only wanted for you to be all right. My father is gone too, apparently.

Without even saying goodbye." She smiled sadly. "We were lucky that Fenix was still there. Without an Earthsinger, you would not be alive."

He felt his silent debt to the Singer in question grow. But was glad the man was gone.

Mooriah leaned against him, placing a hand on his chest. Ember stilled, not wanting her to move. "I don't know where I will go," she said. "I doubt I will be able to stay in Night Snow now."

"We shall see," he murmured and lifted her hand to kiss the back of it.

"I would do it again though," she whispered, voice grave. "A thousand times over, no matter the consequence."

"We are not sure of the consequence yet. Not until we return and face the clan. How long has it been?"

"Half a day. But I don't want to go back yet."

The sooner they returned the sooner he could see about setting this right and ensuring her place in the clan. Maybe they would redo the match or maybe, since Ember had rightfully won, the officials or Crimson would rule in his favor.

"We should—"

She silenced him by pressing her lips against his. Her kiss was desperate, seeking. It ignited a strange energy that had been thrumming through his veins since he'd awakened. He felt more alive, more energetic than he ever had before. He deepened their kiss until he swore he could feel it in his spine and ankles and wrists. Mooriah was everywhere; infused into every cell of his being.

As if to reinforce that thought, she shifted to straddle him.

He was vaguely aware of the drinking bowls tipping over and tea pouring down into the firepit. But if Ember was feeling more animated, Mooriah apparently was too.

She pushed him down until he lay on his back with her atop him. Her hands explored his chest, running across his pectorals, down the ridges of his abdomen, and back up again.

She lowered her head and trailed kisses across him, laving him with her tongue and gently nibbling his skin. Her teeth grazed his nipple and he hissed, hardening to stone. She ground against him, the heat between her legs inflaming his already needy erection.

He took control, rolling them until he was on top of her. She spread her legs wide to accommodate him. Starting at her jaw, he kissed his way down her neck and shoulder. The fabric of her chestcloth was in the way; he tugged at its tie to loosen it. Mooriah rose and removed the offending clothing, presenting her bared breasts to him.

Firelight made her skin glisten. He palmed her breasts, testing their weight and running the pad of his thumb across one, dark nipple. The urge to taste was too strong to ignore. His tongue ran circles around first one then the other, and he grazed her with his teeth, satisfied when she bucked in response.

Then he delved lower, kissing across the gentle curve of her belly, gauging her reaction. His hands cupped generous hips, and he nuzzled their apex through her waistcloth.

Her fingers trembled as she undid her belt and slid out of her remaining clothing. Then she was bare before him, and he could feast.

MOORIAH WRITHED AND squirmed as Ember's tongue attacked her core. He lapped at her with a fervency she would never have guessed possible. She squeezed her eyes tight under the assault and whimpered.

Her legs were mobile, kicking at the air when he placed his large hands on her thighs to still her. Then he resumed his attack with even more urgency.

She clutched the mats beside her as the pleasure rose and crested and she breathed out her emotions, chanting his name over and over again.

All was still for a moment. She no longer held control of her body, it belonged to Ember. He crawled up her body in order to claim it.

If her fingers worked, she would have undone his waist-cloth, but she was lucky that he attended to the task himself, very efficient. She did manage to lift her arm to stroke the thick length of him. The action made him still, his eyes glittering in the firelight.

This brought back more of her fine motor skills. She stroked him again, squeezing her fist around him. He sucked in a breath in response and removed her hand, lowering his weight onto her.

He licked the shell of her ear and kissed her jaw as she wriggled beneath him, eager to rub against his solid hardness. "Mooriah," he said, voice husky.

"Yes?"

"I am yours now. Whatever happens."

She couldn't respond to that and was grateful when he guided himself into her. The slow push inside made her eyes roll back into her head with relief. It felt like he was coming home inside her body.

She gripped him tight, their breathing deepening. He found her mouth, and they kissed messily, then he retreated from her body to enter again.

She wrapped her legs around him and tilted her pelvis to meet his thrusts, urging him onward silently. He met the challenge and soon was pistoning into her. The mats beneath them slid across the ground with each thrust. She planted her heels on the backs of his thighs and gave herself over to the sensations overtaking her.

When she went over the massive crest this time, he was with her. Spilling his seed inside her and shouting his release.

They lay there afterward, clinging to each other. The fire in the pit had cooled to nothing but embers. Ember—the man—shifted his weight, but she squeezed him tighter, not wanting him to go yet. Not wanting him to ever leave her.

Wishing that when he said he belonged to her, it could somehow be true.

~ 14 ~

Enhancement of Vision: Increases patience; nourishes foresight.

Crush phantom rosemary and add two drops of rubia honey. Meditate and await the Breath Father's voice. Only by his will may the spell be completed.

—WISDOM OF THE FOLK

I T DIDN'T TAKE long for Ember to convince Mooriah to head back to the arena. She knew she had to face her fate, and Ember's optimism was endearing but she couldn't stand false hope. She would pay the consequences of her actions, whatever they might be.

The pathways and tunnels of Night Snow were oddly quiet. They encountered no one on the journey to the arena, which she found strange. This was a heavily trafficked part of the territory, and there would normally be dozens around at this time of day tending to their various duties.

But once they entered the arena, the reason became clear. None of the audience had yet awoken. They were all as they'd been over half a day ago, collapsed where they'd fallen when Mooriah unleashed her Song upon them. Their chests rose and fell with their breaths, but they were all still unconscious.

She reached out with her Song and found that virtually everyone present had the amount of Nethersong they should. Whatever she'd done to them had not harmed them in any way. It was just taking quite a bit longer than she'd assumed for the effects to wear off.

In fact, as she and Ember stood there slack jawed and staring, people began to stir, making soft movements and groans of waking.

"Come with me," Ember said, grabbing her hand and pulling her into the sparring circle.

They approached the place where his blood still stained the ground, a congealed pool of it which had dried to an unnatural purple hue, due to the poison.

Ember kneeled, tugging on her arm for her to join him.

"What are you doing?" she asked.

"No one will know what's happened. They can't blame you if this affected you too, can they?" His tone was urgent. Bewildered by this logic, she nonetheless followed his lead.

"Now collapse on top of me like you were mourning me."

It wasn't a stretch. This was the exact position she'd been in before Rumble had angered her. She lay across him, resting on his chest. His scent filled her nostrils as she settled and feigned unconsciousness.

All around them, people slowly awoke and began to chatter in low voices. Murmur begin to stir from his spot not far away. Once the noise grew, she then blinked her eyes open, and sat up hesitantly.

Still monitoring the Nethersong of the crowd, she stilled at the sight of a motionless figure across the circle. Rumble lay there unstirring. Not breathing. His body was full of the Nethersong of true death. It filled him completely. Mooriah wondered if the whites of his eyes had turned black—the mark of death via pure Nethersong.

She took in a shaky breath.

The only thing she'd ever truly killed before was the cougar. Had his wards not worked properly for some reason or had her unadulterated vitriol against him pierced the protective spells?

She searched her feelings to find no remorse. He had fully intended to kill Ember, and had he lived he would no doubt have tried again. Though it was not her place to deliver punishment, had justice prevailed he would have died anyway, and deserved it. Still, if what she'd done was discovered then she would have difficult questions to answer.

As the people shook off their grogginess, the arena soon became abuzz with confusion and whispered theories of what had occurred. No one had any recollection of what had happened before they passed out. And all were shocked to discover how much time had passed. None felt that it had been so long.

Mooriah listened to it all silently, immobile as a boulder in the midst of a rushing river. Ember rose and approached his father who stood over Rumble's body. Glister was there too, staring in confusion at Rumble, and soon a medic was called to verify what Mooriah already knew.

She held her breath and moved no closer, though she desperately wanted to stay near to Ember while she could. But soon, Murmur beckoned her over to where he stood with Oval.

"It seems that no one recalls anything after Rumble stabbed Ember with the poisoned blade," Murmur said.

"Neither of you do either?" she asked.

Oval shook his head. He wore a thoughtful expression which creased his heavily wrinkled brow. "This is a great mystery," he said, voice low and gravelly.

Mooriah swallowed. "Some are saying Iron Water must be to blame. That they poisoned the air."

"That is unlikely but gather what's needed for the Trial of Purity."

She froze, she did not have her satchel, having left it in Ember's hiding place. It was quite unlike her, but the day had been full of the unexpected, and her mind was frayed and at loose ends.

Murmur noted her wide-eyed expression and nudged his own satchel toward her, which lay at his feet. She knelt, shooting him a grateful expression as the two men continued to talk.

"I suspect that this is a message from the Mother," Oval said. "It has been many years since She has sent us communication so clear."

"Or so inscrutable," Murmur added.

"Hmm." Oval strolled over to the chieftain and Murmur crouched down.

"What do you think? Is this one of the mysteries of the Mother?" he asked.

Her fingers shook under his perusal of her. She dropped the packet she had grabbed and scrabbled to pick it up again. "H-her ways are often beyond our understanding."

"True, they are. However, if something like this happens again, certain suspicions may arise." He looked at her significantly. The man who'd raised her and instructed her in the use of her Song was canny, and he suspected something.

She did not want to lie to him but feared his censure. "I—I…" She had no idea what she wanted to say. Fortunately, he glanced away toward the chieftain and his dead son. She finally settled on, "No one was seriously harmed, other than Rumble?"

"No. A few bruises and bumped heads, but nothing major."

She exhaled slowly still searching for the words to admit to him what she'd done. "I'm sorry, I—"

"Perhaps some things should remain a mystery," he said, drawing a line in the dirt with a finger.

Her mouth fell open and her breathing grew even shakier.

"Everyone will have their theories. Some will, no doubt, grow more popular than others over time. So long as this never happens again." His piercing gaze cut through her, and she nodded.

"I'm sure it never will."

"Good." He continued drawing in the dirt—another line

and then three circles, separated by the two lines.

"Why?" He was effectively telling her not to tell him or anyone else what she'd done. Murmur knew more about her power than anyone, but apparently did not want to have any more information to verify his suspicions. He was trusting her to control herself better in the future—which she fully intended to do. She would train and practice even more until not even strong emotion would push her to where she'd been yesterday. But she didn't understand why he would bother to protect her.

"I had another vision." He looked around at the chaos unfolding around them. "I will tell you about it later, but it concerns your future. The path ahead is rocky for you, my dear. It holds happiness—" His gaze moved to Ember. "But also many trials. And your road is longer than you probably expect. You will be needed in the days to come. You must continue to prepare and study."

She nodded, her shoulders releasing the tension she didn't realize they held. "I will. And thank you."

He pursed his lips, his eyes seeing something far away. Maybe recalling his vision. "Don't thank me yet. By the time all is done, you may feel quite differently."

He looked down at his simple drawing. Three globes divided. She didn't know what it meant, and he wiped it away before standing and dusting his palms.

Part of her wondered what his vision would mean for her. But the other part was deeply grateful for the reprieve he'd given.

THE OFFICIAL PLACED the ribbons of victory on Ember's shoulders and stepped away. A chill went through him, and his father stepped up beside him. No one in the audience was paying attention, still chattering away with one another, no doubt about the strange circumstances of their collective comas.

Ember sought out Mooriah and found her standing alone, expression plaintive. He motioned for her to come over, but she shook her head and crossed her arms over herself.

Crimson held his hands up over his head and waited for the crowd to settle and hush. Quiet descended as the clan awaited the words of their chieftain. The energy bubbling around was cautious and curious.

"I know that we all want answers as to the strange occurrences of today. One thing is clear, I have lost a son during the brawl. What the Mountain Mother and the Breath Father give unto us, they also take away."

"*Umlah*," the crowd repeated as one.

Rumble's body was still there laying at their feet. It was not the Cavefolk way to hide the dead with covers as if afraid to look upon them. Ember glanced at his brother's lifeless face. The medic had been shocked to discover that Rumble's eyes were completely blackened but posited that he might have accidentally ingested some of the poison he'd tried to kill Ember with. It was a decent explanation as no one knew what poison it was.

Crimson continued. "The Mother showed favor to my son

Ember, saving him from the poisoned blade. And the prophet Murmur and our shaman, Oval, believe that while She delivered Ember from harm, She blessed the rest of us with sleep so as to keep Her mysteries intact."

Gasps sounded in the audience as this news penetrated.

"It was the Mother's will!" someone shouted.

"We are truly blessed by Her!" cried another. Exclamations of praise and gratitude rose until Crimson hushed them all again.

He gazed at Ember, solemnly. "My heir and your future chieftain is one consecrated by the Mother. Sanctified by the Breath Father who poured breath back into his lungs. Night Snow will be led by a warrior embraced by both our divine parents, and he will lead our clan to heights heretofore unseen!"

The crowd exploded into cheers. People cried out, chanting his name. "Ember! Ember!" He had no idea when Crimson had decided to spin the mystery into some divine selection, and as much as it made him uncomfortable, he had to admit it was brilliantly done.

The mass fainting of the entire clan could make them look weak, both to others and among themselves. It could deplete morale and give an opening to other clans to sow seeds of dissent. But if their chieftain was chosen by the divine parents—then Night Snow maintained its superiority, one touched by sacred hands.

And while to Crimson, this might be fertile ground on which to start another war, to Ember this was the planting ground for lasting peace. This tale could help his quest to eventually unite the clans under one banner and preserve their true strength for as along as possible against the threat of dying out.

As the crowd continued to cheer, he acknowledged their praise with a bow. When he rose, he was pleased to see Mooriah approaching Oval. There was no doubt some type of ritual necessary now that he had been chosen as heir.

He looked around them and found Glister slowly retreating. She was sliding backward through the group of highly ranked clan members that usually flanked Crimson, trying to remain inconspicuous.

He motioned to Coal, the clan Protector, who approached. "Have Glister taken to the detention chamber. She has displeased me." Coal bowed and motioned to a guard who went to apprehend the woman. She had much to answer for.

Ember turned back as the crowd's chanting began to subside and lifted his arms to quiet them. Now that he was the heir, his commands were second only to Crimson's. And there was one thing he needed to take care of immediately.

He stepped forward to address his clan. "I am honored to be chosen as the heir and future chieftain. To serve Night Snow has long been my dream. I would also like to thank the Mountain Mother and Breath Father for their gracious blessings. I also owe a debt to the ancestors for their wisdom, to my mother, Raven, whose sacrifice has served the clan and my father, Crimson, who has led us with distinction for so long."

Applause and hurrahs rang out. But Ember was not done.

"Before the ritual begins, I would also like to show appreciation to our prophet, Murmur, for the gift of his visions and our shaman, Oval, for his protection of our home, our persons, and our spirits. Their work is essential to the clan. And to our future shaman, Mooriah—she has my deepest gratitude."

A hush settled over everyone as he called out a woman as yet unclanned. He turned to her, noting her shocked expression. "And beyond my gratitude, she holds my heart. If she will have me, I would make her my wife."

Mooriah's eyes widened and she blinked rapidly. She didn't appear to be breathing.

Beside him, Crimson hissed, "She is unclanned, son."

Ember smiled. "The chieftain's wife is by definition clan. Once we wed, she will be Lady of the Clan." He approached her, holding out his hands, waiting for her to accept them.

She looked around the silent arena. It was as if everyone was holding their collective breaths, awaiting her next move.

She extended shaking hands to him and grabbed hold. He squeezed her, and a band around his heart loosened.

"Will you have me? Will you be my wife, Mooriah?"

She was quivering, and it took her a moment to speak. "Yes, of course I will." He grinned and pulled her toward him.

Then the crowd began to cheer, more raucous and livelier than ever before. Chants went up of, "Ember! Ember! Mooriah! Mooriah!" They echoed through the stone walls of the arena all the way to the ceiling high above.

Holding her tight in his embrace, he whispered in her ear, "I am yours alone for as long as you'll have me."

"Well, you have me for life," she said, burying her face in his chest.

He was not sure that was long enough. But he would be happy to find out.

Fenix and Mooriah return in *Requiem of Silence* (Earthsinger Chronicles book 4).

If you're new to the Earthsinger Chronicles series, start at the beginning with book one, *Song of Blood & Stone*, to learn more about Yllis, The Mantle, and the war between Earthsingers and the Silent.

Also By L. Penelope

Earthsinger Chronicles
Song of Blood & Stone
Breath of Dust & Dawn
Whispers of Shadow & Flame
Cry of Metal & Bone
Requiem of Silence

The Eternal Flame Series
Angelborn
Angelfall

Standalones
The Cupid Guild

About the Author

L. Penelope is an award-winning fantasy and paranormal romance author. Equally left and right-brained, she studied filmmaking and computer science in college and sometimes dreams in HTML. She lives in Maryland with her husband and furry dependents. Sign up for new release information, exclusives, and giveaways on her website: www.lpenelope.com.

A Memory of Summer

by

Grace Draven

Spinsterhood has never bothered or embarrassed the independent Emerence Ipsan, and the winter festival of Delyalda keeps her far too busy managing her father's shops to worry about matters as trivial as marriage.

Until the arrival of a young Quereci warrior with old eyes and an admiring gaze makes her question that notion.

A MEMORY OF SUMMER is a short novella that takes place in the world of the Wraith Kings series. For those who've read the first three books in the series (RADIANCE, EIDOLON, THE IPPOS KING), this storyline takes place after EIDOLON and before THE IPPOS KING. It runs concurrently with events in the novella IN THE DARKEST MIDNIGHT and reintroduces the Wraith king Gaeres.

"I HEAR YEOMAN Percivus is looking for a wife." Glauca made the announcement as she refilled jars with dried herbs Emerence had sorted for her. "He's a wealthy farmer. He just bought his neighbor's holdings to increase his own."

Emerence sighed inwardly as she weighed dried rosehips on a scale. Her cousin was an unashamed matchmaker. A relentless one as well. "I wish him well. His income will guarantee no lack of candidates interested in becoming the third Madam Percivus.

Glauca clucked her disapproval at Emerence's obvious disinterest. "I've met him. He's pleasant and his children well-behaved. Both of his wives seemed happy. A shame one died in childbirth and the other from lung fever. But that wasn't his fault."

Emerence paused in her task to stare at her with a raised eyebrow. "If I didn't already know you were happily married, I'd think you were considering throwing in your ribbon for a chance at becoming the newest Percivus bride."

This time Glauca sniffed, as if Emerence's teasing carried a bad scent. She closed the lid on the jar she'd filled and reached for another. "I would but as you say, I'm married. You, however, are not, nor are you getting any younger. Yeoman

Percivus would be perfect. He isn't in his dotage, already has several children, and has a purse fat enough to keep you comfortable for the rest of your life with no need to birth more children for him."

"Sounds glorious," Emerence said dryly. She loved her cousin and knew Glauca loved her in return. It was why she remained so persistent in her quest to see Emerence married even after others had given up their matchmaking attempts years earlier. Still, there were times, like now, when Emerence found her efforts more annoying than endearing.

"I'm perfectly content with my life as it is, cousin. I manage two shops, own my own home, and control my time as I see fit." Emerence sometimes envied the companionship other women of her acquaintance shared with their spouses and offspring, but she'd seen a similar envy of her in the eyes of some of those wives and mothers shackled by the demands of marriage and parenthood. She wasn't afraid of such bonds; she just had no intention of rushing toward them just for the sake of avoiding the stigma of spinsterhood.

"But you're almost seven and thirty," Glauca all but wailed, as if such a ripe old age heralded Emerence's impending doom.

Emerence couldn't help it. She laughed and continued laughing despite Glauca's glare. Once her spate of humor subsided, she wiped the tears from her eyes. "You say that as if I'm at death's door. I assure you my life will not end at the arrival of seven and thirty." She uttered the last in a voice pitched low as if another year in her lifespan would thunder past her instead of breeze by as every year always did, hardly marked, barely noticed.

"Don't you want a husband?" Glauca wrenched the lid closed on the jar she held and yanked another empty one toward her. "You can't live with your father and Linnett forever."

Emerence shrugged, dividing her attention between Glauca's task and her own of pulverizing a batch of nightshade in a mortar with a pestle. "I don't live with them," she said. "I live next door as you well know, and I never said I didn't want a husband, only that I won't settle for one."

"Same thing, Emerence."

"No it isn't." She had no illusions regarding the existence of the perfect man. She just preferred to wait for one who was perfect for her. If he never showed, well that was a risk worth taking in her opinion.

The two women fell silent as they continued to work. These were the darkest days of winter, just before the Festival of Delyalda, and those citizens of Timsiora sick with coughs and other lung ailments were numerous. One of the shops Emerence's father owned was this apothecary, and this was its busiest season. Emerence and Glauca had worked long hours already restocking the shelves from the rapidly diminishing inventory of herbs and spices while in the front room where products were displayed and sold, a small army of clerks dealt with a steady stream of customers.

"I just don't want you to be unhappy," Glauca finally said, breaking the silence. She opened a jar of glue and fished a paintbrush from her apron pocket.

Emerence slid her a stack of labels with the names of various concoctions and other herbal combinations written on them. "Do I look unhappy to you?" She was restless at times, more so each year while she lived and worked in the Beladine capital and never went more than a league beyond its walls, but she wasn't unhappy.

Her question made Glauca frown. "No, but we all hide things from each other." She lined the labels up in front of their matching jars, turning the first one to paint glue on its surface and affix a label. "I don't want you to be lonely either. All by yourself in your house at night with no one to talk to."

If Glauca only knew how much Emerence treasured those hours, she wouldn't worry so much. "I deal with people all day, every day, Glauca. Customers, suppliers, caravans, other merchants. By the time I can escape to my house, I'm desperate for the solitude. You worry for nothing."

She hadn't denied being lonely, but everyone experienced loneliness. It wasn't synonymous with solitude. Emerence dealt with her bouts of it by staying busy, so busy that exhaustion kept it at bay, even on those nights when she fell into bed and wondered what it might be like to share the space with a lover and wake to his presence at dawn.

Thankfully, Glauca let the matter of Yeoman Percivus's bride search drop, and their conversation turned to the idle chatter and gossip that made the drudgery of inventory replenishment less wearisome. They were interrupted not long after by a harried clerk who burst into the stock room, eyes wide, face flushed. "Mae Ipsan," he sad on a gasp, using the informal title instead of the more formal "madam" to address Emerence. "Culkhen Goa is back making trouble out front, and there's a group of Quereci here asking for you."

Emerence growled under her breath. Her pity for Culkhen's drunkenness had evaporated when his snake-oil concoctions, sold from the back of his cart, had poisoned a half dozen people. She'd warned folks of the dangers in buying from him, not because he was a competitor but because he was incompetent and dishonest. He blamed Emerence for the loss of his business and had sworn revenge.

"This is the second time in a week he's come calling," Glauca said. Her eyes rounded as did the clerk's when Emerence snatched one of the grabber poles leaned against the corner. "What are you going to do with that?"

"Get rid of a loiterer." Emerence strode out of the stockroom with her clerk tight on her heels.

The clerks and customers in the apothecary's storefront only glanced at her as she passed them with her weapon of choice. The apothecary boasted floor-to-ceiling shelves displaying a large selection of jars filled with herbs, unguents, and tinctures. Those who worked in the store often used a grabber pole to reach the items on the highest shelves. This was the first time Emerence had armed herself with one to do battle with a nuisance.

"Go fetch Guzman," she instructed the clerk who'd brought her the news of trouble and visitors. "Tell him I'll give him a day's wage for a half day's door duty if he comes now."

The boy nodded and shot past her out the door. Emerence followed, nodding and smiling to a few customers who greeted her. She didn't linger, and her hand clenched tighter on the pole as the sound of Culkhen's slurred haranguing reached her ears.

He stood in the middle of the cobblestone walkway, between the apothecary and the drapery, also owned by Emerence's father. He had his back to the apothecary's doors while he bellowed his complaints to passersby and those who sought to enter the shops. "You'll not want to buy from these thieves," he yelled into the street. "These Ipsans will take your hard-earned coin and sell you toad guts for a cough and moth-eaten blankets to keep you warm on a winter's day like today." His glassy gaze returned to Emerence. "Isn't that right, Madam Ipsan?"

She rolled her eyes. The Ipsan family's reputation as honest traders of quality goods was well-established. A drunkard's claims to the contrary wouldn't harm that reputation. Except for a few gawkers, most people ignored Culkhen and went about their business, but his bellowing presence kept potential customers from their doors, and when he clutched the arm of one bolder, would-be visitor she took action.

Flipping the pole in her hand so that she held it like a washing bat, she swung, striking Culkhen's backside hard enough to throw him forward. Caught by surprise, he pinwheeled into the street and fell into the muck churned up by wagons, riders, and foot travelers. Those who witnessed Emerence's attack laughed. She did not. Instead, she glared at Culkhen when he flipped over to stare at her with a bewildered expression that swiftly turned ugly.

"You bitch," he snarled, rising unsteadily to his feet, his front caked in filth from neck to feet. He took a menacing step toward her.

Instinct warned her she no longer faced a loud-mouthed albeit harmless drunk, but she gripped the pole tighter and held her ground. If she fled inside, backed away, or showed any hint of weakness or fear, he'd take it as a signal and only increase his harassment.

"You get one warning, Culkhen," she said. "Plant yourself here again to disturb the peace, and I'll see to it you take up residence at the Zela. Again." She had no idea how she'd make such a thing happen, but Culkhen didn't need to know that.

She must have sounded convincing if the sudden flash of fear in his eyes was any indicator. Her triumph was short-lived. His lips peeled back in a feral baring of yellow teeth, and his hands clenched into fists. He took two steps toward her. Emerence gasped to suddenly find her view of her opponent partially blocked by a tall, broad-shouldered figure.

"You heard Madam Ipsan," her defender said in accented Beladine. "Go your way and don't return."

Stepping to the side for a better view of both Culkhen and this man, Emerence watched as Culkhen swayed on his feet, blinked slowly and executed an unsteady pivot before lurching away. The show over, those who who'd stopped to watch the confrontation continued on their way, a few going into the apothecary and the drapery just as Emerence had hoped.

She released the breath she didn't realize she'd been holding until now and addressed her companion. "I thank you for the intervention, sir. Culkhen is troubled and troublesome."

He turned fully to face her. She caught and held a second breath, this time for a very different reason.

A Quereci nomad. A strikingly handsome one at that.

Swarthy skin made even swarthier by the mountain sun and sharp features that reminded her of a raptor bird, he stood out among the pallid, sun-deprived Beladine crowds like a memory of summer, beautiful and brief in these climes. She guessed him to be in his late twenties, though it was hard to tell. The sun had carved small fans into the skin at the corners of his black eyes. His eyes too seemed older, ancient even, as if he'd witnessed the passing of centuries or stared into a darkness that stared back and showed its fangs.

Those eyes narrowed as his gaze took in her stance and the grabber pole in her grip. "Have you faced him alone before?"

She liked his voice, soft around the edges, deep in the middle, as if he rarely spoke loudly, and if he did, others sat up and paid attention. "No, He hasn't been this bold until now. I suspect he learned my father and half our staff are working at the palace today. He must have assumed he'd only have me to deal with."

"More fool him then." The Quereci tipped his chin toward the grabber pole. "You're good with that stick."

Emerence felt the hot waterfall of a blush descend from her scalp to paint her cheeks and stain her neck and was horrified by her reaction to a polite compliment. The memory of her clerk's words when he first warned her about Culkhen saved her from an awkward response. "I was told a group of Quereci were waiting to see me. I'll risk a guess and say that's you?"

Her champion nodded. He gestured to where a trio of women waited just outside the entrance to the drapery. Bundled for winter weather, they waved with gloved hands. Emerence recognized the one who held up a stack of packages to show her.

"Dahran Omeya!" She strode to the women, leaning in to gently kiss the elderly woman's cheeks and have same done to her.

The Quereci woman perused Emerence from head to toe, finally declaring with a frown, "You shouldn't be fighting men in the streets in this weather dressed like that, Mae Ipsan. At least wear a shawl and cap."

Emerence laughed. In the many years her father had traded with the Quereci, she'd learned of and grown to admire the fiercely independent mountain nomad women. Dahran Omeya had been their principle contact, and Emerence was always glad to see her. The reminder she stood outside in a harsh winter wind with the threat of snow hanging in the air made her shiver.

"Come inside," she said, gesturing toward the drapery's entrance. "There's a fire going in the parlor, and if you've time, I'll serve tea so you can warm up and rest for a time."

They followed her into the shop, past the customers inspecting bolts of cloth and tailors either cutting lengths to order or taking measurements, to the very back of the store. Unlike the apothecary, the drapery's stockroom was a two-story building with its stockroom upstairs. The back had been turned into a parlor where more genteel business negotiations were made over pots of tea or glasses of spirits Emerence's father Tocqua served to his clients.

The drapery had preceded the apothecary. Tocqua Ipsan was a tailor by trade and expanded his trade from working with cloth to importing it and selling it, concentrating on high quality woolens as well as luxury silks and velvets that appealed to the wealthy Beladine citizenry. While the apothecary was redolent with the scents of herbs, spices, and infused oils, the drapery smelled of wool. It was also a warren of smaller rooms with the walls padded in bolts of cloth stacked atop each other to the ceiling.

The parlor Emerence led her guests to was a comfortable room, kept warm by a fire burning brightly in the hearth, a thick rug on the floor and tapestries on the walls to ward off the cold seeping through wood and stone. Comfortable chairs had been placed about the room, along with a pair of tables. She invited her visitors to sit and took Dahran Omega's packages to set them on one of the tables.

The shop's all-maid darted inside before Emerence could call for her. Her glance swept the room, and she raised five fingers in silent question. Five for tea? At Emerence's nod, she disappeared, closing the door behind her.

"We'll have tea very soon," Emerence said, growing increasingly uncomfortable under four intent gazes. She nodded to those women seated on either side of Omeya and to their fierce-looking escort with the golden voice who stood behind the elder's chair. "Dahran Omeya may have already spoken of me, but if not, I'm Emerence Ipsan, the daughter of Tocqua Ipsan who owns this shop and the apothecary next door. I was the one who placed the order for a bolt of amaranthine-dyed wool."

The order hadn't been for her but for the future aristocratic bride of a high-ranking nobleman who wished to include the costly bolt of purple fabric in his bridal gift to her. The Quereci were renowned for their weavers. Her father hadn't trusted anyone else to make good use of the expensive skeins of amaranthine-dyed wool he'd managed to get his hands on from a merchant who traded with the non-human Kai. He'd almost worried himself into an early grave wondering if he could deliver the promised gift on time. Fortunately, the Quereci had arrived, and if Tocqua's luck held, one of those packages Dahran Omeya had brought contained the prized bolt.

The two women who'd accompanied Omeya smiled when she translated Emerence's introduction to them. "This is Dahran Sulti and Dahran Bulava," she said. She pointed to Emerence's erstwhile defender. And that is Gaeres, fifth son of the Kakilo clan's chieftain. Sulti here is his aunt. He's being considered for the position of council *sarsen*." A proud note entered her voice when she included that last bit of information. She looked as if she wanted to say more but Gaeres's warning glance stopped her.

Emerence wondered at the interaction but didn't comment. Whatever silent communication was exchanged between the two, it was neither her business nor her concern. She gave them all a swift bow. "You were very kind to intervene on my behalf earlier," she told Gaeres. "I thank you."

His hair, revealed once he removed his fur-lined hat, was as black as his eyes and fell around his face in tousled waves, tamed at the temples by small braids woven with tiny coins. She'd heard the Quereci people valued their women so greatly it was difficult for a Quereci man to obtain a wife. Emerence doubted this one had any trouble at all and likely had more than one wife waiting for his return to the camps currently wintering on the plains at the base of the Dramorin mountains.

He returned her bow, his gaze never wavering from her face, his expression solemn. "It was my privilege, Madam Ipsan."

Once more the annoying blush she couldn't seem to control heated her face. For the gods' sakes, she was no green girl to turn red under a man's admiring eye, not even a man as handsome as this one. Surely, she must be coming down with one of the fevers that tended to crop up this time of year.

Before she could ask about the packages Omeya had brought, a quick tap at the parlor door signaled the all-maid's return with the promised tea. She let her in and helped her clear the tray of cups, teapot and plate of small pastries, setting them on the table in front of the Quereci women.

Emerence gave the girl instructions before she left. "Go next door and tell Glauca I'll be gone for sometime. She'll have to manage the stores until Papa returns or until I do."

The maid nodded and left. Emerence set to filling cups, waving away Gaeres's surprising offer to help. He insisted on delivering the cups to the women once Emerence had doctored them to their liking with honey, milk, and turmeric and waited until they'd all taken a first sip—including Emerence—before partaking from his own cup.

His actions were so strange to her, she couldn't help but stare. Beladine society was distinctly patriarchal and in the more orthodox families, men weren't only heads of their households, they were small gods. Emerence's father followed a more balanced philosophy, his business acumen overriding any belief of male superiority, at least when it came to running his shops. He'd put Emerence in a supervisory role the first time she turned a profit for him years earlier. Still, he'd never displayed this sort of deference to the women of his family, not even his mother when she was alive. It seemed the rumors that the Quereci were ruled by women might well be true.

Beladine men would sneer at Gaeres's actions and call him weak. Emerence suspected that would be a life-threatening mistake.

"We're different from the Beladine in many ways," Omeya said, her knowing half-smile hinting she'd guessed at her host's thoughts.

"But the same in others." Emerence raised her teacup in a quick toast. "To fine tea, a warm fire, and good company."

Tocqua Ipsan had always believed a client made welcome was a repeat client and a vendor made to feel the same gave one the best workmanship, first pick from a shipment, and the best goods from a coveted lot. He'd built this parlor for that purpose. Hot tea, comfortable chairs, and an inviting fire remained in memory long after negotiations were over, and the return on hospitality was great.

Emerence employed that philosophy every chance she got. In this instance though she simply enjoyed her Quereci guests' company and Dahran Omeya's conversation. Watching Gaeres over the rim of her cup while he drank his tea wasn't a hardship either.

"Tell me of your trip to see us," she told Omeya. "Did you encounter much snow?" She refilled teacups and offered tiny, coin sized pastries to eat.

With Omeya translating at times, the three women took turns describing their journey, which consisted mostly of cold days, colder nights, a great deal of snow, and a small avalanche.

"Gaeres saw the warning signs before it was upon us," Dahran Bulava said. "We managed to get out of the way in time." She gave Gaeres a wide smile. He returned it with a smaller one and the touch of his fingers over his heart in salute to her.

Playing savior obviously came naturally to him, and Emerence liked the fact he didn't crow about it. There was charm in humility.

"It's dangerous this time of year to travel here to Timsiora. My father and I appreciate your willingness to deliver the order, especially with the festival about to start and no lodgings to be found in the city."

Gaeres spoke this time, once more treating her to the sound of his fine voice. "We're camped outside the city walls. We prefer it anyway. Fewer people. Better smells."

He wasn't wrong about that. Timsiora's reek wasn't so bad in the colder months but in summer it was choking. "Will you stay for the Festival of Delyalda?"

Omeya nodded. "For a few days. A dozen of us traveled here. The younger ones want to attend the events as well as the market. Those of us who prefer quiet and an early bed will stay in the camp."

"And I will play escort to my cousins to some of the celebrations," Gaeres said without resentment.

Emerence, who attended a few of the smaller Delyalda

parties each year but eschewed the bigger events, suddenly found renewed interest in the annual celebration. Foolish, foolish old maid, a voice inside her admonished. She ignored it.

"Have you attended Delyalda before?" Gaeres shook his head. "Then you're in for a treat. There are far more events going on than you can possibly attend even were you to stay for the entire festival. I can assure you that neither you nor your cousins will lack for things to do."

"Will you also be attending these celebrations, Madam Ipsan?"

His question took her by surprise, as had many of his actions and statements in the short time since they'd crossed paths. Emerence glanced at Omeya who returned her look with a shrewd one of her own but said nothing. Surely Gaeres wasn't hinting at wanting her company? Then again, she was a logical choice for such help. She was local with in-depth knowledge of the city and the festival, the perfect guide for newcomers looking to attend the best events. Were she not so buried in work, she might have offered to take on the role.

"I've grown too busy and too dull over the years to take part in all but a handful of festival gatherings," she said, giving him a smile so he'd know she didn't really mind that fact. "If you'd like to know the best things to attend, my clerk Kaster is a font of knowledge. I can send him to your camp once his work shift is done and he can give you his recommendation of the best gatherings to visit."

Their respite ended with the emptying of the teapot, and they all turned tot he business at hand. Gaeres opened the packages Emerence had set on the second table in the room, spreading their contents across its surface.

Swaths of wool dyed in both vibrant and muted colors, the weaves tight and durable while still being soft, warm, and light as spiderweb were laid out for Emerence's inspection. Tocqua had ordered several bolts of dyed wool from the Quereci, not just the extravagant amaranthine. Emerence exclaimed over the beauty of each item, imagining shawls and scarves, head wraps and cloaks edged in fur or lined with tiny, semi-precious stones and carved beads.

Omeya opened the last package herself. This was why they'd made the cold, arduous trip from the plains to the canyon in the dead of winter.

"My gods," Emerence exclaimed in a reverent voice at her first sight of the rich purple cloth, nearly black in places where the folds created pockets of shadow.

THE KAI MADE amaranthine, and the skeins they dyed and exported to the Gauri in the south commanded a high price, even higher now as that kingdom still reeled from the aftermath of a demon attack on a massive scale. Tocqua refused to tell Emerence how he'd gotten his hands on the costly skeins this far north, but he'd put them to good use, commissioning the Quereci, renowned weavers, to make this stunning cloth.

"Once more the Quereci prove their prowess at weaving," she said, sliding her fingers along one of the cloth's edges. "This is extraordinary."

Omeya beamed. "You're pleased then?"

"Thrilled," Emerence assured her. "As my father will be.

As the lucky bride will be, and her groom as well. Shall we settle accounts?"

She left them to retrieve her accounts ledger and quill and ink. When she returned, they'd already cleared the table and stacked the bolts of cloth neatly to one side, the amaranthine bolt carefully folded and placed atop the stacks.

Once the sale was recorded and money exchanged, she escorted the Quereci back through the shop and onto the street. Evening came early these days and the air had turned even more brittle. The heavy sky was darker, grayer, and Emerence smelled snow.

"You'll not want to linger behind the walls," she told them. "Or you'll end up trudging through a snowfall to reach your camp." Making your way anywhere in the dark under a heavy snowfall made for a miserable, half-blind journey, no matter how short or long.

Still, the Quereci hesitated. It was Gaeres who explained their hesitation. "The man in the street earlier. Is he a danger to you? Will he return?"

It was thoughtful of them to ask, and while she couldn't guarantee Culkhen wouldn't return to plant himself on the walkway to harass passersby and slander the Ipsan name, Emerence didn't think him a danger. "Culkhen is a nuisance who finds courage at the bottom of a spirits glass. I'll be fine." She tilted her head toward the shops behind her. "And I'm not alone. We'll manage him together if necessary."

Assured by her words, the Quereci women bid her farewell and left to join the diminishing throng in the street. Gaeres lingered, his regard intense, those black eyes reminding her of a bolt of black velvet her father had once presented to her mother as a gift. "Where is your husband to guard you from the likes of this Culkhen, Madam Ipsan?"

Emerence sighed. It always came down to this. She didn't fault him for the assumption. Most women her age were or had been married for years. Those who weren't were widows or embraced partnerships outside the accepted bonds of marriage. Never married, with no prospects in sight or a wish to pursue any, she was an oddity in Beladine society, sometimes ridiculed, often pitied.

"I have no husband," she said without apology. "I've yet to meet one worthy of that role." She smiled to take the sting out of her words though she meant every one. "And you, Gaeres? Does your wife wait for your return?" If he felt entitled to ask about her marital status, then she'd return the favor and ask about his. She tried not to pay attention to the flutters of anticipation and dread in her belly as she waited for his answer. Not that it mattered either way.

A smile curved his mouth, enhancing the prominence of his high cheekbones. "I have no wife," he admitted. "I've not yet been deemed worthy enough for one."

Those flutters in her belly burst into flight. Mortified by her reaction to his words, Emerence thanked almighty Yalda that she was good at hiding her thoughts, though the way Gaeres watched her made her doubt her ability.

"I've no doubt that will be rectified very soon," she told him. "Especially if you're about to be made a council chief as Dahran has said." She glanced over her shoulder to see the figures of the women disappearing into the crowd, obviously not concerned that Gaeres wasn't with them. "You should hurry," she said. "Before they leave you behind."

"And you have a shop to attend to." He bowed to her. "It was my honor and my pleasure to meet you, Madam Ipsan."

The way he said it made it seem more than just a polite, perfunctory farewell. Impassioned almost with the hint of hope they'd meet again. The awful blush plagued her yet again, and she returned Gaeres's bow to hide the fire licking at her cheeks. "Likewise, sir. May you and yours enjoy Delyalda while you're here."

She watched him sprint after the Quereci women, his tall figure fleet as he maneuvered through the crowd to catch up. He was handsome, intriguing, courageous, and courteous. And young. At least too young to consider a woman like her anything more than the role she fulfilled: Beladine merchant. She shrugged. His presence had afforded her a pleasant interlude for a short time, and if she'd imagined the admiration in his eyes, that was fine too. It was good to dream.

She shivered in the blustering wind and retreated to the drapery where fine cloth dyed by an Elder race and woven by mysterious nomads waited to be repackaged and stored for her father's return and inspection. The work day didn't stop, not even for daydreams of future Quereci chieftains.

SHE DIDN'T SEE Gaeres the following day or any days after, though Kaster said the Quereci had returned to the drapery to inquire after her and ask questions about the festival. Gaeres had also spoken to her father who'd been in raptures over the amaranthine wool and regaled Emerence over supper one evening with gossip from the royal palace.

When he left for the kitchen to refill his tankard from the ale ask, his wife Linnett gave Emerence a pitying look. "You realize you'll hear all of this at least three times?"

"How many times have you heard it so far?"

Tocqua's second wife was much like Emerence's deceased mother in character if not in looks. Pragmatic to the bone and just as patient. Emerence had liked her from the first moment they'd met.

Linnett huffed. "Four, and I was there with him, mind, so I saw and heard the same things he did firsthand."

Emerence smothered her laughter when her father returned with his ale and continued with his stories of palace chaos and intrigue as the royal family planned to open the festivities for Delyalda and host a mob of nobles attending the winter celebration as well as the wedding of Lord Sodrin Uhlfrida to King Rodan's niece.

He and his assistant tailors had been run ragged with seeing to the wardrobes of the many lords ordering new finery at the last minute or updating what they already owned. He turned to more serious matters after exhausting the subject of palace gossip. "I was told by more than a few people about Culkhen Goa making an ass of himself, and that Gaeres had to stop him when he threatened you. You should have told me yourself, Em."

Linnett nodded. "Keeping quiet doesn't help anyone."

Emerence pushed her food around her plate. "I'm sorry to

you both, but there really was nothing to tell. Culkhen was deep in his cups and spouting nonsense. I dealt with him and Gaeres convinced him not to linger. I didn't mention it because you would have worried needlessly as this conversation proves."

"You're my child. Of course I'll worry."

"I'm a long way from childhood, Papa."

"But still my daughter," Tocqua insisted. "I'll walk you home when you're ready to leave." His expression brightened. "Or you can just stay the night here and return home in the morning."

"Papa, I live next door. I'll be fine."

Nevertheless, he ended up watching her from his doorway, refusing to budge until she unlocked her door and waved to him before going inside. Culkhen was becoming even more of an annoyance than anticipated if he was motivating her father to treat her like she was five years old.

Her tiny house was a cozy refuge, perfect for one person, two at most if the pair were enamored with each other. The corner hearth was barely large enough to hold a decent size cook pot but when lit, it kept the main room and the alcove serving as her bedroom warm. The rug underfoot, the blankets on her bed and the curtains at the single window near the door worked as barriers against the cold as well. A humble, comfortable home, and most important of all, entirely hers.

She shed her outer garb and cap, lit the hearth and set a pot of tea to boil. She added a warming pan as well to glide over her bed linens once it got hot enough to do the job. She caught a flicker of motion in the corner of her eye and rose from her crouch by the fire to twitch back the window curtains. The window pane's glass was frigid under her touch with a line of frost already painting the edges. The street was mostly dark except for a few puddles of light cast by lamps placed in windows of houses across from her.

People were awake later than usual. Delyalda would start in another day, and many prepared to either host or attend private parties as well as the public festivals. Soon enough the streets would remain brightly lit, crowded, and noisy until dawn.

Every year Tocqua groused about the noise and crowds though he didn't complain about the increase in business. Emerence loved it all. The festival provided a much-needed break from the dreariness of deep winter and the seemingly endless days of bone-chilling temperatures and leaden skies. The Festival of Delyalda bid farewell to the longest night of the year, with an eye toward the preeminence of the longest day, still months away but getting closer with every sunrise.

She finished her tea, dressed for bed, and by the time she banked the fire, her house was toasty. The warming pan turned her bed from a mortuary slab to a cozy haven that invited her to snuggle in and pull the covers over her head, content.

Mostly content, a small voice niggled in her mind. Memories and images played across the backs of her eyelids. Gaeres, tall and burnished, with his hawkish features and black eyes whose expression belonged to an old veteran of brutal wars instead of a young man still sliding into his prime.

She'd found him beautiful. Even his voice, with its rich

quiet tones and the half smile he often bestowed on the Quereci women he guarded, enchanted her. He did indeed remind her of summer with its promise of warmth and the sultry play of sunlight on smooth skin and dark hair.

Drowsiness encroached on her visions, and she welcomed it. To dwell too long on those things not hers, and never would be, invited melancholy. She wanted to fall asleep happy not sad. Still, her last image before slumber overtook her was of Gaeres as he took his teacup from her hand, his brown fingers slender and elegant, their tips the whisper of a caress against her own.

As it was every year, the days designated for celebrating Delyalda were defined by crowded streets and a city swelled to thrice its usual size in population. The weekly outdoor market reflected the same as it crept beyond the edges of neighborhoods, and enterprising citizens with an item to sell or a skill to trade set up shop in their doorways, their parlors even, and earned coin from visitors arriving hourly to celebrate the winter festival.

Emerence split her time between the apothecary and the drapery, helping her father and Linnett manage both. She'd intended to balance the accounts for both shops this day, but the crush of customers kept her far too busy. Tocqua was in his glory, he and his army of tailors frantically plying needle and thread to festival finery while Linnett handled the apothecary and Emerence kept the harried staff of both stores from dropping with exhaustion.

Summer came unexpectedly to the apothecary near noon, golden and warm and dusted with snow. She glanced up from measuring a packet of ground willow bark for a client to see Gaeres standing at the counter watching her. She offered him a wide smile, inordinately happy to find him here but worried for the reason. Those who visited this shop did so seeking relief from or a cure for ailments.

She scraped the order of willow bark into a small cloth bag, gave instructions for dosage to her customer and took payment. She signaled one of the clerks to take her place at the counter so she could concentrate on her Quereci visitor.

"What a pleasure to see you here, sir," she said, meaning every word. "Though I fear why. Is Dahran Omeya ill? The others?"

Gaeres shook his head, flinging droplets of melted snow from his hat onto the floor. "We're mostly well, Madam Ipsan. I'm here for two purposes. Two of my cousins are next door looking at ribbon, and I'm to escort them to the open market later for one of the daytime events. My other cousin woke this morning with a sick stomach. I've been instructed to return to the camp with something to settle it fast so she'll feel well enough to attend tonight's festivities with her sisters." His black eyes warmed. "It was a good excuse as any to see and speak with you once more."

The surprise jolting her at his forthright statement was only surpassed by the heat suddenly coursing through her veins. She didn't doubt his sincerity. A lifetime as a shopkeeper's daughter had trained her ear to know when someone spoke truly or simply tried to charm her into giving them something for free. Even if she weren't so immune to such false wiles, she'd believe him. Her impression of Gaeres thus far had been of a man of upstanding character, and Emerence trusted her judgment.

"I have just the thing," she said and motioned to him to follow her toward the back of the shop and one of the floor-to-ceiling shelves crowded with jars and bottles. She went up on her toes to reach a small vial, swallowing a gasp when slender fingers curved around hers to grasp it.

Gaeres let go almost instantly, but Emerence's hand still tingled from the brief touch as did the rest of her body, especially with him standing so close behind her. She turned to offer him the vial and almost collided with his chest. The apothecary's small confines and the number of people currently shopping inside it enforced even closer proximity. In this instance, she didn't mind at all, and if Gaeres's expression was anything to judge by, he didn't mind either.

She held the bottle up for his perusal. "Candied ginger, suspended in a little honey," she told him. "Chew it or steep it in a hot tea. It's guaranteed to ease the touchiest stomach."

He plucked the bottle gently from her fingers. A clerk and three more customers sidled up next to them, squeezing them into a corner. If Gaeres was close before, he practically enveloped Emerence now. She savored the moment. He loomed above her, half in shadow, half in lamplight, the fur edging of his hat framing his angular face.

"I'm sorry it's so crowded," she said.

"I'm not." His words caressed her. "What do I owe for the

ginger?"

She was tempted to tell him it was gratis, a gift to repay his help with Culkhen days earlier, but she avoided that trap, listening to instinct that warned he'd find insult in that kind of gratitude for his nobility. Instead, she quoted him the price, to which he nodded then grinned. "If we can get out of this corner, I can reach my coin to pay you."

Never before had Emerence been so reluctant to take payment from a customer.

His hands settled on her waist as he maneuvered her away from the corner toward the counter where customers made their purchases.

"Mae Ipsan," a clerk called from the other side of the store. "Could I get your assistance please?"

A sigh of regret escaped her lips before she could stop it. She gazed up at Gaeres who towered over her, his hands a warm pressure on her waist even through her heavy clothing. "I'm needed," she said. "Someone at the counter will see to your purchase." She smiled. "It was a pleasure to see you again, sir."

"Gaeres," he corrected her. "Call me Gaeres, Madam Ipsan." His hands fell away and he edged back enough to give her room.

"Then you must call me Emerence, Gaeres." She liked the way his name fell on her lips. "I may be older than you, but it makes me feel like your mother or your aunt when you address me as madam."

He frowned. "Of the many things about you that have crossed my mind since we met, a comparison to my mother or my aunt was never one of them."

"Mae Ipsan!" The clerk sounded panicked now.

Emerence brushed Gaeres's hand with hers. "Give my best to Dahran Omeya and to your cousin. The ginger and honey will help."

His regard rested soft on her shoulders as she walked away. She watched from the corner of her eye as he paid for his purchase. She missed seeing him leave except for a glimpse of his hat as he passed through the doorway and onto the street.

The remainder of the day was defined by crowds, chaos, and Tocqua Ipsan's glee over the many sales both shops made. Emerence managed to escape the madness shortly before they closed, explaining she couldn't put off balancing accounts any longer.

She didn't lie. The spike in business had delayed her monthly reconciliations and she'd sworn to herself she'd put in a few hours balancing entries before going home. Her stepmother brought her dinner while she worked alone in the draper's office upstairs, and Emerence savored the quiet of the finally empty shop, even as her eyes itched with fatigue.

She finally set the accounts aside after adding a column of numbers incorrectly for the fourth time. Linnett had extracted a promise from her that she'd go home once she finished her meal. Emerence had broken that promise a good three hours ago.

The distant sounds of party-goers celebrating at some of the homes owned by Beladine nobility echoed through the market district's deserted streets. Thick clouds obscured the moon and stars above, and snow fell in a gentle curtain onto the rooftops and cobblestone walkways.

She locked the drapery's front door, checked the door to the apothecary for good measure and turned to walk home. Her heart vaulted into her throat at the sight of a hulking shadow standing across the street, silent, watching. She fumbled for the key she'd dropped into her apron pocket beneath her cloak, as well as the small knife she carried. A tool more than a weapon.

The streets of Timsiora were safe enough if one stayed away from the worst quarters of the city, and she had nothing on her to attract the attentions of a cutpurse or pickpocket, but one could never be too careful. The menacing figure watching her made her glad she carried even the smallest weapon and wish she'd kept her promise to Linnet to leave earlier.

Her small squeak of distress changed to one of relief when the shadow sharpened into details, revealing a familiar tall form. "Gaeres?"

He crossed the street, halting in front of her before offering one of his courteous bows. "Forgive me. I didn't mean to frighten you."

Gladdened and puzzled by his appearance, she looked to either side of him wondering where his cousins might be. "What are you doing here? I thought you were escorting your relatives to one of the evening parties."

"They're attending it now, along with Dahran Sulti who'll see to it they're safe. I'm here to do the same for you." Darkness hid his expression but not the concern in his voice. "Does your father not worry that you walk alone at night?"

Emerence slipped the shop key and knife back into her

pocket. "He always worries, but I've done this many times. It's mostly safe and I stay alert and don't carry money or jewels on me." While moments before her heart sat wedged in her throat, it now beat fast at the knowledge Gaeres had come to escort her home, worried for her safety. "How did you know I was still here?" The windows in the drapery's second story were blocked by concealing curtains, and the light from her desk lamp wasn't bright enough to penetrate their coverings and shine through.

"I didn't. Not at first. I wished to see you again so I left Dahran Sulti and my cousins at the party and returned here. I saw your father's wife bring food to the shop after it closed and assumed you were still working."

She gaped at him. "You waited all that time? Why didn't you just knock? I would have let you in." And cheerfully abandoned battling numbers in favor of spending time with the handsome Quereci.

He shrugged. "I didn't wish to disturb you."

Astonished, Emerence could only stare at him before saying, "That's a long time to wait for someone, especially when you weren't really sure it was me still in the shop."

Another shrug, this one accompanied by a lopsided grin. "Reason and good instincts served me well." He sobered. "I would be honored to escort you to your home or to one of the parties if you so desire."

As fatigued as she was, the last thing Emerence wanted was to spend the rest of an already long evening amidst loud, drunken crowds, no matter how entertaining the venue or luxurious the setting. "Home," she said, delighted by the idea of spending a brief time in Gaeres's company, even if the walk was no more than two streets over from the shops. Hopefully they'd leisurely stroll.

Their breaths fogged in front of them, mingling in a single cloud before dissipating in the frosty air. The snow fell harder, cladding rooftops and covering streets in white. Used to initiating conversation and carrying on small talk with customers, Emerence avoided the awkwardness that came with hunting for topics of conversation.

"The two biggest public parties during Delyalda are hosted by the Ganmurgen and Dolrida families. They've been in competition with each other for more than a decade as to who hosts the best party. Which one did you and your cousins attend?"

Snow crunched under their feet as they walked, and Gaeres held her elbow to steady her as they navigated across a slippery patch of road. "I don't remember," he said. "It was a great house built of white stone, filled with light, people, and music."

Emerence couldn't decide if she heard awe or horror in his voice or possibly both as he described the scene. She recognized his description of the house. "That's the Dolrida estate. Your cousins will be having a fine time there as will Dahran Sulti. You're missing out by keeping company with me." She wasn't fishing for a denial. A young, handsome Quereci warrior would garner a great deal of fawning attention at a Delyalda celebration and be far more entertained than acting as escort to a tired shopkeeper whose idea of the best ending to the night was to drink a cup of tea and fall into bed.

"I disagree," he said. "I've hoped all day I'd find a way to speak with you again. My patience has been rewarded. There's no other place I'd rather be at the moment."

Emerence halted abruptly. Gaeres mimicked her action. "Why?" she asked.

"Why what?"

She held out her hands in a puzzled gesture. "Why did you want to speak with me again? I assure you I'm not known for my sparkling conversation or extraordinary wit." She was just Emerence Ipsan, merchant's daughter. A spinster as well. *"How unfortunate,"* many had clucked to each other, often within her hearing.

Gaeres's expression remained maddeningly obscure in the shadows. Emerence wished the night were clear so the moon's radiance might reveal his features better. "Because I find you interesting and would like to know more about you." He frowned suddenly. "Is this walk of ours unacceptable in Beladine society?"

His question made her smile. Her days of being chaperoned under a matron's eagle eye for the sake of propriety were long over. There were certain freedoms and perks afforded to spinsterhood, and she was old enough now to act as a matron herself. She chuckled and resumed walking, Gaeres keeping pace beside her. "For a woman of my age and status, it's perfectly acceptable." And worthy of at least a month's supply of gossip among any of the crones who loved to mind everyone else's affairs except their own.

"What is your age and status?" he asked.

A blunt question that might be considered rude were it

asked by another Beladine citizen, but Emerence interpreted as Gaeres meant it – innocent curiosity and a wish to learn more about her just as he'd said. "I'm six and thirty," she said. He really didn't need to know she was staring seven and thirty hard in the eye. "And I've never been married."

"Ah. I assumed you were a widow."

Of course he did. Those who didn't know her always assumed such when they learned she wasn't married. "As it is with most unattached women of my age," she said. "It's a reasonable assumption."

"But not why I make it," he countered. "You're beautiful, brave, and competent. What man wouldn't want such a woman?"

Stunned by his compliment and made tongue-tied by it, she stayed silent. He continued with his line of questioning, no doubt emboldened by her silence. "Why have you never married?"

That was an easy question to answer and answer honestly. She wondered if Gaeres would be as startled by her answer as she'd been by his praise of her. "I haven't yet met the person I'm willing to devote myself to. When I do, it will be for all my life, wholeheartedly and without reservation. They will have all of me, and I will demand all of them. It's a great deal to ask of someone and a great deal to give them. Such a person may not exist but I'd rather be alone and content in my solitary state than unhappy in a marriage simply for the sake of being wedded.

If her response unsettled him, he gave no indication of it, and the night hid any tell-tale emotion in his gaze. Even if she had unsettled him, it didn't matter. Gaeres was Quereci, not Beladine. A visitor to Timsiora, a pleasant, very temporary distraction in her daily existence. If he chose to scoff at her words or worse, pity her for them, no matter. The worst that might happen would be she'd send him away and continue her journey home by herself.

Her fascination only grew when he nodded. "That is wise. And admirable. I think there would be many happier people and happier marriages if they thought as you did."

"There would certainly be a lot more unattached people," she said with a grin, relieved despite her logical self assurances, that he didn't mock or express contempt for her beliefs. He'd complimented her yet again, and the warmth inside her chased away much of the cold seeping through her clothes.

They were halfway to her house, their time together almost at an end. Emerence chose to satisfy her own curiosity. "And you, Gaeres, what is your age and status?" She already knew him to be unmarried though not why.

"I'm seven and twenty," he said. She'd guessed right, but having it confirmed made her groan inside. If only he was in the same decade as her. "I remained unmarried because I'm not yet deemed by my clan as worthy to take a wife."

Emerence's eyebrows shot up. Handsome, charming, son of a chieftain, and soon to be a council subchief himself according to Omeya. What could possibly disqualify him as husband material among his own people? "How do you become worthy?" The Quereci were an insular folk who kept to themselves for the most part, their culture mysterious and unknown to outsiders. It seemed she was about to get a peek into their society.

"Through notable deeds, displays of wise council, defense of the clan in times of hostility, hard work, and the building of trust in others through reliability and steadfastness."

She blinked at him. "Those are all admirable traits in anyone, and while we don't know each other very well, I have a difficult time believing you haven't met most if not all of those requirements."

It was Gaeres who halted first this time. He bowed to Emerence. "You honor me with your words," he said. She blushed, grateful for the darkness. "I've tried to meet those expectations. Only one has yet to satisfy the elders, and that one is mostly due to my age. I hope to remedy that when I become a council *sarsen*."

"Wise council," she said. "Wisdom isn't normally the purview of youth."

Gaeres nodded. "So I've been told."

"You're young," she said, "but not a stripling lad." And his gaze was strangely old, she thought. The color and shape of his eyes were arresting, sublime, but their expression was riveting simply for that perennial quality to his regard.

"I hope to still be young by the time I do take a wife," he said without revealing more about Quereci customs.

They resumed their walk a second time, and she steered the conversation back to the festival and more recommendations for the parties he and his relatives might enjoy attending. "Dahran Omeya said you weren't staying for the entire festival. Now that you've attended some of the gatherings, will you change your mind?" She prayed he'd say yes.

He dashed her hopes with a quick shake of his head. "We leave day after tomorrow, early. However, my cousins are insistent we go to the Sun and Rose celebration. Have you heard of it?"

Not only had she heard of it, she'd attended it several years in a row when she was still in her twenties. "It's one of the favorite Delyalda celebrations. Four young men are chosen to represent Yalda or the sun. They dance with every woman participating until the musicians stop the music. The woman still dancing with one of the four suns receives a rose of promise. The belief is she'll find her true love and be married by the time of the next festival."

"My cousins will kill me in my sleep if I don't take them to that particular event," he said on a mournful note.

Emerence laughed. "Trust me when I tell you that you'll have as wonderful time as they will. As long as you like dancing. I used to attend every year. I still go some years. It's as entertaining to watch as it is to participate."

"Why don't you participate? You said you didn't wish to marry until you found someone you considered worthy of your heart. That doesn't mean you can't still dance and hope just as the others do."

Whoever became this man's wife would be one fortunate woman, she thought wistfully. "It's no longer for me," she said. "As I'm no longer a dewy maiden and have never been a widow, me dancing in the Sun and Rose would make me ridiculous in others' eyes. Besides, every woman participating is another woman's direct competition for that rose. Many truly believe in the rose's promise. I've no wish to make it harder when I have no interest in the outcome."

His frown became a scowl. "The Beladine are very different from the Quereci. A Quereci woman, old or young, would be encouraged to participate in such a dance, not mocked for it, and the men would fight for the privilege of representing the god instead of waiting to be chosen. In fact," he continued, "the woman would be the one to pass out a rose to a hopeful Quereci man."

She sighed. "Your people sound amazing, the women so valued in your world."

"They are the heart and soul of the clans," he said. "A Quereci man isn't considered a full-fledged member of the clan until he marries or is sponsored by a Quereci woman. A Quereci woman is born with the status." He smiled. "You don't believe me."

She shook her head. "No, I do. Truly. I'm just amazed by it all. The Quereci men accept this way of things?"

He tilted his head to one side. "Of course. Why wouldn't they?"

She wanted to ply him with more questions but unfortunately they'd reached her house. It sat small, dark, and empty across the street from where she stood with Gaeres. Never before had seeing it not given her pleasure. Until now.

"My home," she said, pointing to the structure. "My father and his wife live next door." The bigger home was dark as well. No doubt Tocqua and Linnett were sound asleep.

Prior to Gaeres's revelations about the strong matriarchal nature of Quereci society, Emerence would have braced herself for some disapproving remark over the fact she owned her home independent of her father or some other male relative. Such a thing just wasn't done. Tocqua himself had been so furious when first learned what she'd done, he didn't speak to her for a fortnight. She didn't regret it then. She didn't regret it now. She might be solitary, but her life was her own, including this humble abode.

Gaeres didn't remark on her home ownership, but his face drew into forbidding lines and his demeanor changed, taking on a mien so threatening, Emerence backed up a step. "Your door is open," he said softly. "And a shadow moves inside your house."

Alarm shot through her and she peered at her door. It was indeed open, partially. The shadows cast from the nearby street lamp had hidden that fact from her on first glance, but her companion had noticed. Her heart thumped painfully fast and hard in her chest. An intruder lurked in her parlor. Were they looking to steal from a house temporarily unoccupied or where they waiting for her to return? The second possibility made her shudder much harder than the first one did.

Gaeres shifted, and suddenly he gripped a wicked looking long knife in one hand. He silently motioned for her to stay where she was.

"What are you doing?" she whispered, a terrible suspicion that he meant to confront the intruder becoming reality right in front of her.

He ignored her question and sprinted across the street on silent feet before she could stop him. He angled away from her door, ending up two houses down before creeping toward her house. As lithe and fluid as any shadow he soon slipped through the doorway.

Emerence jumped at the sudden crash of something break-able, followed by a pained yelp, then a thump and finally a gravid hush. Her door banged open suddenly, slamming against the outside wall as Gaeres emerged, dragging a huddled form by the scruff across the cobbled walk before tossing it into the middle of the street.

The loud noises had alerted her neighbors. Lamplight flared pale yellow in several windows, including those in her father's house. Gaeres bent to pick something up from the ground before stepping into the street. He nudged the intruder onto his back with the tip of his boot.

Emerence gasped, her fear turning to outrage when she saw the face of the person who'd violated the sanctity of her home. "Culkhen Goa, you bastard!"

"EMERENCE," LINNET FINALLY declared, rubbing the small of her back after giving one last swipe of her rag across the small hearth's mantle. "The house is so clean now, if you scrub anything else, it will crumble to dust, including the stone."

Her stepmother was right. Emerence's reason told her it was so, yet she struggled to overcome the revulsion of knowing someone with malicious intent had been in here, touching her possessions, making himself at home in her house, sitting on her furniture as he waited for her to return. For the hundredth time her skin crawled at the thought.

Hours earlier, the small space had been crowded with the

city's constabulary, concerned neighbors, and her furious father demanding Culkhen's head on a plate. Gaeres had stayed only long enough to recount the event and all pertinent details to her father. Culkhen had remained huddled in the street, surrounded by half the neighborhood who threatened to stone him if he tried to get up and run.

Gaeres had handed a nasty looking dagger to Tocqua. "He had this on him. Whether or not it's something he always carries or if he brought it with him just for tonight, I can't say." His gaze settled on Emerence, sympathy gleaming in those black eyes. Anger too. "I can't stay to speak with your constables," he said. "My relatives are probably wondering where I am, but I can return tomorrow if needed."

Tocqua took the knife, and for a moment Emerence wondered if he planned to use it on its owner. Instead he held out a hand and grasped Gaeres's forearm in a forceful grip. "Thank you, Gaeres. Thank you for saving my daughter."

Gaeres returned the clasp, his regard flickering briefly to Tocqua from Emerence. "It was my honor to do so, sir." He let go and bowed low to her. "Madam Ipsan, I remain forever in your service."

He left the small mob in the street. Emerence assured her father she'd be right back and chased after Gaeres. He paused when she called his name and turned.

"A thank you seems so inadequate," she told him. "You've saved me twice now."

Gaeres shook his head. "I defended you twice. There's a difference."

Oh, if only she were younger with different dreams and

goals. Or if he were older, also with different dreams and goals. He possessed the charm of a courtier, but a charm wielded with sincerity and from the heart, its power so much greater than the practiced kind. Fifteen years earlier and Emerence's knees would have melted. Instead, she remained steady and offered him an assurance. "You needn't worry about the constabulary bothering you. My father is a respected Beladine citizen. They'll accept his word and my testimony as well. And Culkhen Goa has already spent many a night locked in the Zela for petty crimes."

Gaeres's eyebrows lowered into that same forbidding expression she found both intriguing and not a little intimidating. "Breaking into your house to wait for you with the intent to commit violence against you isn't petty, Emerence. You'll need to be on your guard when they release him from the gaol."

She nodded. "I know. I will." She'd underestimated Culkhen's drive for revenge or the fiery blame he'd assigned her for slandering his already notorious reputation. She wouldn't make the same mistake twice.

"Come to the Sun and Rose celebration tomorrow night," he told her. At her hesitation, he employed the words that guaranteed she'd show up. "Come so I may have a last chance to tell you farewell before I leave Timsiora."

"All right," she said. "I'll be there, though I don't know when."

"I'll wait for you." His gaze drifted to a point behind her. Emerence didn't need to turn to know what he stared at: all her neighbors avidly watching the two of them converse and trying their very best to overhear what was said. Gaeres winked at her. "Until tomorrow, Emerence."

She watched him go until he turned a corner and disappeared from sight. Even then, she didn't move until her stepmother's voice at her shoulder startled her out of her reverie. "A constable is here to speak with you, Emerence."

Questions and statements by the constabulary and her father's insistence she sleep at his house for the rest of her life made the night long and tiresome. At dawn she was still wide awake and cleaning her small abode with a demon's fury. She'd resisted Tocqua's demands to come home with him and Linnet.

"There's no possible way I'll sleep tonight, Papa," she'd told him. "I just want to clean my house, boil my sheets and get rid of any sense of Culkhen being there."

"You can do that in the morning," he began, only to be interrupted by Linnett who came to Emerence's rescue.

"Remember that time the pair of thieves broke into the apothecary and made off with the emergency fund? Only the coin box was taken, but you had all of us clean the store from top to bottom."

At that reminder, a glint of understanding dawned in Tocqua's eyes. He grasped Emerence's hands. "We can stay to help."

She pressed his hand to her cheek. "Go home. It's late. Get your rest. You can help by giving me the day free away from the shops."

"Done," he declared.

After promising him and Linnett she'd be fine and wishing a good night to the other neighbors who finally dispersed and went home, she returned to her house and began her cleaning frenzy. She'd presented a calm front to everyone and hadn't lied when she'd said she was fine, but every creak of the house or noise in the street made her jump. The arrival of the dawn and Linnett at her door with a basket of cleaning supplies had been welcoming sights.

Several hours later, with her house sparkling and new linens on her bed while the ones she washed dried on a line in her back garden, Emerence took pity on her hard-working stepmother. "You're right. I don't' think there's a spot of dirt to be found." The lingering sense of being somehow violated remained. No mop or cleaning rag would get rid of that, only time.

"May I use your washtub?" she asked Linnett. "I'm attending the Sun and Rose party tonight, and I'm too dirty for a just a sponge bath."

Delighted by the request and the fact Emerence didn't plan to hide in her house from fear, Linnett had readily agreed. When Emerence arrived next door, she found not only a hip bath full of hot water but scented soaps and oils available for her use. And it was Linnett who dressed her freshly washed hair in an intricate knot of braids wrapped in a bun that rested against her nape and was decorated with a sprinkling of pearl hair pins.

She donned the nicest outfit she owned, a gown of forest-green embossed velvet with cuffs, hem and bodice embroidered in silver thread. Her father's eyes widened when she entered the parlor where he sat by the fire enjoying a cup of tea. "Well," he said. "Aren't you a fine sight in the that gown with your hair just so."

She saw the questions in his eyes: why attend a Delyalda festival this year? And why this particular one with its nod to marriage? Had Gaeres been the one to motivate her to go?

He asked all of these with his gaze but kept the words behind his teeth. Emerence gave him an answer that was true and would please him. "I refuse to let street muck like Culkhen Goa turn me into a fearful hermit. Tonight I will attend a celebration and enjoy myself." And bid farewell to a man who'd given her a brief view into what it might be like to fall in love.

Smiles wreathed Tocqua's lined face. "Do you need an escort?"

She almost declined then changed her mind. "I'd love one."

Tocqua wasted no time. He abandoned his tea and hurriedly exchanged his shoes for his boots. He donned his coat and rushed to open the door for her. "Ready?" he said.

They both checked her house before they left. Tocqua had replaced the broken lock earlier in the day, adding a second for good measure. He'd done the same to the door that opened to her back garden. Satisfied the house was locked up tight, they set off for the Sun and Rose celebration.

The host for this popular Delyalda event changed every year, and this year's host was the powerful Jakarin family whose estate sat at the end of Timsiora's market district, surrounded by a high wall that protected a mansion set in the middle of an expansive, manicured garden.

The festival was open to the public for a price. Proceeds went to funding the following year's party at the next host's residence and to repair any damage done at the current residence. The second usage was a rare event. No one wanted to be blacklisted from a Sun and Rose celebration.

Her father left her at the main gate where a huge crowd of celebrants had gathered to wait for entry. "When should I return for you?" he said.

"You won't have to. You know how this works. I'll just join one of the big groups that always travel together. If you're still awake when I get back, I'll knock."

She chatted with several business acquaintances who waited with her outside the gates. Once inside, she paused to admire the gardens decorated for the festival and the great house shimmering with the light of countless lanterns. Hundreds of people strolled the grounds or gathered in clusters to drink or partake from the numerous tables of food laid out in various spots to be enjoyed.

Emerence set a meandering course toward the house, her gaze sweeping the crowd, looking for one face in particular. She spotted him inside in one of the three packed ballrooms, surrounded by a flock of Beladine maidens whose infatuated expressions told Emerence he'd managed to charm them just as quickly and thoroughly as he'd charmed her. She chuckled under her breath at the hunted look he wore.

Dancers swirled around them, and she caught sight of three dressed in garb not of Beladine fashion and similar in style to Gaeres's. The cousins, she was sure, and somewhere among the crush of people a venerable dahran watched them with a hawk's gaze.

This was a young crowd for the most part, but there were

plenty of watchful parents or relatives playing chaperon who were closer to her age as well. Emerence's attention on Gaeres was drawn away by a handsome lord she recognized as one of her father's clients. He asked her to dance. She obliged and soon found herself whirled about by one partner after another until she begged a moment to rest and fled for small corner of the room, away from the crowd, where she could cool off and enjoy the taste of wine from a goblet a servant had given her. The drink was cold and soothing on her parched tongue and throat.

She spotted Gaeres again and this time his gaze met hers across the room. So much for catching her breath. The look he bestowed on her was hot enough to set her clothes on fire. That look made her wonder what it might be like to stretch naked under the light of a summer sun.

Gaeres began shouldering his way through the crowd of celebrants toward her, his gaze locked on her. She'd come here as he'd asked to say goodbye. Maybe if she were fortunate, he'd kiss her hand or possibly her cheek when he bid her farewell. It would be a lovely memory of him to hold.

He never made it to her. The musicians playing on a second story balcony overlooking the ballroom struck up a familiar tune. The crowd bellowed its excitement and surged together like the inhalation of a great, heaving beast. The dance of Sun and Rose had begun.

Emerence no longer saw Gaeres in the crowd. He was tall but so were many other men in attendance, and it was easy to lose sight of someone among so many. The sea of people broke up into four huge circles. A master of ceremonies held up a bowl to pick the first of four names, men who would act as avatars for Yalda, god of the sun and creation. The four would dance with many of the Beladine maidens in attendance until the music stopped and the lucky woman still dancing with one of the Suns received a Rose of blessing as a token of luck that she might be married by the following Delyalda.

Emerence abandoned her place in the corner, not to join the dance, but for a better view of the dancers, and a better chance of seeing Gaeres in the crush of bodies. She laughed aloud when his name was one of the four called to act as one of the Suns. He wore a resigned expression as he stepped forward to the crowd's cheers and wagged an admonishing finger at an older woman Emerence recognized as Dahran Sulti. No doubt it had been Sulti who'd entered his name into the lottery.

Emerence almost pitied Gaeres. He and the other three men chosen were in for a long slog of it, fun though it was. While the women either waited their turns to dance with the Suns or bowed out after a time, the men acting as the Suns danced continuously. It was a grueling exercise in stamina, especially when the crowd was this large.

The master of ceremonies raised a hand and signaled for the musicians to begin again. Just before Gaeres's first partner approached him, he found Emerence. The tiny tilt of his head encouraged her to join the circle. She refused with a quick shake of her head and a smile. As she'd told him before, this dance was no longer for her though she was happy to watch.

He was a graceful dancer, even when it was obvious he was learning the steps as he went. Even as the dance grew progressively faster and wilder, with partners switching at increasing speeds and the musicians played with a gusto only matched by the crowd's enthusiasm and the dancers' flying feet, Gaeres didn't falter or stumble. People in the crowd shouted encouragement to their favorite dancer and the four Suns, two who looked ready to faint from exhaustion.

When the master of ceremonies finally called a halt, the musicians could hardly be heard over the crowd's roar. A deafening cheer went up, along with a round of applause for the Suns who managed to make it through the entire event and the four women who'd won their Rose of blessing. Emerence clapped and whistled her approval at discovering that Gaeres's final partner was one of his cousins. He gave her a brief hug, then nudged her toward the master of ceremonies who presented her with one of the roses.

It was Emerence's turn to be enveloped by the crowd, and she lost sight of Gaeres a third time. Hemmed in from all sides, she managed to shove her way to the perimeter of the ballroom where a set of doors led outside to the gardens. Spotting freedom from the crowds and the heat, she slipped outside, grateful for the shock of cold air that suddenly buffeted her face and cooled her skin.

Snow continued to fall, blanketing the gardens so the white landscape took on a sparkling, ethereal quality. It was only a matter of time before the cold became too much, even for her heavy dress, and she'd retreat inside once more. Until then she followed the line of neatly manicured bushes iced in white to where they stopped just shy of a towering conifer whose sloping branches defied an accumulation of snow so the tree stood tall and black against a night sky made charcoal gray by snow-heavy clouds.

"Emerence."

She turned at the sound of her name behind her. Gaeres stood nearby. She'd hadn't heard him come outside. He stood in a pool of lamplight, dressed in the warm colors of autumn, his dark hair tousled from the wild dancing, his hawkish features burnished by the light.

"You finally escaped the crowds too," she said, walking toward him.

He met her halfway. "It was a battle hard-fought but worth it. I found you again." His gaze swept over her. "I didn't think you could be more beautiful. I was wrong."

She blushed at the compliment. "You're very kind."

"No, I'm very honest."

"Then I will be as well," she said. "You look magnificent in your finery, and I know I wasn't the only woman in that room to think so. Was your cousin happy to win one of the roses?"

"Ecstatic." He angled his body ever so slightly toward hers as she drew ever closer. "She's the envy of her sisters at the moment and will be bragging about her rose the entire trip home, much to their disgust I'm sure. She was also the one who was sick."

"Then the honey and ginger worked." Emerence clapped her hands. "I'm delighted for her."

Gaeres's expression turned somber with a shadow of disappointment overlaying it. "I'd hoped you would join the dance so I could dance with you."

"You know my reasons why I didn't." She touched his arm.

"I would have liked to dance with you as well."

Gaeres surveyed their surroundings. "We can dance together here," he suggested. "Though we have no music."

Anticipation beat delicate wings against her ribs. "I can hum the tune."

His grin surely matched her own. "Well then," he said and held out his hands to hers.

Their fingers entwined and soon they swayed and spun to the tune she hummed. There was no change in tempo to signal a switch in partners, and they danced together as the snow fell ever heavier on and around them.

Emerence forgot the cold as with each step that separated them, then brought them together again, Gaeres drew her ever closer until they no longer spun but only swayed, breast to chest. His arms wrapped snug around her waist, his hands pressed warm to her lower back. Emerence slid her arms over his wide shoulders to rest her fingers against his nape.

He was big and warm, solid and comforting in her arms. His breath tickled her neck and ear as he bent closer to whisper, "I hold the stars."

She fancied herself too old to go weak-kneed over sweet words, but her knees shook and she sagged in his arms. Gaeres gathered her close until there was no space between them. Emerence leaned back to stare into his eyes. For a moment an odd trick of the lamp light seemed to edge his irises in a thin band of glowing blue. She blinked and it was gone. Only the soft blackness stared back at her.

"You've stopped humming," he said softly.

"You can't kiss me if I'm humming."

Gaeres didn't hesitate. He swooped down, captured her mouth with his and kissed her until she thought all her senses would explode from sheer pleasure.

He tasted of sweet wine, his lips firm but also soft, his tongue a deep caress that filled her mouth and invited her to do the same to him. Muscled arms held her not as if she were something fragile and easily broken but as something he desperately wanted to sink into, be enveloped by, revel in until he was exhausted. Sated. Her light moan only made him hold her tighter, kiss her more deeply.

"Gaeres?"

His name sounded from the direction of the doors. Emerence abruptly ended the kiss and Gaeres groaned a low voiced protest when she jerked out of his arms.

She stared at him wide-eyed. That was Dahran Sulti's voice, and by the tone of her question, she hadn't spotted her and Gaeres where they'd ended their dance by the giant conifer.

When he answered, his voice was calm, giving nothing away and completely at odds with his intense expression as he stared at Emerence. "I'm here, Aunt. Stay inside. The snow is coming down harder."

"We're ready to leave," she said.

"I'll join you in a moment."

When the doors closed with a click, Emerence exhaled a sigh. "I don't think she saw us."

His regard didn't lighten. "Would it have mattered if she did?"

The question took her aback for a moment and she hesitated before answering. "No," she said. "Not for me at least." She was neither embarrassed nor ashamed to return Gaeres's affections, no matter how fleeting. If he'd been able to stay longer, she'd invite him to continue.

His expression eased and he coaxed her back into his arms. "Nor I," he said and brushed a second, lighter kiss across her mouth. "I wish could stay, kiss you more, kiss you longer. Walk you to your house and see you tomorrow morning and all the days to come after, but we have to return home."

"I would like that too," she said, sliding a lock of his damp hair through her fingers. "But your family awaits you, and as you say, you must return. Thank you for the dance." She trailed her thumb across his lips. "And for the kiss."

She stepped out of his hold once more. If she didn't put some distance between them, they'd end up locked in another passionate embrace. He let her go. Slowly, reluctantly.

"I don't know if or when I'll return to Timsiora," he told her. "If I do, may I escort you home again?"

Kiss you again? Dance with you again?

Emerence heard all three questions in the one he spoke. She smiled, a difficult expression now that melancholy shadowed her heart at his leaving and the very real possibility she might never see him again. "Come back to Timsiora and I will answer you," she said.

He captured her hand and kissed her fingers. "Summer," he said as he backed away. "Look for me when summer comes, Emerence Ipsan." He bowed and left the garden to find his aunt and cousins.

Emerence listened for the door's click. Only the towering conifer bore witness to her promise. "I will wait as the seasons turn. Wait and remember."

ALSO BY GRACE DRAVEN

World of the Wraith Kings
https://gracedraven.com/world/4

World of Master of Crows
https://gracedraven.com/world/3

The Bonekeeper Chronicles
https://gracedraven.com/world/2

The Fallen Empire
https://gracedraven.com/world/5

Other Works
https://gracedraven.com/world/1

About Grace Draven

Grace Draven is a Louisiana native living in Texas with her husband, kids and a big, doofus dog. She has loved storytelling since forever and is a fan of the fictional bad boy. She is the winner of the Romantic Times Reviewers Choice for Best Fantasy Romance of 2014 and 2016, and a USA Today Bestselling author.

gracedraven.com
facebook.com/GraceDravenAuthor
www.instagram.com/grace_draven

9 781945 367762